She was trapped and she had to get out. *Now.* Léa tugged at the latch desperately. The chain finally gave in to her efforts. S _____ d out onto the porch

Her bare foot h _____ m step should have be _____ rive painfully up in _____ on the wet grass and s _____ to her face.

For a moment, lying there trying to regain the breath that had been knocked out of her, Léa didn't know what had hit her. Then, as she tried to roll to her side, there was a dark figure looming over her.

"Don't move."

Pain was shooting up her leg from her foot. She was still trying to force some air into her lungs, but she searched the ground around her for anything she could use as a weapon. The man's hand was on her shoulder, restraining her, and the rain was pounding into her face.

A baseball hat, pulled low, completely shadowed his face. He crouched by the steps and tried to work her foot free from where it remained caught in the broken stair.

"Are you a neighbor?" Léa managed to ask as she felt her foot come free.

"Yeah, I live next door." His face turned toward her and, despite the darkness and the rain, she realized she knew him. The rush of relief was almost overwhelming. At the same time, she wished a hole would open up beneath her and swallow her, for she suddenly felt incredibly foolish.

"You're Mick Conklin."

"That's right." He looked up. "Been a long time, Léa."

Jan Coffey
Twice
Burned

MIRA®

RECYCLED PAPER
RECYCLED PAPER

ISBN 1-55166-919-6

TWICE BURNED

Copyright © 2002 by Nikoo K. and James A. McGoldrick.

Visit us at www.mirabooks.com

Printed in U.S.A.

To the Kepples...our extended family.

Prologue

Bucks County, Pennsylvania
Friday, May 19

In waves as palpable as mist, the chill from the river radiated through the night air. Settling on the skin, on the scalp, it was a feeling, a sensation, a living presence…almost. In time, it would seep through to the bone.

It didn't matter where it was. The black endless void of the sea. A silent mountain lake. Even in a place known since childhood—a river's bank, the pond's edge—one sometimes felt it. It was a brush of damp on the face, the arm.

In the light of day, one could think that moments like this gave birth to tales of Grendel and his kind, of monsters that rose out of swamps and lakes and oceans to destroy and to devour.

But now, as one stood by the water at night, the chill raised the hackles on the neck. The sounds of night birds became omens. The glow of fireflies became warnings. The shadows of rocks and trees became death traps.

The low gurgling hiss of the river hid any sound of footsteps. Protected by a moonless sky, the intruder left the path along the bank and moved quietly beneath the trees. Above, leaves made rasping sounds in a solitary night breeze, shivering slightly before tumbling through the darkness.

The air was cool, heavy, and stretched like the dark coil of some huge and motionless snake across the grounds. The trespasser, now one with the deep shade, stopped and stared up past the lawns at the unlit windows of the house, and waited.

A sports car sped down the road. The garage door opened automatically and the driver pulled in sharply. In a moment, silence again reigned. Moving noiselessly, the shadow stepped out from beneath the trees and crossed the lawn to the house.

"Help with your sister, Emily."

The sleepy-eyed five-year-old stared blankly at her mother's profile in the dim light of the car and then nodded off again. Marilyn Hardy switched off the engine and punched the remote for the garage door to close. Twisting in the driver's seat, she found both girls asleep again.

"Emily!" she snapped. "Come on, girl. Wake up."

She touched her older daughter's knee and gave it a firm shake. The child opened puffy, red-rimmed eyes and groggily tried to focus on her mother's face.

"We're home. Hear me? Home. Now get moving." Pushing open the driver's door, Marilyn cursed as it hit a new tricycle, jamming it against the garage wall. "Christ, Emily! How many times do I have to tell you to put this damn thing where it belongs?"

Marilyn snatched the girls' packed bags off the front seat, letting them drop onto the cement floor before reaching for her purse. The thin handle strap caught on the gearshift on the center console. Losing patience, she tugged hard to free it. The clasp snapped open, and the contents poured out onto the seat and floor.

"Shit!"

She threw the purse aside and, backing out, wrenched the seat forward. Marilyn glared at Emily's nodding head.

"I *told* you I need your help." The child snapped awake

immediately and reached over to undo the seat belt holding her younger sister.

Without opening her eyes, Hanna cried and kicked her foot crossly. As her mother reached in to take her out of the car seat, the three-year-old twisted away and whined angrily.

"Save that crap for your father," Marilyn hissed, grabbing the child roughly under the arms and pulling her out.

Hanna uttered a soft complaining cry and opened her eyes, looking over her mother's shoulder at her older sister. Emily fetched the small stuffed tiger from the back seat and stretched on tiptoes to hand it to her. The younger child tucked the precious toy beneath her chin and nestled her face against Marilyn's neck, closing her eyes again.

The door of the car slammed shut with a loud bang. The tricycle was kicked out of the way. Emily stayed right beside her mother as the timed lights went off in the garage and the space was pitched into blackness.

"No more tears. No more whining. I don't want to hear one more goddamn word out of you two tonight. You hear me?"

"Yes, Mommy," Emily whispered, clutching a corner of Marilyn's jacket as they moved quickly toward the door leading from the garage into the house. The girl kept her eyes on the three orange dots of light from the buttons that opened the garage doors. The door into the house was right next to them.

"And I'd better not *ever* have to deal with you making a scene like that again. You will never—hear me?—*never* question me in public like that again. Got it?"

"Yes, Mommy," the little voice barely squeaked.

The door was unlocked, as always. The wide hallway leading to the stairs was dark, but Marilyn didn't bother to turn on the lights. She only paused for a second to kick off her high heels before going up the stairs.

In the hallway on the second floor, she walked directly

to the girls' bedroom. Without being told, Emily slipped
in front of her mother and pulled back the quilt and sheets
on Hanna's bed. The younger girl was already asleep when
Marilyn laid her down.

As Marilyn straightened up, the sound of the phone
yanked her head around.

"Christ! What now?" She stormed out of the room,
giving Emily a sharp glance as she went. "Take her shoes
off. And get yourself ready for bed."

Marilyn turned on the light in her own bedroom and
snatched up the phone beside the bed an instant before the
voice mail kicked in.

"What."

The voice on the other end was barely more than a snarl.
"Look, Marilyn, I don't know what this shit is you're
trying to pull, but I made plans with the kids for this weekend and I am coming for them right now."

"Over my dead body, Ted," she snapped. She could
hear the sound of traffic through his cell phone. "I told
you before and I'm telling you now, you aren't taking *my*
girls anywhere near that crazy woman."

"My aunt has Alzheimer's, damn it! She is not crazy.
And if this is all part of some trick you're trying to pull
with that new lawyer of yours to keep the girls away from
me…"

"Daddy?" The soft whisper of Emily's voice on the
phone line jerked Marilyn's head toward the hallway. The
light from the bedroom stretched across the carpeted floor.
The little girl was holding the phone to her ear with both
hands. "Daddy, are you coming after us? Please, Daddy…?"

Marilyn marched angrily toward her daughter.

"I am, sweetheart." Ted Hardy's voice gentled instantly at the other end. "Don't cry, sweetie. I am calling
from the car. I'll be there before—"

Marilyn snatched the phone out of the little girl's hands

and slammed it down. Emily looked up, terrified, pearl-like tears rolling down her round cheeks. "He…he's coming. I can get Hanna ready. I promise not to be any—"

"I told you to get to bed," she barked. *"Now!"*

For a split second, a spark of defiance showed in the blue eyes looking up at her. Marilyn raised her hand to slap her but Emily darted back down the hallway, closing the door tightly behind her.

Marilyn raised the phone to her ear as she glared at the closed bedroom door.

"If you ever—" he was saying. "Do you hear me, Marilyn? If you *ever* lay a hand on my children again—"

"Go fuck yourself, Ted."

She punched the disconnect button on the phone and dumped it on the long table in the hall. Thinking she'd heard the far-off sound of a car's engine, she turned her back on the girls' door and started down the stairs.

The front hallway and the living room were dark. Marilyn padded across the thick plush carpet to one of the front windows and peered out at the quiet street. There was no car in sight. Crossing to the front door, she locked the dead bolt and hooked the chain. She moved silently through the house and, a moment later, bolted the door from the garage, too.

At the bottom of the stairs, she paused and listened. The only sound was the tick of the grandfather clock in the living room. Satisfied, she pushed her hair back over her shoulder and walked down the long hallway to the kitchen.

That room was dark, too, but just as Marilyn reached over to flip on the lights, she froze at a movement beyond the island separating the kitchen area from the spacious den. Her heart nearly stopped as she stared at the gauze curtain gently fluttering by the patio door.

With prickles of panic washing over her, she glanced at the light above the stove. The light was always left on…but not now. She watched as a breeze lifted the curtains again. And then, for the first time, she sensed the presence of someone else in the room.

Marilyn flipped the switch and turned around.

"Oh, it's you."

"I don't know how it happened, Léa. She was sitting right there watching TV."

The heavyset woman pointed to the worn recliner in the corner of the small living room. The television, nestled into the bookcases and cabinets that lined the opposite wall, was still on, making somebody a millionaire. Léa switched it off.

"I was standing right in the kitchen," Clara continued, flustered and upset. "I was talking to Dolores on the phone and fixing Janice's dinner tray. When I brought it out, she was gone."

Léa checked the two bedrooms again, the closets, the small bathroom. She even pulled back the shower curtain and checked the tub. In the coat closet, she saw the walking shoes and tan overcoat her aunt always wore when she went out.

"I am *so* sorry!" Clara blurted tearfully as soon as Léa came back to the kitchen. "I know you told me to watch that she doesn't go out. But she seemed so good tonight. She was happy, chatting away about Ted and the girls coming over tomorrow for her birthday. She said Ted got tickets to the Phillies game…that you were all going down to—"

"Clara, can you please stay here until I get back?" Léa grabbed her car keys and purse off the pile of books she'd just dumped on the kitchen table. Her aunt's dinner still sat on the table on a plastic tray. "In case Aunt Janice comes back on her own, you have my cell phone number."

"Sure." The middle-aged woman glanced at the clock

on the kitchen wall. "I can stay until it's time to wake up my son. He's on third shift now, you know."

"Right," Léa said, going out of the kitchen. Clara followed her through the small apartment toward the front door.

On impulse, Léa stopped at a small table and picked up one of the picture frames. It was a photograph of Janice, with Ted and the girls in front of the Liberty Bell. She quickly slid the felt-covered backing out and removed the picture, tucking it into her jacket pocket.

"Do you want me to call the police or something? I know it hasn't been more than an hour since she's been gone. But you never know…in the city, with all those punks on every corner these days…and poor Janice in her slippers and housedress…" The older woman stopped and dashed away a tear.

"Let me check the building and go around the block first." Léa opened the door. "I'll call them myself if I can't find her."

Léa didn't tell Clara what a waste of time calling the police had been last week. The time she'd spent explaining everything on the phone and answering the dispatcher's canned questions had been for nothing. In the end, Léa had called Ted and he'd driven into the city. The two of them had scoured the streets until they'd found her, at about 2:00 a.m. in an alley nine blocks from the apartment. A tight knot forced its way into Léa's throat as she recalled how terrified Janice had been, crouched beside a Dumpster and weeping softly like a lost child.

Léa stepped into the narrow street and decided against taking her car. She had already decided not to call Ted. She knew how excited he was to have Emily and Hanna for the weekend, and with everything he had on his plate next week, he didn't need this, too.

The line of row homes stretched down the block. An old van turned onto the street and drove slowly past. A man's angry bellow from the van, followed by a woman's screechy laughter, startled Léa. Clutching her car keys tightly between her fingers, she strode quickly to the end of the block and turned the corner. Peering into every shadow and doorway, she headed toward the place where they'd found Janice last time.

A church bell clanged ten o'clock a few streets over. Two blocks up, she passed a rowdy group of men just coming out of a corner bar. One made some crude remark in her direction that drew laughs from his buddies. She quickly walked by.

Léa thought of the talks she had been having with Ted about their aunt. Two and a half years ago, after retiring from a lifetime of teaching, Janice had decided that she wanted to live closer to her only family—the niece and nephew that she'd raised since their teenage years.

The first year and half had gone very smoothly. With Léa working as a social worker at one of the city's public schools, and Ted and his wife and children living an hour north of the city in Bucks County, life was going well.

But then everything had started falling apart.

First, it was Ted and Marilyn's marital problems and their separation. Then Janice had been diagnosed with Alzheimer's. A couple of weeks after that, the school budget had been cut, and Léa's job with it.

Léa crossed Broad Street and dodged a speeding car that obviously had no interest in stopping for red lights. She prayed that her aunt was where they'd found her last week.

She had moved Janice in with her and started a graduate program at Temple at night, while trying to make ends meet with part-time day jobs. Ted had moved to a place just north of the city, too. Many nights, while Léa was taking classes, he'd come in and take care of Janice. But Ted felt that living here in the lower end of South Philly was not the best situation for Janice.

Léa agreed. Janice's illness was advancing more quickly.

Soon, Léa couldn't afford the "luxury" of being a part-time student/part-time worker anymore. She needed a full-time job and a place where dangers didn't threaten their aunt every time she walked out of the house. She needed to find a place where people would know the older woman.

Though it would put a bit of distance between them and Ted, Léa felt strongly that she needed to go back to the town in Maryland where Janice Hardy had lived and worked her whole life before coming to Philly. Léa had sent a few resumés out to people she still knew in the Baltimore suburb. From the couple of phone calls she'd already received, the response was positive, but she didn't want to get her hopes up too high, yet.

As she stopped at the end of the alleyway where they'd found Janice before, a chill settled in the pit of Léa's stomach. The narrow alley was dark, lit only by a single light over a door halfway down. These were mainly the back doors of lunch places and shops, closed up tight now. Léa realized it was overly optimistic to think that her aunt would be here again, but she couldn't give up hope. She had to take a look.

Glancing across the street, she saw two women sitting on the steps of a row home about halfway to the corner. Nine or ten teenage boys and girls were listening to a rap song on a boom box a little farther up the street. Léa put her hand into her jacket pocket and exchanged her keys for a small can of pepper spray and started down the dark alley.

The graffiti-decorated Dumpsters that lined the alley were overflowing with garbage. Broken bottles and empty cans and more garbage were scattered everywhere. A cat peered out at her from between two of the Dumpsters as she passed, its eyes gleaming at her without fear. Léa searched carefully, covering every shadowy inch of the alley. Every doorway and trash pile. When she'd nearly reached the end, relief washed over her as she spotted a small shape huddled against a brick wall.

"Janice," she called out in a low voice. "Aunt Janice."

No response.

As Léa drew closer, her foot inadvertently kicked an empty bottle, sending it skittering loudly along the pavement past the sleeping form. As the bottle shattered against the wheel of a Dumpster, the figure sat up, glaring and hurling a string of violent obscenities at her in a graveled voice.

"Sorry," Léa murmured apologetically, backing away from the homeless man. "I thought you were someone else."

Quickly, she retreated down the alley. Feeling genuinely panicked now, Léa looked up and down the street when she reached it. The two women were gone. The beat of the music drew her gaze to the teenagers still hanging on the steps up the street. She started toward them. A couple of them turned their backs to her as she approached. The girls glared with open hostility.

Léa took the picture out of her jacket pocket. She folded Emily's and Hanna's faces under.

"Excuse me. Could any of you guys help me?"

Someone turned the volume of the music up. Two girls lit cigarettes and walked down to the corner.

"I was wondering if any of you might have seen this woman around here tonight?" She held out the picture and walked to the middle of the group.

One of the boys strutted over to her and put his arm around Léa's shoulder, looking with exaggerated interest at the photo. "What'd she do, hon, steal your man?"

She gave him a sharp jab in his bony ribs and shrugged off his arm, drawing a laugh from the rest of the group as he complained loudly.

"Look...I've got ten bucks." Léa pushed the picture

toward the others. "Maybe you passed her on the street. She's lost and…"

"You're kidding, right?" Someone snickered behind her back. "Maybe if you try fifty, lady…"

A black kid who had just joined the group stepped toward her and took the picture. "Let me see."

He walked a couple of steps toward the streetlight with it.

"She's wearing a flowery housedress," Léa said, following him. "Pink slippers. She's short. This high. Very thin. She wears her white hair tied in the back, in a ponytail."

The teenager brought the picture closer to the light.

"Have you seen her?" Her voice must have shown her desperation, because the boy's dark eyes looked up. He gave a cool shrug.

"What's it worth to you?"

"I don't have fifty bucks on me," Léa whispered. "I only have ten. But help me find her, and I'll get you the rest tomorrow."

"Yeah, right." With only the slightest hesitation, he shrugged again and motioned for Léa to follow. She did, ignoring the laughter and comments behind them.

"Jamal got himself a white girl…."

"She is as old as your mama, Jamal…."

"Didn't mean to ruin your reputation, Jamal." Léa tried to make light of the situation despite the worry that was eating away at her insides.

"She your mother or something?" He handed the picture back to Léa.

"She might as well be. She's my aunt. She raised me."

"What's wrong with her? She crazy or what?"

"No, she's not crazy. She just…sometimes forgets her name…and where she lives…and gets lost."

"Alzheimer's?"

"Yes."

"My grandmother's got it."

"Oh. Sorry." Léa hesitated a second as Jamal turned down a very rough street. A fire had burned four or five houses on one side, and two or three others looked abandoned. She eyed the half-dozen derelict cars along the broken sidewalks. "You *have* seen her, haven't you?"

"Yeah." At the end of the street, he stopped and nodded his head toward a bus stop across the way. "Right there. She was sitting there when we went by before. Kind of just talking to herself."

Léa's heart leaped at the sight of her aunt rocking back and forth on a bench near the corner. Her slippers were dangling from her thin feet. Her face had a wild expression as she kept glancing up and down the street in search of something. Léa started crossing, but then whirled around.

"I'm sorry. I almost forgot." She reached for her purse.

"Forget it." The kid gave another shrug and waved her off. "Just take better care of her next time."

Before Léa could insist or even try to explain, the teenager had turned and was walking away. As she crossed the street, there was a bitter taste in her mouth. She did her best…and Aunt Janice was *not* being neglected.

The older woman didn't even see her approach. But when Léa slid onto the seat next to her, Janice's gray eyes brightened with recognition.

"Good thing you got here. The bus is coming any minute." She glanced up the street anxiously.

"Where are you taking me, Auntie?" Léa turned her head and saw a bus was indeed coming.

"We're going to pick up Ted. He's waiting." Janice grabbed Léa's hand and stood up when the bus pulled to the curb. "Come on."

"But he's already coming to the house. We don't have to pick him up." Léa shook her head at the bus driver when he opened the door. Gently, she put an arm around

Janice's shoulder and turned her down the street. "Ted and the girls are coming over tomorrow morning."

"Who?"

"The girls. You remember…Hanna and Emily."

The older woman glanced anxiously at the departing bus. "Ted won't find the way."

"He will, Auntie. Don't worry. Ted never gets lost. He'll be here tomorrow." Léa linked Janice's arm in hers and started for home at a slow pace. "In fact, let's talk about tomorrow. Did you know I love birthdays?"

"Whose birthday?"

"Mine!"

Janice laughed heartily, and Léa felt her own emotions surge through her. She loved this woman.

"*Whose* birthday?" she repeated with a wide grin.

"Yours!" Léa patted her hand. "But no peeking at the presents until tomorrow."

Despite the attempt at humor, it was obvious that birth dates were just one more thing that Janice no longer remembered.

They took their time walking back to the house. The more they talked, the less confused and suspicious Janice seemed to be. By the time they reached the front steps of the row home where their apartment was located, the older woman was calm and reasonably lucid.

Clara was still waiting for them when they came up the steps. The television was on again. "You gave this poor girl a heck of a scare, Janice. You really shouldn't—"

Léa shook her head at Clara. After taking her aunt to her favorite chair, she walked Clara out. "There's no point. She doesn't really remember what she did or where she went, or even why."

"Maybe I shouldn't be saying this, dear, but you should be thinking of putting her in one of those homes or something. If she's going to just disappear like that, she'll be too much to handle for you, and for your brother. And you can't expect somebody my age to be watching her anymore, either.''

"Janice had a bad night. That's all. She's not like this all the time. Thanks for staying, Clara.''

"That's okay, Léa. But you should think about—''

"I know. I will,'' she said, biting back the sharp edge that was creeping into her voice. "Good night, Clara.'' She closed the door on the older woman's back.

Janice was standing by her chair, her eyes glued to the television set.

"Ted is not coming,'' she said.

"Of course he is, Auntie.'' Léa locked and latched the door and headed for the kitchen. The protectiveness she felt had every nerve in her body humming. She was *not* going to send Janice to some institution where she might be ignored and neglected. No matter how severe her illness got, Léa knew they could work through it themselves, as a family. They would work through it the same way as her aunt had done when she and Ted had been dropped in her lap.

"Léa!''

"Why don't you sit down? I'll get us something to eat,'' she called, throwing away the cold meal on the tray and reaching inside the fridge.

"Ted's not coming,'' the old woman called, louder this time. There was a note of panic in her voice.

"You're right. He's not coming tonight. But he and the girls will be here for breakfast.'' She took out a plastic container of soup and set it in the microwave.

"Not coming…not coming…''

The mournful chant of the older woman brought Léa out of the kitchen and across the living room. Tears were rolling down Janice's cheeks. She was shivering.

"Come on, Auntie.'' Léa sat down with the older woman on the sofa and gathered her like a child into her embrace. She was already well accustomed to these sudden mood swings that were part of the illness. "You and I will have a nice meal together, and before you know it, tomorrow will be here and..."

"Not coming..."

The television's reflection in the glass front of a cabinet caught Léa's attention. Something familiar passed across it. She turned to stare at the television screen. A news reporter was standing on a dark street with fire trucks and police cars behind her. What remained of a burned house was visible beyond. The woman was recapping the story.

"...what we know. A triple murder here in the peaceful bedroom town of Stonybrook, Bucks County."

Léa felt every inch of her body go tense.

"Thirty-three-year-old Marilyn Foley Hardy's body was discovered in the kitchen. We've just been told the partially burned bodies of the two little girls have been discovered upstairs."

Aunt Janice's face turned to the screen again. Léa couldn't breathe.

"The preliminary reports already indicate that the mother was stabbed to death before the fire was started...."

Léa couldn't move. Couldn't say a word. A wrenching sound escaped her throat, but she still couldn't breathe. Stunned, all she could do was to stare at the television.

"The woman's estranged husband, Ted Hardy, was arrested on the scene an hour ago. He is being held in custody...."

Janice sobbed and looked into Léa's face. "I told you Ted is not coming."

One

Two years later

Half bent over the toilet, Léa leaned against the cold metal wall of the bathroom stall and tried to will her stomach to stop heaving. Her nerves were shot. Her stomach was now, as always, the first thing to break down.

She flushed the toilet again and lurched out of the gray stall. Leaning over the old porcelain sink in the courthouse bathroom, she opened the cold-water faucet wide, washed out her mouth and splashed handfuls of water onto her face. The frigid water on her skin did little to ease the fevered burn.

The door opened to her left, and Léa immediately pulled some paper towels out of a dispenser. She kept her face buried in the coarse brown sheets as the newcomer's high heels clicked toward one of the bathroom stalls. When the lock on the stall snapped shut, Léa hazarded a look at her own reflection in the mirror. She looked like hell.

All that was left of the little makeup she'd applied that morning was a couple of smudged black rings under the swollen slits that once were eyes. Her nose was red and her lips colorless. Her skin was blotchy.

At the sound of the toilet flushing, Léa reached into her purse for her sunglasses. A younger woman, coming out of the bathroom stall, stared at her openly as she walked to the adjacent sink.

Léa pulled on the dark shades and cast a final glance at the beleaguered stranger that she had become. Forcing herself to be calm, she walked out of the bathroom to face the inevitable.

She felt her knees wobble as she entered the nearly packed courtroom. The clock on the wall showed a minute before four. She focused her attention on her own seat and tried not to be affected by the pronounced hush that came over the place with her arrival. Marilyn's mother, Stephanie Slater, said something aloud, but Léa didn't bother to spare the woman a glance. Weeks ago, she'd given up responding to her taunts and thinly veiled threats.

The district attorney and his three assistant D.A.s entered the courtroom a minute later. Ted's lawyer, David Browning, walked in with his team at 4:06. Browning was, as usual, sporting a starched white button-down shirt that highlighted his impeccable tan. His suit today was charcoal gray, and Léa didn't think she'd ever seen this one. He gave her a friendly nod that she ignored.

Last week, she'd received his latest bill. Browning was a junior partner in a decent law firm in Philadelphia, but she couldn't help but wonder how many of his tan and manicure sessions had been folded into the mind-blowing sum she now owed. And then there was the young lawyer's collection of Armani suits—each a different but oh-so-conservative shade to cover every day of the week.

Léa dropped her chin to her chest, knowing that she was looking for any excuse to explode. David Browning just happened to be an easy target.

As a door along the wall to her right opened, cold claws of fear ripped at her insides. She watched two court officers escort her brother into the courtroom. He had lost so much weight. She looked into his drawn face, at the coarse blond-and-gray beard that covered his once-vibrant and handsome face. He was only thirty-five, but he looked fifty-five…maybe older. His eyes had once sparkled with life, but now there was no light, no hope.

He, too, looked like a stranger.

Ted Hardy was not waiting for any twelve jurors to decide on his sentence. He had given up hope long ago. She knew he'd already given up the first time she'd seen him after his arrest two years ago.

Tears burned Léa's eyes, but she blinked them back. Ted sat down at the defendant's table without looking at her. She understood what he was doing. He was severing this last bond—this last connecting lifeline—and she felt more lonely and lost than she'd ever felt in her life.

There had been no question of Ted attending their aunt's funeral last week. Even if he'd been allowed to, he wouldn't have gone. As Léa stood to deliver the eulogy before the small congregation, she had looked out at the faces of her aunt's lifelong friends. They had come out to lend their support to her, but her only thought had been that this had to be the lowest point a life could go and still be bearable. Until now.

As the court proceedings continued, Léa hardly noticed her surroundings, now so familiar that they were a part of her dreams. She only became alert when the court crier asked permission to receive the verdict.

The courtroom became deadly silent. Léa kept her gaze on the back of Ted's head, her hands fisted in her lap.

"Will the foreman please rise?"

Léa's gaze drifted to juryman number eight, an older businessman in a navy suit who was rising to his feet. She lifted the sunglasses off her face and looked intently into the face of the man. There was no hint of what he was about to say. Nothing.

"Jurors, have you agreed upon a verdict and penalty?"

"Yes, we have." A chill washed through her at the calmness of the answer.

"Do all twelve agree?"

"Yes."

Léa realized that she was tapping one shoe on the ground. She pressed a hand on her knee, trying to keep herself under control.

"Having found the defendant, Theodore John Hardy, guilty of murder in the first degree of Marilyn Foley Hardy, guilty of murder in the first degree of Emily Hardy, and guilty of murder in the first degree of Hanna Hardy, what is your verdict as to penalty?"

Léa held her breath.

"Death."

Someone gasped out loud in the courtroom behind her. She thought she heard Stephanie crying on the other side of the room. There was a loud buzz of people talking behind her. She heard the footsteps of a few who bolted out. Reporters. Léa felt the burn of tears in her eyes and pulled on the shades again. A lump the size of a fist formed in her throat.

"Thank you. Please be seated, sir," the court crier said loudly over the noise as the judge hammered away with her gavel, demanding silence in the crowded courtroom.

"We request that the jury be polled, your honor." David Browning's request received a nod from the judge. Léa was watching for some reaction from her brother. Nothing.

At the judge's order, the court crier turned to the dozen jurors again. "When your name and number is called, you will please rise and in a full, clear, audible voice announce your verdict."

Léa felt the knot in her throat choking all life out of her. Repeating the crimes again and again, the crier polled each juror in turn. Eight women and four men stood one by one and repeated the same word to the roomful of people.

And to Ted, who appeared to hear nothing.

Death… Death… Death…

She didn't want to remember the crimes. It crushed her

when she thought of the fresh, pretty faces of Emily and Hanna. So young and alive. But Ted couldn't have done it. He could never have set fire to the house knowing his own daughters were sleeping upstairs.

Death.

As difficult as Marilyn was, he had once loved her enough to marry her. They'd had children. Planned a life together. He could never have stabbed and killed her.

Death.

"Your Honor, the jury has been polled..." The court clerk's voice rang out in the court, but Léa was no longer a part of the proceedings.

He couldn't have done it.

Her entire body was trembling. She felt as if a bullet had torn through her. From a gaping wound in her soul, she was bleeding emotions and memories she'd worked so hard to repress.

In her mind, time was repeating itself. The memory of another murder pushed forward, blocking out the present, scorching her insides with unbearable heat. Léa had been eleven, Ted fifteen, when they'd come home to find them. She could see it now as clearly as if they were at this very moment lying on that kitchen floor in front of her. The blood. Her own anguished cry. She also remembered Ted's horrified face—his absolute silence as he'd stared at their parents' dead bodies.

Stonybrook officials had called it a murder-suicide. John Hardy had stabbed his wife twenty-seven times before retrieving his revolver from the desk drawer in his study, sitting down at the kitchen table and blowing his brains out.

Without hesitation, Janice Hardy, the only surviving relative of Léa and Ted, had assumed full responsibility for the two children. Taking them to the small town in Maryland where she lived and taught school, she was determined to erase the nightmares afflicting these two young people. They all knew, though—social workers and doctors alike—that Ted and Léa would carry painful psychological scars for their entire lives.

The judge's voice cut momentarily into her thoughts. "Ladies and gentlemen of the jury, the Code of Judicial Ethics prevents me from commenting one way or the other on your verdict. And that is the way it should be…"

Léa tried to focus on the black robe of the judge. On what was happening now. Despite the verdict, despite the link Browning himself had suggested between this murder and their parents' violent deaths, she could not believe that it was possible for Ted to kill his own family.

Ted had been the one sure thing that had helped Léa survive the painful years following their parents' deaths— and all the years since. Ted and his undying support. Ted and his sense of humor. Ted and his unwavering loyalty to his sister and his aunt. Ted and his love of his family.

Léa looked at her brother, sitting motionless at the defense table, staring at nothing.

Her attention was drawn back to the courtroom. The jury had been dismissed, their chairs sat empty. The judge was speaking directly to Ted.

"…and this court wishes to advise you that you have an automatic appeal to the Supreme Court of Pennsylvania."

In a monotone voice, the judge read the script explaining the automatic appeal. Léa had already read everything there was to read on this phase. This was not the end. She wouldn't let it be.

"However, before that appeal can be heard, certain posttrial motions must be filed and disposed of within ten days of today."

Léa stared at David Browning. Their lawyer. Their advocate. He looked slightly bored. She wondered if he was even listening. He was definitely not writing any of this down. His pair of twenty-something-year-old lawyers sit-

ting with him looked only slightly more engaged. Then,
as she stared at their backs, one of them closed his briefcase with a snap, looking suddenly ready to bolt for the
door.

A flush of rage sent blood rushing to her face. Halfway
through the trial, Léa had realized that Browning was
nothing more than a talking head. But she'd had little
choice and little time to make a change, considering Ted's
total lack of cooperation and the severity of Janice's illness. The final straw was the totally ineffective appeal to
the jury during the penalty phase.

Sitting beside the lawyers, Ted continued to stare
blankly at the table while the judge continued to spell out
the specifics of what was needed, including the date, time
and place for the disposition of any posttrial motions. Still,
Browning's pen never even scratched at the legal pad before him.

She was getting a new lawyer. Their old family house
in Stonybrook *had* to sell. Then she'd use the money to
hire the person who would make a difference.

"In the interim, the court will order a presentence psychiatric examination to be performed on Mr. Hardy. Anything else, counselors?"

Everyone was so calm. So businesslike. Ho-hum. Just
another day. Just another human being sent to death row.
No questions. No comments. Nothing.

She clenched her fists, wanting to throw something at
Browning. *Say something!*

"All right. This court stands adjourned."

Ted still wore that same lifeless mask as two court officers came around to escort him out.

"Ted!" Léa found herself leaning forward in the chair
and calling his name. He froze for an instant but never
acknowledged her. He rose to his feet and turned his back
to her.

The lawyer said something quietly to Ted. The condemned man shook his head once. This was the only response that Léa had seen her brother make at all during these last days of the trial. Browning leaned forward, obviously insisting on whatever he had said before, and this time Ted turned to him sharply.

"You have my answer. Now, leave it go."

The bitterness of his tone caused Léa to shrink back in her chair. She still couldn't tear her gaze from Ted's face as he was finally led out of the courtroom. He was not helping with his own defense. David Browning had made a point of telling her repeatedly that her brother was not cooperating in any way. Léa knew that Ted had resisted the psychiatric examination that had been done right after his arrest.

"Miss Hardy?"

Léa turned around at a touch on her shoulder. She looked questioningly at a woman dressed in a court officer's uniform. Léa knew her. She had seen her standing by the door of this particular courtroom a number of times before.

"You must have dropped this on your way in."

Léa looked at the white envelope that the woman held out to her. The courtroom was nearly empty. She didn't remember dropping anything. She didn't recall having any envelope in her possession. All the same, she reached out and took it.

"Thanks." She glanced around and found Browning talking to one of the prosecutors, an attractive redhead who had presented the physical evidence for the state during the trial. His own assistants had already beaten the crowd to the door. Léa needed to speak to Browning before he left, but he didn't seem to be in any hurry.

Léa looked down at the sealed envelope in her hand. Her name and the courtroom number were typed on the front. Curious, she tore open the flap and took out the single folded sheet of paper. The contents took only a moment to read, and she turned around and searched the empty seats behind her. With the exception of the court officer walking to the door, there was no one else left. She looked again at the piece of paper in her hand, reading the words again.

Ted is innocent. I know who did it.

"But it's *another* of those letters!"

"I see that. Did it come to your hotel?"

"No. It was dropped outside the courtroom door. Today."

"I'm sorry, Léa." Browning darted a glance at her as they descended the stairs. "It's a sick joke. I think you should hand this one over to the police, too."

"I'm handing *nothing* over," she said tersely. "In fact, I want everything back that I've given them."

"That won't look good."

"Won't look good for whom, David?"

"Look, there are procedural issues that need to be considered. A progression of steps we need to follow."

"And if we don't?" she snapped. "Who are we concerned about now? Have you already punched the clock on Ted's case?"

"An attitude won't help anything."

"Do you want to see an attitude?" Léa grabbed the sleeve of the lawyer's jacket and tugged hard, forcing him to stop on the stairs. "I am sick and tired of you and those cops and your useless assistants and everybody else. You couldn't care less about saving Ted's life! Why the hell did you accept this case when you clearly don't give a damn, David? Aren't you afraid that your precious partnership will go right down the toilet when your bosses find out what a useless piece of shit you were in court?"

"Léa...I know you're upset." Browning let out an exasperated breath and looked up and down the wide marble stairs before turning his full attention back to her. "Listen,

I know you've been under a lot of stress. I'm very sorry about your aunt. And I meant to come to the funeral last week, but—''

"Damn it, this is not about some social obligation. My brother was sentenced to die in there. Do you understand? Death. A lethal injection. *The end.* For God's sake, you're his lawyer. You are supposed to be on his side."

"I am—"

"Then why have you done *nothing* to help him? There was not a single goddamn day that you were prepared. You sat there like a log and didn't make a peep while the prosecutor presented his witnesses. And then you let him walk all over your case. Why didn't you pursue anything I told you about Ted as a person? He's *not* the monster these jerks made him out to be. He was a loving father and a good husband. Marilyn was the one who got restless. *She* was the one who wanted a divorce. You, of all people—his own attorney—just sat there and acted like this case was a hopeless cause."

"That's not true."

David shook his head in disagreement and, in his usual manner of avoiding confrontation with her, started down the stairs again. No emotions, no passion...and no integrity. It had taken two years, but she'd finally figured him out.

"You know what?" Léa said, going after him. "I don't think you would do a thing even if someone stepped forward and admitted to stabbing Marilyn to death and setting the house on fire. I don't believe you want the complication. You put in your time. You think you can just put it all behind you now and move on."

"That's completely unfair." He glanced at her. "But what do you think are the chances of that happening? Of someone admitting to something like that, especially this late in the game?"

"*Here's* a chance. Right here in my hand," she said

stubbornly as they reached the bottom of the stairs. "This
letter is one chance. And there are at least a dozen more
like this one that probably went right into the circular file
of your friendly police detectives."

A few heads turned in their direction. Léa recognized
one of them as a newspaper reporter who had been hound-
ing her for an interview for the past couple of months. As
the man started toward them, David took her by the arm
and led her toward a clerk's office on the first floor.

Closing the pebbled glass door in the face of the approaching reporter, the lawyer looked at the empty desks
behind a high counter. The clock on the wall showed it
was nearly six.

"Now, listen to me carefully, Léa," he started. "I know
your emotions are running high." As she opened her
mouth to object, he raised a hand in defense. "And you
have every right to be like this after all you've been
through these past couple of months. Past couple of years,
even. But before you race out of here, looking for this
jerk—this letter writer that you think will save the day—
you need to address something more pressing that might
actually help your brother."

The lawyer's calm, monotone voice was enough to drive
Léa over the edge again. All of her insults were not
enough to get his blood flowing. She bit back the new
wave of temper, though, knowing full well that, as it stood
this minute, Browning was Ted's only attorney.

"What do you mean, 'pressing'? What could be more
pressing than a death sentence?"

The man brushed a speck of lint off his jacket sleeve.
He glanced at his watch. "I really didn't want to say anything to you until I'd exhausted every possibility. Until I
had a chance to talk to Ted again."

Léa moved to the side, forcing the lawyer to look into
her eyes. "What are you talking about, David?"

"Ted refuses to allow any appeals to go forward. He's

told me that I cannot file anything on his behalf. He won't take visits from either the ACLU or Amnesty International or anyone else active in capital punishment cases. He knew…he was certain what the sentence would be today. He wouldn't change his plea to avoid the death penalty. He wouldn't help me in any way. And now he doesn't want to drag this thing out for five or ten years. He won't waive his right to appeal, but he says he won't be part of any circus.'' Browning put a hand on Léa's shoulder. ''Those were his exact words. He wants the governor's signature on the warrant of execution. Your brother wants to die.''

Léa felt the walls tilt slightly. ''This is the depression talking. He has never recovered since the murder. That attempted suicide last year should be enough of a clue. He needs genuine psychiatric counseling. In his state of mind, he can't make that decision for himself.''

''Yes, he can. In the eyes of the court, he was fit to stand trial, and he's fit to make a decision like that. And I can put off letting him do it for only so long. In high-profile cases like this, lawyers get disbarred for what they do or don't do. But that's not going to happen here.''

Léa leaned against the high counter, too upset to respond, while thousands of arguments boiled up inside of her.

He gentled his tone. ''Listen, Léa. I've also learned that in this business you should never give up hope. I plan to talk to Ted again tomorrow about the appeal. I think you should talk to him, too. You are the only family he has left. Work on his conscience. On his guilt about abandoning you. Beg him, if you have to. I think you're the only one who can make him change his mind. His life rests in *your* hands.''

She shrugged off his touch and straightened up.

''Don't you worry. I *will* talk to Ted. We're not giving up.''

* * *

"Eight hot dogs, two pretzels, three popcorn..."

"We need two more hot dogs, Hardy."

Ted tossed a half salute at his friend by the souvenir booth next to the food stand and turned apologetically to the cashier.

"Can you add two more hot dogs to that order?" He handed her the money.

"Ted? Ted Hardy?"

There was a feathery touch on his shoulder. Ted turned in the direction of the voice and stared for a second into the vaguely familiar and very beautiful face of the woman standing back a little in the next line. He and every man within fifty feet had noticed her when she'd approached the concession stand. She was dressed in a short, white, wraparound dress, and it hadn't taken much imagination to see she was wearing nothing underneath. Definitely overdressed...or perhaps underdressed...for a baseball game.

Now, looking for the first time into her face, Ted struggled to remember.

"Marilyn!" She had a beautiful laugh. *"Marilyn Foley. Don't tell me you've forgotten!"*

"Oh, yeah! You and I went to school together back in Stonybrook," he said quickly, feeling his ears go red even after so many years. How could he have forgotten? The only daughter of the number-one family in town. As an adolescent, he'd drooled over her for two years before she'd agreed to go out with him on one date. And one date had been the extent of their romance, too. Fifteen-year-old Ted had made a total fool of himself that night. She'd been experienced, and he'd been clumsy and overeager. It had been a disaster.

"Your food, sir?"

Ted turned for the trays.

"You need a hand with those?" Without waiting for an

answer, she forfeited her spot in line and came to help him.

"Thanks. Are you here alone?"

"No, I came with a friend and his kid. They're some-where out there." She tilted her head toward the ballpark seats and smiled. "He's into that father-daughter bonding stuff. It's getting just a little boring. Do you have any kids?"

"Yes. Ten of them." Her shocked expression was price-less. Ted couldn't hold back his smile. "But only for today. A friend of mine and I have a group of inner-city kids out with us."

"Oh…like a charity."

"No, it's more like mentoring." He dropped the food by a condiment table and motioned to the loud group mak-ing their way slowly toward them. "They're a great bunch. We're going out for pizza after the game. If you want to bring your friend and his daughter, you're welcome to join us."

"Too many people." She shook her head and handed him the tray. "So, do you live around here?"

"Yeah. Center City."

"Have a business card?"

He reached inside his pants pocket and was surprised when Marilyn's eyes followed the movement of his hand as he took a card out. She stared down at it.

"Pharmaceuticals. Impressive. Actually, there are a few things about you that seem…pretty impressive."

The comment and the body language that went with it were one hundred percent sexual.

She reached inside her purse and took out a pen. "What's your home number?"

As Ted gave it to her, she turned the card over and pressed it against his chest, trying to write the number down. Their bodies brushed. Her scent filled his head.

"I'll call you," she whispered tantalizingly. *"And you can take me out on a date."*

All Ted could do was nod. All he could think of when she walked away was what she would wear...or not wear...on their date.

He couldn't wait to find out.

Two

Léa went out ahead of Browning into the first-floor lobby. The reporter had disappeared, and nearly everyone else had cleared out, as well.

"Do you need a ride back to your hotel?"

"No, I'm all set," Léa answered curtly. As they walked out side by side, it was impossible to remain civil to the lawyer. Of course, Ted's life depended on her. On *her* and not the ineffective legal dog-and-pony show Browning and his people had put on.

"I'll call you tomorrow."

"You do that." She turned away as soon as they reached the sidewalk. Léa felt like a woman possessed. She was racing against time.

Angry at the world and at herself for not acting sooner, she turned her steps toward the small hotel where she had been keeping a room on a monthly basis during the trial.

There was a message waiting for her when she got up to her room. This morning, before leaving, she'd tried to get hold of the real estate agent who was selling their house in Stonybrook. The woman's voice and message were crisp and businesslike, and gave no indication of whether she had good news to convey or not. The Realtor just said that she would be working late in the office, if Léa could call her.

Their family house—the same one that her parents had died in so many years ago—was the only asset they had left. For years following the tragedy, the house had been rented out by a local agency, providing a small but steady income. Though Léa couldn't see any point to hanging on to it, Ted had insisted they maintain and keep the property. Léa didn't share her brother's sentimentality about the place, but she had let him have his way.

As the years passed, Léa had thought less and less about the house. She hadn't cared at all what happened to it, and she had never gone back there.

But now she did care, for all of her plans depended on the money she could get for that house. Whether it was finding a new attorney, or paying David Browning's outstanding bill, or even hiring a private investigator to see who was sending her these letters, she had to sell the house.

The house had been sitting empty for a year and a half. Though the last tenants had apparently trashed the place, Léa put it on the market as soon as it became evident they'd need the money for Ted's defense. The real estate agents had told her on the phone that the property was a "perfect fixer-upper." But "perfect" did not mean a quick sale. In fact, they hadn't received even a single bid on it.

Léa dialed the real estate office. The woman was out on an appointment, another agent told her, but he'd have her call when she got back.

While she changed out of her suit, the local television news broadcast a ten-second clip on Ted's sentencing with a promise to report more after the commercials. She shut it off, knowing that she couldn't fall apart now.

Léa hung up her suit, trying to think what the real estate agent might have to say to her. The last time they'd talked was two months ago, and at that time Léa had again agreed to reduce the price.

Dropping the mail that had been forwarded from Maryland, she picked up her notepad and a thickly stuffed manila envelope the real estate agency had sent to the hotel address. With a sigh, Léa stretched out on the bed. She hadn't had a chance to go through any of it yet.

Before opening the large envelope, she looked at the pad of paper with her own scribbles on the top sheet. Her budget…though it hardly deserved the name. The miniscule income from her job was based on a ten-month contract tied to the school calendar. She wouldn't see another paycheck for two more months, when she went back to work.

Léa pulled a folder out of a briefcase beside the bed and opened it. She already had the name of a possible lawyer to replace David Browning. This time, she had done her homework. She'd even sat in on one of the woman's cases when it had gone to court, during the same week that one of Ted's hearings had taken place. In court, attorney Sarah Rand looked sharp and powerful. The woman exuded confidence and credibility. Léa knew the lawyer also had an excellent record in homicide cases. But there was another interesting facet to Rand's credentials that Léa couldn't help but consider an asset. Married to Owen Dean, a movie actor and television star, Sarah Rand was also a local and national celebrity. And to Léa's thinking, forcing Ted's trial into that kind of spotlight was a way of avoiding the neglect Ted had faced the first time in the courtroom.

From the folder, Léa pulled out a paper with the estimates she'd been given by the attorney's office. Of course, all of it was contingent on whether or not Sarah Rand decided to accept the case.

The phone rang, and she picked it up on the first ring. Betty Walters, the real estate agent, was on the other end. The woman was polite but formal. Léa was certain she must have already heard about Ted's sentence.

"Ms. Hardy, early this week we sent a file on your property to the hotel address you gave us."

"Yes, Betty, I got it." She reached for the manila envelope and shook it out, leafing through the items quickly. "Sales flyers. Advertisements. Notices on the reduction of the price. The clippings from the local newspaper ads. You've put a lot of work into this. I really appreciate it."

"Then you received our letter, too."

Letter. Léa leafed through the other mail and found an envelope. "Can you hold on a sec?"

Tearing it open, she pulled out a folder with a letter clipped to the front. Quickly, she scanned the contents. The agency was sorry, but considering the condition of the house, they recommended taking it off the market until the property could be put into a more marketable state.

She stopped reading and let out a frustrated breath. "So you...no longer wish to represent us in selling the property."

"No one can sell it, Ms. Hardy. The house has been in the multiple listings database for nearly two years. We've done everything imaginable, but there has not been so much as a nibble."

"But I've been reading all about how the economy is so good in Stonybrook—about the building boom that is going on there. *Someone* must be looking for a house that needs a little work."

"We are not talking about a *little* work, Ms. Hardy. If...if you would drive down and take a look yourself, you'd see the extent of—"

"Unfortunately, my schedule right now won't permit it," Léa replied, trying to keep the frustration out of her voice. "But I am still very much interested in selling this property. So if you have any...ideas? You're the expert in this field. There must be something creative that we can do. From all I hear, you *are* the best, Betty."

The praise seemed to have some effect, for there was a pause on the line. "The only other option that you might consider is to put the house up for auction."

"Auction," Léa repeated, suddenly hopeful with the prospect. "That could work."

"Yes, it could, possibly. The only problem that you should know up front is that the final selling price might be far below what you are asking."

Léa grabbed up the sheet with her estimated expenses scrawled on it.

"How much less?"

"No way of telling. It may go for half the present asking price. Maybe even less. You see, in this case, we would have to set the minimum bid very low. Otherwise, no one will show up."

Half the asking price would give them just enough to pay off Browning. There would be no money for anything else. "No, I can't live with that option."

"Then, I am sorry, Ms. Hardy, but I'm afraid there is nothing more that we can do...."

Léa listened to the woman's polite explanations for a moment more and then said goodbye. Frustration stabbed away at her as she dropped the phone back in its cradle.

"Nothing can go right, can it?" She lay back on the folders and envelopes, and stared up at a long, thin crack in the plaster ceiling.

She remembered uttering these same words to Ted the summer that Janice had been diagnosed with Alzheimer's. In their family, she'd complained, good luck came in tiny spoonfuls while bad luck came in buckets. Before she could go on about the injustice of life, Ted had painted her a picture of the positive side of all of it—of the importance of a close family and of returning some of what they both owed Janice. And how lucky they were to be in the position of being able to help the older woman.

As always, Ted the optimist.

Every challenge, he'd asserted, every setback, could only make them stronger. They had their health. They had each other. They should be grateful for that and try to build on it each day.

"Ted the wise." She smiled bitterly, knowing that she had to use his own words to convince him that there was reason to fight. Guilt, coercion, begging—whatever it took—Léa had to convince him to allow the lawyers to file the appeal papers. And then she had to be ready with other plans.

She reached for the real estate package again. Every day, there was another article in the papers about the real estate boom in Bucks County. Stonybrook was at the center of it, since it was the perfect commuting distance to Philadelphia. It was a seller's market.

She considered what it would take to do a little cosmetic work and approach these agents again. From the time she was a teenager, she'd liked painting and doing little fix-up jobs with Ted and Janice on their place in Maryland. She'd even put in some time with Habitat for Humanity while she was in college. There was no way she could afford to hire someone else for the job. But it meant she'd have to go back to Stonybrook and try to do the work herself.

Léa pressed her fingers against her temple. Just thinking about walking back inside that house made her head pound. She forced herself to find the single white envelope she'd received in court today. Pulling out the letter, she stared at the words again.

Ted is innocent. I know who did it.

All the other letters had been mailed to her apartment address in Maryland. She'd checked the post office stamps and knew that some were mailed from Stonybrook. Others were from neighboring towns, all in Bucks County. She ran her fingers across the words again. The police detective that she had first spoken to about the letters—one of David Browning's friends—had told her that receiving this type of thing was very common. He warned her that there were people out there who got a kick out of doing things like this. They enjoyed seeing a family member build up their hopes, only to have the world come crashing down later. Browning and his people had sent off those letters to the Stonybrook police, but nothing had ever come of it.

Léa was not convinced, though, that someone's twisted sense of humor could keep at it this long. That was why she was dead-set on hiring someone to look into it. A professional. She searched through the pile on her bed again, looking for the investigators' brochures.

A stack of identical envelopes peeking out of the Realtor's folder caught her eye.

Léa pulled them out. Six white ones, neatly typed, addressed to her. All mailed to the Poplar Street address in Stonybrook. She checked the faint postmark imprint. The dates varied from early last year to this past spring. All were postmarked from Stonybrook. She ripped open the first one.

Ted is innocent. Come to town and I'll tell you who did it.

She reached for the next one. There was dirt on the white envelope. She opened it.

I saw him get there. But she was already dead.

Léa sat up on the bed and grabbed the next envelope.

He didn't hate her as much as the rest. Come to town.

"The rest? The rest *who?*" She pulled open the last of the letters. They all said the same thing.

Come to town...

Despite the police reports, Léa had been certain that someone other than Ted had been there that night. The real killer. But now the idea of a third person—someone who had witnessed everything—sent her hopes soaring.

She pulled out the cover letter from the real estate agent. At the end of it, Betty mentioned the enclosed mail. The envelopes had been found inside the door of the house since the last tenants had moved out.

She reached for the first letter again. She read it out loud.

"Ted is innocent. Come to town and I'll tell you who did it."

Léa had to go back. It was up to her.

"You are playing with my head," Marilyn whispered when Ted pushed her chair in and went around the table to take his own seat.

"How's that?"

"All of this!" She touched the loose rose petals strewn on the table. *"The wine. The candlelight dinners. The music. Taking me so many places these past couple of months. We're already having great sex, Ted. Why are you going through all of this?"*

"Because I think you've been missing it."

"I've had sex before."

He laughed.

"Not sex, Marilyn…romance." His fingers entwined with hers, and her gaze was drawn to his handsome face. *"You act tough. Talk tough. You even claim sex is the only thing you're looking for in a relationship."*

"That's the truth."

"Is it?" His thumb made small circles on her palm. *"Then what are you doing here? How come you haven't gotten tired of us? Moved on?"*

He was doing it to her again. Making her think. Making her remember how lonely her life was every minute that she wasn't with him.

"I understand you, Marilyn. For all of your life you've been pressed to conform because of your family name. You've mastered the elegant public persona of what it takes to be Marilyn Foley. But in private, you rebel in every way you can. You shock. You even hurt people. But I know you do things to get attention. It's all part of a deep need you have to be noticed. To be cherished."

It was all part of wanting to be loved. As if that were possible. A tight knot was growing in her throat. Her fingers tightened around his.

"You can't reform me, Ted. No matter how hard you try. I'll always be me...and you'll eventually end up hating me, too."

"Have faith in me, Marilyn. Have faith in yourself. We've been cursed with the family names we were born with. But we can change anything."

Three

The bell above the glass door jingled, and Sheila Desjardins knew she was not quite done for the day.

"I'll be right with you," she called from the rear of the hair salon.

Quickly folding the last towel, Sheila put the clean pile between the hair-wash sinks. Squirting some moisturizing cream on her hands, the hairdresser came around the divider and then paused in surprise.

"What are *you* doing here?" She smiled at the man standing by the register.

Mick Conklin pulled the Red Sox cap off his head. "Nice welcome. You still cut hair here?"

"I didn't mean that." Sheila laughed self-consciously. It was amazing, even after knowing Mick for practically all of her life, how flustered she got when she unexpectedly came face-to-face with his raw, masculine looks. Heck, it wasn't only her. Most of her female customers—and a few of the men in this town, she'd wager—shared her sentiments. With intensely blue eyes that looked right into your libido and a stubborn mouth that made a girl dream, Mick had been Stonybrook's own heartthrob for close to three decades. Brian Hughes referred to him as a tall Paul Newman. And just like the actor, Mick was only getting better as he got older.

"Then what did you mean?"

"I just thought you would have gone to Doylestown for Ted's sentencing. Everybody else in town went."

"Afraid I'm not much into public hangings." He tossed the hat onto the coat tree in the corner.

"Nice shot." Sheila motioned him to follow her to the back of the shop. "I guess you heard about it, though."

"Yeah. I heard on the radio." Mick sat in the chair. She draped a towel on his shoulders, and he leaned his head back into the sink.

She started testing the water. "I think it's horrible they gave him the death penalty. I know I'm probably the only one in town who thinks it, but I still say he didn't do it."

In a moment, she was working the shampoo into his thick, sandy blond hair.

"Rich makes fun of me. I know he arrested Ted and all, but I have this thing inside of me—this sixth sense for judging character. And I say Ted Hardy just couldn't be a cold-blooded killer and suffer like this at the same time."

"That right?" Mick said without opening his eyes.

"Absolutely. Rich took me down to the courthouse a couple of times during the trial. I couldn't believe how horrible Ted looked. Honey, anyone looking at him can see that he is in pain. And, my God, last time I was there, I didn't even recognize Léa. You remember her, don't you?"

"They were our next-door neighbors. Of course I remember her."

"Oh, that's right. Well, I don't really know how she turned out in looks when she grew up and all that, but seeing her in the courtroom, all washed out and wearing those dark glasses all the time, I would have tripped over her and not recognized her as the same leggy little thing that used to tag along after her brother." She rinsed off the shampoo and started patting Mick's hair dry with the towel. "I remember you used to let Ted hang around you and the other older boys when you were in school. Did you get down to the courthouse, at all?''

"No." Mick followed Sheila to the front room and sat in the chair she spun around for him.

"Well, I'd say you're the only one in town who didn't." She combed through his hair. "The days I went, it was like Main Street on Memorial Day. Everybody, I mean *everybody,* was there. Reverend Webster and his wife and son. Brian and Jason. Gwen and Joanna from the flower shop. Some of Doug's crew. I even remember seeing Andrew Rice there one day. And Rich said it was no different any other day. How do you want me to cut it?''

"Short. Buzz it."

"No! You *can't* do that!" Sheila ran her fingers through the wet curls and stared at him in the mirror. She arranged a few of them on Mick's high forehead. "Women *love* this reckless, bad boy look. Come on, hon, let me do a little trim job, and I'll work some mousse into it...."

"Jerry in the barbershop charges half your price, and he doesn't give me any grief."

"That's because Jerry's the only barber in Bucks County who's blind in one eye and got his license through the mail."

"Cut it short, Sheila." Those blue eyes were unnerving when they made a demand.

"I still say it's a crime."

She reached for her clippers with a sigh and started in. In no time, sandy brown hair covered the floor around the chair.

"So, how are you getting along with Heather?"

"Okay."

"I haven't seen her come downtown at all since she's moved back in with you. What's it been...two weeks now?"

"She's hanging around the house. Trying to get settled in again."

"Sure. It must be tough for her. Not that I'm blaming *you*," she added quickly, holding the clippers away and looking at him in the mirror. "But it's not like your ex lives in the next town. That poor girl, going from Pennsylvania to California and back again. A year here, two years there, and now being sent back this way again. What happened? She didn't get along with your wife's new husband or something?"

"Heather likes East Coast weather better."

"And if you think I believe that…" Sheila laughed and met Mick's guarded gaze in the mirror. "How old is she now, anyway?"

"Fifteen."

"That's right. But not for too long. Her birthday's near the end of the summer, isn't it? Around Labor Day weekend?"

"Yeah."

"Heather didn't get down to the courthouse, either, did she?"

"Not likely."

"Well, actually, when I think of it, that makes three of you. You, Heather, and Dusty." She moved around him, looking critically at her handiwork. Even with his hair short, he still was a fox. She changed the head on the clippers.

"Dusty hasn't left town in fifteen years, at least."

"I know. But Dusty was really close to Marilyn. You knew that, right?"

Mick didn't answer.

"I mean, who'd figure it? Here's a homeless weirdo that no one wants to get within a mile of—"

"He's not homeless."

"I know that, Mick. I'm just making a point. Who'd figure on Marilyn, of all people—the perennial homecoming queen—regularly giving him food and money and God knows what else."

"I have to get back to work."

"Oh, yeah. Almost done." Sheila blushed, realizing that she'd stopped cutting and was just talking. She started on Mick's sideburns. "I hear your company got the contract for the renovation job on the old Lion Inn?"

"You hear everything."

"Of course!" Mick bent his head so Sheila could shave the back of his neck. "Did you know Marilyn used to rent one of the inn's cottages by the lake up there year-round?"

"Rich tell you that?"

"Everybody knew it!" She stood behind him and eyed the sideburns to make sure they were even. "But why do you think she'd be needing that, when she was staying at her own family's house on the edge of the town? Don't answer—I know, I know—she had to be discreet while she was fighting Ted for custody of the girls."

She brushed the hair off Mick's neck.

"Now, there were some juicy rumors going around about…certain people…she entertained at the inn."

"I like the haircut," Mick said casually, pulling the towel and apron away from around his neck. He stood up and reached for his wallet, following Sheila to the register.

She punched in some numbers. "I know we're supposed to believe that this great judicial system works and everything, but everyone in this town knows there was a lot of dirt in Marilyn's past that never surfaced during the trial. Some of it might have mattered, too."

"Nice way for the girlfriend of the town policeman to talk."

"I'm serious. I mean, if somebody really took the time to look at Ted and Marilyn, they would have seen that she had more screws loose than he ever did…in spite of everything."

Mick handed her the money, waiting for the change.

"Everybody says you got to know her pretty well after

your divorce, Mick…before she married Ted. What do *you* think?"

"I think you're barking up the wrong tree. Your boy-friend was the guy that did most of the work on the murder."

"I know, I know. But you know Rich. He was born and drug up here. He's as loyal as an old dog when it comes to this town and the people we grew up with. I think the biggest thing going against Ted was that he was a Hardy. Do I need to say anything more?"

Léa glanced up at the gray clouds racing in from the west.

"…the band of severe thunderstorms will cross the area in the evening hours. Heavy downpours and wind gusts of up to fifty miles per hour have been reported in Berks and Montgomery Counties…."

"Oh, please." She switched off the radio. "I really don't need this now."

The first drops of rain hit the windshield of her eight-year-old Honda as Léa pulled off the highway and turned down the country road toward Stonybrook.

She passed a motel that looked like something out of another era, but the place had its neon No Vacancy sign lit. The parking lot was packed with small trucks and antique cars wrapped in canvas covers. Who would have thought there'd be a car show and a balloon festival in the area the same weekend that she wanted to work on the house? Léa had heard all about it on the local radio station. There was not much point, she decided, in driving up and down these roads hoping to find a room somewhere else. Her sleeping bag and the house on Poplar Street would have to do…at least for the night.

She passed a fancy carved sign with gilt lettering welcoming her to Stonybrook, but the very sight of it caused Léa to tighten her fists on the steering wheel. The houses started coming closer together, with well-manicured lawns ending right at the road. She'd had to look at a map this morning to jog her memory. Twenty years was a long time to be away, but the recollections were coming fast now.

Léa forced her fingers to relax on the steering wheel and tried to think of everything she had on her plate right now. The past few days had been a constant push. The meeting with Ted hadn't gone well. As she'd pleaded with him, he just sat and stared at his hands. She might have been talking to a rock. And yesterday, two full days after the sentencing, she'd found out that David Browning still had not contacted his client.

The one bright thing that had happened since the sentencing was that she'd spoken to Sarah Rand on the phone yesterday afternoon. Even through the phone line, the attorney's questions about the case and about Ted, his past and the type of person he'd been, had made Léa realize what a loser Browning really was.

Rand had been willing to read through the trial transcripts over the weekend to see if she might be interested in the case. She would talk to Léa on the phone again on Monday.

Léa had gone overnight to Maryland to clean up some loose ends with Janice's things and the apartment. But she was now back in Bucks County, hoping to revive the albatross of a house hanging around her neck. She had little more than a single weekend to do it. Hiring someone like Sarah would mean Léa had to liquidate fast.

"Never say it can't be done." She turned the radio back on and changed the station until she found an oldies station out of Allentown.

The drops of rain turned into a downpour just as she reached the edge of the downtown area.

Léa stopped at the red light before turning onto Main Street. Waiting for the light to turn, she realized she was not in any hurry to drive directly to the house. The early years of her life had been spent in this town. Almost perversely, she wanted to see it, to see if she could remember some good to go with the bad. She wanted to see if the town had changed, as *she* had.

In truth, she wanted time to build up her courage before facing the house where her childhood had exploded in a single afternoon.

On her left, she looked at the old movie theater. No glittery chrome-and-plastic cinemaplex, the place still showed one movie, with one showing each day. Cheap and safe, the theater used to be a good hangout for teenagers on Friday and Saturday nights. Léa smiled as she saw a van park at the curb, with a half-dozen kids piling out and running for cover under the marquee.

She turned her attention to an impressive new two-story office building on her right. An out-of-town bank branch occupied the bottom floor.

The light changed and she made the turn. The downtown was straight ahead, and she drove slowly through it. Despite the years and the teeming rain, the solid beauty of this street was just as she remembered it. Large half barrels of flowers every few yards on clean sidewalks added color. Signs of hunter green and black and royal blue with gilt letters hung out from above the shop doors. Wooden benches sat under a green-and-white awning at the ice cream shop.

No cheaply done, homemade signs. No lit-from-within stuff. No neon. Nothing to jar the quaint effect. No troublemakers in this downtown to ruin the image of stolid, conservative affluence.

Thinking back to her childhood, Léa didn't remember ever seeing anyone poor or homeless walking along this street. Not for all the years she'd spent in Stonybrook. Even Dusty Norris knew better than to hang around Main Street. The Vietnam vet who came home with his wires crossed had probably been warned off, she thought now.

Everything in Stonybrook's downtown was in order. It always had been, she realized. Safe, orderly, refined. With one exception. Her family.

Léa slowed the car and crawled past Hughes Grille. How many nights, she wondered, had John Hardy stumbled drunk out of that place and lurched along these sidewalks? There was a new awning. Hanging plants by the door. The windows were no longer smoked. Nonetheless, the place was still here.

On the next street corner was Bob Slater's bank, the Franklin Trust, where his wife's money—made from the mill that had once been the backbone of this town—probably sat moldering in a musty vault. Léa's father had once run that mill, in spite of his alcoholism. And then Ted, so many years later, had married Marilyn, the product of Stephanie Slater's first marriage to Charlie Foley. Marilyn would have been the sole heir to that fortune.

She sped past the bank, but stopped at the next intersection as a couple of pedestrians ran from the large park that stretched out behind the buildings on the left. She stared at the people as they crossed the street to get out of the rain, wondering if she once had known any of them. Darkness had descended with the onset of the storm, and the few people left on the sidewalk were rushing to get where they were going.

Léa's attention was drawn to the police station to her right. Regardless of his episodes of drunkenness and a quick and sometimes violent temper, John Hardy had never been brought down here. But then again, Lynn, Léa's mother, had never complained, either. And in the end, she'd paid the ultimate price for her silence.

Léa turned left at the library and drove across the river. Slowing the car on the bridge, she looked downstream. There was a paved bike path along the river now, and she knew that if you followed it down beyond the closed mill, you would come to a burned-out house where a woman and her two innocent children had died horrible deaths.

Thunder rumbled overhead. Strong gusts of wind swept across the park and covered Léa's windshield with sheets of rain.

Her vision blurred momentarily, but she stabbed away at the tears and continued on, following the road up around the park that stretched out now to her left. The street was completely deserted on this side of the park. She pulled the car to the curb and wiped the fog from the driver's side window.

The small lagoon was still there. Léa recalled the winter afternoons when she would follow Ted down here to ice skate. The wind and rain swept across the water. Old birch trees bowed submissively by the gazebo on the far side of the lagoon. In the murky light, she could just see the backs of the Main Street buildings in the distance.

Some of the best memories of her childhood involved this park. Léa remembered the concerts the town used to put on here. Even now, she could see herself and Ted and her parents sitting by the water's edge on a summer evening, listening to the brass band as the stars came out.

She pushed back the nostalgia and turned her attention to the line of buildings facing the park. The stone-steepled Presbyterian church. Beyond it, the huge old neoclassical mansions with their white columns. These had been the homes of the families that had built Stonybrook, but Léa remembered reading somewhere that over the years they had, for the most part, been changed into luxury apartments.

She flipped the windshield wiper to High before pulling back on the road.

At the upper end of the park, she turned right and drove up a tree-lined street into the old neighborhood where she and Ted had grown up.

Oak Street. Cedar Street. Willow Street. Birch. Spruce.

Léa smiled. All the streets were named after trees in this section of town. Poplar Street came up too quickly, and she stopped at the intersection, gathering her courage before turning onto the street where they had lived.

A bolt of lightning lit the sky over the downtown, over the park, and she saw the reflection of it in her rearview mirror. A split second later, a loud crack of thunder startled her. It felt so close.

The rain pounded down on them as they trudged up the hill from the bus stop. They were both soaked. The clothes, the shoes, the hair, the schoolbags. Léa's sneaker slipped on the first step as she got to the front porch, but Ted caught her arm, stopping her from falling on her face.

The front door was closed. The windows were tightly shut and the curtains drawn. A chill ran through Léa's body as she reached to turn the knob on the front door.

"Take your shoes off," Ted warned, kicking off his own and pushing his way inside ahead of her.

Suddenly, Léa was frightened. It was only midafternoon, but she didn't want to be left outside alone.

The living room was dark. Ted's call was answered by silence. He dropped his schoolbag and shed his jacket by the steps. Léa was shivering as she started toward the kitchen.

"Mom?" Her voice scratched and clawed up a slippery well. She'd seen their car in the driveway. Their father was home. He was always home these days. Always fighting with her mother about something. "Mom?"

"Maybe she's not home." Ted reached the kitchen doorway at the same time she did.

Their parents were there. They were both there.

She hadn't walked back into that house since the day her parents died. She didn't want to be here now. But her life had never really been about choices—well, not about good choices. Only hard ones.

Léa turned onto Poplar and pulled to the curb. Peering down the street through the rain and the gathering dusk, she saw well-groomed yards and nicely maintained houses. Bright lights shone out of large windows.

She had to loosen her grip on the steering wheel and take a deep breath before turning and looking at the house where she'd been born.

In architectural style, their house at one time might have been called Victorian, though it lacked the gingerbread trim and the fancy decorative shingles that most of the neighboring houses had. But it was also so uncared-for that she almost cried just looking at it. The wide porch that wrapped around the front and side seemed to be sagging dangerously, and she noticed the stair tread of one of the front steps was completely missing. She looked up at the broken windows and the dangling shutters of the second floor, at the peeling paint, at the missing shingles of the roof extending over the porch. Her gaze traveled over the overgrown grass and shrubbery and took in the ancient carriage house that sat like a hulking ghost behind the house at the end of the gravel driveway.

Lightning ripped open the sky directly behind the derelict place. The inside of the house came to life momentarily with the flash of light.

"My God," she murmured. "It looks haunted."

Léa felt what remained of her courage seeping out of her.

"Okay. This is it. Now or never."

Turning off the engine, she grabbed her purse and cell phone, and jumped out of the car. Out of habit, she paused in spite of the drenching rain to lock the door before running for the front steps.

A dog barked from the porch of the next house.

Léa stepped over the missing step, but the second one,

too, groaned and gave way a little. Cringing, she mentally added it to the list of things that would have to be fixed immediately.

Léa's shirt was plastered to her skin and her hair was dripping by the time she stood on the porch.

"I wish *I* had a dog." She glanced curiously at the large golden retriever, still barking noisily at her. With his front paws on the porch railing, he didn't look like he was about to let up any time soon. Léa's hands were trembling, but she somehow managed to find Ted's key to the house deep in her purse. She put it in the lock, but it wouldn't turn.

"Come on." Wondering if they'd changed the lock and not told her, she glanced around for a key box with a combination that some real estate agents used, but there was nothing. Frustrated, she dropped her purse and phone on the porch and, holding the old doorknob with one hand, tried to jiggle the key with the other.

The door swung open.

It hadn't been locked, and Léa stood for a moment, smelling the musty scent and peering into the too-familiar darkness.

"Heather, could you bring Max in?" Mick called from his study. Without looking up, he continued to plug the last numbers into the computer. He wanted to finish the estimate. If there was one thing he hated, it was having paperwork slow down a job.

A sharp flash of lightning was followed by another clap of thunder, and the dog's barks became more furious.

"Heather?" he called again, but there was no answer.

Mick closed the computer file. Just as he punched the power button on the machine and pushed away from the desk, the lights in the house flickered.

"Heather!"

Walking out of his office, he looked in the kitchen first. All the dishes still sat on the table. The pots and pans on the stove hadn't been touched. Nothing was cleaned up. But he should have figured that, considering their argument during dinner. He marched into the front room.

"Heather!" he shouted from the bottom of the stairs.

This had been a bone of contention between them since the day she'd come back to live with him again. Moping around all day. Refusing to leave her room, for the most part. Never lifting a finger to help with anything. He'd asked and then ordered her to come down for dinner tonight. She'd showed her face, but then had sulked and picked at the food and found something wrong with everything he'd made.

Granted, Mick wasn't ready to fill in as guest chef at Le Bec-Fin or any other fancy restaurant in Philly, but he was pretty damn sure his dinners were more normal than anything she'd been getting in her mother's house.

Finally, he'd lost his temper and stormed away from the table, telling her to clean up.

And as a result, his dinner was still sitting in a lump in his stomach. Hers remained untouched on the table. Nothing like a nice, quiet family dinner.

The dog's barking was getting on Mick's nerves. Opening the screen door to the porch, he called the animal. Max looked once at Mick and then went back to barking.

"In!"

Reluctantly, the golden retriever took his paws off the railing and came across the porch. Tail wagging, the animal shoved his ninety pounds of wet fur and muscle through the door. Mick reached for the towel he kept in the wicker basket by the door but was too late, as Max proceeded to shake himself in the middle of the living room.

"You *are* an idiot," Mick said gruffly, wrestling the towel around the playful animal before wiping up the worst of the puddle on the floor.

Standing up, he glanced wearily toward the stairs. Nat-

alie had warned him about this on the phone when he'd
suggested having Heather come back and stay with him.
Remarried for less than a year, his ex-wife, a successful
pediatrician, couldn't deal with their daughter's rapidly de-
teriorating attitude any longer. Natalie, unwilling to jeop-
ardize her new marriage, was ready to send the fifteen-
year-old to an exclusive boarding school in New Orleans.
But that was a choice that just didn't set well with Mick.

He started up the stairs. He didn't know what had gone
wrong or when, but he hadn't recognized the purple-haired
young woman he'd picked up at the Philadelphia airport
earlier this month. Dressed in black from head to toe, she
had enough pierced jewelry to double for a lightning rod.

In fact, it was probably a good thing she was under
cover with this storm.

At the top of the stairs, Heather's door was closed.

Strange-colored hair and earrings and nose rings and
eyebrow rings and Lord knows what other kinds of rings—
Mick could live with all that. Hell, the way he saw it,
years ago he'd been plenty rebellious himself.

What he somehow had to learn to get past was
Heather's "I don't give a damn about anyone or anything" attitude. That was something else entirely.

He knocked on the door. No answer. He knocked again.
"Heather?"

No music blasting. No "go the hell away." Maybe
things had improved since dinner. Max appeared next to
his master's leg and nosed his way in.

The room had clearly been shaken, turned upside down,
and then shaken again. Shoes and mixed piles of dirty and
clean clothes and half-emptied suitcases and stacks of
books covered practically every inch of the hardwood
floor. Mick stared at the mess and found his temper rising
again. His daughter was lying on the bed, her face to the
wall.

A bolt of lightning lit the window, the clap of thunder following immediately.

"Heather!" he snapped, stepping over a black trench coat lying in a heap in front of the door.

The lights flickered and went out for a moment. When they came back on, the red numbers of the clock on the bedside table started flashing. Heather hadn't moved, though.

"You didn't do one thing that I asked you to do down there. I don't know what you've been used to, living with your mother, but I am *not* going to hire someone to come in and pick up after you every day." He kicked a sneaker out of his way. "I'm not asking a lot. Just basic stuff. Like looking after yourself. Picking up your own mess. Simple things that separate us from the animals."

Still no response.

Max jumped on the bed and nestled his wet fur against her legs as lightning flashed again. The house shook with the ensuing boom of thunder, and she started. She definitely wasn't asleep.

Mick didn't know what was happening to her. To them. Her mother had warned him about Heather's change in behavior, about the problems at school, but still he hadn't been prepared for this.

"But aside from this mess, every now and then you might show me that you can act normally. Walking and occasionally carrying on a conversation would be nice." He gentled his tone, trying a different approach. "Look, Heather, I know teenagers need a lot of sleep, but I don't think I've seen you do much of anything else since you've been back."

The dog sighed a complaint of his own as he laid his muzzle on her hip. Mick frowned, realizing that this approach wasn't much better. He was still carping at her.

"Hey, I know I'm a terrible cook, but you used to put up with it before." He gently touched her purple hair and stared at her pale profile. Her eyelids moved, but she wouldn't open them. "I wasn't too pleasant tonight, ordering you around, but I am just tired of this new attitude. I want the two of us back the way we were."

Nothing. He withdrew his hand and picked up a leather jacket. Under it was an empty bag of Oreos. Max moved slightly to inhale the crumbs.

"Come on, baby. Why can't you at least talk to me? I know something must be wrong. Whatever it is, we can take care of it…together."

Heather pulled her knees into her chest but didn't say a thing.

Frustration was burning a hole in his stomach. He looked at the bright flowery curtains, at the matching wallpaper, at the bedroom set that his daughter had picked out herself three summers ago. Her old teddy bear sat up by the headboard. She'd been a happy, loving kid. How had everything gone so wrong?

He looked down at her young face again.

"We can't go on like this, baby. Tomorrow is Saturday. Except for dropping a couple of things off here and there, I'm gonna take the rest of the day off. You and I will just spend a few hours together. We can go for a ride, if you want. We'll just talk, and figure this new 'us' out. How's that sound?"

When he leaned over to brush a kiss on her cheek, she turned and buried her face deep in the pillow. It felt like a kidney punch.

"Good night, baby." He pressed a kiss into her hair and straightened up. Watching her as he moved to the door, Mick switched off the light before going out. Max stayed behind, snuggling contentedly against her legs.

The storm was continuing to light up the windows as Mick descended the stairs. He felt totally inept in dealing with his own daughter, and that bothered the hell out of him. Although it was nine years since he and Natalie had divorced, they'd both done their best to stay in touch and remain involved in Heather's life, despite the three thousand miles that separated them. But somehow, during the last couple of years, everything had gone sour.

Cleaning up the kitchen was what Mick needed to sort out his thoughts. It took only a few minutes to wash the pots and load up the dishwasher, but he was already feeling a little better as he switched off the light over the sink. Looking out at the rain pelting the kitchen window, he noticed the light on in the Hardys' house across the lawn. He stood for a moment and watched. A shadow passed in front of the light, and he remembered Max barking.

Mick had run into Betty Walters downtown when he was having a late lunch at Hughes Grille one day last week. She'd told him they were going to give up trying to sell the house for the family, and had asked Mick again if he was interested in buying it. He could probably get it cheap. He still wasn't interested.

Someone passed in front of the window again.

Pulling a flashlight out of a drawer beside the sink, Mick started for the back door.

"I'm pregnant."

Ted's breath caught in his chest. The joy he felt at the news was almost overwhelming. But he remained still. He couldn't let her know how much this mattered to him. He couldn't let Marilyn guess how much he'd be hurt if she decided not to keep their baby.

"I've been on the pill for years. I don't know what happened. I think I must have become too relaxed since I've been…well, only with you."

For the first time, she looked vulnerable. Frightened, even. Ted walked to her and gathered her in his arms. "Did you want this to happen?"

She nestled against his chest. "I…I think I did. I do. I wanted to get pregnant. I wanted to have your baby."

He couldn't hold back his emotions anymore. *"I love you, Marilyn. God, I love you."*

"I want to run away and get married. Now. I want to do everything right for our baby."

Four

No wonder they hadn't been able to sell the house.

To say that the place was a dump was being pretty darn generous, Léa thought. The last tenants hadn't even taken their broken furniture when they'd left. After that, there had been no one around to haul out the trash and clean up.

Léa made a quick run through the upstairs. The sink and tub and toilet in the small bathroom were heavily stained. Despite the rain, she opened the window wide to let out the dank odor. From what she could see by the light in the hallway, the condition of the three bedrooms was not much better, either. Garbage bags of what she only hoped were old clothing were heaped up here and there. Broken furniture, a ripped box spring and a number of stained mattresses were scattered about.

Renting a Dumpster would be at the top of the list of things she would need to do.

At least someone—most likely the Realtor, Betty Walters—had made an attempt at making the downstairs rooms presentable. The three connecting rooms had been swept, with more broken furniture and boxes and bags of junk piled in one corner.

Léa walked toward the back of the house. Standing in the doorway to the kitchen, she fumbled with a shaking hand for the switch on the wall for the overhead light. She found it and tried to turn the light on. It wasn't working.

She peered into the darkness and felt the cold wash through her trembling body. She'd kept control over herself, walking through the rest of the house, not thinking of the fact that *this* room had been her room, or *that* room had been her parents' room. She hadn't allowed herself to think of the time she had tickled Ted in the bathroom and caused him to split his lip on the sink.

No, she had successfully detached herself from the reality that this was the place where she had spent her childhood. This was the place where her life had been formed. This was the place where her parents had…

But now, looking into the darkness of the kitchen, realizing that *everything* was the same, Léa felt the clawed hand of panic gripping her stomach. She backed out of the doorway and practically ran through the family room toward the front parlor.

The lightning seemed to be all around her as she made a couple of quick trips to the car. Her sleeping bag. An overnight duffel. A small bag of groceries that she couldn't bring herself to take to the kitchen. That was everything that she would need for the night. Léa wished she had brought a flashlight.

She stood dripping inside the front door, with her insecurities, her fears, her grief all crushing her.

But she was not about to let herself fall apart. She had come too far. A job needed to be done. She only needed to wait for the morning to get started.

There was no locking the front door, so she latched the tarnished old chain. As for the back door, she couldn't bring herself to pass through the kitchen to check. Tomorrow was soon enough to look into the cellar.

Many things obviously hadn't changed in Stonybrook. People still didn't lock their houses, it seemed. The townspeople still carried the sense of security that nothing could go wrong. No theft, no breaking and entry, no drunkenness or drug abuse, no assault, no other crimes worth mentioning.

The residents of Stonybrook just kept on living in a dreamworld, despite the wake-up call her family seemed destined to sound over and over.

Léa pulled off her wet sneakers and socks and spread the sleeping bag on the floor by the wall. There were no draperies or shades on the windows, but she didn't mind. She didn't want to feel shut in and alone in the house. Léa opened the windows looking out onto the porch. She breathed in the smell of rain. The old-fashioned screens were missing from the windows, and she wondered vaguely if they were stored in the basement with the storm windows. A spark of memory from years ago passed through her mind. She thought of her father, religiously changing the screens for storm windows every year on Columbus Day. She looked out past the overgrown bushes, down the street, at the line of Victorian houses set back gracefully from the road.

It appeared that now, even after twenty years, Poplar Street had kept its look of respectability. A doctor, two retired schoolteachers, an architect…she couldn't remember all of the neighbors' jobs, but they all had been solid, responsible, important. John Hardy had fit right in at one time, running the mill. Even Léa's great-grandfather, who had lived here before them, had owned and run the only pharmacy in town.

They'd belonged here on this street, in this town, as much as anyone else, Léa used to remind herself. But still she had sat by this same window so many nights, wondering what the other families on the street were like inside the walls of those respectable homes. When she was much younger, she'd wondered how mean other fathers got when they drank. She would sit and wonder if the other kids' mothers were like her own, saying they were too sick to come out of their rooms, hiding their bruises and their shattered illusions about love.

Léa pushed away from the window and ran her blood-less hands up and down her arms. Her clothes were wet. She was cold. She didn't want to be here. Her gaze wandered inescapably to the door of the dark kitchen. She felt goose bumps standing on her skin.

Her mother's unseeing eyes were open when Léa and Ted walked into the kitchen that afternoon. There was blood on her face, on her neck, matted in her dark blond hair. There were deep gashes on her chest, on her arms. But Lynn Hardy's eyes were open, as if she were waiting for her children to get home. A sob formed in Léa's chest, and she pressed a hand to her mouth to control it. She blinked back the tears and saw her father leaning against the doorjamb, his revolver in hand, ready to take his own life, as well.

There was a flash of lightning somewhere very close to the house. As the clap of thunder exploded an instant later, the hall light went out completely. Léa's heart froze in her breast. She couldn't move. For an agonizing minute, she could not tell reality from the imagined.

But then, with sanity came the fear that toed the electric edges of panic. Thoughts of another being in the house… perhaps cutting the power…raced through her mind. She scrambled for her purse and the can of pepper spray.

Crouching, with her back to the wall, she glanced out through the windows. Everything—every house and street-light—was enveloped in the same blanket of darkness. The storm had knocked out power in the entire area. For several moments she remained where she was, breathing deeply and forcing back the panic.

Then, just as her pulse rate dropped to the level of a mere drum roll, she heard a noise from the rear of the house. From the kitchen.

Léa's actions were instantaneous. Grabbing her purse, she ran for the front door. Yanking it open, she lost her grip on the handle and stumbled backward as the chain latch snapped tight. She threw herself against the door, slamming it hard and trying to work the latch free. Her fingers had suddenly become numb. She couldn't undo the chain.

Behind her, a loud knocking sounded through the house. A man's voice. But Léa was in no mood to listen. She was trapped, and she had to get out. *Now.* She slapped and tugged at the latch desperately. The chain finally gave in to her efforts. She jerked the door open and dashed out onto the porch and down the steps.

Her bare foot hit the slick ground where the bottom step should have been, and Léa felt something sharp drive painfully up into the flesh. Her other foot slipped on the wet grass and slate walk, and she tumbled hard onto her face.

For a moment, lying there trying to regain the breath that had been knocked out of her, Léa didn't know what had hit her. Then, as she tried to roll to her side, there was a dark figure looming over her.

"Don't move."

Pain was shooting up her leg from her foot. She was still trying to force some air into her lungs, but she searched the ground around her for anything she could use as a weapon. Her purse was gone, out of reach. The man's hand was on her shoulder, restraining her, and the rain was pounding into her face.

"I knocked at the kitchen," he growled, "but then I heard the front door bang open. Don't move."

A baseball hat, pulled low, completely shadowed his face. He crouched by the steps and tried to work her foot free from where it remained caught in the broken stair.

"Slide back toward the step, if you can. That's it."

The bright beam of the flashlight he'd dropped in the

grass was shining on the splintered wooden boards of the steps.

"Nobody's used the front door in two years. This step was busted before the last tenants moved out."

"Are you a neighbor?" Léa managed to ask as she felt her foot come free.

"Yeah, I live next door." His face turned toward her, and despite the darkness and the rain, she realized she knew him.

The rush of relief was almost overwhelming. She felt like crying and laughing. At the same time, she wished a hole would open up beneath her and swallow her, for she suddenly felt incredibly foolish.

"You're Mick Conklin."

"That's right." He looked up. "Been a long time, Léa."

It was flattering to think that he remembered her name. At the age of eleven, she'd had a horrible crush on Mick. She'd been certain at that time that he hardly knew she existed.

"I...I had no idea any of the old neighbors would still be around."

The rain continued to pelt down on them. Trying to salvage something of her dignity, she sat up and brushed the mud off her bare arms.

"Actually, though, driving through the town tonight, I was surprised to see how little everything has changed."

His hand was wrapped around her ankle, and he didn't appear to be in any hurry to give it up. He shone the flashlight at the scratches on her leg and her foot.

"I think you might have some splinters in there. When was the last time you had a tetanus shot?"

"I don't know. Recent enough, I suppose." She was sitting in a puddle of water that was getting deeper by the minute. "But I think I have more of a chance of drowning than dying from an infection."

His smile was unexpected. More startling, though, was the immediate jump in her pulse.

He nodded toward the dark Victorian-style house next door. "Come in and let me check out your foot."

She wiggled her toes and flexed her foot, trying to hide the pain that shot into her ankle from the sole of her foot. Whatever she'd stepped on was still in there.

"I'm okay. Plus, this is closer." She glanced up the steps at the open door. "If you wouldn't mind lending me a flashlight or a couple of candles, I'll be all set."

"I guess they didn't tell you."

"Tell me what?"

"Your house is under quarantine because of the bubonic plague."

"So...another Dr. Conklin. You went to med school after all?"

"I went, but I never finished." He put a hand under her elbow and started helping Léa to her feet.

"Too many cadavers in the labs for you?"

"Too many sunny days outside. Can you walk or you want me to carry you?"

"I...I'm really okay." To prove her point, she took a step away from him toward her house. But whatever was in her foot dug in sharply when she put her weight on it, and she winced with pain.

"You're coming with me." In a matter-of-fact manner, he looped his arm around her waist. "Of course, it's been years since I did any kind of surgery."

"I thought you said you never finished medical school?"

"I didn't. But as you said, I had plenty of chances to work on cadavers."

Léa smiled. "Well, that just fills me with confidence. Just a sec," she said, spotting her purse on the ground. She gathered it up and tucked it under her arm.

Before he could put his arm around her again—or do

something unthinkable, like really carrying her—she started hopping and limping toward his front yard.

"You're almost there." He wrapped his hand around her elbow.

"But I'm not going in your house. Call it vanity or whatever, but the way I look right now—" She pushed the wet hair out of her face. "I'm not going any farther than your front porch. So if you want to play doctor, we'll just have to do it in the open, where everyone can hear me scream."

"Now, that's a thought."

Léa glanced up at him, hearing the tone of amusement in his voice. She blushed and quickly searched for something else to say before she got herself in any deeper.

"Is your father enjoying his retirement?"

Maneuvering up the three steps of the porch was difficult, and she found Mick's arm around her waist.

"You knew he retired?" he said with surprise. "I guess you haven't been too much out of touch with Stonybrook."

"Right after Emily was born, I remember Ted saying how disappointed he and Marilyn were that your father was—" Léa paused, realizing that she'd forgotten for a moment that her brother was in prison and his family was all dead. "Ted…Ted said Dr. Conklin had sold his practice and retired."

"My father was the only show in town for too many years. But he and my mother are having a great time traveling around." Mick helped her sit down on a wide wicker chair on the porch. "Every time I talk to him on the phone, though, he still brags that it took a general practitioner, two pediatricians and a physician's assistant to fill his shoes."

"Really?" Léa asked.

"To a point. Things are growing around here. In fact, we have a bit of a boom going on. New schools, new developments, all kinds of new people. Most of it is on the outskirts of town, but it's all the same area."

The excited whimper of a dog on the other side of the screen door drew Léa's attention.

"Don't move. I have to go and sharpen my knives."

She took the flashlight that he handed her. Léa smiled as he struggled past the bouncing form of an animal blocking the doorway.

"I like dogs, if you want to let him out."

"You asked for it." He opened the screen door and a blur of dark gold bounded toward her. Mick stood by the door for a second, obviously making sure she was going to be fine with it. "His name is Max."

She started petting him. "We met at a distance when I first pulled into the house tonight."

"I have to boil some oil, too. I'll be right back."

"Take your time."

After Mick went in, Léa rubbed the dog's ears. The animal actually moaned with delight. "You're all bark and no bite, aren't you?" She scratched his sides and back, disregarding the clumps of hair sticking to her wet body and clothes. She laughed in surprise, though, when Max jumped up onto the seat next to her and stretched the top half of his huge body over her legs.

"Oh, a lap dog," she said, scratching his muzzle and broad face.

Mick stepped back onto the porch with his arms full. "Get off, you beast."

"But I just got comfortable."

His smile was gratifying, and Léa's blood warmed in her veins. He'd shed his baseball hat and jacket inside. This Mick Conklin was older and more strikingly masculine than the eighteen-year-old she remembered. He'd been on his way to college the last time she'd seen him.

"Off, Max."

Grudgingly, the dog got down from Léa's lap and

huffed off to the edge of the porch stairs. Throwing himself down, he peered out into the darkness. Defending his kingdom, no doubt.

"He loves storms."

Mick handed her a towel he had tucked under his arm. Léa thanked him as she took it and dried her face and hair and arms with it. The lightning seemed to be moving away, but the rain continued to come down hard. Léa felt oddly protected here on the porch. She looked at Max, who rolled over on his side with a sigh.

"I have to get a dog."

"Borrow him for a couple of days. That should cure you."

She watched Mick move about the porch. He lit a couple of candles in large jelly jars and placed them on a table beside her seat. He grabbed a wooden stool from a corner formed by the porch railing and sat on it, facing her.

"Give me your foot."

"Let me take a look first." She crossed her ankle on top of the other knee and tried to reach for the flashlight, but he pulled it out of her hand.

"Don't be a coward. I won't hurt you too much." He wrapped a large hand around her ankle and pulled it onto his lap. Without another word, he opened the first aid kit and placed it on her lap.

Léa hugged the towel tightly to her chest. She didn't know how to deal with the prickles of heat that were washing in waves down her spine. There was an intimacy in his touch that she was hardly accustomed to. She moved back on the wicker seat, trying to create some distance between them. But the heat spread even deeper when his fingers began massaging her heel and the ball of her foot.

After a moment he put the light on the floor, angling the beam upward, and then took something out of the first aid kit.

In an attempt to retain some slight grasp on reality, she looked down at the kit. From there, her gaze wandered to the furniture neatly arranged on the wraparound porch. In the next instant, however, she found herself fascinated by his long lashes, his short-cropped hair. She couldn't help but admire the fit of the T-shirt across his chest and shoulders.

"Ouch!" She practically leaped out of the chair, but he didn't let go of her foot. "What are you doing? A root canal?"

"I just wanted to make sure you were awake." He gave her a half smile and went back to his prodding with the tweezers he was holding in his hand.

"Okay, I'm awake."

Mick poked at the sliver again, and she squirmed on the seat.

"Wait a minute, I didn't agree to any exploratory surgery. I mean…I'm an organ donor, but that is supposed to be after…"

"Quit moving your foot around. It's almost out."

Léa jumped again at the pain. "It's supposed to be a sliver. I—"

"Actually, it was a tree." He held the tweezers up where she could see the long and ugly-looking piece of splintered wood. "Now, sit back, I have to clean it up."

She leaned back and hugged the towel again to her chest. "Thank you. The way you were going there for a minute, I was sure you weren't going to settle for anything less than amputating."

"Yeah, well, I'm not done yet. It looks like we got it all, though."

Whatever it was that Mick used to clean up the wound, it stung like crazy, but Léa bit back her complaint. Max came over again, this time carrying a chewed tennis ball he'd retrieved from somewhere, and dropped it in her lap. She bounced the ball on the wood flooring, and he caught it on the first bounce. "So, you need someone to watch him for a couple of days?"

"Not really. Heather does that when I'm out on a job." He reached for a tube of ointment and lowered his voice. "That beast is so spoiled that I have to threaten him constantly. Watch this. Dog pound, pal!"

Léa didn't think Max looked too scared as he ignored his master entirely and dropped the ball again in her lap.

"Heather is my daughter. She moved back in with me a couple of weeks ago. Her mother lives out in L.A."

Léa didn't look up but continued to rub the dog's ears as Mick put a large adhesive bandage on the bottom of her foot. She *was* curious about Mick—about what he had been doing for all these years, about what had gone wrong with his marriage, about what his daughter was like. But at the same time, she'd been so focused for so long on her responsibilities in life that she'd never had much time for socializing, or even making good friends. And this wasn't a good time to be starting, either, she told herself.

She put her foot on the floor as he started packing up his supplies.

"Thanks, Doc."

"No problem."

It was surprising how easy it had been to let down her guard for a few seconds. To be herself. But she was in town for only a couple of days. A week at the most. Only long enough to sever the last ties she had with Stonybrook.

"Well—" Léa came to her feet when he did.

"You don't have to go yet. I'm only putting these things back in the kitchen."

She smiled and shook her head. "I have a big day planned for tomorrow."

"Don't you want to at least wait until the lights come back on?"

As if the world had been awaiting his signal, the lights in the house and on the street came back on in one sweep.

"I see you have the power," she said in jest. She gave the dog a final pat on the head and started toward the porch steps. "You could have made a fortune during the West Coast power shortages."

"Hold it. You can't step out there barefoot and ruin my handiwork."

"I am not eleven, Dr. Conklin, and this is not a life-threatening emergency."

"You sure know how to bruise a guy's ego." He put a hand on her arm. "But wait…I'll get an umbrella and walk you to your door."

It was unnecessary, since she was already wet, but Léa kept her comment to herself and watched him reach inside the screen door. She heard the first aid kit hit the floor, and he reemerged with a pair of black shoes and an over-sized umbrella.

She eyed the high-platform clogs he dropped in front of her. "I'd hate to wear these. Are you sure you won't need them to go out later?"

"Very funny. Don't worry, they're Heather's, not mine, and she's done for the evening."

Léa smiled and slipped her foot into the shoes. "I feel like I'm walking on stilts."

He opened the umbrella, then took her by the elbow as they started down the steps.

"How long are you staying around for?"

"Just for the weekend, I think."

"And you're roughing it in *there?*"

"Yeah, it'll be easier getting things done that way." She made a conscious effort not to trip and fall or limp. Arriving at her decrepit front steps, she looked up and saw the door wide open, just the way she'd left it.

"Are you sure you want to go up this way? The back door is a lot safer."

"No, this will be just great." Léa climbed over the missing step and onto the landing, slipped the shoes off and handed them back to Mick. "Please thank Heather for me."

"Maybe you'll meet her this weekend."

"Maybe."

Léa gave a little wave and turned to peer in the doorway, wondering suddenly why she'd been in such a hurry to come back to this dismal death house.

Marilyn fidgeted in the seat on the stage. The windy old politician had been droning on forever. He'd bored her to death ten minutes ago. The handing out of the Foley Scholarship certificates promised to be even longer and more tedious.

Her feet were swollen and hurting. She glanced down at her stomach, which had popped out like a balloon with this second pregnancy. She wanted to sleep all the time, but having a toddler running around the house made that totally impossible.

Nobody in the audience was looking at her. Other than the usual "When's the big date?" or "How are Ted and Emily?" no one at all had commented on how she looked. She couldn't even remember the last time anyone had glanced down at her breasts or checked out her ass.

She shot a resentful look at her mother, sitting so dignified next to her on the stage. Dressed in a stylish navy suit, Stephanie looked young, beautiful and well taken care of. Marilyn's gaze went to Bob Slater, sitting in the front row. That stuffed shirt only had eyes for his wife.

Her gaze wandered down to his crotch, and she wondered idly how easy it would be to get him to go hard. One touch, probably. She shivered with the thought of giving Stephanie a reminder lesson about infidelity.

The back door of the auditorium opened, and she saw them walk in.

Ted had Emily in the carrier on his back. The room was large, but Marilyn had no doubt that her husband's atten-

tion was only on her. *She felt her entire body begin to relax.*

Marilyn returned his warm smile and once again let that weird feeling of contentment creep through her, forcing out the bitterness.

Ted loved her more than anyone else.

Five

The storm had moved through, but the air was still heavy and damp. Mick stood on the walkway, listening to the crickets and watching Léa walk into the empty house and close the door behind her. Finding her at the bottom of these steps tonight had been like getting thrown back in time. Léa had always been the brave little hazel-eyed girl next door, always watching the world around her at a careful distance. He closed the umbrella.

Years ago, as a teenager, he'd regularly been worried about her. Everyone on the street—hell, everybody in *town* knew that there were some serious marital problems in that family. And everyone knew the children were suffering for it. As a kid, Ted was tough and outgoing and personable, and brushed off everything with what may have been a pretense of not giving a damn. It was hard to tell about him. Léa, on the other hand, was less able to hide her feelings. She never could help showing her sensitivity or her vulnerability, no matter how hard she tried. To everyone…well, to Mick, anyway, Léa had always been carrying her family's problems on her back.

Through the front windows, Mick saw Léa walk up the stairs with a duffel bag in one hand. He whistled for Max, and the dog bounded down the steps. Mick took the ball from the retriever's mouth and threw it between the two houses into the backyard.

She'd surprised him tonight with her sense of humor

and her easygoing manner. But he'd also been a little surprised at his own immediate attraction to her.

A pickup truck rounded the corner and came slowly down the street. Mick turned and watched it warily. When it pulled up to the curb where he was standing, he saw it was the police chief, Rich Weir, behind the wheel. He was not in uniform. Rich rolled down the passenger window and gave Mick a half salute.

"What's going on there?" he asked, flicking his eyes toward the Hardys' house.

Mick didn't know where it came from, but he found himself mildly annoyed.

"You on duty or off, Rich?"

"You know we're always on the job."

Mick smelled Chinese food. There was a small cardboard box full of containers on the seat.

"And that job would be...delivering meals for the Peking Dragon, huh?"

"Cute, Conklin. I'm on my way to Sheila's."

"Tell her I said hi." Mick whistled for his dog and started back toward his own house.

"Seriously, Mick," Rich persisted, now eyeing the car parked in front. "Do you know who is staying in the house?"

Mick turned and glared at him. "Léa Hardy is staying there for the weekend."

"I thought so." The policeman frowned. "What the hell did she come back here for?"

"Any law against someone staying on their own property, Rich? We haven't passed any new ordinance about that, have we?"

The chief fixed his gaze on Mick thoughtfully. "I asked a simple question. Got a bug up your ass, pal?"

Mick leaned on the truck's open window and looked into Rich's square face. "Maybe I do. But this is a free country, Rich, and she isn't doing anything even mildly out of line. And considering all the grief this woman has had to put up with, I think you should respect her privacy and quit skulking around here.''

Rich let out a low whistle. ''Pretty little speech there, pal. If I didn't know better, I'd say it sounded like you and her have something going on.''

''There is *nothing* going on between Léa and me.''

''Sorry, Mick,'' he said wryly. ''You must just *sound* pissed off.''

''As a matter of fact, I am pissed off—and do you want to know why?''

''Can't wait.''

''Because you've already decided to check up on her for no goddamn reason.''

''No reason, Mick?'' The policeman glared back. ''I'm paid to keep order in this town. I want this Hardy thing over and done with. I want this town back on an even keel. If she's here to stir up trouble, then that's reason enough for me to keep an eye on her. A *close* eye on her.''

''Let me tell you something, Chief. Léa Hardy's no troublemaker. She came here knowing the shit this town was sure to dump on her front step. This woman's got guts. You *might* consider respecting that in her.'' Mick straightened up from the truck. ''Good night, Rich. Your delivery is getting cold.''

The static from the police scanner whined and crackled off the cheap paneled walls of the old trailer. Dusty Norris reached over and adjusted the knob until the dispatcher's voice came through clean again.

''Russo called again. He says some teenager has parked on Maple Street, partially blocking access to his drive-way....''

Beneath the bare fluorescent bulbs, a Doylestown news-paper was spread on the card table Dusty used as a desk.

Painstakingly, he followed a straight line as he cut the latest murder trial article from the damp pages.

"Jeff, can you check it out? I'm on the other side of town."

Laying the article to one side, he went to work cutting out the picture of Léa Hardy from an inside page. He paused for a moment and stared at the picture. She was wearing a dark business suit and glasses, and was crossing the street to the courthouse.

"This is two in a row you owe me, Robin. You know that guy only complains because he's sweet on you, girl."

Dusty picked up the two newspaper clippings and walked to the corkboard hanging beside the door of the old trailer. The board was full of other newspaper pieces he'd collected from the trial. He adjusted and moved some of them around before finally finding just the right position for the new clippings.

"It's not me. Old Man Russo has a hard-on for you, boy...."

"Finally, you're getting it right," Dusty muttered toward the radio as he walked back to his ancient swivel chair and dropped his weight into it. He swung his booted feet up onto his desk. "It's about time you assholes figured out he likes the boys better."

A large hunting knife and a half-carved piece of wood—a rude depiction of a feminine figure—sat on an upended wooden barrel next to him. He brought them onto his lap.

"There's no car blocking anything here. For chrissakes, he's waving me in from his porch. Guess I'm going in."

"If you don't come out in an hour, Jeff, we'll send in backup units." The dispatcher's snicker over the radio made Dusty's lip curl.

"Good luck, Jeff. Asshole. Be sure to keep your pants zipped."

The razor-sharp blade of the knife shaved through the wood, and the edge of a smile stayed on Dusty's unshaven face. He paused and looked up at the wall of pictures and newspaper photos above his desk.

They were all of Marilyn. She'd always loved having her picture taken, and it was quite a collection. A veritable montage dedicated just to her. In the center, a wedding photo from which Ted had long ago been excised. Marilyn, beautiful in a sexy white dress, was looking straight at the camera. Straight at Dusty. His gaze wandered to the other pictures.

"Remember when I told you about seeing Russo flashing those boys at the pond?" Marilyn's high school prom picture smiled back at him. "You laughed, but you had to add him to the list." He jutted the point of his knife at her graduation picture and looked into the sparkling eyes. "You knew I was watching by the woods behind your house when you hired him to do some gardening for you. You knew I was there."

He stared at a yellowed newspaper clipping of a young Marilyn winning a town tennis tournament.

"When you came out in your bathing suit and sat on that lounge chair on the patio, I thought the old bastard would croak." Dusty started laughing. "But it wasn't enough. You had to take your top off." He turned the carving in his hand. His thumb caressed the curves and hollows of the breasts, the buttocks. "You rolled over and had him rub oil on your back. On your legs. I know you were telling him just what to do. But you shouldn't have made him slide his hand up your thighs. You shouldn't have let him touch you there."

The blade of the knife sliced through the wood and a shaving dropped to the dirty floor.

"*I* wanted to do that, Merl. I got so hard watching you." His voice grew husky.

"I think you liked having me watch you. I think that day with Russo—" Dusty's gaze was drawn to a picture of Marilyn in a little bikini lying on a beach. "I think you knew I came in my pants watching you. You knew I couldn't help it…I couldn't wait.''

The dispatcher's voice filled the trailer again. *"Robin, I need you to check out a dog barking over on Ridge Avenue."*

"Jeff's still in there, huh?" she responded.

Dusty felt a couple of drops of water hit him on the shoulder, and he looked up at the water-stained ceiling as he wheeled his chair a little to get out of the way. With his boot, he pushed a metal bucket to catch the drips.

"Robin, maybe Russo's gonna keep Jeff until you agree to marry him."

"Fat chance. He can keep him for all I care. I'm heading over to Ridge now."

Dusty looked to the left of a tiny window where he'd taped scores of clippings and pictures of Marilyn with other people. There was a newspaper photo of Marilyn hanging a medal around Robin's neck. Her hand just happened to be brushing the police officer's breast.

"Yeah. You always liked having me watch you, Merl.'' He could feel his hardening erection pressing against his pants. He carefully placed the knife and the carving on the barrel and unzipped his fly. He looked back at the beach picture. "Like the time you brought your friend from college back to town that Christmas. Yeah…sure it was worth it to give her a tour of a closed-up mill in the middle of a snowstorm.'' He wrapped his hand around his pulsing erection and pulled a rag from his pocket. "The two of you…on the desk in the upstairs office. I saw you two…each of you doing the other…''

His breathing was getting shorter as his hand moved along his shaft. "You saw me, Merl. You put your head back. You…you looked right into my eyes…when you came.''

"I'm back…and my virginity is intact."

Dusty grunted as he exploded into the rag.

"More than we needed to know, Jeff."

"Sure, be that way, Robin. You can go in there next time."

"Knock it off, you two," the dispatcher broke in with a chuckle. *"Jeff, since you're in the neighborhood, take a drive down Poplar Street."*

Dusty wiped himself with the rag and threw it into a corner.

"What's going on there?"

"The chief called. The Hardy girl is back in town."

He paused as he zipped his pants, his every nerve wired and alert. A rush of anger surged through him.

"No shit? Léa Hardy?"

"The very same. The chief wants a patrol car circling the neighborhood all night."

"Is Rich expecting trouble?" Robin chirped in.

Slowly, Dusty reached for the knife until his fingers curled around the hilt.

"Damned if I know. But that family is nothing but trouble, far as I can tell."

With a flash of movement, the chair swiveled around, and Dusty fired the knife at Léa's picture on the board across the trailer. His accuracy was dead on. The tip of the blade cut the image in half and buried itself deep in the trailer wall.

"Not this time," he muttered. *"No Hardy's coming close to my Merl this time."*

"You could renovate the old house on Poplar Street. Or, if you prefer, you can move into the place where Marilyn used to live. Hell, if you don't like either of those two, Stephanie will probably build a mansion for you if that's what it takes to convince you to bring those babies back to Stonybrook." Bob Slater put a hand on Ted's shoulder. *"Just look at her. She becomes the very picture of a doting grandmother every time she gets near them."*

Ted watched his mother-in-law giving a bottle to month-old Hanna, while Emily played at her feet. He smiled but shook his head.

"We can't live in Stonybrook."

"Come on, Ted. This is not that Hardy thing, is it? Nobody who lived there then remembers. And the rest don't even know about it."

Marilyn walked in from the kitchen, and Ted saw his wife's gaze go immediately to Stephanie. The flush of anger colored her face in an instant.

"Ted, I said I wanted you to feed Hanna." She charged toward her mother and took the infant roughly out of her arms.

"But Marilyn…" Stephanie pleaded.

"Bring Emily, Ted. It's time for her nap." She fired a hard look at her mother as she started out of the room. "Sorry, visiting hours are over."

Ted wouldn't move back to Stonybrook for a million bucks. And it wasn't a Hardy thing.

Six

Heather pulled the black T-shirt over her head and shoved her arms through the sleeves. She stood before the mirror and put on a layer of black lipstick.

The black-clad girl with purple hair staring back at her had dark circles under her eyes. Other than that, her face showed nothing.

Heather turned and grabbed a backpack off the floor. Moving about the room, she quickly stuffed her old teddy bear into the pack. She picked up her favorite CD, rap covers of Kurt Cobain songs. She shoved it in as well, followed by a Metallica T-shirt she'd picked up at a concert in L.A. Going to her dresser, she searched the top until she found the diamond studs her mom had given her for her fifteenth birthday. She pushed those to the bottom of the bag and turned toward the door.

On her way out, she grabbed the leather jacket off the floor and stuffed it in the backpack, too. She couldn't get the flap of the bulging pack to clip closed, but she slung the thing over her shoulder, anyway. Remembering her cigarettes, she rooted around on the shelf of her closet and took down a pack and a lighter. Tucking them into her pocket, she quietly slipped out into the hall.

She could hear the shower running in her father's bathroom as she hurried past his door. Max appeared at Heather's side at the top of the stairs. Ignoring the dog's enthusiastic greeting, she went down the steps with the golden retriever at her heels.

The hands of the grandfather clock were straight up and down, and the chimes started to ring six as she reached the bottom. Glaring at the antique piece, she slipped her platform clogs on. With a quick glance up the stairs, she walked through the house to the kitchen and out the back door. The dog almost pushed his way out behind her, but she shut the door tightly.

The early morning fog was thick and dreary in the yards. The grass was wet and the wisps of mist looked like smoke in the air. She couldn't even see the stone wall at the back of the property line, never mind the houses beyond it. Coming down the steps, Heather could barely distinguish the outline of the flower garden or the top half of the mulberry tree. Most of the beat-up house next door was hidden, too.

This was just the way she liked it.

Adjusting the backpack on her shoulder, she tapped a cigarette out of the pack and lit it before cutting across the backyards. The rain on the grass wet her shoes as soon as she took the first step. It got worse when she crossed into the Hardys' backyard, where the long wet grass immediately soaked her pants up beyond the ankles.

The old carriage house, its gray wood showing almost black through the large sections where the paint had peeled off, looked soft, soggy. As Heather approached, she thought it seemed to have taken on a bit more of a lean overnight.

She started for the path behind the carriage house, but stopped when she saw a possum through the fog, waddling along the stone wall ahead of her, and decided against cutting behind the building to the next yard.

Heather took a drag of her cigarette and directed her steps up the gravel driveway next to the Hardys' house, toward Poplar Street. Her mind was racing as she walked. She used to sleep a lot, but now—despite her pretense of it—she couldn't sleep at all. All she did was think. Think and get disgusted and mad at her mother for not loving her anymore. For kicking her out. At her father for not realizing that she wasn't a two-year-old anymore. He still thought she could be babied and won over by some nice present or a day at work with "Daddy."

Of course, she found she got plenty mad at herself, too. It was just so hard to care about anything. Or do anything. She was just getting dumber and lazier as every day went by. Other than a sugar kick here and there, she didn't eat anything healthy, either. And she *was* getting fat. Her ass was too big and her chest was too flat. She was tired of the purple hair, but the reaction she got from people who knew her father or her grandparents was too good to miss. She'd become an asshole, and she hated herself for it.

What it all came down to was life sucked, and Heather was *so* goddamn tired of it.

She wasn't half done with the first cigarette, but she took out a second one and lit it and threw the first one into the wet grass. She took a deep drag and ignored the growl of hunger in her stomach.

"Good morning."

The cigarette fell out of her mouth as her foot slipped out of one of the wet clogs. In an instant, she was sitting on her butt, with the gravel digging into the palm of her hand where she'd landed. With her heart beating in her ears, she quickly jumped to her feet and looked around wildly through the fog.

Years ago, somebody had told her that the Hardy house was haunted. She should have believed them.

"Are you all right? Sorry to scare you. Over here."

This time Heather saw the figure of the woman leaning over the side railing of the porch. She was waving and looked concerned. Gathering herself together and brushing the gravel from her hand, Heather slipped her foot into her clog and moved a couple of steps closer.

"Weird weather, don't you think?"

Heather's usual reaction at a time like this would be to blow the blabbermouth off and hit the road.

Her feet, moving up the driveway, seemed to have other plans.

"I'm Léa Hardy."

"No shit." She hadn't meant to say the words aloud. But they were out, and Heather found herself gaping at the plain-looking woman still leaning over the railing. She had her hair pulled tight in a ponytail and didn't have a stitch of makeup on her pale face. The Hardy woman smiled, and Heather decided maybe she wasn't ugly plain, just didn't-know-what-to-do-with-herself plain.

"I guess everybody in this town knows me or has heard of me." She looked down at Heather's shoes and extended her hand. "I think I might have heard of you, too."

She stared at Léa's extended hand and decided not to take it. "I gotta go."

The woman put her hands on the railing again. "Thanks for the use of your shoes."

Surprised, Heather looked down at her wet clogs. "What?"

"I had kind of a crazy night last night." Léa laughed a little. "I got here right in the middle of the storm. I was actually scared to death of going in. I haven't been back here for twenty years. Anyway, right in the middle of my Amityville horror, the lights went off."

Heather had no clue what an Amityville horror was, but she noticed that Léa Hardy looked sort of wound up. She got plenty wound up herself, sometimes.

"Anyway, I ended up with my foot stuck in that bottom step."

Heather glanced down at the missing stair.

"You're Heather, aren't you?"

She gave a wary nod.

"Your father was nice enough to help me out and sit me on your front porch while he took out the stump of the tree that was sticking into the bottom of my foot. Anyway, that's how I ended up wearing your shoes. From there to here.'' She motioned to their porch and back to hers.

Through the slats of the railing, Heather saw the woman was wearing a pair of ankle socks. But there were scratch marks on one shin.

"Sorry to babble on.'' Léa straightened up. "It felt kind of good walking out here and seeing somebody alive in the yard.''

Something about her openness kept Heather from bolting off. "You here to stay…or something?''

Léa shook her head. "I need to sell this place. Hopefully, soon. You know…for money reasons.''

"It has to do with your brother, doesn't it?''

"As a matter of fact, it does. I need to hire a new lawyer for him.''

In Heather's experience, most adults treated teenagers either as kids or as morons. This one was fairly cool.

"By the way, do you think it'd be okay if I snuck over to your house and picked up my purse?'' Léa glanced over that way. "I think I left it on the front porch last night.''

"Sure. Whatever.'' She adjusted the backpack on her shoulder. "I gotta go.''

"Thanks for stopping by.''

Heather gave an indifferent shrug and started walking again. At the end of the driveway, though, she turned around and stared at the Hardy woman, who was still on the porch.

"Um…good luck finding a good lawyer. I hope your brother gets out.''

Léa nodded once and then stared down at her white socks. She actually looked flustered.

Heather turned on her heel and started walking up Poplar Street. She didn't know what got into her to say that.

No, she knew why. The first summer she'd been babysitting for Emily and Hanna, Ted used to come around a lot. He was a real cool dad, the kind her own father had been when she was little. And the girls really liked Ted.

The girls. Heather swallowed the painful lump in her throat and lit another cigarette. She didn't want to think about them now. She didn't want to think about Marilyn, either. Even though she was *glad* that someone had knocked off the bitch.

Her steps led her toward the park. Still, she didn't know why she'd been nice to Léa. What did she care what Ted's sister thought of her?

Shit, it was too late for being nice. Too late for being anything. Because after tomorrow it wouldn't matter what people thought of her.

It probably looked as if she'd swallowed her tongue, but Léa was genuinely touched by what Heather had said. And somehow, she could tell…she could feel that the words had been spoken in earnest.

She waited until the fog closed in behind the teenager's retreating figure before pulling on her sneakers and edging carefully down the steps. Around midnight, when she'd had another panic attack, Léa had realized she'd left her purse on the Conklin's front porch. Without her keys, her wallet, her cell phone or even her pepper spray, she'd felt horribly vulnerable. But there'd been no escaping the house. She had nowhere to go. And sneaking out there and having Max wake the neighborhood with his barking had been out of the question, too. So Léa had forced herself to wait out the dark.

Reaching the sidewalk, she turned around to take her first good look at the house in the daylight. Even through the soft layers of the fog and mist, the broken windows and peeling paint and sagging porch looked as ugly as before.

Léa headed toward the Conklins' house. The neatly kept yard that she and Ted had played in was badly overgrown. If she wanted to make a better first impression on potential buyers, she had to clean the yard up first.

Behind the screen door, the beveled-glass front door

was closed. Léa peered through the railing. Her purse lay by the foot of the wicker love seat, where she'd dropped it last night.

She went up the porch stairs on tiptoes, but Max's barking inside the house told her that he wasn't fooled. As she hurried to pick up her purse, her only consolation was that Heather was already up and out. Maybe Mick was an early riser, too.

She had her purse under her arm and was making her escape when the front door opened.

"Léa!"

She winced guiltily. "Me again."

"How's your foot?"

"All better. In fact, I'm back to normal." She peeked at the man and the dog standing behind the screen. Mick's hair was wet. No shirt. She looked down at Max, but found herself admiring the muscles of Mick's hairy legs beneath the khaki shorts. She looked up in embarrassment, forcing herself to look at his face.

"Sorry to sneak up on you. I left this here last night." She held up her purse as proof. "When I saw Heather just now, she said it was okay if I came over and got it."

"You saw Heather?" Without waiting for an answer, he pushed the door open. Dog and man were on the porch in an instant. Max excitedly circled her once before bouncing down the stairs and into the yard to relieve himself.

Léa focused her attention on the dog, then the railing and finally the professionally trimmed bushes. She tried to think of anything but the expanse of Mick's shoulders or how low the tan on his back went.

"She was out?"

"Heading that way." She pointed up the street.

"Fifteen. She's fifteen," he muttered before turning to her. "I have to keep reminding myself that she's old enough to go out for a walk if she feels like it."

From experience Léa knew not to say anything. This

was exactly what parents sometimes needed. Somebody to hear them out.

"And I suppose it doesn't really matter that I was planning for us to spend the day together." There was definitely a touch of regret in his voice. "But this is exactly what I've been on her case to do. To stop moping around the house and get out more. Of course, I didn't expect her to be going visiting at six in the morning, either."

He turned his attention back to her.

"Sorry to unload this on you. My daughter and I are just going through an adjustment period. You've got your own troubles."

Léa shook her head. "That's okay. It was nice meeting her."

"She actually talked to you?"

"Well, when I gave her a chance, she did hold up her end of the conversation."

"Conversation, huh? Are you sure this is the *same* Heather that we're talking about? Purple hair—"

"Pierced eyebrows, ears—" she touched her lip "—I'm not sure, but I thought she had a stud on her tongue. Maybe she didn't. Same shoes I borrowed last night."

Mick laughed and his face grew pensive. "So how does she compare?"

"Compare with what?"

"With all the troubled teens you deal with in your job?"

Léa tried to hide her surprise that Mick knew what she did for a living. "Looks alone don't shock me anymore. It's very common for adolescents to experiment with strange styles of dress and manners. They're trying to separate themselves from the family unit. It's the same in every generation."

"Is this what she is trying to do?"

"That's what most teenagers do."

"You are being evasive. My question was about Heather."

"Mick, I know as a parent you want someone to give you a straight answer. But I exchanged only a few words with her this morning. I don't really know Heather, so it would be impossible for me to differentiate between what is normal teen rebellion and what is over the line."

Immediate concern darkened his expression. "What do you mean, 'over the line'?"

"Never mind I said anything." Léa shook her head guiltily. She had no right to worry him with something that wasn't there. "I was only talking shop. People like me have a hard time leaving their jobs at work."

"What do you mean, people like you?"

"You ask an awful lot of questions. You didn't by any chance go to law school after you flunked out of med school?"

"I didn't flunk out of med school." Now a hint of a smile tugged at his lips. "But you still haven't answered my question."

People like me. People who had no personal lives of their own, whatsoever. But she could not say this to him.

"I tend to get emotionally attached to the troubled teens I work with." She waved him off as he started to respond. "I know that is *not* a particularly good thing for someone in my profession, but that's the way I am. And on that note, I will make my exit."

"Have you had breakfast yet?"

"No," she said before thinking. If she had taken a second before answering, she could have lied. Already, she was feeling things she didn't want to feel, thinking things she didn't want to think. And Mick Conklin was definitely out of her league. "I'm heading out to grab something now."

"Where to?"

She gave him a narrow glare. He was rubbing a spot on

his chest, and it was distracting. Léa had to force herself not to stare down at the crisp curls of blond hair.

"Is this a twenty-questions thing?"

"Hardly. Just trying to be a good neighbor. Where are you going for breakfast? And can I come?"

"Are you trying to hit on me?" Léa immediately looked away. It took a couple of seconds to swallow the knot of embarrassment choking her. "Sorry. I don't know why I said that."

When she looked back at him, Mick was studying every flaw in her face.

"Now, Ms. Hardy," he said, a mischievous glint in his blue eyes. "If I were hitting on you, I'd do it this way. First, I'd invite you to come inside for breakfast. Then, after making a couple of phone calls to cancel my appointments for the day, I'd make some of my world-famous raisin bread French toast with applesauce. And let's just say, that would only be the start."

His tone was light, but she knew he was serious. Léa tried to ignore the heat spreading from her belly all the way up to the tips of her ears.

"Oh, the old 'world-famous French toast' line, is it?" she said flippantly. "Can I place an order to go?"

His rumble of laughter made her smile. "You sure know how to put a man in his place."

He was right about that. Léa was an expert at turning down offers. A lifetime of practice had perfected her technique. She looked down as Max ran back up onto the porch.

"In all seriousness, with everything I have on my plate for today and tomorrow, I won't have time for any sit-down meals." She smiled warmly. "I am grateful, though, for what you've done for me already. I'll see you around."

She walked down the steps and crossed the lawn before that six-foot temptation behind her succeeded in clouding her thinking. She frowned as she headed toward her car, knowing it might be once in a lifetime that a man like

Mick Conklin would pay any kind of attention to someone like her.

Well, maybe in her next life she'd get the chance to take him up on it.

"What's so difficult to understand, Ted? I'm not happy." Marilyn *couldn't bring herself to look at him. She wouldn't allow his hurt to play on her guilt. She went back to packing the suitcases on the bed.*

"You accuse me of working too much. Fine, I'll try to cut my hours. You claim that I don't give you enough attention. We can fix that. I'll ask Léa or your mother to come and stay with the girls, and we'll take a trip. You miss living in Stonybrook." He threw his hands up in frustration. *"We'll move back. Running away is no answer!"*

"I am not running, Ted. I'm moving out. Moving out of this house. Away from you."

"Marilyn!" His anger seethed in the edge of his tone. *"How am I supposed to make you happy when you don't give us a chance? How can you give up on us when we have so much at stake?"*

He was talking about the girls. Everything was about them. The center of his universe had become them.

"I'm taking Emily and Hanna with me. You can come and see us as often as you like. I'm not filing for divorce, so think of this as a break. I need a break from you. And you need a break to clear your head and think of a way to convince me our marriage is worth it."

Seven

The gas station attendant stared at her across the empty lot. Heather turned her back to the rows of gas pumps and continued to wrestle with the Goodwill box sitting near the edge of the pavement.

As it was, the backpack would not fit into the metal chute. No amount of shoving, twisting, even cursing worked. Frustrated, Heather dragged the bag out and pulled it open.

The black leather jacket had been a Christmas gift from her father. She looked at it, remembering how excited she'd been that he had actually picked the *right* thing—without her asking for it, or giving him any ideas. She'd even forgiven him for not coming to California for New Year's as he'd promised her over the phone. Regardless of the warm spring days in L.A., she'd worn the jacket to school every single day for the rest of the school year.

She stuffed it into the chute and watched the box swallow it up.

The Metallica T-shirt and the CD were from the first concert she'd ever gone to. Heather had felt like such a grown-up, getting invited to go with some of the older kids of one of Natalie's friends. Those went down really smooth.

Something pulled in her chest when she looked at the old worn-out teddy bear. He was her oldest friend. For as far back as she could remember, he'd always been there.

During all her trips back and forth across the country,
Teddy had always traveled with her, tucked under her arm.
It hurt to think that he wouldn't be there tonight for
Heather to cuddle with when she went to bed. She hur-
riedly pushed the stuffed animal down the chute.

After tomorrow, none of it mattered, anyway.

Heather spotted the pair of diamond earrings at the bottom of the bag. One of her friends had told her that they
were a carat or something each—like Heather knew the
difference. But it was so typical of her mother to buy
something that outrageously expensive for her just because
Heather had asked for earrings. Natalie wanted everything
simple. She didn't have time to do any thinking or planning. She never even attempted to surprise her daughter
with anything original. She herself always ate in the same
handful of restaurants. Always vacationed on the same island. Drove the same type of car. Always bought whatever
Heather asked for.

More than a few times over the past few years, Heather
had wondered how was it that Mick and Natalie had lasted
together as long as they had. In so many ways, they were
total opposites.

She decided against throwing the earrings away indi-
vidually. Instead, she just clipped the bag shut and slid it
down the chute. No problem this time.

"Heather!"

From somewhere behind her she heard a teenage boy's
voice, but she didn't turn or answer. She shook another
cigarette out of the pack and lit it.

"Heather, is that you?"

Ignoring the persistent voice, she started down the sidewalk. The engine of a car roared to life somewhere in the
gas station, and she heard it chugging up next to her.

"Heather, it's me, Chris Webster!"

She experienced a momentary lapse in judgment. She
turned and looked. Behind the wheel of an ancient station

wagon, a young man's face split into a huge grin. *Great.* How had she ever been stupid enough to consider this dork her first love?

"I heard you were back in town. God, I can't believe it. You really are back."

She wanted to tell him that how stupid it sounded, the way he kind of repeated the same thing. But she didn't, because she didn't want to encourage him to hang around. She took a another drag off her cigarette and turned her steps down the street again.

"Hey, you got a minute?"

He didn't wait for her to answer, but pulled the car into an open parking space on the street, killed the engine and hopped out.

He was much taller, and his chest had really filled out. Heather noticed his face had changed, too. The kid look was pretty much gone. He'd actually gotten kind of cute without those ugly glasses he used to wear. All the freckles were still there, though, and the bright red hair. Okay, he wasn't a dork.

"My God, you look different."

She had to stop, since he was now standing in her way.

"So do you. Big deal." The only reason why she answered him at all was because he hadn't ogled her breasts as soon as he got out of the car. Standard operating procedure for most boys, in her experience.

"I heard you were back in town."

"You already said that." She took another puff of the cigarette.

He hesitated. "Are you mad at me or something? I mean, for not calling you when you got back?"

She shot him an incredulous look. "Why would I be mad at something like that?"

He shrugged and stuffed his hands in the pockets of his jeans. "How would I know? Who knows why girls act the way they do. I mean…if we were going out together or something…it'd be different."

"Yeah, well, we're not."

His baby-blue eyes turned soft. "But I sort of thought…we *were* going out the last time you were here. But then you never answered any of my e-mails. And anytime I was on instant messenger, you wouldn't talk to me. And—"

Heather threw the cigarette on the sidewalk and crushed it out. "Well, it was nice talking to you, but I gotta go." She pushed past him.

"Hey, can you come out with me tonight?" He fell in beside her. "Remember Kevin? Anyway, he and a couple of other guys started this band last year, and they're playing tonight, and I can get out of work early and—"

"I can't."

"Okay. Then can I call you? Say Monday?"

"Don't bother."

"Why not?"

"Because I won't be there."

"I heard you were staying around for the summer, even for the school year."

She started crossing the street toward the park. He kept pace with her.

"Oh, I know! You meant you won't be there on *Monday.* How about Tuesday? I can call you after I get out of work."

Heather whirled around to face him by the entrance to the park. "I won't be there on Tuesday. Or Wednesday. Or Thursday. Or any day after that. And no, you can't send me e-mail or try to talk to me on instant messenger. Just drop it, Chris. Just chalk me up as permanently unavailable. Period!"

Pulling into the jammed parking lot of the Bucks Equipment Rental, Mick realized why he never came down here at 8:00 a.m. on Saturday mornings. All the do-it-yourselfers were out in force. He had to go around the building and park in the back. As he got out of his truck, he saw a couple of Doug's guys wrestling a hitch onto an old Honda. An open trailer behind the car already had a lawn mower and a shop vac, a floor sander, hedge clippers and a bunch of other hand power tools loaded into it.

"Hey, Mick."

"Looks like somebody's planning a relaxing weekend," he joked, giving a cursory glance at the inside of the car. Cans of paint, brushes and pans and rollers, drop cloths and other odds and ends were all piled up on the back seat.

One of the men stood up and jerked a thumb at the car. "Only if this old rice-burner will pull it all."

"Haven't you heard these cars are made in America now?"

"You don't say!"

Mick shook his head at the pair and headed toward the back door. "Doug in?"

"Yep, and I heard he has a line on that backhoe you wanted for Monday."

"About time."

As he reached the shop door, he paused with his hand on the doorknob and cast another glance at the car. From this angle he could see the license plate. Maryland.

The door moved against his hand, and he turned to face Léa coming out.

"I am *not* stalking you."

"That's what they all say." Her smile reached her hazel eyes, and Mick felt the same strong pull of awareness between them. The tendrils of blond hair that had pulled loose from the ponytail were dancing around her face. The effect was to make her look much softer, younger.

"So where are we going next?"

Her smile turned to laughter.

''All I can say is—'' her voice dropped down low ''—I'm glad you told me you're *not* hitting on me.''

She stepped past him. He let the door close.

''And if I were?''

Her gaze flitted away. As he watched the color rise prettily into her cheeks, Mick found himself admiring her soft skin. The way her chin curved so delicately upward to the full lower lip.

''Then I'd say I wouldn't have much of a chance.'' With a shy glance in his direction, she turned and walked across the lot toward her car.

Mick stood for a full minute, watching her and realizing that something had just happened to him.

The stirring that he was feeling a few inches below his belt was not unfamiliar, but that other something—that connecting spark that just leaped from one contact to the other—*that* was the stunner.

He continued to stare, admiring the perfect fit of her butt in the tight jeans shorts, the long and shapely legs. He remembered how seeing that compact little body of hers in the wet T-shirt and shorts had affected him last night. He'd done his damnedest to hide it.

''You coming in, or should I come out?''

Mick turned to see the heavyset owner of Bucks Equipment Rental holding the door open. Doug looked over at Léa, who was now leaning over to help the two guys with the hitch.

''Nice ass!''

''Mind your manners.'' Mick took a hold of the door himself and motioned the proprietor back into the store.

''What? Just because you're single, you think you have a monopoly on every attractive woman in this town?''

''It has nothing to do with that. She's a customer, for chrissakes. How the hell do you expect to run a business when a woman can't feel comfortable walking in here without getting harassed?''

Doug led the way to the small office behind the counter. "I wasn't harassing her. Hell, I didn't even help her. Gracie did. I just admired her…uh, physique—and not to her, but to *you*." He sank down in his chair as Mick leaned against a dented file cabinet. "And quit giving me so much shit. There's no law against looking…."

Gracie poked her head unceremoniously into the office. "Can you believe it? That was Léa Hardy."

"Ted's sister? No kidding?" Doug pushed to his feet and went to the window, pulling up the blinds. "What do you know about that!"

"She rented quite a few things." Gracie looked from Doug to Mick. "Wanted to know how to go about renting a Dumpster for this weekend. I told her she was dreaming if she thought she could get one inside of a month."

Gracie moved next to Doug and started peering out, too.

"She's doing some fixing up of that house they own before putting it back on the market."

"Dumpster, huh?" Doug said thoughtfully. "She's gonna need more than a Dumpster for that place. Nobody from around here would want that house if she was giving it away. That place is just bad luck."

"Are you two renting equipment or running a real estate office here?" Mick frowned fiercely at them. "What do you say, Doug? Are we going to get to my jobs, or what?"

With a flirtatious smile at Mick, Gracie left the office, but Doug kept looking outside.

"Forget it." Mick started for the door.

"Wait, wait. I have it right here." Doug picked up a paper from the tray of the printer. "Backhoe on Monday. Two Dumpsters by 7:00 a.m. at these two addresses on Tuesday. Let's see…I had this other list someone from your place faxed me yesterday. Where the hell is it?" He went behind his desk and started pawing through the paperwork, but his gaze kept drifting to the window.

Mick took the step to the window and pulled the cord. The blinds dropped with a snap.

"You know what you said earlier?" He planted his hands on Doug's desk and leaned toward him. "Guess what? I am single. And yes, I may just be planning on monopolizing this one. Do you have any objections?"

Surprised, the heavyset man eyed Mick for a long moment. "I guess not."

The stack of old sneakers in the corner filled the teenager's room with a certain unmistakable aroma.

The flip side of Chris's organized and responsible behavior, his mother thought, was his inability to throw old shoes away. Patricia Webster left the door open and dropped the basket of folded laundry on her son's bed. Pulling up the blinds, she opened the windows wide.

The fog had finally burned off outside. She took a deep breath of the morning air.

The phone rang next to the bed, but before she could reach it, she heard her husband answer it downstairs.

She took a pile of neatly folded clothes out of the basket and put it on the dresser next to the other pile that Chris had not yet put away. She also moved the half-dozen socks he'd left beside the computer on his desk and put them with the other piles. Patricia thought their son worked too hard. But her husband still kept pushing him.

Every Saturday, year-round, he worked behind the cash register and stocked shelves at the pharmacy downtown. In addition to that, twice a week during the summer months, he mowed lawns and trimmed hedges and did all kinds of outdoor work with a landscape company in town. And if that weren't enough, he was now washing dishes at Hughes Grille whenever Brian's regular guy didn't show up—which was practically every other night.

She put the empty laundry basket on the floor and stared

for a moment at the shelves of trophies and certificates and pictures lining the wall.

The phone rang again. This time Patricia didn't even bother to reach for it. Her husband would take care of whatever the caller wanted. More and more, Allan seemed to be taking care of everything in their lives.

Patricia smiled as she started putting the clothes away for Chris. Every drawer was perfectly organized. Boxers at one end of one drawer, undershirts at the other end. Collared shirts separate from the T-shirts. Everyday T-shirts separate from the nicer ones. So much like his father. She couldn't help but wonder if someday Chris might even decide to take after Allan and become a minister.

She opened the overflowing bottom drawer where Chris put his socks. So unlike him, she thought. Everything was a total mess here.

"Finally, you left something for your mother to do." Patricia knelt down on the rug with the clean pile and got to work. She took out handfuls of the jumbled mess. As she pulled out more and more socks, she reached deeper into the drawer. Then her fingers brushed against something at the back. Frowning, she backed up a little and pulled out the drawer a little more. It was a worn and partially folded envelope.

Patricia's heart sank. She knew what it was before she even took it out, and her fingers were trembling when she reached for it. She turned the envelope over in her hand and opened it.

She stared at the half-dozen pictures that dropped onto the rug when she took out the handwritten letter.

"No! Please, no." Her body rocked back and forth. Her fingers shook so badly that the words were a blur, but she forced herself to read.

Dear Christopher,
Here is a little something to keep you smiling until

next week.

   I'll be waiting.

                                                         Marilyn

"You bitch. You whore," she cried in anguish, tearing the letter into shreds. "Why don't you leave us alone?"

The photos might have looked innocent enough to someone who didn't know better, or who hadn't seen them before, or who had not heard explained in graphic detail what events followed the taking of them.

Marilyn standing behind Chris and peering over his shoulder at the camera. The remote that allowed her to take the picture was in one hand. But with her other hand, she was reaching around him and holding onto his belt buckle. In the next, he was sitting at her kitchen table and she was leaning over him. Her breasts were pouring out of her low-cut blouse beside his face. There was one by the car. Another one of Chris alone, stretched out on a bed, smiling.

"No! Dear Jesus, no!" Patricia sobbed. With tears coursing down her cheeks, she picked up the pictures one at a time, tearing them in half, then in half again, and again, until they were shreds scattered around her knees.

"I was on the phone. I heard you cry out. I ran up to see…" Allan's large frame filled the doorway. He tried to catch his breath. "What's wrong, Patricia?"

The tears continued to fall. "She's not dead. Not dead, I tell you." She raised a hand helplessly toward her husband. "Marilyn is *not* dead."

He came to kneel beside his wife, gathering her slight frame against him. "Don't talk rubbish, my love. Don't! The woman is *gone*."

Patricia shook her head. "An envelope. A letter." She motioned to the shreds scattered everywhere on the floor. "They were the same pictures she promised to destroy. She promised me, Allan. We talked. I went back again. I begged her. She told me she wouldn't put her filthy hands on our son again. And you...you told me the Lord takes care of things. You said you would make sure she never comes back.''

''She is not coming back, my love. Everything has been taken care of. She is *never* coming back. Believe me, she is never going to hurt us again.''

Come to town and I'll tell you who did it.

Léa was back in town; now she had to make sure everyone knew it. Making a stop at the busy newspaper shop on Main Street was a last-minute thought. She pulled the car and the trailer into a double parking space and hurried across the street.

She picked up a paper and paid the heavyset woman behind the cash register. ''The last time I was in town, this was an ice cream parlor,'' she commented conversationally.

''That must have been a long time ago.''

''I guess it was...well, twenty years ago. I should introduce myself.'' She stretched a hand across the counter. ''I'm Léa Hardy.''

The woman shook her hand with a pleasant smile, but Léa noticed a few heads in the shop turn in her direction. *Mission accomplished.*

A couple of minutes later, Léa left the store and started for her car. As she strode across the travel lane, a gray Cadillac lurched away from the curb and accelerated rapidly. Hearing a sharp warning, she jumped for the curb as the car sped past.

''Jeez!'' She saw Stephanie Slater driving the car. Her heart racing, Léa stood on the sidewalk, staring after her.

A bicyclist pulled up beside her. ''That was close. Did you get the license plate?''

''No, I didn't.''

''That lunatic almost ran you down!''

"I'm okay," Léa whispered, with a grateful nod to the man. He was obviously an out-of-towner and didn't know it was no crime in Stonybrook to run down a Hardy.

"I'm sick of her. I'm tired of this marriage."

"You can't give up on her, Ted," Stephanie pleaded.

"She's left me no choice." He crumpled the letter Marilyn had left him. *"I'm not going to rise to her bait. No more. She can do whatever the hell she pleases. I don't give a damn."*

"Please, Ted. Tell me what happened. When she called to ask me this afternoon to come and watch the girls, I got the impression that she was going out with you tonight. I thought maybe…maybe she was coming to her senses and realizing how difficult this whole situation has been on you and the girls."

"That makes two of us." He flung the crumpled paper into the fireplace. *"She asks me to come over for dinner, only to leave a note saying she is going out on a date and doesn't know when she'll be back. Every time…she reels me in to arm's reach so she can slap me."*

"But you know this is her way of doing things," Stephanie reasoned. *"She thinks by making you jealous, she'll get more attention."*

"Well, she already knows that doesn't work. This is not the first time she's tried to pull this shit." He paced restlessly across the room. *"I can't do it anymore. I'm not putting up with her games, with her lies, with the blatant screwing around. I'll file for divorce. I was naive once. I thought she could change, but she was right about that one. She said I'd learn to hate her. And I have."*

Stephanie sank down on the chair. *"This will be so hard on the girls. They're so attached to you."*

"I'll take them with me."

"But she won't let you. She knows how much they mean to you, so she'll fight you for them."

"Let her," Ted said coldly. "But she won't win. She's negligent and incompetent as a mother. Christ, she's incompetent as a human being. I'll have my lawyers get a statement from everyone who knows her. I can play hardball, too, if that's what it takes to get custody of my children. She'll have no choice."

Eight

It had taken about half a dozen tries. Every time she started the lawn mower and began to tackle the hayfield she once called a lawn, the engine would simply cut out. Finally, Léa was convinced. She would have to raise the blades and cut the grass a couple of times. There was no quick way of doing anything, it seemed.

She was on one knee beside the mower and raising the blades when a police cruiser pulled to the curb in front of the house. The officer was eyeing the car and trailer, which were also parked at the curb in front of the house. He started talking through his two-way radio.

Léa's distrust of the police force in Stonybrook ran deep, but she forced herself to keep a clear head. She stood up and wiped a spot of grease from her hand onto the seat of her jeans. Walking toward the young man getting out of his patrol car, she noted that at least she'd never seen this one testify in court.

"Good morning, officer."

"Is this your vehicle, ma'am?" He motioned to the car and trailer.

"I rented it this morning. Not even an hour ago. I needed it to bring these things back from the equipment rental place." She gestured toward the lawn mower behind her and the other things still in the trailer. "Is there a problem with it?"

He took a pen and his book of tickets out.

"Is this necessary?" Léa tried to keep her tone good-natured. "I mean, if there's a problem…?"

The policeman looked at her through his mirrored sunglasses. Talking slowly, as if she were incapable of comprehension, he went on to explain her violations. She was parked heading in the wrong direction on a two-way street. The nose of her car was marginally blocking the driveway of her neighbor to the left. The trailer wheel was approximately twelve-and-a-half inches from the curb. There was a minute crack in the red plastic of the trailer's left brake light.

"Look, I'm sorry I pulled in like this. I had every intention of parking in the driveway, but I thought I'd unload the lawn mower first and…and…" She looked away, trying to control her frustration. "Would you give me this ticket if I told you my name was Liz Smith and I really lived on the next street over?"

"Yes, Ms. Hardy."

Sure. They knew who she was. They had already decided to give her a hard time. Léa couldn't help but wonder if the building inspector and the fire marshal would be stopping by next. She held out her hand for the ticket.

"Have a nice day, officer."

She took her keys off the front porch and went to move the trailer. The policeman sat in his cruiser, watching her intently as she got into the car. Obviously, intimidation was going to be part of the approach.

It would be easy enough to go around the block and park on the right side of the street or even pull into the driveway. But they'd probably stop her for something else like the trailer's temperamental brake light the rental place had warned her about. Or they might just give her a noise-ordinance ticket for squeaky brakes. God only knows what they'd think up.

"You're not going to do this to me," she muttered under her breath. "I'm not going to feel as if I have to look over my shoulder every time I turn around."

Léa slapped her hand on the steering wheel and turned off the engine. Getting out of the car, she walked purposefully toward the police cruiser still parked behind. The officer was talking on his two-way radio but put the mouthpiece down as she approached. He lowered his window.

"I am so glad you are still here, Officer…Officer…" She looked at the name badge. Thomas Whiting. "Tom."

As he looked at her in annoyance, she plastered a nonthreatening smile on her face. "I know you're a *great* driver, so I was wondering if I could ask your opinion on something…well, car related?"

"We're here to serve and protect, ma'am."

"Exactly." She half turned to face the trailer. "You see, all those things in the trailer are rented, so I figure it would be safer if I pulled it into my driveway. But I can't pull the car in head first, because I might have a problem backing out. But backing into the driveway is too hard, too. Do you think…well, could you possibly explain to me how I can do it without causing a lot of damage to everything? I don't want to take out all of the hedge that's encroaching on the driveway. You must be so good at doing these kinds of things. I mean, you look like an outdoorsman. You must have experience with boat trailers."

She looked at him hopefully, and after a moment he nodded and stepped out of the cruiser. She must have touched his male ego just right, for he immediately launched into an elaborate explanation on how far to bring the car out into the street and when and how to turn the wheel as she backed up.

"Are you're sure I won't hit the house or anything?" she asked in winsome tones. "I'd hate to do any damage to anything."

"It's really not too difficult, Ms. Hardy."

"Please, call me Léa," she said pleasantly.

"Right. As I said before, all you have to do is—"

"Tom, would it be too much trouble to ask *you* to move the car for me?" She looked at him hopefully. "Sorry, never mind I asked that. You must be so busy. It was totally wrong of me to keep you here as long as I have."

"No, not at all." He took Léa's keys and, as she stood there watching, backed the trailer and car into her driveway.

Léa had used exactly the same approach years ago when she'd started as a social worker in a run-down high school in South Philadelphia. All the teachers explained how unsafe the classrooms were and told her what to expect with regard to ongoing damage to her car. Léa had managed to get to know some of the toughest kids right off the bat, and they'd ended up being her best allies. Those years had given her a very good foundation for working with difficult teenagers. This adolescent in uniform was no different.

When the officer came back out, she maintained her smile. "Thank you, Tom."

He gave her a polite nod and handed the keys back. "Don't mention it, ma'am…uh, Léa."

She went and stood beside the lawn mower and waved a goodbye as the policeman drove off. She waited until the cruiser made a left at the corner.

Shaking her head, she pulled the cord of the lawn mower and listened to it roar to life.

At the sound of the car wheels on the gravel drive, Bob Slater closed the program on the computer. By the time he heard the sharp click of Stephanie's shoes on the kitchen tiles, he had the computer shut down and his electric wheelchair was purring through the house to meet her.

He stopped in the wide doorway to the kitchen and watched his wife's agitated movements as she upended a large grocery bag on the counter. Something had upset her. Again.

The cut flowers in a cellophane wrapper ended up under the bread and large cans of something else landed on top of them before rolling off the counter and across the floor. She quickly hunted through the rest of the stuff and pulled out the carton of cigarettes. Her hands were not moving fast enough. He saw her shoulders shaking.

"W-what's wr-rong?"

"She's in town." Stephanie's hands attacked the carton, tearing it open and scattering packs of cigarettes everywhere. "Léa is in Stonybrook."

"Wh-who t-told you?"

"I saw her," Stephanie snapped, lighting a cigarette before finally turning around. "And she is going around town…to the hardware store, the gas station, the grocery store. Shopping. Talking to everyone like there is not a goddamn thing wrong. Like she's not even related to that murderer. Like she belongs here."

She'd been crying and long streaks of mascara stained her face. Her shaking fingers never moved the cigarette more than an inch away from her lips. She took another drag.

"She killed my…my grandchildren."

"S-Steph, T-Ted killed them. N-not Léa."

"She is on death row. Where she belongs. She is going to fry for killing my babies."

"N-not her. T-Ted."

She couldn't even hear him. Her delusions were back in full force.

"Rich said they would let me watch. I want to see her dead. I want to see the pain in her face. In her eyes…"

Bob didn't bother to correct her anymore. She clearly wasn't hearing him. Stephanie continued to puff away at the cigarette. She had stepped over the threshold to her other world again. The place where she confused people, places, times. But she always remembered that Marilyn and the girls were dead. Bob had seen her go there many times in the past two years, but he thought she seemed to be improving. Until now. She crushed out the cigarette in the sink.

''She's out.'' She immediately lit another cigarette. ''She is walking the streets. In broad daylight. She must have escaped.''

Bob pressed the button and moved his chair near the wall.

''I...I have to...to call the police. She...she has no right to be here. The killer. The murderer.'' Stephanie reached for the phone on the counter. ''I'll call Rich. He'll take care of it.''

Without checking for a signal on the phone, she punched in the numbers. She waited, puffing on the cigarette, while one more black tear rolled down her cheek and dropped onto her stained white blouse. She kept waiting.

Bob let the line that connected the receiver to the phone jack drop down onto the kitchen floor. He moved his chair toward his wife. Everyone thought Stephanie was the one taking care of him since the stroke. But he was taking care of her, too.

They weren't going to put his wife in any hospital just because she went off the wall every now and then.

No, Bob would always make sure Stephanie was protected and cared for. He owed her that, at least.

Heather took out the prescription slip from her back pocket and walked into the drugstore. The pharmacist's counter was all the way to the back. As she started that way, though, she spotted Chris stocking books and magazines on a rack halfway down. Quickly, she changed direction and walked up the next aisle.

There were three people sitting in the waiting area. Another woman, holding a fretting infant in her arms, was pacing a six-foot path back and forth in front of the counter. Heather saw the pharmacist, Mr. Rice, at one end talking on the phone while punching something into a computer before him.

Andrew Rice had been the pharmacist the last time Heather was in Stonybrook. He was the only black pharmacist she'd ever known, even in California. He knew her father, and many times, when she'd picked up a prescription for Marilyn or the girls on her way over to baby-sit, he would stop to talk to her. Not today, though. He never even took a second to look up.

"Can I help you?"

Heather's attention turned to the clerk who was running the cash register behind the prescription counter. The girl looked as if she'd just scrubbed her face with soap and water.

"Yeah." She laid the paper on the counter. "I want this filled."

"Is this the first time you're filling a prescription here?"

"No, I was living here a couple of years ago. All the insurance stuff is the same."

"We have a new computer system now, and—"

Heather dropped her insurance card on the counter and went on to recite birth date and address and phone number. "I'll wait for it."

"Oh! I'm sorry, but we are so backed up that unless it's an emergency…"

"What if I say it is?"

The girl cast a look at the pharmacist, still on the phone. "You can wait for Mr. Rice and explain it to him, if you want. Or you can have your doctor call us, and—"

"How long of a wait would it be if I decide to come back?" Heather asked, irritated.

The girl looked at the clock on the wall. "Midafternoon, I think. There are a lot of prescriptions ahead of yours.

About three? I can call you if you want. Or we even deliver, if you can wait until Monday morning.''

"Never mind. I'll be back at three."

Heather ignored the curious looks of the other customers and stalked out of the drugstore, avoiding Chris Webster again as she left.

Well, that was that, she thought. By three o'clock this afternoon, she'd have everything she needed. Everything she'd ever need.

Mick called home a couple of times during the morning, but the answering machine was all that he got. Not that Heather would ever consider answering the phone if it rang. Still, though, he was starting to get a little apprehensive about her whereabouts.

After his last appointment at twelve-thirty, he headed directly home. Turning onto Poplar Street, the first thing he noticed was the change in the Hardys' house. The lawn was cut and the evergreen shrubs around the house and along the driveway had all been trimmed back.

But with the good came the ugly. As he got out of the truck, he stopped and looked at all the chipping paint and warped clapboard and missing pieces of trim. It all showed a lot more, now that the house was exposed. It was kind of like getting a buzz cut at the end of the summer. The tan line was brutal.

As Mick went up his porch steps, he saw Léa dragging a blanketful of grass and hedge clippings toward the back of the carriage house.

He knew it would only be neighborly to offer her the use of lawn equipment and whatever else she wanted out of his shed down by the back wall. But by helping her, Mick knew that he would be getting involved. And not just in the selling of the house, but in the complication of Ted's defense.

He didn't know how he felt about any of that, right now.

Max bounced around him like a puppy when he walked in.

"Heather!" he called up the stairs. No answer. He held the dog for a moment as he listened. "Wait a minute, you maniac."

He walked through the house, dumping his keys into the kitchen drawer. There was no sign of her and no note.

"Heather?" Mick went up the steps three at a time. Her bedroom was empty and in the same condition that she'd left it this morning. He stood at the top of the stairs, thinking and vacantly petting the dog. As far as he knew, she had not called any of her old friends since being back. Nobody had come here, either.

As guardedly pleased as he'd been this morning to find out Heather had finally decided to get out of the house, he was worried now about where she could have gone.

He checked again to see if there were any messages left on his cell phone. There were none. He did the same with the answering machine downstairs. With the exception of his own messages, there was only one other. Andrew Rice had called, asking Mick to call him at the pharmacy.

By the time he was done listening to the messages, the dog was all over him, anxious to go out.

Mick looked up Andrew's number and took the phone with him as he let Max out the back door. Standing on his back porch and watching the dog go about his business, he dialed the number. After being put on hold for a couple of minutes, he heard the pharmacist's voice on the other end of the line.

"Look, pal, you told me it's okay not to start the second-floor addition to your house until October. Don't tell me you want us to start tomorrow!"

"Tomorrow?" Andrew laughed. "I want it started today and *finished* tomorrow."

There was a series of clicks on the line.

"Hey, can you hold the line for a minute, Mick? I have a call coming from a doctor's office."

"Sure thing."

Tucking the phone in the crook of his neck, Mick descended the back steps and threw Max's Frisbee. The dog made a flying catch by the Hardys' property line and ran back toward Mick, eager to play.

Léa was walking back from behind the carriage house with an empty blanket. Mick gave her a friendly wave.

"Are you still there, Mick?"

"Yeah." He tried to get ahold of Max's collar, but the beast escaped and ran toward Léa.

"This place is crawling with sick people today. I better get down to business. God knows when the next call is coming."

Léa dropped the blanket and motioned to him that she was okay with the dog. Mick watched her scratching and petting the excited animal.

"So, what's up?"

"Heather dropped off a prescription to fill this morning. Before she picks it up this afternoon, I wanted to make sure you knew about it."

Mick's instant relief that his daughter had not run away was immediately overshadowed by the thought that she was sick. "What's the prescription for?"

"Some low-dose sleeping pills. It's on your wife's prescription slip, and it looks like she signed it. Just to be sure, I already made a call to her office in L.A., but the answering service told me she's out for the next couple of weeks. This is a routine thing we do, Mick. You know, with all the stuff going around with teenagers. It's probably nothing, but, well, she is still a minor and these pills do have some kick to them."

"I appreciate that you called, Andrew. And no, I didn't know about it." And the whole time he'd been thinking Heather just slept too much. "Natalie *was* her doctor when she was in California. But I'd like to talk to Heather *and* her mother about it.''

"I can just hold on to it until you get back to me, if you want."

It was a reasonable-enough solution, but Mick didn't want to erect more of a wall between them. Especially if Heather really needed these things. Still, sleeping pills for a fifteen-year-old? It just didn't figure. He turned away from watching the playful antics going on between Max and Léa.

"Is there a way you could do a partial fill? I'm trying to buy some time until I get hold of my ex-wife or take Heather to a local doctor here."

"No problem, Mick."

"But I don't want Heather to know this was my suggestion."

The man's voice turned confident. "She won't. We run short on drugs occasionally on Saturdays. You can call me when you want us to fill the rest of the prescription."

Mick's mind was already racing. It was true that Natalie couldn't seem to find enough time in her life for their daughter, but she was by no means a negligent mother or slapdash physician. She was strictly straight arrow.

"I appreciate the call, Andrew. I'll let you know."

"Like I said, no problem. By the way, I hear your next-door neighbor, Léa Hardy, is back in town. If you see her, tell her hi for me. She and I were classmates back in… I've got another call. Sorry, Mick. Gotta run."

For a long minute, Mick just stared at the phone in his hand. Then he immediately dialed Natalie's home number. The answering machine picked up. Instead of leaving a message, he tried her cell phone. Again, the same thing.

He couldn't operate his life like this. He and Heather had to start to talk. He dialed the number for Natalie's mother's house. He was almost surprised to get a live person at the other end, even if it was the housekeeper. But at least the woman knew who Mick was and didn't hesitate to answer his questions.

Natalie and her husband had gone on a two-week trip to one of the islands in Hawaii. No, she didn't know what island. But he could call back later and talk to Natalie's mother.

Mick looked tiredly about him in search of the dog as he hung up after the last call. Only a few steps away, Léa was crouched beside Max and holding him by the collar. Her gaze was on Mick, though.

"Nothing's wrong!" he said a bit more sharply than he intended.

"I didn't ask." She let go of the dog and rose stiffly to her feet.

Watching her pick up the blanket, he suddenly felt like shit. She was heading back toward the hedges along the driveway.

He caught up to her as she was picking up a rake. "Look, I'm sorry about snapping your head off just now. It wasn't you."

She put a hand to her forehead and then tilted her head from side to side. "I *think* it's still attached."

Mick was fascinated by how good she looked, with twigs stuck in her hair and dirt smudged on her already-sunburned face. There were grass clippings all over the sleeveless T-shirt.

"Guess I'll have to try harder next time."

She smiled but never stopped working, raking the cuttings onto the blanket.

"Where would you go in this town if you were fifteen and didn't have too many friends and just wanted to hang somewhere outside of the house?"

Mick knew why he'd asked this question of Léa. She, too, had been a loner. In a way, like Heather.

"The park. Probably I'd hang out by the lagoon and feed the ducks."

Nine

The seat of her pants was wet from sitting on the rain-soaked ground, but Heather was beyond caring. She glanced down at her watch again. One-thirty. Another half hour, she thought, and she'd head over to the pharmacy again. They always had things ready before they told the customers.

She stared into the empty take-out bag. There was nothing left of the order of French fries she'd picked up from the fast-food place up the hill, but the ducks didn't seem convinced. A couple of them continued to stand a foot away from her shoes, making little complaining sounds as they stared at her with cocked heads. A half-dozen Canada geese were grazing by the edge of the lagoon. They kept an eye on her, too.

She shook a foot at the ducks, but they only trotted off a few steps and then edged back toward her.

Heather turned her thoughts to the few things she needed to do tonight. Letters. She wanted to write goodbye letters to her parents and her grandparents. They all deserved to know why she was doing this. She also wanted to write letters to a couple of the friends she used to hang out with in ninth grade in L.A. And then there was Chris. She hadn't thought about writing to him until today, but she realized now she had to. She needed to explain. She crumpled the empty lunch bag and shot it at the green garbage barrel. It went in.

She planted her elbows on her knees and stared at a couple of younger kids kicking a ball around across the lagoon.

Heather also wanted to write a will. She'd already dumped the stuff she cared most about in the Goodwill box. But there were other things that she wanted to give to people.

The two ducks suddenly erupted in a flurry of quacks and wings and feathers. Turning, they half ran, half flew down the bank into the water. The geese, too, turned as a unit and swam out into the lagoon.

"Was it something I said?" Heather called after them. A split second later, though, she heard the enthusiastic breathing of the golden retriever racing down the river walk toward her. She glanced up the path and felt a knot of worry form in the pit of her stomach. Her father was coming, too, with Max's leash dangling from his hand.

She turned her attention back to the lagoon and put a bored look on her face. Nothing like a little attitude to put off the interest of an adult.

Max, though, wasn't discouraged at all, and Heather braced herself. The knucklehead knocked her over all the same.

"There's a leash law in this park, you know," she complained loudly, pushing herself back up. Her father was taking his time catching up to the dog.

The excited animal was all over her, licking her face, tugging and pulling at one of her shoes until he had it in his mouth. She tried to reach for him, but he backed just out of her reach, waiting with his butt in the air, his tail wagging sixty miles an hour.

He looked so cute, but Heather couldn't bring herself to say it out loud. "Give that back to me," she said crossly. "Now! Bring it *here.*"

"He missed you this morning." Mick took the shoe

from the dog and dropped down on the grass next to her. "And so did I."

This was her cue to say something nice, but Heather couldn't bring herself to do it. Not this late in the game. "Don't kid yourself. The two of you are *much* better off without me."

She could feel him staring at her face. She didn't turn to look at him but kept her eyes on Max, who was swimming out into the lagoon after the geese.

"I don't know why you say that."

"Because it's the truth."

"But it's *not*." He let out an exasperated breath. "Heather, you are my daughter. I *wanted* you to come back and live with me. I have been *waiting* for the chance to get close to you again. But I'll be honest. I'm having a hard time understanding this new you."

"It shouldn't be too hard to understand," she said sharply. "It's the fact of recognizing that you were much better off before I came back. That your life was much simpler before I got here. More manageable, easier to deal with, routine, pleasant…call it whatever you want. But that's the fact."

"How do you figure that?" His expression showed the hurt. But he wasn't giving up. The blue eyes were piercing when they met hers. "What have I said or done that could possibly make you think that?"

When Heather started shaking her head, he put a firm grip on her arm and drew her attention back to him again.

"And what makes you think a *simpler* life is what I am after? How could I ever want to replace my daughter with *simple?*"

"Mom did."

"I'm not your mother."

"I know that," she retorted. "And maybe *simple* is the wrong word. But look at you. Your life *has* gone downhill since I came back. You're thirty-eight. A healthy, single, good-looking man that most women drool over. How come all of a sudden you don't have a girlfriend?''

His laugh lacked conviction. ''You're upset because I am not going out with somebody right now?''

''You haven't had a date since I came home.'' She picked up a pebble and threw it into the water. ''I was a fifth wheel when I was living with Natalie, and I knew it. And now you're ruining your social life so that I won't feel the same here. I'm not a kid anymore. I'm old enough to notice things. I'm old enough to know that I don't belong here.''

''You miss your mother, don't you? That's what all of this is about—being homesick. Is that right?''

''Jeez, Dad! You are so thick sometimes.'' She shook her head. ''You've been too far away from her for too long. Natalie is only good for *stuff*. I ask and she buys. It's a simple arrangement. And it's just the way she likes it.'' Heather met her father's gaze dead-on. ''But I don't need *stuff* anymore. I don't need *her*. In fact, I don't need either of you.''

Heather jumped to her feet and took the shoe out of her father's hand. Stuffing her foot in it, she started up the path.

''Wait a minute, Heather. This is *not* the end of this conversation.'' Whistling for the dog, Mick quickly caught up to her. In a minute, Max was trotting a couple of steps ahead of them, his coat dripping. ''I can see there are misunderstandings that we have to sort out between us. That we have to force ourselves to—''

He stopped talking when she took the cigarette pack out of her pocket. She shook one out and lit it.

''When did you start smoking?''

Heather intentionally smiled at the note of disapproval she heard in his voice. ''Get real. This is nothing new.''

''You're fifteen, for God's sake. Have you heard of lung cancer? Do you know the damage you are—''

"Save it, Dad." She quickened her steps and took another drag off of the cigarette.

"It's not even legal! Does Natalie know you smoke?"

"Of course she does," Heather lied. "But with all the other stuff I've gotten myself into...you know, drugs and sex, hooking up..." She shrugged. "Heck, smoking was nothing."

Heather was surprised when he snatched the cigarette out of her mouth. She was really shocked, though, when her father took her by the arm and spun her around until she was facing him. She'd never seen him this angry before.

"You listen to me," he growled. "I don't know what it is you're trying to sell me here, but I am *not* buying. Now, I know your mother is busy and has a very important career. But in spite of all that, I know she wouldn't be sucker enough to buy this, either."

He crushed the cigarette under his foot.

"From now on, there are rules that you will follow. Basic. Got it? And you *will* respect these rules. And I don't give a damn how wild you were in L.A. I don't care what you got away with out there. You're back here with me now, and you *will* change this ugly behavior. Now, do you understand?"

"Perfectly!" She shook her arm loose and took a step back. "Keep dreaming."

As she walked away, she heard him behind her. She should have known he wouldn't let her escape on that note.

"Heather!"

Léa was bone tired by the time she settled down on the front porch. And disgusted. And her joints ached. The night was overcast, and there was no breeze. The long, cold shower she'd taken and the light, sleeveless sundress she'd put on did little to cool her off. She could still feel a bead of perspiration dripping slowly downward between her breasts.

The whole thought of putting this house in shape to sell was starting to overwhelm her. All day, she'd been cutting and hauling and raking in the yard. Scraping chipped paint from the outside walls. Pruning and clipping hedges. And despite working her butt off, she hadn't even started on the inside.

But that wasn't all that was pressing on her. Every time she'd come around from the backyard, she'd checked the mail slot in the front door, thinking that maybe there would be another letter. She'd come back here as he—or she—had told her to do.

"Stupid girl!" she mumbled under her breath as she wiped the sweat off her brow with the back of one hand.

Léa took a deep breath, knowing that she needed to stop herself from thinking about it all, if only for a few minutes. She needed to make herself push Ted and the trial and this house and Stonybrook and all those damn letters out of her head. For just a few minutes, she had to force her mind and her body to unwind. To cool off. To recover.

She stretched her bare legs out on the old blanket and leaned back against the clapboard wall of the house. With her eyes closed, she tried to picture something totally striking in her mind's eye—a sleek white sailboat slicing through a sparkling blue sea. Bold. Free. Fearless.

"Asleep?"

Léa opened her eyes with a start at the sound of the low whisper. She immediately relaxed when she recognized the voice. Mick stood on the front lawn, looking at her over her porch railing.

"Asleep? No! I only take power rests."

"Oh, sorry. I'll go away."

"Don't! I'm well rested already. In fact, I'm a new woman."

His smile was so powerful that she felt the kick of it in her stomach.

"That new woman wouldn't be hungry?"

Starved, she thought, for human company. "I had a sandwich for dinner."

"Good. Because I didn't bring you dinner. But I did bring something more important. Can I come up?"

"If you can manage the front steps."

"No problem."

Léa watched him come up onto the porch. He was carrying a plate in one hand and had something else tucked under an arm.

"Sorry, I'm not really equipped to entertain." She pushed a couple of the paint cans next to the railing as a place for him to sit if he wanted to.

"I don't need to be entertained."

He was barefoot and dressed in old jeans and a T-shirt. "I want you to know this is the first time in a long while that I've felt safe walking across that lawn barefoot."

Léa smiled and took the two bottles of beer that he handed to her. As he started lowering himself onto the blanket beside her, she slid over to make room for him.

"By the way, do you drink beer?"

"On occasion."

He filled the space, and she found herself very content with it.

"Then let me ask this question. Are you sure you're old enough to drink?"

"You should know." She peeked under the aluminum foil covering the plate he put down between them and immediately let out a sigh of pleasure when the smell of it drifted upward. "Chocolate chip cookies! And still warm. Did you make them?"

He shrugged. "I like to bake. And, if I may say so myself, I'm a pretty decent cook."

"Yes, you warned me about that this morning." She stole one and took a bite. "Mmm. Out of this world."

She popped the rest of the cookie in her mouth.

"But you have to wash it down with this." He opened the two bottles and handed one to her. "Beer and cookies. Nothing like it."

She shook her head doubtfully but took a sip. He was watching her, so she let the taste linger in her mouth, then took another sip. She reached for another cookie.

"Not bad, huh?"

"My first impression? I thought it would be foul enough to use in a Mothers Against Drinking campaign." She took a bite and followed it with a swallow of beer. "But I've learned not to trust first impressions. So, to give you an honest opinion, I'll have to taste a few more…just to make sure." Léa finished the rest of the cookie and reached for another one.

"If this is a trick to finish the plate and not leave me any cookies, I'm on to you."

"And here I was thinking that you brought the whole plate just for me."

"Actually, I did." Mick took a swig of his beer. "I was hoping you'd let me pick your brain about something."

Léa saw the uneasiness that had crept in his face. It was something in the set of his eyes. "This is about Heather, isn't it?"

He nodded.

"Mick, if you need a sounding board, someone to talk to, I will gladly be that. But I want you to know, I am *not* a licensed psychologist or therapist." She softened her tone and lightly brushed the back of his hand with her own. "If anything, I'm only good at *identifying* problems. And I might be able to find the names of qualified professionals in the area that you could call."

"I think—" he paused "—no, I *hope* all I need is somebody to hear me out. I guess I want to make sure that it's not only me, that all parents go through this. And I'd prefer not to talk to some stranger. I want to talk to you.''

Léa felt butterflies inside her, and they were not just stretching their wings. They were churning up a storm in there.

Mick gently tapped her bottle with his. "What do you say? Can you give me a couple of minutes?"

"I'm all ears."

He squeezed her hand once before releasing it. "It's kind of tough knowing where to start, considering I didn't really think Heather and I even had a problem until this afternoon."

Léa watched his profile. The tension was there. In his jaw. Around his eyes. In the thinning of his lips.

"You met her. You saw the look, the image or whatever it is that she's trying to present."

"You mean the defiant teenager look?"

Mick nodded. "My ex-wife, Natalie, warned me about it, so I was ready when I picked Heather up at the airport. And, to be honest, her look didn't really worry me. I know we all go through stages." He put the bottle aside. "But the thing that totally took me off guard was her attitude. The 'I don't give a damn' attitude. The laziness. The lack of interest in anything. Staying in her room all the time. Not eating, unless it's a two-liter bottle of soda or a family-pack of Tastykakes. Not talking to me. Not expressing any feeling, good or bad. I mean, bringing Heather back here wasn't like throwing her into a new town or a new home. It isn't like she doesn't know anyone. The last time she was in Stonybrook, there were at least half a dozen kids that she hung out with. She rode her bike everywhere. She had a summer job. She was a happy kid. Certainly, a different one."

Mick ran a hand through his short hair and rested his wrist on a knee.

"I didn't know how long I should let it go. I just figured

that I'd go with the flow. But it's been almost three weeks she's been back and there's still no change in her attitude. So last night, I blew up and gave her a long lecture. Then, for whatever reason, she did come out of her room. But not for long. Pretty soon, we were right back where we'd started.''

"Then she went out early this morning."

He nodded.

"What happened this afternoon?"

"I went to the park." He turned to her. "You were right. She was there, by the lagoon, even feeding the ducks.''

Léa remembered how, at a much younger age than Heather, she, too, had discovered and used that park as a refuge.

"She was very vocal today."

"That's a good start."

"Not really." Mick shook his head. "Not in any constructive way. She just blasted me. She was mad at me, mad at her mother, mad at the world. She told me we were all better off without her. That she didn't need any of us, either. Whatever 'I don't give a damn' attitude she had before, today she turned it all into anger. And then, when I tried to talk to her, to explain, she stuck a cigarette in her mouth and walked away." He turned sharply to Léa. "How many of your teenagers smoke?"

"A few, I'm sure. But never on school property where *I* can see them.''

"Well, Heather told me today that with all the sex and drugs she's been involved with, smoking should be the least of my concerns. She used the term *hooking up*. What is *that* supposed to mean?"

"It means having casual sex with someone you don't necessarily know.''

"Great.''

"What did you say when she told you all this?''

"I lost it. I went after her and barked out a list of expectations about a mile long. Things I told her would be mandatory behavior for as long as she was living with me. I blasted her with everything. I even hit her with the guilt thing because of how she's hurting everyone with this rejection phase, including her mother and me."

"But she wasn't listening."

"No. But that didn't stop me. I went on and on about how important family is. How she should cherish what she has, rather than throwing it away."

"What was her response to that?"

"She didn't say anything." Mick looked out at his house across the lawn. "She just stepped right into the street. And she would have been killed if that woman had been speeding or hadn't been able to slam on the brakes fast enough."

Léa's attention was sharply focused on him, on everything Mick had just said. "Was she *trying* to kill herself?"

"No! She just wanted to scare the hell out of me. She wanted to shut me up. To leave her alone." Mick closed his eyes and rubbed the bridge of his nose. "And she succeeded."

"Where is she now?"

He nodded toward his house. "Upstairs in her room, probably with music blasting through her earphones."

"Has Heather been taking a lot of risks lately? Giving things away? Talking about death?"

"What are you getting at?" He suddenly looked angry.

"I'm talking about warning signs, telltale things we look for when a kid might be in trouble."

Mick looked more upset than before. Léa pushed the plate of cookies and her beer aside and moved to sit cross-legged on the blanket, facing him.

"Look, I'm just a social worker. I'm not qualified to advise you. But hearing you talk, I think it's possible

Heather might be struggling with a case of teenage depression."

"But she has so much going for her. People who love her. Things that every teenager dreams of. She's smart. Beautiful, in spite of doing her best to hide her looks. Why should she be depressed?"

"I hardly know her, so I can't really say. But I can tell you from what I've seen in my work that many adolescents end up fighting depression just because they feel unable to articulate their feelings. And their feelings are often anger—or sorrow—over some loss or shame or dashed hope. Depression is a world of numbness...of *no* feeling."

"I don't know..."

"But look at what you just told me. Heather got angry today. She blasted you. That's a very good thing, because it means—for a while, anyway—she found the voice to express her feelings."

"But we didn't get anywhere. When we were done, I walked away more frustrated than before. And I don't think she was any better off, either."

"I didn't say you solved all your problems today. All I am suggesting is that communication, in any form, gives you a place to start." Léa knew Mick would fight her next suggestion, so she gentled her tone, tried to present it in a practical sense. "It looks like Heather has resisted having any structure to her life. Unlike many kids her age, she's not contacting friends. I'm guessing she wasn't involved in any activities or sports in California, either. Nothing that provides any sense of routine in her life."

"She's not a five-year-old anymore. I can't tell her to go outside and kick the ball, and I can't very well drag her to quilting class."

Despite the sharpness of his tone, Léa nodded her understanding. "Another possible way to address a situation like this—and this is a recommendation I often make to kids' parents—is to get their son or daughter into some kind of therapy.''

He didn't say anything right away, but the rejection of the idea was etched on his face. Léa could almost read his thoughts. She and Ted had had years of therapy, and she knew firsthand that most people still attached a negative label to it. Most people didn't know how much relief it could bring.

''This doesn't even have to be a one-on-one session,'' she persisted. ''Just having her take some classes on identifying feelings or on developing some sense of assertiveness might be enough to bring Heather out of her shell. She very well might need someone other than her parents to help her out of the slump she's in.''

''Those questions you were asking before about taking risks or talking about death. Don't you think you might be overreacting a little?''

His tone was accusatory, but Léa recognized that she was no longer talking to Mick, her big crush next door. She was counseling a concerned father who was possibly in denial about his troubled teenage girl.

''I warned you before we started, Mick. I am not the most qualified person for a situation like yours. I make recommendations about the teenagers I work with only after spending many, many days with them. I really don't know Heather, and whatever overreacting you think I am guilty of, it's only based on what you've told me.''

''That's good.'' He rose to his feet. ''Thanks, Léa. This was quite educational.''

''You're welcome,'' Léa murmured, feeling as if she'd been kicked, inside and out.

As she watched Mick walk back to his house, Léa silently upbraided herself. She should have expected this. Of course. She was back in Stonybrook. Here, only the Hardys had problems. The rest of them were picture-perfect.

On the surface, anyway.

* * *

He was the last one left in the kitchen.

Chris finished rinsing the large, double stainless-steel sink and used a towel to dry and shine it, just the way Brian wanted it.

Finishing there, he wiped the top of the stoves and the counter, then ran a clean rag over the front of the refrigerator and freezer doors. The large mixing bowls were put away in order by size. The pots and sauté pans hanging from their hooks. The utensils lined up in the drawer. Chris shut the cabinet doors tightly and picked up the mop to run it one last time over the tiled floors. Brian would have nothing to complain about.

In addition to being the second-generation owner of Hughes Grille, Brian Hughes was also the chef. At forty-something years old, the man took great pride in the establishment he'd worked hard to improve, and he had strict rules that all his employees had to follow. Cleanliness and order were at the top of the list.

Sister Mary Brian, some of the help called him behind his back. But not Chris.

The floor gleamed from the wash. Satisfied with it, Chris dumped the bucket into the sink by the back door and rinsed everything out. Storing the mop and bucket, he saw a sports car parked by the screen door. The teenager glanced toward the double doors leading to the restaurant and wondered if Brian knew that Jason was back.

Chris never had any problem getting along with Brian, as fussy and particular as he was. But putting up with Jason Shanahan was something else again. It wasn't that he had any problem with the restaurant owner being gay, either. Brian was a solid guy and he seemed committed to his relationship with Jason, the same way most married couples in town were committed to each other.

But Chris saw how Jason acted behind his partner's back, and it only increased his dislike of the man.

The teenager's apron was soaked, and he tossed it in with the rest of the kitchen laundry for pickup tomorrow. His own car was parked in the back, but he decided to poke his head in and let Brian know he was done.

He punched out and worked his way back through the kitchen to the alcove that led to the darkened dining room. After the kitchen's bright fluorescent lights and tile, the darkness and the carpet made the dining room seem startlingly tomblike.

As soon as the swinging door of the kitchen closed behind him, Chris could hear clearly the argument that was going on in the front bar area. He approached cautiously, unsure of how to make his presence known.

"…took care of it!" The restaurant owner was unhappy. Very unhappy.

"So *what* if I made a mistake? That was two goddamn years ago! Water over the dam, remember? You're getting all bent out of shape over nothing, Brian."

"Nothing, my ass! When the hell are you going to get it in your thick head that as long as there is proof out there, fingers can get pointed at us? At me?"

"The scag is dead. Her husband is gonna fry. And if *I* can't find that shit, nobody else is gonna, either." There was a long pause. "And remember, nobody's looking for it. So there we go. Now stop your damn nagging and let's lock up. I had a tough day."

"No, you can't brush it off just like that. Listen to me, Jason." Brian's voice dropped down low, and Chris could hear the worry in it. "It was all over town today that Léa is back. She'll dig it up, damn it. And if she…"

As he moved closer to the bar, Chris's hip brushed against the corner of a table. The delicate flower vase fell over with a soft thud, and water spilled out onto the tablecloth. He quickly righted the vase, but the dining room lights came on instantly.

Jason peered in suspiciously from the archway leading to the bar. "Oh. What do you want?"

"I'm finished in the kitchen. I came in to tell Brian I'm on my way home. Is...is he out here?" Chris used one of the cloth napkins set out in preparation for tomorrow's lunch to soak up the water. "I...I'm sorry. It was so dark in here, I just couldn't see a thing."

"Leave it go, Chris." Brian appeared behind his boy-friend. His face was flushed. "It's late. Your parents will be worrying. I'll take care of it."

With an appreciative nod, Chris backed out the same way he'd come in. Before disappearing through the swinging door, though, he cast a final look over his shoulder. Jason had disappeared into the bar again, but Brian was changing the wet tablecloth.

Chris couldn't recall ever seeing Brian Hughes quite so upset.

"Get me the names, damn it," Marilyn screamed through the phone at her attorney. "I want the name of every goddamn traitor in this town who's given a deposition to Ted's lawyers about me."

She slammed the phone down.

"You want to play dirty? I'll show you dirty."

Ten

What else could she expect from a hole-in-the-wall pharmacy?

Heather added the three paltry pills to the larger bottle she'd been hiding on her closet shelf. She crumpled the bag after looking once more at the note telling her the rest of her prescription would be available by Tuesday.

"I'll be six feet underground by then," she murmured, tucking the bottle in the front pocket of her pants.

She didn't need them, anyway. Her mother had given her the original prescription in California six months ago, and Heather had gotten it filled right away. She'd had Natalie write this prescription slip for her just before coming east, but it didn't matter. She had enough here to do the job.

Heather glanced around the room one last time. All the letters—the envelopes clearly marked with the recipients' names—were taped to the dresser mirror. The piles of clothes on the floor were more or less cleaned up. She didn't want to waste any time putting them away, so she'd just stuffed them into the closet. The effect was good enough.

She checked her watch. It was 2:10 a.m. Plenty of time. She slipped out of her bedroom into the dark hallway.

Tonight, Heather had come to the conclusion that taking the pills here in her room wouldn't be right. Considering the way her father had acted today, she decided he couldn't handle it. He'd freak, pure and simple. And even though the house had been in their family for a couple of generations, she figured he might not be able to live here anymore. Not if she died right here in the house.

As always, Max followed her step-by-step as she went silently through the house. In the kitchen, Heather took a couple of cans of soda out of the fridge and a big bag of Oreos out of the cabinet. Max whimpered softly as she reached for the back door. Instead of trying to go out ahead of her or grabbing his leash in his mouth or jumping at the door, he sat back on his haunches with his big chocolate brown eyes staring at her.

Heather crouched down and gave him a big hug around the neck. He was always a smart dog.

She slipped out the back door before the tears came.

A cut branch dangled from the hedge, brushing against the driver's side window. Léa's eyes vacantly watched the hypnotic back-and-forth swing of the leaves in the breeze while her mind skimmed along the thin edge of sleep.

She was curled up on the front seat with her back to the house. Her legs were draped over the center console. The key was still in the ignition, her purse on the floor. Léa's eyelids closed for a second, and she gratefully felt the first waves of oblivion advancing.

Out here, at least, she might be able to sleep. She didn't have to be afraid. She didn't have to listen to every creak in the wood, certain it was some stranger's footstep. Out here, she didn't have to stare at the shadows and imagine her father alive again. Preparing to do the unthinkable. Out here, she could escape. She was safe in this car.

A muscle jumped in her leg, and her foot pressed involuntarily against the driver's door. And her eyes were open again.

"Please!" Her quiet appeal was to no one but herself. Exhaustion had her on the edge of tears, and she had no

one to blame but herself. Why, after all these years, was she still unable to block out the demons of the past.

"It's too hot in here." She balled up the blanket that was partially covering her legs and threw it into the back seat of the car. As she did, she saw the shadow pass through the backyard and disappear inside the carriage house.

The chill that washed down Léa's spine froze her. For one confused moment, she stared, questioning what was it exactly that she'd seen. The night was very dark. The equipment in the trailer, still hitched to the back of her car, partially obscured her vision. As she tried to clear her head, she could not grasp clearly whether what she'd seen was real or imagined.

The shadow of a tree branch, she told herself. Clouds racing across the moon. Léa knew her best choice was to ignore it and go back to sleep, but she could not tear her gaze away from the carriage house. Her mind wouldn't stop thinking the worst. Someone lying in wait in the yard. A stalker watching the house. Watching her.

Or maybe, she thought, a teenager meeting someone. Or a young woman hiding in a place where she wouldn't be found for a while.

Léa suddenly felt sick to her stomach. Her hands were shaking when she reached over and took the keys out of the ignition. Her heart was hammering in her chest as she scrambled out of the car and stood in the dark driveway.

She took a step toward the carriage house, then stopped. Reaching inside the car, she fished her pepper spray out of her bag. She could be wrong, and years of having to be street-smart were engrained in her.

Léa edged along the car and then the trailer toward the carriage house. Every sound, every movement seemed un-naturally distinct. The summer breeze riffling through the leaves. The scrape of branches overhead. The barking of a dog far across town. Even the slight grind of her sneaker-clad feet on the gravel.

By the time she reached the shadow cast by the carriage house itself, serious doubts about what she'd seen caused her to pause. Through a wide crack occasioned by one of the warped wallboards, she peered in. Everything inside was still and dark. Any number of creatures, wild and dangerous, could possibly be making their homes inside this place. Léa remembered her newly purchased flashlight. It was sitting on the back seat of her car.

A soft noise like the popping sound of a plastic bottle drew her attention back to the inside of the building. Someone was in there. She moved quietly toward the side door. It was slightly ajar. Still holding the pepper spray tightly in one hand, she grasped the latch and pulled the door open a little more. A narrow strip of dim light widened inside. At the very edge of it, Léa spotted the tip of one dark shoe.

"Heather?" she whispered softly.

The shoe immediately pulled back into the shadows. Léa paused by the partially open door and stared into the darkness. The sound of her own nervous breathing was blocking any sound from inside. The sudden doubt that Mick's daughter might not be the shadow lurking in the dark chilled her blood. Léa took a hesitant step back.

"Bitch!" The whisper came from behind. As she looked over her shoulder, she spotted the dark object flashing toward her head.

The blow was sharp, and Léa's head bounced against the door like a rubber ball as she went down hard in the grass.

Before his mind was clear of the gray layers of sleep, before he even realized who was screaming, Mick was out of bed and running down the hall.

In a moment, he was standing in his daughter's doorway. The room was empty. Downstairs, Max was barking furiously, and Mick looked in confusion at the empty bathroom at the end of the hall.

The screams subsided, but he could now hear Heather calling for him. Urgency bordering on panic infused every cry. He realized that the cries were coming from the open window in his daughter's room. Crossing the room, he yanked the window all the way open. A shadow was hunched over by the carriage house on the Hardys' property. Heather cried out for him again.

He was down the steps and through the house in seconds. Max was barking and scratching at the back door. Mick switched on the floodlights in the backyard and charged out the door behind the dog.

"Heather?" Mick ran across the yard.

"Daddy, it's Léa."

"What's wrong?"

"She's…dead. Léa…is dead.…" She half turned in his direction. Her hands were shiny with blood. Her eyes were wild. She was nearly hysterical. "Pushed her…hit the door. She's bleeding.…"

"Go back to the house. Call 911." Mick crouched down beside Léa. To his relief, he found the pulse beating strongly in her neck. Heather continued to sob raggedly next to him. "She's alive. Get moving. *Now!*"

The teenager scrambled to her feet and ran toward the house. Max continued to bark furiously by the stone wall at the back of the property. Mick moved so that the bright lights from the back of his house were shining on Léa's face. Blood covered her forehead, and he gently lifted her hair. There was a long gash right below her hairline. The blood was continuing to ooze out of it. He listened and felt for respiratory movement. She was breathing.

Léa moved her head and said something unintelligible under her breath.

"You'll be okay, baby."

Mick checked her shoulders, arms, hands, legs. Looked for any broken bones. Her fingers clasped his hand.

A neighbor from two doors up came trekking across the backyards in his bathrobe, a flashlight in one hand. "Is everything okay here?"

"Heather..." Her voice was weak. Mick's attention turned back to Léa. Her eyes were open, and she was trying to focus on his face. "Where...is Heather?"

He was relieved to hear her talk. "She went inside to call for help."

"What the hell is going on here, Mick?" The neighbor leaned over them, his gray hair standing up like a thistle pod.

"Is...she okay?" Still holding on, Léa tried to sit up, but then winced and brought a hand to her forehead.

"Lean against me," Mick told her, moving around to support her head against his shoulder. "The ambulance should get here any minute."

The neighbor pointed the flashlight into Léa's face. "I should have figured it was this house."

She brought a hand up to block the light. Mick shoved the man's hand away. Immediately, the sound of sirens could be heard in the distance. "Ray, go in front and wait for them. Send them back here."

As the older man started for the street, Mick turned his attention back to Léa. She was cold, and he rubbed his hands up and down her bare arms. She moved closer against his chest.

"Is...Heather okay?" she asked again.

"She's fine." He entwined his fingers with hers and held her hand at her waist when she tried to touch the cut on her forehead. "What happened here, Léa?"

Emergency vehicles came to a screeching halt in front of the house.

"Someone...someone hit me."

"Who?"

"I don't know."

Before he could ask anything else, the backyard exploded with activity. Mick moved back as a couple of medics took charge. A uniformed officer was talking to the neighbor near the house, and two more were approaching and directing the beams of their flashlights around the backyard. Looking around, he spotted Heather sitting on their back step, holding tightly to Max's collar. Even from this distance, she looked terrified.

Now that the backyard was starting to fill up, Mick figured he should probably put on something more than his boxer shorts. He glanced at Léa and found her talking to one of the officers as the medics continued to check her out.

He started across the lawn, but one of the uniformed cops approached him. Mick recognized him. He was one of the newer members of the force.

"Mr. Conklin, do you know what happened here?"

"Léa told me someone whacked her on the head." He glanced again at Heather. "I have to put some clothes on. I'll be right back."

Without waiting for the man's response, Mick crossed the lawn to his daughter.

"Come on inside."

Her eyes were still tearing when she looked up. She'd washed off the blood from her hands. "Will she be okay?"

"I think so." He took hold of Max's collar. "But I need to talk to you. Come on."

She gave him no argument and went up the stairs ahead of him. In the kitchen, he let go of the dog and pulled on a T-shirt and a pair of running shorts from a basket of clean clothes sitting by the laundry room door. When he turned back to Heather, she was sitting on a chair at the kitchen table, hugging her knees to her chest.

"What happened out there?"

"I thought she was dead."

"Did you see it happen?"

She buried her head against her knees and shook her head.

"You went out after she was attacked."

She nodded without looking up at him.

"Léa was scared—for you. She asked if *you* were okay." Mick crouched before his daughter. "Did you see anyone else out there?"

She gave a quick shake of her head. "I…I thought she was dead."

"Are you okay, baby?" he asked gently, taking hold of her chin and lifting it until he was looking into her tear-stained face.

She nodded.

"I have to go outside to talk to the police and check on Léa. You stay right here and—"

"I'm coming." She sprang to her feet.

Mick looked at his daughter for a moment. There was no point in refusing her. He pulled on a pair of sneakers and, leaving the dog inside, went out the back door with Heather on his heels. More of the neighbors had now gathered in small groups by the street. Every light in every house on the street seemed to be on. Léa had a bandage wrapped around her head, but she was sitting up on the stretcher, talking to a female police officer.

"And you say she's not here to stir trouble."

Mick turned to face Rich Weir but Heather went past them, heading straight toward Léa.

"You seem to be a little confused about who's the victim here, Chief."

The square-faced police chief shot him an annoyed look and took out a pad of paper and a pen from his back pocket. "Do you or your kid have anything to contribute to the report on what happened here or not?"

"Heather came out after Léa was already down. I heard my daughter calling me and came out after that."

"Is that her room?"

Mick looked up at the window where Rich was pointing. It looked down over the Hardys' backyard and the carriage house. "That's the one."

"Did she see anyone?"

"She said she didn't."

The chief put the paper and pen back in his pocket and started walking toward the street. Mick went after him. "What do you have?"

"Nothing. She slipped and banged her head against the door." He waved impatiently in the direction of the three police cruisers and the emergency vehicle that were blocking the street. "All this manpower wasted, it seems to me. Next time, just take her to the emergency room, why don't you? Save us some tax dollars."

"I think Léa knows the difference between banging her head and having someone attack her." He stepped in front of the chief and lowered his voice. "Listen, Rich. Don't have me lose all my respect for you in one night. You're brushing this thing off because she's a Hardy."

"What do you want from me, Mick?"

"Check into it right. Are there footprints? My dog went after something at the back wall when we came out. Did you look for any kind of blunt instrument lying around? Fingerprints? How the hell do I know what you should do? This is your job." He glared fiercely at the chief. "But how can you honestly think a young woman could walk into her own backyard at two in the morning and injure herself that badly."

"Because Hardys are walking time bombs. They're trouble." Rich looked away, frustration showing on his face. "You tell me why this woman was camping in her car when she has this big house to sleep in? You can't. I'm telling you, this goddamn family is flat-out screwed up. For all I know, she probably woke up and thought that carriage house was the goddamn outhouse!''

He stepped around Mick and then stopped.

''Next time, don't bother calling us.''

''Emily scratched up her elbow and her knees when she fell off the swing in the playground. There were at least half a dozen other parents there. They saw it happen.'' Ted tried hard to control his temper. ''I would never intentionally hurt my daughter.''

The Family Services worker, accompanied by a police officer, wanted the names of the witnesses. Ted gave them everything they were looking for.

Marilyn had called the police. She'd called Family Services, the hospital, her lawyer—every stinking person she knew—to accuse Ted of abusing their child. Just because he'd put a couple of Band-Aids on Emily's elbow and knees.

She was sick. Ted now understood it. Accepted it. And episodes like this made him more determined than ever to take his children away from her.

Eleven

With every word the woman said, it felt like a gong was being struck and left to vibrate in Léa's head. She knew she couldn't take much more of this. The medics were looking on in curious disbelief, but the officer continued to ask her questions.

"One more time. Why did you say you were sitting in the car?"

"To cool it. To get away from the fumes of the house. Because I couldn't sleep." Léa spoke thinly, tiredly. She peered at the name on the officer's name tag. "Listen, Robin."

"Yes, ma'am."

"Can you tell me what all these questions about me being in my car have to do with the person who whacked me on the head?"

"We're trying to figure that out now, ma'am." The woman jotted something down on her paper again. "Now, you said you saw something run through the backyard and that's when you came out here. Could you please be more specific about what you saw?"

"I've already explained everything I know to you and to your partner." Léa closed her eyes and wished the pounding would go away. She just wanted to curl up and go to sleep.

"Do you remember the approximate shape or size of this 'thing'?"

She shook her head.

"Could it have been a stray cat or a dog?"

Léa opened her eyes and noticed Heather standing a couple of steps away, near a medic who was no longer hiding his impatience. "I don't know. Maybe."

"Is it possible that you maybe tripped over this thing—this animal?"

"Someone hit me on the head." She turned her attention back to the officer.

"But there is blood on the latch, ma'am. It looks like you cut your forehead on the old door."

"I didn't trip. I must have hit the door on the way down."

"It appears as if you were unconscious for a couple of minutes. How can you be so sure what you remember?"

"I didn't imagine the voice. Someone cursed at me from behind. I turned and—"

"But you are not certain if it was a female or male voice. Maybe it was a chirp of a bird or a dog's bark. Or an owl—"

"She's *not* lying, if that's what you mean." Heather's sharp protest was totally unexpected. The officer and the medics turned to the teenager. "I...I mean...I found her. She was covered with blood. Ask these guys." She motioned to the medics next to her. "There must be a lump on her head. She was really hurt. You can see she still is...."

"Now, back to this noise you heard," Robin said to Léa, turning her attention from Heather. "Do you scare easily, Ms. Hardy?"

"Don't bother, Officer," Léa said weakly. "You must have decided what happened before you even got here. I'm done talking to you." She looked up gratefully at the teenager. Heather looked as upset as Léa felt.

Taking his cue, one of the medics leaned down and told Léa that they were taking her to the hospital for some stitches and maybe an X ray, depending on what the doctor there would recommend.

Léa felt herself fading rapidly. The police officer went on to ask a few more questions, but Léa paid no attention to the woman. She was drained, emotionally and physically. Closing her eyes, she held on to the sides of the stretcher as they wheeled her across the lawn. She couldn't allow herself to remember how vulnerable she'd been, but the word and the sharp blow kept echoing in her head. Someone had been after her. Someone had intended to scare her. Hurt her. Maybe kill her.

Léa put a hand to her forehead as the gurney stopped. A steamroller of emotion was crushing the breath out of her, it seemed, and doubts about what she wanted to do and her ability to do it suddenly washed through her, bleeding her of what little strength she had left. She was lost.

She felt a hand, strong and warm, wrap around her cold and bloodless fingers, and she opened her eyes. Mick.

"We're following the ambulance to the hospital. You won't be alone."

Léa couldn't stop the tears from trickling down.

"Heather," she managed to get out. "You need to stay with Heather."

"She's coming, too." With his thumb, he gently brushed the wetness from her face. "Everything will be okay."

Her own soft sobs awakened her.

Without moving, Patricia Webster opened her eyes and stared up through the darkness at the ceiling.

Again. That horrible dream again!

Upset, trembling slightly, she turned and took a tissue from her bedside table. Her face was wet. The tears had dampened the hair at her temples; she patted it dry.

She glanced at the clock. The red numbers showed it

was only 4:12. She turned to where Allan should have been. His side of the bed was empty.

Patricia sat up, suddenly concerned. The door to the bathroom was open, and the light was off. She stared again at the turned-back sheet and leaned over to touch her husband's pillow. It was cold and smooth. She wasn't certain he'd come to bed at all last night.

She slid off the bed and pulled on a robe, knotting the belt tightly at her waist. The large house was very quiet as she padded barefoot down the hall. By Chris's closed bedroom door, Patricia paused. She'd gone to bed before he got home last night. Allan had been working on his sermon and promised to stay up and wait for the boy. In a moment of panic, she wondered if something had happened to their son. She pushed the door open slightly and peered in. From the dim light coming in from the window, she was relieved to make out the silhouette of Chris's body sprawled on the bed. It was difficult not to go in—not to touch his hair and pull up the covers. It was impossible to let go.

Despite the urge, Patricia backed out into the hall and quietly descended the stairs.

The television set in the family room was off. There were no lights on in Allan's office off the living room. He'd not fallen sleep in his favorite chair reading in preparation for the Sunday service. She didn't recall hearing the phone ring, and besides, he always let her know when he received an emergency call and had to leave in the middle of the night. But then again, she hadn't heard Chris coming in, either. Perhaps he *had* awakened her and she just couldn't remember.

In the kitchen, Patricia put the kettle on the stove to boil some water for tea. She didn't bother to turn on the lights. She welcomed the darkness, the safety of her home, the tranquillity of night. Tranquillity was an increasingly elusive feeling, of late.

In his practical way, Allan was always pushing her these days to get involved with some committee or the next. He was forever trying to push her out of the house. The thought occurred to her that men rarely understand what women really need. How could she explain to him that *this* was what she needed? What made her feel safe. What made her happy. Her house. Her family. Why was that so difficult?

She made a cup of tea for herself and went and sat down on the cushion in the large bay window that overlooked the yard and the pathway leading down to the river walk.

She'd been sitting only a minute or two before she saw the figure striding up the path. At first she didn't recognize him, and Patricia stared hard at the man, a sense of uneasiness gripping her. He was moving quickly, a stout walking stick in his hand. In a moment, though, she breathed more easily. For as he drew nearer, his pace slowed and she made out the glasses, the thatch of gray hair.

Patricia saw her husband stop by the pile of wood they kept stacked beside the shed. She smiled when he tucked the stick he was carrying behind the pile. Allan did so many curious things lately, it seemed.

He took a couple of steps toward the house, but then stopped and just looked up at the sky. She'd seen him do this before when something was bothering him. He would just stand there—like he was doing now—and stare up at the sky as if he could see God up there. As if he could really talk to him.

She took a sip of her tea and then turned on the floor lamp next to the window.

It was less than a minute before Patricia heard the kitchen door open.

Allan's face was flushed when he came through the house.

"You're up early." He peeled off the light windbreaker and smoothed back his hair.

"And you're staying up too late." She wrapped her hands around the warm cup of tea.

"Not really. I dozed off working on my sermon and woke up only a couple of minutes ago. I just thought I'd step out and get some fresh air."

"I'm worried about you, Allan. Worried about us. About…everything."

He gave her a confident smile and pressed a kiss on her forehead.

"There is nothing to worry about, my love. I have everything under control."

Mick started the car and shook his head.

"You are *not* checking into any motel, and you are not driving all the way back to your hotel room in Doylestown, either. Sorry, Léa, but you've been outvoted. You're staying with us."

As she leaned her head against the backrest, obviously trying to think of her next argument, Mick reached over her, pulled the seat belt across and locked it.

She sighed audibly. "I'm not helpless, you two."

There was a snort from the back seat. Mick glanced into the driver's rear mirror and caught Heather rolling her eyes. Something about the expression—the simple response to this situation—made him smile. It was a glimpse of his old Heather.

He pulled out of the hospital parking lot. Dawn had somehow shoved the night aside while they'd been waiting inside, and the sun was now showing its face in the east.

"There is no way I can repay you two for what you've already done for me. I mean, there was really no reason for you…well, to hang around all this time. And I just feel so embarrassed to be the cause of all this trouble for you. I could have taken a taxi—"

"Did they give you any prescriptions for sedatives that we should have filled?" he deadpanned. Despite the crownlike bandage on her head, Mick saw the narrow glare he was getting in return. "I know the pharmacist in town. I could call him up and—"

"You're not calling anyone on my account at this hour. Besides, I'm supposed to stay awake. In fact, the doctor said I should try to keep talking for the next few hours. So are you sure you don't want to drop me off at the nearest bus stop?"

"Did we ever buy Max a muzzle?" Heather's question was so unexpected that Mick burst out laughing. Glancing in Léa's direction, he saw the smile tugging at her lips, too.

"Fine! If you're going to gang up on me, I'll be quiet now."

Despite her effort to be brave, Léa looked dead tired. And that was on top of being bruised and cut and interrogated and sewn up, all in the span of just a few hours. One of the nurses told Mick that Léa had ended up with eighteen stitches. She also was sporting another goose egg a couple of inches from the blow she'd taken to the hairline. That she could have sustained two injuries from one fall, as Rich Weir wanted to believe, was just too much.

No, that dog just won't hunt, Mick thought. He was no detective, but he knew enough about medicine and injuries to figure it was highly unlikely that a simple fall could have done that much damage.

It was understandable that Léa's return to Stonybrook would be a little threatening to some people in this town, but the police chief's response was way over the top. Sure, a few people might be afraid that she could open up a can of worms, but until tonight Mick would never have believed that someone would actually go so far as to try to hurt her.

He glanced out at the park as they drove by it, and his

blood ran cold as he remembered Heather out in that yard, crying her heart out. Alone. Afraid. Needing him while he slept. Some father.

Mick looked at his daughter in the rearview mirror. Her gaze was riveted on Léa. Tonight and this morning, she'd been more responsive—more engaged—than he'd seen her in a long time. She was genuinely concerned about Léa's condition in that hospital. He had a feeling she was not done worrying even now.

Mick couldn't ignore the gnawing feeling that maybe Heather had seen more than she was admitting. He turned the corner onto Poplar Street and pulled the car in front of his house.

The police cars were gone. There were no signs of last night's disturbance anywhere. An empty street and quiet houses. Just an ordinary Sunday morning.

"You take her in, Dad. I'll go and get her bag." Heather opened the car door and jumped out before either of them could say a word.

"I'm really okay," Léa said immediately. "There's just too much I have to do today and—"

"The only thing you have to do is take it easy and get some rest."

"Says you."

When he wrapped his hand around her wrist, he could feel her pulse racing. Mick's gaze was drawn to the smooth skin of her neck, to her parted lips, to the ridiculous-looking bandage on her head. Something welled up inside of him, and he couldn't figure out how she did it to him, even when she looked like this.

"Don't make me get rough with you. You *will* lie down for a couple of hours. After that, you'll be in a better condition to decide."

She smiled, and Mick suddenly found himself fighting the urge to lean over and taste those lips. Fighting and losing.

The sight of Heather on Léa's porch drew his attention, though, and the thought that he shouldn't have let her go alone rocketed through him. He watched her push the front door open and walk in. Through the curtainless windows, he could see his daughter walking around.

He'd never been concerned about Heather's safety in Stonybrook before. But now he found himself as alert as a prison guard at riot time.

"It's ten of six now. I'll stay until eight o'clock, but that's my limit." Without waiting for him, Léa pushed open her door and tried to get out. "I really have work to do."

"Stubborn, aren't we." He jumped out quickly and came around to help her. She had already taken a couple of steps on the sidewalk before he reached her. But Mick saw her wobble, and he looped an arm around her waist and pulled her against him. "Not too fast."

For a long minute she remained nestled against him. Her arms had naturally wrapped around his middle, and her cheek was pressed against his chest. Mick felt her need. She just wanted to be held, and this whipped up in him a whole new blend of sensations.

Suddenly, she pulled back. "I...I'm sorry. I must have stood up too fast."

A deep blush was spreading on her cheeks. He didn't remove his arm from around her waist. Heather appeared on Léa's porch and came across the lawn toward them. She had a duffel bag draped over one shoulder and something in her other hand.

"Is this *all* of your things?" he asked.

Léa didn't answer. Mick looked down and found her face had turned ashen in the morning light. She was staring at Heather's hand.

"I found this letter just inside the door. It has your name on it."

* * *

The crotch of the oversized pants practically reached the boy's knees. The black T-shirt he was wearing under the unbuttoned sport shirt had *Luzer* emblazoned across the chest. He'd left his old van running and now leaned against the passenger door.

Bob Slater balanced the wallet on his knee with his partially paralyzed left hand and took out a fifty-dollar bill with his good hand. "Does th-this cover it, T-T.J.?"

"Sure, for last night's work." T.J. stuffed the money in his front pocket and moved around the front of the van to the driver's side. "Send up a flare when you need me again."

Bob watched the teenager get inside the old van and drive around the circular gravel drive. As the vehicle disappeared beyond the gate, the retired banker glanced over his shoulder at the house. He directed his electric-powered chair down the walk toward the backyard.

The morning had been startlingly clear, more like September than June. The dew that had glistened on the finely manicured lawns had evaporated an hour ago, and the sun was high.

He stopped on the brick-paved patio. The river, brown from the mud that had washed in with the storms, was still running high beyond the lawns and the gardens and the carefully placed groves of trees. Tomorrow it would be running clear and the smooth rocks, now hidden, would be breaking the surface, channeling the waters, creating movement and life. Solid, unmoving…and yet potent, still.

He drove his chair to the edge of the bricks and considered taking the chair across the lawn to the river walk. It would be good to go down there, to feel the fresh, cooler air from the water on his face. As he pressed the control knob, he heard the door from the kitchen slide open behind him.

He stopped.

"Who was the kid out front?"

Bob turned his chair around. Stephanie was already puffing away at a cigarette as she walked across the patio. Last night's makeup was still smudged around her eyes and she was wrapped in a green Japanese-print robe.

He'd bought that robe for her years ago. She used to look stunning in it, especially when she wore it with nothing underneath. It'd been a long time since he'd thought about sex. Even longer since he'd thought about sex with her.

"L-lives in the n-neighborhood." He touched the bag of newspapers that was hanging from the side of his wheelchair. "G-gets me these. You know th-that."

The little jerk of her head was more acknowledgment that he'd spoken than agreement, but Bob had no interest in pursuing that subject.

"I called Rich this morning." She threw the cigarette into a planter situated at the edge of the brickwork, and reached into her robe pocket for another one. "I told him about Léa being in town."

Her eyes glittered with hate as she lit the cigarette.

"He said he's taking care of things. He said she'll be leaving…very, very soon."

Twelve

"**Y**ou have the choice of sharing this bathroom with Heather, or you can share mine. But that means you have to walk through my bedroom."

Standing in the narrow doorway of the decoratively tiled bathroom, Léa could feel the heat of Mick's body behind her. She turned and looked up at him. He hadn't had a chance to shave yet this morning, and she was fascinated by the blondish growth on his chin, and by her urge to touch the stubble.

"I'm only staying for a couple of hours. I might not need to use a bathroom."

"Well, I know you are not supposed to get those sutures wet, but a long bath will do you a load of good." His gaze traveled down the front of her wrinkled and stained dress before meeting hers. "I can run the water and help you undress."

With everything on her mind, it was almost shocking how her body reacted to him. It was as if a violin string, running from her brain to somewhere deep in her stomach, had been plucked, and the vibration was simply humming throughout her body.

"I think I can manage it myself." She bit back her smile. "But thanks for the offer."

A couple of steps back up the hall, directly opposite Heather's room, was the guest bedroom. A set of old-fashioned twin beds covered with colorful quilts were set against each wall. A braided carpet and a rocking chair in one corner gave the place a sense of homeyness. The single window looked out on a vegetable garden in the next-door neighbor's yard.

"You'll have to share this with Max."

As if proving his master's point, the large dog appeared and pushed his way between them. He settled comfortably on the rug. Léa turned and looked past Mick for any sign of Heather. The teenager had volunteered to take Max out for a walk when they'd first arrived.

Mick put the duffel bag on one of the beds and showed her where the linen closet was. "You can sleep, but I'll have to wake you up every so often to check for—"

"Drowsiness, nausea…I remember the instructions, Dr. Conklin." She leaned against the doorjamb. "I'm tougher than the average patient. Really, you don't have to fuss over me."

"But I want to."

Léa's breath hitched in her chest when his hand touched her face.

"Even if it's only for a couple of hours, I think it's about time you let someone else take care of *you* for a change."

Stunned and speechless, she stared into his blue eyes. A knot rose in her throat at the sincerity she saw there. The letter she was clutching in her hand slipped between her fingers and dropped onto the hardwood floor.

Mick reached down and picked it up. Smiling, he held it out to her. "I'll have your breakfast—raisin French toast with applesauce—ready when you come down."

Did he say 'come down' or 'calm down,' she thought as he turned away. This light-headedness she was feeling, she knew, had nothing to do with the blow to the head she'd taken last night. It was Mick Conklin, pure and simple. It was impossible to tear her gaze away from his back as he disappeared down the stairs.

The feel of the letter in her hand, though, was a slap of reality.

Léa walked into the guest bedroom and started to close the door. Looking at Max, she left the door partially open to give him a chance to get out if he wanted to go. The dog seemed perfectly contented, though, curled up on the floor.

She hadn't dared to open the letter outside for fear of getting Mick and his daughter more involved than they already were. Heather probably had her reasons for not admitting anything, but Léa was sure that the teenager had been in the carriage house last night.

She was also fairly certain that it was because of Heather that she was alive now.

Léa sat down on the edge of one of the beds and stared at the typed address. The envelope was not stamped. Some time between the hour she'd gone out to her car to spend the night and this morning, when she'd come back from the hospital, someone had slipped this letter through the mail slot of her front door.

She carefully opened it. There was a single typed sheet inside.

Ten o'clock Monday morning sit on the bench by the Main Street entrance to the park. You'll meet Marilyn's Hate Club. They will all be there.

Léa turned the page over. Nothing else.

There was a soft knock on the door, and Heather poked her purple head in. Léa immediately folded the letter and replaced it in the envelope.

"I'm up. I'm fine. No dizzy spells."

"Well, that's not good. You're supposed to be down and not feeling so good. That way I can go get my dad."

Max went to the door to greet the teenager.

"Did he put you up to this?"

"No way. I thought of it all on my own."

Léa tucked the letter in an outside pocket of the duffel

bag. "Well, in spite of what everyone else wants, I am way too wound up to lie down. Come on in."

Heather gave a noncommittal shrug, but then walked in, anyway, and stretched out on one elbow on the bed across the way.

"I—

"I'm—"

They both started talking at the same time, and they both stopped at the same moment. Léa laughed self-consciously. "Okay, you first."

Max was standing and resting his large head on the bed in front of Heather. The girl looked down at the dog, scratched his ears and stroked his muzzle for a minute. Finally, she looked up and met Léa's gaze for an instant before looking away.

"I was really scared." Her blue eyes were identical to Mick's. "I thought you were dead."

Léa had to suppress the urge to go to her. She didn't want Heather to stop talking.

"I…well, it wasn't just the attack, though that was when I started screaming. It was the blood. I thought this was it. The end. Some creep just deciding to end it all for you. And not just you. All these other people who must be counting on you. People like your brother." She dashed a tear from her face, and Léa could see she was trying very hard to be tough. "Seeing you like that made me realize that I couldn't even imagine what…would happen…if someone hurt my dad. I don't know what I'd do."

"I'm sure your father feels the same way," Léa said softly. "I mean, if something were to happen to *you*."

Heather didn't say anything, and Léa let the silence build for a couple of minutes before she spoke again.

"I know that a lot of us, at one time or another in our lives, think of death as an answer to problems. The sad thing is that it isn't an answer. It only shifts our problems to someone else. To those who survive. I know about that.''

"I guess you would," Heather said quietly.

"But then, a thing like this...attack...this accident just reminds us how fragile life is, how permanent death is, and how much love we have inside of us to give."

Heather's cheeks showed red beneath the makeup. She glanced at the door, looking ready to run.

"And in my ripe old age, I've discovered there's such a big difference between reality and romanticizing."

The teenager turned her gaze on Léa. "What do you mean?"

Léa looked around the room. She wanted to gain the teenager's trust, not put her on the spot. Most of all, she didn't want to be the cause of her sinking again into her previous gloom. A church bell rang somewhere in the distance.

"What I'm trying to say is that we are surrounded with romantic images of death in our culture."

"Oh, you mean like rock and roll. That was before my time."

Léa smiled and shook her head. "No. I'm talking about other things that are around us day to day. Like religion. When I was a kid and went to Sunday school, we were taught that crucifixion was a gift, sort of. Jesus loved us so he died. And it's true across the board with most religions. Some Muslims and even some Christians still believe in self-flagellation as a way of purifying their souls. Others believe dying in battle will send them to heaven." The church bell continued to ring. Léa glanced at the window and gave a broken laugh. "But I'm not talking against religion on a Sunday morning. All of those religions also *welcome* life. What I am getting at is that romanticizing death is everywhere—in books, music, movies. I can't even count how many different versions of *Romeo and Juliet* I've seen over the years."

Heather's attention seemed to be focused on the dog, but Léa knew she was listening to every word.

"I didn't mean to give a sermon. But what I am getting at has to do with my own life. With my own family. Actually, with Ted's situation." She once again had the teenager's attention. "A jury out there found him guilty of killing his own family. But I believe he didn't do it. And I also believe that his continuous silence…his depression…his lack of wanting to fight for his innocence…it's all part of a father's grief over losing those he loved. To me, that's the reality of death and what it does to those who are left behind."

"There's nothing romantic in that."

"You're right."

Léa wiped her cold palms on the quilt. There was a lot more that she wanted to say. If Heather *had* seriously been thinking of ending her life, then she needed a lot of support and counseling. This was all conjecture, though, and Léa didn't want to press her and have the teenager retreat into her shell.

Léa smiled up at her. "What *I* was about to say was thank you. Thank you for being out there. I know you saved my life."

The teenager's blush got deeper, and she stood up. "I guess I better let you sleep or something."

Léa noticed that Heather didn't deny being out there. "I think I might try to take a shower or bath instead. I must smell like a hospital room."

"Actually, you look worse than you smell."

Léa stood up, too. "Are you always this honest?"

"Only with people I like."

She started for the door.

"By the way—" Heather paused by the door "—I'd tell if I saw who did this to you."

"I know." Léa nodded and watched the girl and the dog disappear into the hall.

* * *

Like most everything in Stonybrook, the Miller Flower Shop had always been closed on Sundays.

Tradition notwithstanding, for several years now Joanna Miller had been insistent on opening the small nursery greenhouse in the back seven days a week during the planting season. She needed it. Not for the money, necessarily—though a few extra dollars never hurt. No, she needed it for herself.

For Sundays were all Joanna's. Around seven o'clock, from March to June, she brought her little cash box out of the flower shop, along with the old coffee urn and a tray of pastries, and opened the place. And the customers came. Trickled in, at first. But then word got around and things improved. Nowadays, business was pretty darn brisk some Sundays.

Joanna loved it. She took care of customers. She chatted and laughed and visited with friends and neighbors who stopped by for coffee or just to say hi. Sometimes they bought little flats of tomatoes or peppers or herbs or annuals, but Joanna never pushed anyone. It was just a pleasant way for a Stonybrook oddball to spend a pleasant morning.

As she plugged in the coffee and took the plastic off the tray of pastries this morning, she knew that one of the real pleasures of these Sunday morning was not having to deal with her older sister Gwen looking over her shoulder.

With a little more money—maybe next year, even—Joanna figured they could replace some of the plastic-covered greenhouse with glass, the way it had been originally. Then she could make this vernal tradition a year-round thing.

But that was all just maybe, for the business was really Gwen's, and her older sister was already unhappy about what she considered pure extravagance on Joanna's part.

They were only twelve years apart, but there were times

when Joanna felt Gwen was twice that. She'd felt that way this morning.

"It wasn't the crummy croissants, and you know it," she murmured to herself. Even though Gwen had been a pain this morning about buying croissants instead of doughnuts, Joanna knew darn well that wasn't the issue.

It was jealousy. Gwen was ticked off at Joanna because she had a life. She was liked by people in this town. She had a sex life, for God's sake. She stood with her hands on either end of the pastry tray and stared at the colors of the ivy geranium in the rows of hanging baskets until her frustration began to ebb.

"You're winning the battle. Don't give up."

"I hope you're right." Joanna was smiling before she even turned to see Andrew Rice. "I didn't hear your car."

"I was out jogging and decided to stop by."

He turned to look at the neat lines of herbs in the planting tables, and Joanna let her gaze linger on the muscular brown legs, on the broad powerful shoulders in the sleeveless shirt.

"You look wonderful, Andrew. I like that shirt on you."

"Thanks." The quick smile made her heart rate double. He touched his perfectly flat stomach. "I've lost ten pounds but have five more to go. It's getting harder and harder to lose the winter fat."

Joanna was disappointed to see him turn his attention to the hanging baskets.

"I was thinking of sending some flowers to a friend who's back in town."

She moved close to him.

"These would be nice for a housewarming." Joanna leaned in front of him to point to a group of planters filled with assorted perennials. Her breast brushed against his arm, and he took a polite step to the right.

"It's not really a housewarming. Actually, it's more like

a welcome back.'' He gave her a half glance. ''It's for Léa Hardy. I hear she's back and is working on the old house on Poplar Street. I thought she could use some cheering up.''

''I'm sure. I heard she was back, too.'' The stab of envy ran surprisingly deep. ''I have some things here that might make an appropriate gift.''

He followed her to the next row of tables. ''Mums? I thought they were fall flowers.''

''We have spring mums, too. And in the Italian culture, they are considered funeral flowers. Particularly appropriate, don't you think?''

''Joanna—''

''Or I can put together a nice arrangement of sunflowers. The American Plains Indians put those on the graves of their dead. Now gladiolas, or carnations, even roses are more universal in nature. But I don't have any of those outside.''

''Jo—''

She shook off his touch on her arm and pointed to a pot of flowers. ''Here. Snapdragons might be the perfect gift. They're supposed to offer protection from curses—''

''Jo! You're being totally immature. Stop.''

She glanced back at him, at his handsome face and the stubborn set of his mouth. ''What, you're not happy with my recommendations?''

''I'm not happy with the way you're behaving.''

''You're right,'' she said. ''I'm sorry. Seriously, though, I have a much better selection inside. Come in and take a peek.''

''But the shop is closed on Sundays.''

Joanna looped her arm through his and pulled him toward the back door of the shop. ''That schedule is for everyone else. But you are an exception.''

''And why am I an exception?''

''Because you're my *favorite* customer,'' she said

brightly. ''And because you are not leaving until we find just what you want.''

She took a key out of the pocket of her sundress and unlocked the door.

''We haven't had much luck with what I want lately.''

''Which just means we have to try harder.''

The shop was dark, but Joanna didn't bother to turn on the lights. Instead, she pulled him in and pushed the door shut.

''Please.'' Her mouth attacked his lips. Her fingers moved up over his chest. ''Make love to me, Andrew. No one will be in for a half hour.''

''Jo—''

''Andrew, I've missed you so much.'' She kissed his lips, his cheek. She pushed him back against the door and bit at the salty skin of his neck.

''Jo, you've been seeing me around town every day. You haven't missed me.''

''Yes, I have.'' She let her hands feel the contours of his back, the curve of his firm buttocks.

He placed his hands firmly on her shoulders and forced her to look into his dark brown eyes. ''You've missed sex, Jo.''

She bristled. ''That's not true. Despite what you may think, there are plenty of available men in this town.''

A frown pulled at his lips. ''Then what are you waiting for? Go ahead.''

''Because that's not what I want!'' She wrapped her arms tightly around him and pressed her face against his chest. ''Please, let's not fight. I'm sorry. Please. These last two weeks have been horrible. You don't answer my calls. We see each other around town, but you look right through me. Like I don't exist at all. Like all the time we've had together means nothing. Andrew, I've been hurting.''

It seemed like an eternity before his arms wrapped around her. ''Jo, I've been hurting, too. But I don't want

to go on the way we were. I told you before. I'm ready
to move on to the next step. The fooling around is not
enough anymore. I want to take you on real dates, where
people see us together. This is not the 1950s. We can sleep
together. Wake up together. We can spend our weekends
together.''

''I don't deserve you.''

''That's bull, and you know it.'' He nestled her head
beneath his chin. ''It's time to get out of that morgue your
sister calls home. It's time for *you* to bloom. I want to
spoil you, Jo. Is that too much to ask?''

''We will. We will do all those things.''

''When?'' He took hold of her chin and forced Joanna
again to meet his troubled gaze. ''If this thing between us
is going to work, then I'm through having to do 360-
degree surveillance before holding your hand.''

''We've only done that because of Gwen. She'd freak
if she found out…found out…''

''That you have a black boyfriend?''

''That I have *any* serious guy. It's all about Cate and
her suicide.''

''Come on, Jo—''

''Gwen is not over it yet. And I know she'd be de-
stroyed if she thought I was deserting her now.''

''Jo, you had a sister who died tragically, but that was
four years ago. I respect Gwen's grief. But I think she's
making a lifetime career out of working on other people's
guilt.''

She tried to look away, but he held her chin.

''Look, it doesn't matter a damn if Cate was a lesbian
or not. It doesn't even matter anymore if it was Marilyn
that started the tongues wagging in this town.''

''Marilyn was the one who ruined Cate's life.''

''Maybe she was. But your sister committed suicide ten
years after leaving Stonybrook. And you told me yourself
you don't know why she did it. Gwen, on the other hand,

made it her life's mission to blame Marilyn...right up to the day she was murdered.''

Joanna looked away. Andrew's words rang too much with the truth.

"Cate is dead. Leave it go."

"I *have* left it."

"Maybe you have. But Gwen is not done yet. She started on you the day Cate left. You couldn't leave this town—or that house, for God's sake! You went to the community college because Gwen didn't want you to move away. And when you were done with your degree, you had to keep right on working in this shop. What does she expect you to do? Just work here like a slave, under her thumb, forever?"

"Come on, Andrew—"

"I'm serious. How long are you going to let her control you, Jo? I mean, haven't you sacrificed enough? I don't kn—"

A knock on the door behind Andrew stopped them both. Flustered, Joanna immediately reached over and switched on the overhead lights. At the sound of a key turning in the door, she immediately moved across the room to one of the refrigerated cases.

"Good morning, *Dr.* Rice. What brings you here on a Sunday morning?"

Joanna watched her sister look over Andrew. Gwen always made sure to acknowledge his professional title. The problem was, she seemed to use it to limit the extent to which her sociability could go. Always formal.

"Your sister was kind enough to recommend a floral arrangement for a friend."

On cue, Joanna found herself reaching inside the refrigerator and picking out a large and exotic arrangement of wildflowers. "This was the one I wanted you to see. It's my favorite. If you'd like, I can drive it over to your house this afternoon...since you don't have your car."

"That won't be necessary," Andrew said coolly. "I'll arrange to have it picked up tomorrow. So long, Gwen."

Joanna's steps moved of their own accord toward the door, following him out. Something had turned in their relationship, and a sense of cold dread washed through her. But she wasn't going to lose him. She couldn't let him walk out of her life. She loved him.

Gwen's hand wrapped around her wrist.

"I need to talk to you, Joanna. I've had a very rough morning."

"My name is on every goddamn charity push in the county. Half of my time is spent going to boring lunches or dull dinners. Every time I turn around, there is another hand stretched out looking for another check." Marilyn *placed her hands on her new lawyer's desk and glared down at the distinguished-looking man.* "Now, are you telling me that all that means nothing when it comes to beating Ted for the custody of the girls?"

"I didn't say that," *the man replied calmly.* "But your husband has drummed up some very strong support from members of your own community."

"Who?" *she seethed.* "I asked before. Who does he have?"

The man opened a file on his desk. "Gwen Miller. She gave a deposition declaring that you created a scandal with regard to her sister some years back."

"Unbelievable! That same, old, ancient history, school-girl crap. Well, I can give you enough information to knock the wind out of that completely."

"Of course. The courts understand that there is always another side." *He went back to his files.* "Brian Hughes, a restaurant owner in Stonybrook. He says that he has seen you drinking heavily and behaving roughly with your children while in the company of a number of men in his* *establishment. There is also a very strong deposition from a Reverend Allan Webster—"*

"I can take care of those, no problem. They'll withdraw their statements." She'd make sure they did.

"Yes, I'm sure any emendation they make will 'clarify' everything." The lawyer looked up at Marilyn. "But the greatest harm to your position comes from this next statement in which you are termed an 'unfit mother.'"

"I don't believe it. Nobody would dare say such a thing about me."

"I'm afraid they have."

"Who?" she fumed.

The man hesitated for a long moment before answering. "Stephanie Slater. Your mother has stated unequivocally that she believes your husband should get custody of both of the girls."

Thirteen

As Heather came in the back door with the dog, Mick glanced over the top of the open newspaper.

"Is Max sick?"

"No. Why?" Heather opened the refrigerator door. He watched her move a few cans of soda from the cabinet to the fridge. She kept one out and opened it up. He struggled against the urge to tell her it was too early in the morning for soda. Hell, he'd drunk worse things than soda in the morning when he'd been her age.

"Well, because you've taken him out three times already."

"I think his hours must be mixed up or something. He doesn't know if it's day or night. I feel the same way."

"Do you ever have trouble sleeping?"

A guarded expression immediately came over her face. "Why do you ask that?"

Mick decided on the direct approach. "I had a call from the drugstore yesterday. About a prescription you dropped off."

"They were checking on me." She took a long swallow of the soda. "So, what did you tell them? Not to fill it?"

"No, I didn't say that." He folded up the newspaper and laid it on the table. "I trust you, Heather. And I also trust your mother. I think she's a damn good pediatrician. Which brings me back to why I asked the question to start with. I've made an appointment for you to see a doctor in town tomorrow afternoon. He's a general practitioner.''

''What for? I'm not sick or anything.''

''I didn't say you were. But with you going to school here in the fall, you need a local doctor.'' The suspicion was still evident in her face. Mick sat back in his chair. ''Also, I was hoping you could check this guy out for Léa. At the hospital this morning, they told her she should see her own doctor in a couple of days to check on the stitches. But I don't think she knows any local doctors anymore. So, if you give us the lowdown on this guy...''

''Sure, let's use Heather for a guinea pig.''

''Hey, this guy was recommended by your grandfather. I just want to know if he's good with women.''

Heather seemed to think about that for a moment and then put her empty can of soda by the sink. ''You think she's gonna stick around?''

''Reading what's in today's paper, it looks like she might.'' Mick pushed the newspaper across the table.

''What do you mean?''

''They have an article on her life in the Philadelphia paper. I didn't finish reading all of it yet.''

Heather reached for the paper and spread it out on the table. She leafed through until she found the page. ''Horrible picture. She looks like the walking dead. A Question Of Appeal. Good title. Very catchy. Did they interview her or something for this?''

''No, they say she wouldn't agree to be interviewed. But there's plenty of material from everyone else she ever worked with.''

''Cool! Here's a picture of her house. It even has the corner of *our* house in it. Does it say she's gonna hang around Stonybrook?''

Mick hesitated for a moment. His daughter was actually enthused.

"It says she may be looking for new representation for her brother. And it mentions that her house was on the market until last week. The two might be related."

"She *is* trying to sell it. For the money for a new lawyer. She told me so herself." Heather's blue eyes snapped up to Mick's. "Why don't *you* help her? With the house and all that. Just take it over. It'd take your people no time at all to fix it up."

The same question had crossed Mick's mind as he'd read the article. Everything was clearly on Léa's shoulders now. Her devotion to her brother was the only appealing part of this whole trial, though. Two years ago, he'd made up his mind that he wasn't getting involved. It was none of his business. He had nothing personal at stake. He'd even refused to form an opinion on whether or not Ted was capable of killing his family.

The article gave a clear picture of what her life had been like in the past couple of years. Caring for a dying aunt. The trips back and forth between Maryland and Pennsylvania. The pressures of her job, the trial, the financial burden. And there was no end to it yet. Even these jaded reporters plainly felt that the performance of Ted's attorney during the trial had skirted the edges of competence. Which meant she needed immediate financial support for a new attorney. Of course, Mick couldn't believe fixing and selling the house would provide money quickly enough to make a difference. Hell, the lawyer she had now probably already threw a lien on the place.

"Well, Dad? What do you think?"

Mick got up to pour himself another cup of coffee. "I don't think Léa would appreciate it if I tried to take over her life. Besides, selling the house right away might not be the answer to her problems. We have no way of knowing what's going on with her."

"But there must be a way you could help her. You have

friends. She has nobody. Like this morning in the hospital. If we weren't there, she would've had nobody to call to come and pick her up.''

''The last thing she needs now, though, is to think that we feel sorry for her. She might be down on her luck these days, but she's never lost her pride.'' He poured a glass of orange juice and brought it back to the table, putting it in front of Heather. ''I think we can help her by just being here. I'll offer my help, though. Whether it's repairs on her house or making contacts with other attorneys or whatever, or just supporting her as a friend. At the same time, we've got to respect her decision about how much she is willing to take us up on any of it.''

''You know, this is one of the big differences between you and Mom. She'd just write a check.''

''Are you saying I should write a check?''

''No.'' She closed and folded the newspaper on the table. ''You…you think of people's feelings. You give it thought, and try to do the right thing.''

''How your mother and I do things may just have to do with our jobs. With our lifestyles. Maybe with where we live.''

''No. She'd be the same wherever she lived. And you don't have to defend her.'' She picked up the newspaper. ''Can I take this upstairs and read it?''

''Are you going to come downstairs later and eat breakfast with us?''

''Do I have to eat your cooking?''

''There's always cold cereal.''

She gave him a narrow look and tucked the paper under her arm. ''Maybe. I'll think about it.''

Mick watched her pick up the glass of orange juice and carry it out of the kitchen.

Orange juice. They'd definitely crossed another milestone.

* * *

Léa was too restless to lie down. The five-minute bath and the two Tylenols had actually done her a lot of good, though.

The trial appeals and the lawyers' fees and the sale of the house and some nutcase's strange letters were still pressing. And since last night, the matter of some creep trying to knock her out had to be added to the list, too.

But on top of all of that, her suspicions about Heather possibly being suicidal were the most disturbing. She already knew what Mick's reaction would be if she approached him with her suspicions. The only answer right now was for Léa herself to keep an eye on Heather while she was still around.

Dressed in her last clean T-shirt and a pair of denim shorts coveralls, she packed her duffel bag with her laundry and straightened the room. A few minutes ago, she heard Heather's bedroom door close. Léa decided to seize the opportunity and started downstairs.

Max met her at the bottom of the stairs, tail wagging, rising up slightly on his hind legs like a puppy. She petted him and then took another appreciative glance at the beautifully done rooms on the first floor as she followed the dog to the kitchen. She found Mick working in his office, a room to the left of the kitchen.

"Good morning."

His eyes lifted from the paperwork on his desk, and he immediately stood up. "What are you doing up already? You're supposed to be resting."

"I did rest."

"Did your head ever hit the pillow? Did you get in bed at all?"

She leaned against the doorway. "I think beds are over-rated."

"Depends on what you use them for."

"I really need very little sleep."

"That leaves a lot of room to be creative."

Léa glanced at the press of his hip against the desk. The stretch of his long legs in the faded jeans. The bare feet. She looked up and saw the teasing gleam in his blue eyes.

"Are we talking about the same thing?" she asked innocently.

He pushed away from the desk and came toward her. "I was talking about sleeping. How about you?"

"Yeah. Me, too." Léa backed out of the room before he reached the doorway. "So, all those promises about breakfast. Was that only talk or can you really cook?"

"You hungry?"

"Starved."

His gaze rippled over her quickly, like water over pebbles, covering and touching everything. "Yeah. Me, too."

"Just tell me what to do." She turned and moved quickly ahead of him. The strangest sensations were racing through her. She wanted to run, to create space between them, for she could feel her system going haywire. At the same time, she knew she really wanted to be caught. And *that* was a first.

"You can set the table and pour some juice. By the way, tea or coffee?"

"I smelled coffee. If you have enough, I'd love a cup."

Mick poured her some and then showed her where everything was. As he went about making breakfast, Léa took the opportunity of saying what she had on her mind.

"I was wondering if you would object if I were to offer Heather a job?"

"What kind of a job?"

"Helping me with some projects next door." Léa folded and refolded the same napkin. "I have no choice but to stick around for a while. So I thought, if it's okay with you, since she seems to be home for the summer, I could talk her into maybe doing some painting. It would all be inside. I promise to give her only safe jobs. No high-ladder work. No power tools…''

She saw the hesitation in his face.

"Mick, I absolutely understand if you're against it. I haven't mentioned any of it to her, anyway. Actually, now that I think of it, with this thing happening last night—" she touched the bandage on her forehead "—it was wrong of me even to—"

"Heather's darn good with power tools."

Léa couldn't hide her delight with his response. "Is she?"

"I taught her myself. I'm not too bad with power tools myself."

She threw him a suspicious look. "It must be a man thing. You *all* claim to be good with power tools."

"Well, I just happen to be better than most." He dipped the raisin bread into the batter and put it on the griddle.

She went to a drawer to get some silverware. "If this is one of those lines for impressing the girls—makes great breakfast and is good with power tools—you don't need it with me."

"So, nothing about me impresses you, huh?" His free arm wrapped around Léa and she was pulled snugly against his side.

The shock of his act caused the breath to catch in her chest. He'd showered and shaved. Léa was drawn to the faint scent of his cologne, to the full curve of his bottom lip, to the deep blue eyes that were staring at her lips. More than anything else, she realized, she wanted him to kiss her in that moment.

"Contrary to what you think," she whispered, "everything about you impresses me."

The sizzling of butter on the griddle broke the moment, and he released her to flip the French toast. She forced herself to move out of his reach and return to the breakfast table across the room.

What was wrong with her? She laid out the knives and forks.

"I use the stuff as part of my job, Léa." He glanced around at her. "Power tools. I'm a contractor. A builder. We renovate people's houses or businesses for a living."

"You are?" She was genuinely surprised. And then it all dawned on her. "Of course you are. The truck you were driving yesterday…" She moved to the window that looked out over the driveway to the left of the house. Next to the black Volvo he'd used to bring her home from the hospital, there was the same red pickup truck she'd seen him driving yesterday. "The name on the side. Stone Builders. I wasn't thinking. That's great! So you really do this for a living?"

He placed the first batch of toast on a metal platter and put it in the oven and started on a second batch. "Yes, and yes. I left medical school to use my hands for other things and to work in the sun and be my own boss. Pretty unimpressive, isn't it?"

"Absolutely not." Léa shook her head incredulously, going back to setting the table. "But don't make me give you one of my long speeches on the importance of *every* career. I go through this every year with my ninth-grade kids. Actually, what I've found out over the years is that *they* have it right and the so-called grown-ups have it wrong. The kids look at jobs as a way to get pocket money. They work to live. Most of their parents live to work."

"Where do *you* fall on that scale?"

"I guess I've been sliding between the two ends for a while. At least since Ted's trial started, I've had to work for financial reasons. At the same time, there were many days that I couldn't wait to get back to my job as a way of escaping that reality." Léa didn't want to think of that. She didn't want to remember it was still the driving reality in her life now. "Enough about me. How did you get hooked up with Stone Builders? They've been around for a while, haven't they?''

''Some fifty years.'' He came over with the coffeepot and topped off her mug. ''I bought them out.''

Léa wasn't actually surprised. Mick's mother had come from a lot of money and his father must have made his share during the years of practicing medicine in Stonybrook. And Mick was an only child. The golden boy.

''It was a second-generation thing. The founder's son had practically bankrupted the business, so I worked there and eventually ended up running it for them for over seven years. When he had a name worth cashing in again, I was the one he approached. So that's what I really bought— the name.''

She paused, feeling guilty. Mick had been fighting a lifetime of labels, too. And she was no different from anyone else at jumping to conclusions.

''Which brings me to where we started.'' He flipped the French toast. ''Léa, if you're open to it, I can arrange to have some of my people work on your house. They can do the bulk of the work for you in no time.''

The objection in her was immediate. ''Mick, you and Heather have done enough for me already. I can't accept something like that.''

''You can treat it as a kind of a loan that you can pay off down the road. Look at it as a business proposition.''

''Then you're a poor businessman. I can't let you do that.'' Léa shook her head when he started to argue. ''I do appreciate what you are trying to do, but I don't even know myself how long I'll be around, or how much work I will be doing on the house, or if I'll be putting it on auction, or if I'll rent it or whatever. Too many things are up in the air right now. And hiring some part-time help is really the extent of any commitment I can handle.''

''Okay. I just wanted to offer. And I have no problem if you want to ask Heather.''

"Thank you." His consent meant his trust, and Léa was grateful for that. She leaned on the fridge door, watching him add spices to a cooking pot of applesauce. "It'd be great if she'd consider it."

"Heather told me you are also looking for a new lawyer. Have you found someone already?"

"I have. Or at least, I hope I have." She took a half step back as he opened the oven and added more French toast to the trayful staying warm in there. "She has an excellent reputation. But I don't know yet if she's going to take the case or not. She's looking at trial transcripts over the weekend, and I'm supposed to call her tomorrow afternoon."

"What's her name?"

"Sarah Rand. She isn't originally from around here. From what I hear, she moved to the area not too long ago. She's already making a name for herself, though."

"I know her."

"You do?"

"Yeah. And her husband. She's married to Owen Dean, the actor. Actually, he's producing now. She's the same woman the police thought had been murdered by a judge friend of hers a couple of years ago. Up in Rhode Island. Owen somehow helped her out and when the whole mess was resolved, they ended up getting married. Their names and pictures were on every newspaper in the country, I think."

"I knew she was married to Owen Dean, but none of the rest of it. Just shows you how out of touch I've been. But you really know them personally?"

"I built an addition onto a stone farmhouse they bought last year. It's about a half hour from here, in Buckingham." He turned off the burners under the griddle. "Initially, they were going to be away in Rhode Island for most of the summer. But Owen was involved in some movie that was being shot around here with Mel Gibson in it. So they were down here living in the house while we worked the job. I got to know them pretty well.''

"Wow, now I'm really impressed.''

"They're good people. Very normal. And you're right, word is that she's a very capable attorney.''

"That's wonderful to know.'' She let out a wistful sigh. "Now I have to cross my fingers and hope that she'll want the case.''

"Everything is ready. Are you going to pour some juice or what?'' Smiling at her, he moved to the kitchen doorway and called up to Heather.

Léa forced herself to clear her mind of everything except this kitchen, these people, this breakfast. She opened the refrigerator door and stared at the selection of juices. "What do you want to drink?''

"Let me see? Choices, choices.''

He was standing close to her, so close that she felt the tickle of his breath on her neck. She shivered and then her back was pressing against his chest.

"Are you cold?''

Léa shook her head. He looked as if he couldn't make up his mind. "You like to take your time, don't you?''

"I do. How about you?''

"Hypothetically, I'd say I like to. But in my life, time is a luxury I haven't experienced in a while.''

"Then we'll have to work on that, won't we?''

Léa glanced over her shoulder and found him looking intently at her lips. She didn't know how badly she needed him until he brought his face that much closer and put his mouth on hers. It was like a dream, so she didn't dare close her eyes for fear of everything disappearing when she opened them again. His lashes were long, his blue eyes smoky, and in an instant the taste and smell of him swept Léa into a whirlpool of sensations.

Mick pulled back from the kiss too soon, but his eyes lingered on her lips.

"Have you…decided what you want to drink?" she somehow managed to ask.

"Yes, I definitely know what I want."

Léa smiled and turned slightly in his arms. Mick kissed her again, as if sealing his decision. But this time she kissed him back, stroking his jaw, his ear, running her fingers through his short hair, feeling the warmth of his skin as they stood in front of the open refrigerator.

She came alive with the embrace. The kiss deepened and a strange exhilaration danced through her. Léa felt the exact second Mick began to lose control. His head tilted, his arms closed tightly around her, and there was a deep, satisfying sound in his throat.

Max's scratching, tapping footsteps turning the corner at the bottom of the steps were followed by Heather's grumble about something that the dog had done. Léa and Mick leaped apart like two guilty adolescents. Léa practically crawled inside the fridge, while Mick moved to the front of the sink and turned the water on the dirty dishes.

"Are you two okay?"

Fourteen

Neither of their answers sounded even slightly coherent. Heather looked from her father's back to Léa's and then at Max's head, which was practically resting on the breakfast table. She dropped the folded newspaper on the counter.

"Nice article." She reached inside a cabinet and started pouring herself some cereal. "It makes you sound like some superwoman or something. By the way, why didn't you agree to talk to this guy? He sounds pretty fair and obviously thinks you are the next Mother Teresa."

Léa peeked at her over the top of the open fridge door. "What guy?"

Heather thought she looked flushed. "Are you hot or something? Feverish?"

"No. I'm fine. Can I pour you some juice?"

"Soda. Don't bother with a glass."

"She'll drink orange juice." Her father put the platter of food and a bowl of applesauce on the table. "I'll have the same."

Heather watched with interest the way Mick's gaze was slow to move from Léa. He was checking Léa out, she thought, a little surprised. He actually waited for her to come and sit before he sat down himself. He didn't do that when the two of them were eating. His hand brushed against Léa's a few times, and when Max tried to jam himself under the table, Heather glanced down there and found their bare feet touching.

She hid her smile and poured the milk on top of her cereal. She couldn't remember the last time she'd felt this normal. She couldn't remember the last time she'd eaten cereal!

"You don't have to hide your hanky-panky from me, you know. I think it's a good thing for both of you."

Léa blushed and smiled, then hid her face behind the coffee mug.

Mick shook his head and grinned. "I thought I'd take you up on your advice."

"It's about time." Heather reached behind her and picked up the newspaper again, glancing at the picture there and then at Léa. "But we *have* to do something about a publicity photo for you. I mean, if we're going to hang out, then we're talking about *my* reputation, too."

"What are you talking about?"

"I don't think there's much she can do about it for a while. Not with all those stitches and the bandages." Mick took the newspaper from Heather and looked more closely at it. "Actually, I don't know why you don't like this one. She looks very professional."

"I am totally lost. Let me see that." Léa reached over to take the paper, but Mick stole a kiss before he handed it over.

Heather thought it was cute that Léa actually blushed.

"Uh, excuse me. Let's not go overboard with this, okay? I would like to keep my breakfast down." She was stunned to have her father lean over and kiss her, too. Stunned and pleased. "Oh, let's just get totally warped while we're at it."

The phone rang.

"I'll get it," her father said. "You two eat."

Heather watched Mick's expression become serious as he listened to whoever was on the other end, and her nerves kicked in again. She'd gone out looking in that carriage house three times this morning and still hadn't been able to find the bottle of sleeping pills. If she could help it, she didn't want anyone asking her any questions about them, even though she had a legitimate reason for having the medication. Just in case, she'd quickly thought up a story, though. The bottle had fallen out of her pocket the afternoon before when…when she'd chased Max inside there…or something.

The label had her name on it, and all she could figure was that one of those police officers must had picked it up early this morning.

It was a privacy thing. It was none of their business that she had the pills. She'd committed no crime, Heather reminded herself as Mick left the kitchen and took the phone with him to talk privately in his office. The only lie had been that she'd come out *after* Léa was already down. But even being that close, she hadn't seen the creep who had done this to her.

Heather looked across the table at Léa's bandaged head. The woman's gaze immediately lifted off the paper and met hers.

"Just reading this little bit, I'm amazed. So in what part of the article does he drop the bomb?"

"He doesn't. It's actually pretty good."

Léa still shook her head doubtfully before putting the paper aside. "I think I'll just take your word for it."

The applesauce Léa was spooning on the French toast looked edible. Heather took a spoonful of it and put it on her cereal.

"There must be a genetic defect in this family. Your father likes beer with his cookies. You like applesauce on your cereal. Both of you are good with power tools."

Heather shrugged but couldn't hold back her smile. "So you've heard."

"He is definitely the proud father—and with good reason, from what I can see."

The warm feeling spreading inside of her was surprising. This morning was just full of surprises. All Heather could think of was how close she'd come to ending her life last night. She stared into the bowl of cereal and felt herself choking up. The wide swing of her emotions over a few short hours was kind of scary.

"I was wondering…no, actually I was hoping." Léa paused until Heather looked up. "Would you consider doing some work for me over the next couple of weeks?"

"Doing what?"

"Work on the house. I don't know, maybe some scraping and painting."

"That's pretty boring."

Léa pointed a fork at her. "You do a good job with that, and I might let you move up to sanding floors."

"Does this mean you're going to stick around awhile?"

"I'm considering it."

Heather tried not to show her delight at the news. "How much are you gonna pay me?"

"What's the going rate these days?"

"Let me see." She took a sip of her father's coffee and then nearly turned inside out. There was no sugar in it. She added two heaping spoonfuls and stirred. "How does twenty bucks an hour sound?"

"Like highway robbery." Léa crossed her arms on the table and faced Heather. "How does five sound?"

"Make it six, and I might consider it."

"Done." Léa picked up her knife and fork and attacked the food on her plate again. "I am really impressed. This is really good. What makes the French toast so good?"

"He puts vanilla extract in the batter and thinks he's Chef Boyardee."

Heather considered trying some of the French toast. She

used to love it before, but instead she took another sip of the coffee. It needed more sugar.

"I have some conditions. Call it fringe benefits or something." She added another spoonful of sugar and stirred.

"Was your father the one who taught you how to negotiate, too?"

"It's in our blood. Back to my conditions for work."

"I'll give you work gloves and goggles. What more could you possibly need?"

"I start whenever I get up in the morning. And you don't give me a hard time about drinking."

"I assume you mean soda."

Heather gave a half-committed nod.

"You want to rot your teeth and ruin the lining of your stomach, it's okay by me."

"Save it. I've heard it all before." She took a piece of French toast and dipped it in the applesauce. "So what do you say?"

Léa shrugged. "Go ahead. I'm not paying dental insurance. You can pick your dentures out next time you're downtown."

Heather bit back her smile. "And the second thing is you don't give me any shit about smoking."

"Nope. No way." Léa shook her head. "That stuff can kill you, and I don't want any part of it."

"You didn't say a thing when you saw me on the driveway yesterday." She took a bite out of the bread.

"I wasn't offering you a job then. Plus, I was too far away. No danger of secondhand smoke."

"Don't try to tell me you're afraid of secondhand smoke."

"As a matter of fact, I am," Léa said flatly. "Plus, I'm fixing that house to sell. I don't want the smell of smoke in there when all the potential buyers line up to see the place. The stuff stinks and sticks around for a long time."

Heather considered calling the whole thing off. But instead, she put another spoonful of sugar in Mick's cup. She had to admit, it would be kind of fun to get up in the morning and go to work. It would be even more fun to hang with Léa all day. She was cool.

"So what are you going to do? Think about it?"

"I don't have to." Heather tried the coffee again. It was too sweet, even for her. She put it back by her father's plate. "I'll take the job. But it's not because I like you or anything, or because I buy that stuff about smoking and all that. I'll do it...well, because I think it's pretty cool that you have a brother on death row."

Léa stared at her with a startled look on her face for a moment. Then Heather saw her hand reach across the table and take her own.

"Thanks," Léa said softly.

Her hazel eyes got misty, but Mick came back into the kitchen at that minute, and Léa busied herself straightening the folds on the paper. One look at him, though, and Heather knew something wasn't right.

"There's a problem on one of the jobs. I have to leave you two to your own devices this morning. Think you can handle looking after each other?"

"I don't need a baby-sitter," Heather said defensively.

"I know *you* don't, but she does." Still standing, he took a bite off his plate and picked up his coffee to wash it down.

The expression on his face was priceless as he drank a mouthful. He couldn't spit it into the sink fast enough.

"I couldn't drink it, either," Heather said innocently. "Way too sweet."

"Clean up the kitchen, brat," Mick ordered, glowering at her. "I need to talk to Léa."

"No problem." Heather pushed her soggy cereal aside and casually pulled the applesauce and French toast in front of her. As she picked up a knife and fork, she watched her father lead Léa into his office and close the door.

"I want you to stay here."

"Sure! Heather and I are going to spend the whole morning together. She agreed to help me next door."

"That's great. But I'm talking about staying here with us while you're working on your house." Mick leafed through a file cabinet and found what he was looking for. He dropped the folder on his desk. "I want you to use this house as your base, where you stay and sleep. I don't want you to be alone over there at night."

She crossed her arms and leaned against the door. "I'll be fine, Mick. Nothing would have happened to me last night if I hadn't gone out there in the middle of the night."

"Yes, it could have." He turned on his cell phone and put it on his belt and started pulling on his sneakers. "Please, Léa, do this for me. Something crazy is going on around Stonybrook, and I'd feel much better if you were somewhere where I could keep an eye on you."

Léa straightened up immediately. "This has something to do with the phone call, doesn't it? Has something happened on one of your jobs because you've been helping me?" She didn't even let him respond. "I am so sorry, Mick. I should have stayed away from you and Heather. It's been so wrong of me—"

"There's no connection between you being here and some jerk vandalizing a job site. But I still want you here."

When she started shaking her head, he took hold of her chin. Her skin was so soft. The thought of the kiss they'd shared in the kitchen came flooding back, but she was hurt and tired. Mick knew better than to take advantage of her when she was this vulnerable. He put on his business face.

"Let's look on the practical side of things. Your house

is not livable as is. Everything will go much faster if you are not struggling to live and work in the same rooms.''

''I can stay in a motel. In fact, I had planned on that originally, but—''

''That won't work.'' He looked from her bandaged head down to her lips again. All his good intentions disappeared in an instant. ''You don't want to have Heather all alone here just because I can't stay away from you, now, do you?''

She blushed and he felt the shields starting to go up. ''Mick, about that. I don't think you and I should…make anything more…''

The moment his lips brushed against hers, her fingers clutched at his shirt and he could almost hear those shields crashing to the floor. She held him close.

''I think we absolutely should.''

There was no starting slow this time. The taste and feel of her were intoxicating. She had an incredible mouth. Mick thought he could go on and make love to her mouth like this for hours. But that was before Léa tucked her fingers in the waistline of his jeans and backed up to the wall, pulling him with her.

Mick's blood pounded and his body hardened, and he pressed and molded himself to every curve of her beautiful figure. Their mouths played and tasted and tormented, and their bodies strained to fit closer.

Léa's fingers moved beneath his shirt and up his back. Mick managed to push down one of the straps of her overalls and cup her breast through the T-shirt. She was wearing no bra, and her nipple hardened beneath his thumb.

''You are full of surprises.'' He smiled before delving deeper into the kiss. Léa's hips moved restlessly against his. She wanted him as much as he wanted her.

His cell phone started ringing, and she tore her mouth away. Neither of them could catch their breath for a moment.

"You...you must be late."

Cursing, Mick looked down at the incoming call flashing on the tiny screen. It was from the same job site.

"I am." He tipped her chin up again. Her face was flushed, her lips a little puffy from their exchange. "Promise you'll stay?"

"We'll talk when you get back." She pulled the strap over her shoulder and opened the door for him. "Be careful."

On the hill just beneath the ridge that bordered Stonybrook to the north, the long-dead patriarchs and matriarchs of many of the well-to-do families of the town lay in their ornate family vaults and looked down over their children's struggles. Each granite-and-marble resting place vied for attention with its neighbor. Angels with spread wings. Crosses with inlaid gold. Enough clusters of little cherubs to make even Raphael blush.

On the edges of the cemetery, following the ridge east and west, the newer plots were not nearly so ostentatious. Granite headstones for the most part. A few low crypts in evidence here and there. All of them carved with the same family names of those far, far more important personages who went before.

Turning off the steep road leading to the ridge above the town, the gray Cadillac glided through the cemetery's stone gate pillars. The vehicle moved slowly past impeccably groomed lawns and into a small parking lot.

The driver of the Cadillac killed the engine and sat. From the perspective of the town below, this place—and everyone and everything in it—was all part of the distant past. Tucked away. Forgotten. No bells rang in the ancient stone chapel by the road, even during the occasional burial service. Almost no one came here. Only some chance tourist following a genealogical trail, or an art historian, curious about one sculpture or another. From the town, no one bothered to come up that hill.

Except Stephanie.

She picked up the two small bouquets of summer flowers—daisies and irises—off the seat and stepped out of the car.

The sun shone high above. A gentle breeze made the growing heat of the day almost bearable. With the exception of an old van laboring slowly up the hill beyond the gates, there wasn't a living soul for as far as the eye could see.

Stephanie stepped out of her high heels and threw the silk scarf she'd wrapped around her throat back inside the car. She carefully locked the car and started along one of the paths. As she went, she smelled the flowers in her hand. They didn't have the same bright scent they used to have when she was a girl.

This was more than a habit for her, this trip up here every Sunday morning. It was now her religion. Indeed, Stephanie thought as she walked, it was a grandmother's duty to visit with her grandchildren.

"A yellow ribbon for you this week, Emily, and a very pretty pink one for Hanna."

Sitting on each side of the headstone, the long ribbons and fresh flowers only accentuated the dark gray color of the granite. As she looked at them, Stephanie noticed little cuttings of grass adhering to the girls' headstone. She got down on her hands and knees and started brushing the grass off. She ran her hands over the entire stone. It was cool to her touch. Surprisingly cool. All the while, she talked about the new dresses she'd seen in a catalog and the new toys that were being advertised on TV.

"You know you have to start making your Christmas list. It's never too early for girls as good as you two." Her hands were covered with dirt when she finally sat back on the grass. The knees of her white trousers were already stained. "Emily, you'll have to do the writing for both you and Hanna. But I'll help you, if you'd like."

As she talked to them, the breeze riffled the flowers on Hanna's side. Stephanie reached across and straightened the arrangement.

"And since you've been such good girls, I thought we could open our presents on Christmas Eve. We don't want that fat old Santa Claus getting any credit for what Grandma's bought for her precious girls."

Another breeze brought with it an odor. Every nerve in Stephanie's body went on alert as she immediately recognized it. She scrambled to her feet and looked about the cemetery wildly.

Standing by the path, Dusty was watching her.

For a moment, panic took control of her as she stared at the devil. She glanced about her feet desperately for something to use as a weapon, but there was nothing.

He was still staring at her. Staring right through her. And as always, when it came to him, she was fully exposed.

Stephanie summoned all her courage and stood guarding the two small graves as he drew near.

Dusty reeked with a smell that was all his own. His clothes were more ragged than ever, the diseased skin on his face showing through his beard in large red patches.

None of this frightened her. The sight of him—the smell of him—only filled her with revulsion.

But when he looked from the children's graves to Marilyn's beside them, the way those dark eyes turned cold with hate caused her to shudder.

"Where are Merl's flowers?"

Stephanie tried to collect herself, and she stepped back to the children's gravestone, creating a little distant between the intruder and herself.

"Where are Merl's flowers?" When he stepped toward her, she backed up involuntarily.

"I don't know. There was nothing here when I arrived."

"You didn't bring her any?"

She brushed the dust and pollen off the top of the granite stone. "I'm here to see my grandchildren. That's all."

Dusty crouched down and scooped up the two bouquets of flowers.

"Get your filthy hands away from those." She moved with the quickness of a cat to him, trying to snatch the flowers away.

He shoved her away and moved the flowers to Marilyn's grave. "For you, Merl. Your mother is a stupid bitch, but she really does love you."

"Give those back to me. She doesn't deserve them." Stephanie tried to reach around him, but he shoved her away—this time harder than before.

As she landed on the ground, her hand struck the headstone and she winced with pain.

"You deserve better, Merl." He ripped the ribbons off one of the bouquets and started spreading the flowers on the grave. "Lots of flowers. Pretty…like you."

"She is ugly!" Stephanie cried out, rubbing her hand. In her mind's eye, she could see Emily sobbing in her bedroom while Marilyn slammed the door shut in the child's face. She remembered coming into the yard to find Hanna sputtering and nearly drowning in the backyard pool while Marilyn casually walked back into the house, her phone pressed to her ear. "She's vile and ugly! Do you hear me?"

"My pretty Merl. So pretty." Dusty started on the second bouquet. "You don't believe anything she says. She loves you, Merl."

The repulsive image of Marilyn on her knees flashed in her memory. On her knees and sucking Charlie's dick in their living room. The slut had been counting on Stephanie walking in on them. Her face had said it all.

"I hate her. Do you hear me? I *hate* her." Crawling on her hands and knees, Stephanie scrambled toward her daughter's grave. "She's nothing more than a whore."

"She's jealous of you, Merl." He ran his fingers on the inscription carved in the headstone. "The stupid bitch is old and bitter, and we know why."

"You're disgusting."

"It's because I like you better. Because now I do it with you."

"Shut your filthy mouth." The tears started to come. She took fistfuls of flowers off the grave and put them back on the children's graves.

"She is jealous. Jealous!" He croaked out a laugh and sat back on his haunches, watching her fall apart. "Should we tell her, Merl? Please, please let me tell her."

Stephanie twisted the yellow ribbon around a couple of the daisy stems. She wound it tighter and tighter. It was easy to imagine wrapping it around Marilyn's neck. The stems snapped.

"The girls?" He continued his conversation with the headstone. "No, we don't want to tell the girls now. They'll whine and cry, and I don't want any of that shit going on before we do it. We want them older, anyway. We want them the way you were. How old were you when we first did it? Fifteen?"

"Shut up!"

"The summer before?"

"Shut up!" Every nerve in her body was taut and sharp as piano wire. The world was tilting around her head.

"Yeah. Fourteen." He laughed again. "You'll have to bring them one at a time…first. After a while, after they're used to—"

"You won't touch my babies!" She sprang at him, toppling him in the grass. "You won't come close to my babies, you bastard." Her fists were flying at his face.

He caught her hands, but she continued to fight him.

"I'll kill you. I'll dig your eyes out with my bare nails. I'll stab you until you're…"

When she tried to bite his hand, Dusty rolled Stephanie onto her back and threw his body heavily on top of her. There was blood trickling from his nose, but he didn't seem to even notice. His breath was foul when he breathed in her face.

"You stupid bitch. Don't you think I have as much right to those girls as you?"

She looked at him in horror. "They are *my* grandchildren," she gasped. "*My* babies."

His eyes were slitted with hatred. "They are Marilyn's girls. So they are mine, too. Or have you forgotten, Stephanie?"

"Marilyn has become more vicious than she ever was before. And everyone around her is paying the price."

"She is not hurting Emily or Hanna, is she?" Ted asked with concern.

"She is inflicting a different kind of bruising on them. Not the hurt that people can see." Stephanie started crying. "I came here to see you because I know what she is capable of. I know the extent of her anger. The depth of her hatred. And I know how far she is capable of going to get what she wants."

"The first hearing is in two weeks. My lawyer thinks, despite all of Marilyn's lies and accusations, I still have an excellent chance of getting custody of the girls."

"Even though you were married to her, you don't know her. You don't understand the…the bad seed that she is from. Revenge is the only thing that drives her. For years, I was her main target." Stephanie took Ted's hand before he could respond. "I have something to tell you. Dusty Norris is her real father."

"Dusty?" He knew nothing about that.

"And from the day Dusty told her the truth, her life's

goal became punishing me. But her target now is you and everyone who takes your side. Everyone that you care for. She is vicious, and she will not stop. I'm her mother, Ted, but I'm telling you…Marilyn is evil.''

Fifteen

The cottages, set into discreet notches along the lake's edge, had been popular with summer tourists from the day the Lion Inn had them built back in the fifties. The lake was long and curved, deep in the middle and a favorite place for fishing and boating. The last owner of the Lion had given the cottages names like Nairobi, Mombasa and Victoria, furnishing them with safari-themed pictures and furniture that were both plentiful and cheap then, thanks to the postwar economy.

From early on, the cottage called Serengeti had proved the most requested. More secluded than the others, it offered privacy that honeymooners and lovers had sought with a regularity that did not surprise the succession of hotel managers. But for almost a decade now, a certain individual's year-round rental of the place had permanently removed this cottage from the available lists.

Driving up to the inn, Mick knew somehow the problem would be in Marilyn's cottage. As he stood frowning in the open doorway of the place, his foreman Chuck shifted uncomfortably behind him.

"This place didn't look *nothing* like this when we went around in April to do the estimate." Chuck leafed through the folder Mick had brought with him and pulled out the sheet of photographs. "I'm glad we took these pictures."

The stench inside was from something more than the closed-up, musty smell they regularly encountered in renovations of old buildings. This one smelled like stale beer. Or dog piss.

"This sets us back a couple weeks at least, boss." Chuck looked at his clipboard. "In Serengeti, the owner only wanted fresh paint on the upper walls and a coat of varnish on the wainscot, and new flooring for the kitchen and bathroom. But with all this damage...I figured we'd better not touch a thing till you got here."

"Did you call Evans like I told you?"

"Yup. He wasn't at home and not up at the inn, either. I left him messages both places."

As Mick carefully picked his way through the large open sitting area, his gaze was drawn to the deep slashing cuts in the wainscot. The insides of the wood, covered by decades of stain and varnish and age, showed through startlingly white, like the flesh in a deep wound the moment before the blood comes.

"Did you check the rest of the cottages again? Any damage anywhere else?"

"Two of them we weren't supposed to touch until these were done. They have people in them now so I couldn't check. But the rest of the cottages are okay, with all the furniture moved out and everything. They look ready to go. It's just this baby."

Mick looked closely at the countertop in the small kitchenette. The same deep cuts marred the surface. They were too wide to have been done with a knife. More like a crowbar or something similar.

"If you ask me," Chuck said, "it looks like somebody went nuts in here."

"I'd say they did." He looked up at the ceiling. The fixture was dangling down. There were big dents in the plaster on the walls, like someone had hammered again and again against the plaster. "What did you do with the crew you brought in on overtime to work on this one?"

"I got them started on the cottage closest to the inn's

dock." He looked at his clipboard again. "Mombasa. They're scraping and pulling out the carpets and the old linoleum in it. We could start painting in there today if you want."

The folding doors to a pantry closet had been ripped out and broken to pieces. Inside, all the shelving had been torn from the walls and lay scattered on the floor.

He peered inside the bathroom. The mirror had been shattered into about a million pieces, and there was glass everywhere on the ancient linoleum flooring.

"Did you touch anything when you first came in?" Mick asked, noticing the red splatters of what could have been blood on the plastic shower curtain.

"The front door. But I only got as far as the kitchen and I knew some serious shit was going on around here. I came right out and called you. Then I left the messages for Evans and put the guys to work in the other cottage. After that, I called you again to give you an update."

Mick reached for his cell phone and dialed the number for the police. In a minute, he was giving the information to the dispatcher.

Nothing could have prepared him for the sight and smell of the bedroom in the back of the cottage. Blood-red paint had been splattered on the walls and part of the ceiling. There were small congealed pools of it at the base of the walls. The light fixtures had been smashed. The damage to the plaster was similar to what they'd seen in the other rooms. Across the bedroom, the sliding glass doors overlooking the lake were cracked, the fissures extending to the outside of the panes of glass like spiderwebs.

"Holy shit!" Chuck motioned to the ceiling and the walls. "It looks like a butcher shop in here."

Mick stared at the dark splotches on the gray carpet and the stains on the wall.

"I'd say whoever did this thought this room was a urinal.'' The smell was disgusting, and the two men backed out of the room. ''Any damage outside?''

''Nothing.''

''When you first came in, did you use the master key?''

''Yup. I picked it up at the inn office. It works on all the cottages.''

''So the place was locked?''

''Tight as a gnat's ass.''

They went outside. The greenery of gently rolling hills around the lake looked like the Garden of Eden after what they'd seen inside. Of course, Mick thought, there was a snake in every garden.

He circled the cottage with his foreman on his heels. From the shingled siding to the high small windows, everything seemed perfectly normal from the outside. They pushed past a grove of evergreens to the edge of the lake and stopped. With the small dock behind them, Mick stared at the place. Even from this angle, all anyone could see was the cracked sliding glass door.

''Let me see those pictures again.''

Mick peered at the date imprinted underneath. April. Unlike the rest of the cottages, this one had been emptied of furniture when he and Chuck had gone through the places with the owner. It was easy to see the intact walls, the new carpeting in the bedroom. Evans had had the old flooring replaced when the police had turned the cottage back over to the inn after Marilyn's murder.

An ache was beginning to pound in Mick's head as they started back toward the cottage. Two months ago, when he had been preparing the estimate to renovate the Lion Inn, he'd been thinking about two things: Heather's arrival from California and his company.

This type of job was perfect for Stone Builders. Spread over two years, the entire renovation was very manageable for a company his size. The owner wanted the cottages done first; the work on the main building, with its more serious structural repairs in addition to the cosmetic work, was done during two off-season periods. They'd build a new boathouse and renovate the docks next summer. The project offered large bonuses for every month that they could finish ahead of schedule. It was ideal.

Amid all the details and arrangements that Mick and his people had gone through, though, he'd put aside something that had seemed very strange to him on his initial tour of the place.

This cottage, Serengeti, had been unavailable to the owner for months after Marilyn's murder. Mick had been told that Stonybrook's police had removed mountains of personal items belonging to the dead woman from the place. Then, after the cottage had been turned back to the inn, some minor renovations had been done. But despite the expense, Serengeti had not been rented. Why?

"You say something, boss?"

"Talking to myself."

"I oughta go check on the crew. See you in a bit."

Mick nodded absently and found himself standing by the front door of the cottage again. *Mountains of personal items taken by the police.* He recalled what Sheila had mentioned when she was cutting his hair. *Certain people Marilyn entertained at the inn.*

How much of this had been presented at Ted's trial, he wondered, suddenly wishing he'd paid closer attention to the news reports.

A few minutes later, Mick still wasn't happy with himself when Chief Weir arrived on the scene alone.

"Did you and your brother really find them dead here?" Heather's voice echoed though the empty house.

Léa looked at the full garbage bag she'd just brought downstairs. Leaving it by the front door, she trudged reluctantly toward the kitchen.

She had yet to step in that room.

About an hour ago, the two of them and Max had come over to the house. Léa had decided to bag and haul some of the trash from the upstairs while Heather and Max had been content to browse around on their own.

Léa stopped at the kitchen door and stood next to the teenager. The instant flash of memory was painful, but she fought off both the panic and the tears.

"Yes. We stood right where we're standing now. My father was at the kitchen table, and my mother…on the floor." She pointed and looked away.

The old linoleum flooring was a different ugly gray than the marbleized one she remembered from her childhood. All the kitchen cabinets were painted in a horrible shade of yellow that she realized might have started out as white sometime during the years she'd been away. But a glance around the room showed that everything else seemed so much the same. The oven, the fridge, the wooden shelf on the opposite wall.

Their mother always kept at least a dozen flowerpots of African violets on that shelf. Léa could still remember standing on a kitchen chair, still recall the smell of the plants and the soil. A pyramid of empty beer cans was the decoration now.

Léa's gaze was drawn to the cheap metal table and the bent and broken folding chairs. They were exactly where the Hardys used to have *their* breakfast table and chairs.

"Did you come back here at all after that day?"

She shook her head. The words were slow to come. "No. Not…not once."

Heather turned her blue eyes on Léa's face. "You look kinda pale. Are you sure you are not pushing yourself too much?"

The back of her throat burned with the surge of emotions she tried to contain. "I'm…fine." When the teenager's hand gently slipped into hers, the tears escaped.

"I'm sorry, I shouldn't have…I…" Heather cast around

for words. "This is the last thing you need, somebody asking you stuff like this."

"No. It's okay. I *want* you to ask." Léa smiled weakly and stabbed away at the tears. "I've been putting off facing this room. But now, with you here…maybe I can deal with it. Maybe I can even get a little closer to figuring out who I was, and what I've become now. It's okay, Heather. It's time to let go of this."

Let go of this. So easy to say. Léa went to the front room and picked up a couple of empty trash bags, some rolls of paper towels and a spray cleaner. How do you let go of something that has haunted you year in and year out for most of your life? How do you let go of such a loss?

She started back for the kitchen, realizing that she had never even thought about who had cleaned up the kitchen after her parents had been taken away. She had no idea who had washed the blood from the floor. She had no idea who had closed her mother's eyes.

Heather and Max had already moved into the kitchen, but Léa hesitated again in the doorway.

She'd come back to Stonybrook with one thing on her mind. To be done with this house. To use it to help Ted. And yet, she was not done with it herself. All the hurt inflicted here—all the pain endured here—had never been resolved. It lay untended, open like a deep gash, for all these years. Even now.

Heather came over and took one of the bags and held it open. "Are you sure you're okay?"

"I am. I'm ready." Léa took the first steps in and started by clearing the shelf of its empty beer cans.

Clean the wound.

"Go ahead. Ask away," she said encouragingly. Heather's expression showed her reluctance.

"People say that every family has a skeleton in their closet. Ours happens to have lots of garbage!" Léa dropped the last can in the bag with a flourish. "Now, if only the people of Stonybrook would believe how innocent we really are.''

"What is it about the Hardys and this town?'' Heather leaned back against a cabinet, watching Léa. "I remember hearing that Marilyn and Ted eloped and never had a real wedding here. I know they lived twenty minutes away and that she only moved back after they were separated. I mean even before…well, Marilyn and the girls were murdered…there were always whispers of stuff whenever your family came up in conversation. More than what happened to your parents' deaths, I mean.''

"There is some serious history there.'' No Band-Aid can cover a twelve-inch gash. Léa knew she'd have to dig deep before every piece of the dirt would be out of this wound. "I guess you could say people were even talking about the Greenwoods—that was my mother's family— before they got going on the Hardys.''

"Why?''

"Well, my great-grandfather Greenwood owned and ran the pharmacy in town back in the thirties, forties and fifties.''

"The one that Andrew Rice runs now?''

"The very same.''

"That's cool.''

"I thought it was when I was young.'' Léa sprayed a shelf and started wiping it. The fact that they had once been respectable—that her family had *belonged*—had lifted Léa's spirits many times as a child.

"What did the Greenwoods do wrong?''

"Back in the spring of 1947, the Greenwoods' only child, a girl who was sixteen but already very beautiful, came home from a finishing school in Connecticut pregnant.''

"What's so shocking about that?''

"We're talking 1947. Remember the time and the town. And she would never admit who the child's father was.''

There had been many times in Léa's life when she had
wanted to blame all their troubles—all their bad luck and
struggling through the interim years—on Liz Greenwood's
mystery man. If he had shouldered his responsibility, if he
had been there for her—perhaps, if he had known. Léa
straightened up from cleaning the shelf and decided that
she liked this last explanation the best. It was the easiest
to accept and forgive. He must not have known.

"So this was your grandmother?"

"Yes." Léa looked over her shoulder and found
Heather climbing onto one of the rickety chairs to clean
off the top shelves of two of the cabinets. "You don't
have to do that."

"No sweat. Seriously." Heather waved her off. "Did
she keep the baby?"

"Of course. My mother, Lynn Greenwood, was born
some four months later."

"That hardly seems juicy enough to keep harping on
after all this time."

"I agree. But the baby wasn't even six months old when
her mother left her baby behind and ran away."

"She left her baby?" Heather looked across the room
at Léa.

"My guess is that she must have been feeling some
pressure in this house. And in town, too. At any rate, she
was gone." Like everything else in her past, Léa had questioned this, too. Had her mother been better off raised by
her grandparents? If the unwed mother had stuck around,
would she have been capable of improving her daughter's
life at all? These were answers Léa would never have. And
she knew it was time she stopped asking.

"Did she ever come back?"

"No, I don't think so. But the story was that four or
five years later...I am not exactly sure now, but I was told
that she was killed in a car accident on the West Coast."

"That's so sad. So your mother never knew her parents?"

Léa shook her head. "My great-grandparents raised my mother. But by then, they were both pretty old. I guess they were very suspicious and very, very protective of her."

And they were hurt. And they were suffering. And they had lost their only child. She had never even thought of what it could be like to lose a child until she saw how such a tragedy had affected Ted. Léa understood it clearly now. She dared herself to open the fridge door and peer inside. She was relieved to find it empty.

"'Once burned, twice shy,' my grandmother says," Heather replied, going back to work on the cabinet shelves.

"I think that's right."

"When did your dad come into the picture?"

Léa had to fight a new surge of emotions at the mention of him. She had to remind herself that he had been kind once. He had been loving. If she went back enough years, she could remember a time when he'd treated her mother right. "John Hardy came to Stonybrook back in the early sixties to run the mill. He was good-looking and in his late thirties when he met my mother. He was an old bachelor."

"Late thirties makes him an *old* bachelor? I can't wait to tell my dad that."

Léa smiled. "Your dad is anything but old. But my father had lived hard. There is a huge difference in the way people age when they abuse their bodies." And his hard living had not been solely a matter of choice, either. There were many things that Léa had learned about John Hardy after going to live with Aunt Janice. There had been a tough upbringing there, too.

"Drinking?"

"Yes."

Heather nodded knowingly.

Léa wasn't as lucky with the oven as the fridge. She pulled out a couple of old frying pans. The top one had the remains of some prehistoric dinner in it and the other was missing its handle. She didn't look too closely at them before dumping the whole thing into the trash bag. This was the same way she had to deal with the baggage of her father's history. He was gone. Dead! She had to let go of the blame and the guilt and tie the knot on the bag.

"How old was your mom when they met?"

"Nineteen."

"*That* is very warped. He was old enough to be her father."

Léa straightened from spraying cleaner into the oven and nodded. Deciding to let go made it much easier on her conscience. She could talk about them now. "After being isolated and watched for most of her life, I believe she was desperate."

Heather jumped off the chair and moved it a few feet to the right, starting on another pair of cabinets. "At least, I hope…well, he was nice to her in the beginning."

"I believe my mother walked into that marriage with her eyes wide open." Léa searched for the right way to explain this. "It all had to do with choices. As far as my mother knew, her only two options were staying home and having her grandparents keep watch on her around the clock, or marry John Hardy. Apparently, he was about the only guy who ever showed any interest."

"Because he was an out-of-towner."

"I guess that may have been part of it."

"So she married him."

Léa nodded. "But, as bad luck would have it, my great-grandmother got sick soon afterward, and they all ended up living in this house, where my mother could care for everybody. And now she had three sets of eyes watching her day and night."

"That's horrible. When were you and Ted born? I mean, was everybody still living here then?"

"I was just a baby when my great-grandfather died. After that, my great-grandmother moved to a nursing home for a couple of years before passing away. I don't remember too much about her." And this was so much like a Hardy and Greenwood tradition. Lynn Hardy losing people she loved. Her husband finding himself without a job soon after. The downward spiral of bad luck. Her children not old enough to defend or help her.

"And then what happened?"

"Ted and I grew up in this house. My father worked at the mill until it was shut down and everyone got laid off. My mother always stayed home, and we went to school like all the other kids around here."

Léa twisted a tie around the first full garbage bag and hauled it to the back door.

"When you were a kid, did you know my dad?"

"Of course." Léa yanked open the drawer under the oven. She more than knew Mick Conklin. She couldn't stop thinking about him. Carefully, she pulled out and dumped the greasy and bent cookie sheets and utensils she found in a new garbage bag.

"Okay, so tell me. What was he like?"

"Who?" Léa said, pretending she didn't know who they were talking about.

"My father!"

"Oh. He was older...seven years older. I just watched him from next door while I was growing up. But, to answer your question, he was very good-looking, and he was *very* popular with girls. I think your grandparents had their hands full from the time he was about twelve years old."

"Did you have a crush on him?"

"Every girl in town did."

"Did *you?*"

"I was the puny little kid next door. Trust me, we were not even in the same universe."

"Come on. Fess up," Heather demanded, stamping her foot on the chair. Léa cringed, certain it would collapse under the teenager.

"Okay, okay. I did. Are you happy?"

"I thought so." Heather smiled and turned her attention back to the cabinets.

The recollection of Mick's kisses this morning flooded Léa's body with warmth. For the thirty-one years of her life, there hadn't been a single moment that she remembered feeling as alive and vibrant as she'd felt during those few minutes in his arms. The few dates she'd had in college and since had not even come close.

"Did you and Ted see the thing with your parents coming?"

The question jarred Léa back into reality.

"No. I mean, they had troubles. My father was an alcoholic, but we never imagined anything as horrible as that." She shook her head. "If we did, we'd have done something—I don't know what—but *something* to stop it from happening."

"I didn't mean it like it was your fault or anything." Heather paused in her work and looked down over her shoulder. "I only asked because I think sometimes we can see trouble coming. We guess something horrible might happen...will happen."

Léa leaned against the counter, focusing on Heather's expression. "Are you thinking about your parents' breakup?"

"No, actually. I was thinking about Marilyn."

"What do you mean?"

"I used to baby-sit for the girls, off and on, the year before she was murdered. And I saw things that I just knew were not too good. The girls were constantly neglected. And there were all kinds of strange guys hanging around Marilyn. And a couple of months before she died, there were these angry phone calls from God knows who. It was kind of like waiting for a bomb to go off. But there was nothing I could do about it.''

She watched tears gather in Heather's eyes.

"You couldn't.'' Léa went to her. "You should never hold yourself responsible for anything like that.''

The teenager's hands were shaking. The mood change from cheerfulness to sadness had come quickly, but Léa could understand why.

Heather turned on the chair and sat down on the counter. "I think it's so not right that Emily and Hanna had to die because *she* was such a mess. I couldn't have cared less if Marilyn had jumped off a bridge or broken her neck, but those girls were...were so innocent. They were only babies. I watched them after school that Friday afternoon. They were so excited about spending the weekend with their dad. She shouldn't have brought them back to the house that night.''

Léa could not hold back her own tears. The sweet little faces were all around her. The memories. She clutched Heather's hands tightly in her own.

"It wasn't your fault.''

"But...but it was!''

"No, it wasn't.''

"I should have told somebody...about her. I should have...I don't know...told Ted or my dad...someone... how horrible she was and what she was doing...'' The words broke down into sobs.

Léa gathered her tightly in her arms. "It *wasn't* your fault, Heather. It wasn't you.''

Heather clutched at Léa, not saying anything, just crying.

As her own tears fell, Léa remembered the guilt that had haunted her way through her own teenage years. She had let herself believe that *she* could have stopped her parents' deaths.

But that was all behind her now. She was done with it. The wound was clean. Covered. Healing.

Or at least starting to heal.

"I need a cigarette," Heather croaked, pulling out of the embrace. "I'll be on the back porch."

"Can I come and sit with you?"

"Are you going to give me shit for smoking?"

"Probably, but I still want to come."

Heather wiped away her tears. "Okay."

Robert Evans, the middle-aged owner of the Lion Inn, waited with Mick outside as Rich Weir and two of the police officers the chief had called went through the Serengeti cottage.

"Have you ever had a problem with someone breaking into these cottages before?" Mick asked him. Evans had arrived about a minute after the police chief. They were both standing by the wooden picnic table and the open barbecue pit near the front door.

"Not in the nine years that I've owned it. I mean, sometimes we catch kids partying by the lake at night. And every now and then some college kids will rent one of these places for the weekend and try to jam about fifty of their friends into two small rooms, but it's never anything like this. This is pretty bizarre. I can't understand it at all."

"Who was the last person to rent this place?" Seeing the hesitation in the man's face to answer, Mick decided to reword the question. "I mean, *when* was the last time somebody stayed in this one?"

"I know what you're asking." Evans shook his head. "And there's no reason to hide it. Nobody has stayed in this cottage since Marilyn Hardy's murder."

"Why is that?"

"No reason in particular. It's just been one thing or

another. First, the police had it forever, it seemed. Then we did a little work on it with the intention of letting it out to vacationers. But my lawyer was quick to remind me that Marilyn had signed another two-year lease on the place just before she died.'' Evans took a handkerchief out of his pocket and wiped his forehead. ''She was dead. She was paying no rent. But the paperwork, and returning the deposit money, and some other problems with her family…the whole thing just bogged down. It took us six goddamn months to sort it out. Well, by then we'd been approved by the Bucks County Historical Society people for the loan on this renovation job. It wasn't worth messing around with it.''

Mick put a foot up on the wooden bench and rested his elbow on it. ''How many people do you think have a key to the place?''

''Christ, I don't know. You know Stonybrook. I don't think we've *ever* changed the locks on any of these places. There might be a few floating around.''

''How about the last time one of your people checked inside of it?'' Mick persisted. ''Two months ago, when you and I walked through, everything was kosher.''

Evan's frown deepened. ''Now that you mention it, I asked my maintenance guy to check all these cottages out a couple of weeks ago to make sure they were ready for you guys to start the job. He didn't say anything about any of this. So it had to be since then….''

Mick's attention was drawn to the door of the cottage as Rich Weir came out and headed toward them.

''So what have I got, Chief?'' Evans asked. ''Devil worshipers bleeding their pigs in there, or what?''

''No. I'd say nothing so dramatic.'' The big man glanced over his shoulder at the door as one of his officers walked out, carrying a briefcase in one hand. ''That's just paint in the bedroom.''

"Was that paint in the bathroom, too?" Mick asked.

The police chief only glanced briefly at him, directing his comments at the inn owner. "We took some samples, fingerprints, pictures, things like that. My guess is that some high school kids' party traveled from one of the private cabins on the lake. I'll send a couple of my guys around after we are done here. We'll have a report ready by tomorrow afternoon, if you want to pick up a copy for your insurance company."

"Did you take a close look at the kitchen counters and the wainscoting, Chief?" Mick asked, finding himself once again growing irritated with Rich's nonchalant attitude. "You figure a couple of beer bottles left grooves that deep?"

"What a treat, Conklin, seeing you so many times in one weekend."

"And wouldn't it be something if all these things were somehow related?" Mick challenged.

"Okay, so what did you do after you hit Léa Hardy with that two-by-four last night? You came out here and pissed on the rug?"

"Well, if you don't actually get some of this stuff analyzed, I guess you'll never know if I did it or not." Mick met the officer's glare. "But I can tell you one thing, Chief, you can't pin it on a Hardy this time. Between the doctors and the nurses in the emergency room and yours truly, she has plenty of people to serve as her alibi."

"You know, Conklin, I don't know what the fuck is going on with you these days." He shook his head and turned to the inn's owner. "You'll have to excuse my French, Mr. Evans. This ornery son of a bitch has been frying my bacon for two days now."

Mick pulled his cell phone off his belt and strode away. This was the last straw. As of right now, he was officially involved.

* * *

Marilyn opened the sliding glass door and walked out onto the small landing looking over the dark lake. The air was heavy, a storm brewing in the distance. Flashes of lightning streaked over the distant hills. Flashes of her blossoming plans for revenge raced through her mind. Finally, she was taking every one of them down. And Ted was going down, too.

But why was it, then, that she felt so miserable and alone?

"Nobody's coming to see Merl tonight?"

She saw Dusty standing in the shadows of the trees. "No. No one is coming."

"Nobody loving Merl tonight?"

"Yes." *She undid the belt and pushed the robe off her shoulders, letting the satin material pool around her feet.* "Daddy is."

Sixteen

Heather walked back into the living room with two tall glasses of iced tea, and then paused at the sight of Léa, curled up and sound asleep in the big leather chair by the window. The paperback she was reading was tucked at an awkward angle under her chin, but the teenager didn't dare touch her for fear of disturbing her badly needed rest.

Her father had called twice today. The first time, he'd left a message on the answering machine just before noon. The second time, about six, they'd been here and he'd talked to both Heather and Léa. Something about the job at the Lion Inn holding him up. He wanted to check that Léa was staying, though, so they would be sure to eat dinner.

That was so much like him. Like they were kids or something and needed him to tell them they had to eat or go to sleep, Heather thought with a smile. She put the drinks on the coffee table and picked up a magazine before stretching out on the sofa.

It was the strangest thing to feel this okay for so many hours in a row. It was even weirder not feeling like a smoke. She'd had one cigarette on Léa's back porch this morning, and that had been it. She hadn't even thought of it till now, and she still didn't want one.

They'd talked as much as they'd worked today, but Léa said it was no problem. Even though they hadn't gotten as much done on her house as she'd planned, she said it was good for both of them. It was kind of a healing thing. That saying goodbye to grief was something they both had to learn how to do.

Heather didn't care if there was a name for it or not, but she did feel better than she had in a long time.

She found herself smiling again as she looked at the sleeping woman. Léa was twice her age, but Heather felt more comfortable with her than she'd ever felt, even with her friends. And she'd told Léa things about her life— things that made her sad or frustrated or angry—that she would never consider telling her own mother.

The thing was, Léa didn't lecture her. She didn't butt in. She didn't offer to fix things. She listened. And then she'd just sort of encourage Heather to feel and to express whatever feeling she was holding inside. And at the same time, Léa would share stuff about her own past—about the years after leaving Stonybrook.

It was definitely an eye-opener to hear how difficult life could be when you lost both parents. It made Heather think. Even if they were a pain in the butt most of the time, at least she still had both of them.

By the time they'd come back here to call in for some pizza, she believed it when Léa said they'd both helped each other.

The headlights of her father's truck reflected off the walls for a second as he turned in the driveway. Heather sprang to her feet and followed Max to the back door to greet him.

A big smile broke out on Mick's face when he walked in through the kitchen door and found her waiting there.

"Hi."

"Kind of like the old days." He petted the dog and looked up and smiled again. "I've missed them."

Heather saw the struggle on his tired face. He was not too sure what he was supposed to do. Well, for tonight, anyway, she didn't give a damn what was cool and what wasn't. She went to him and gave him a big hug. And then she quickly stepped back before things got too mushy altogether.

"Have you had dinner yet?" she asked quietly.

"I ate something on the road."

"Dead squirrel?"

"You know I'm partial to fresh roadkill." He grinned and dropped his keys in the drawer. "How about you two?"

"Pizza."

"Where's Léa?"

"She passed out in your chair in the front room about an hour ago. Keep it down when you go in there. She was dead tired."

"I guess she didn't take it easy today, did she?"

"I tried to distract her as much as I could, but she's a tough one." She saw him stretch the muscles in his shoulder. "Can I get you something to drink? Beer? Iced tea? Glass of milk?"

"Uh, sure. I'd love some iced tea."

He looked at her as if she'd grown two heads as she headed for the fridge. Of course, she couldn't really blame him. She'd definitely been a megabitch lately.

He took a couple of cookies out of the jar on the counter and took a bite out of one. "Sorry I got hung up all day. How did things go here?"

"It was pretty okay." She handed him the glass. "We spent most of the day next door. I helped Léa haul most of the junk from the upstairs, the downstairs and the kitchen out onto the driveway. There's some heavy stuff in the basement that I think she'll need your muscles to move. Also, I think she's gonna need a Dumpster, or at least the back of your truck, to get rid of this stuff."

He planted a hip on the corner of the kitchen table. "I can have one of my guys come over and take it all to the dump tomorrow."

"Also, I know she was sort of worried about returning that rental stuff. It was all supposed to go back by five o'clock this afternoon. But we were working and talking and lost track of time. She left them a message on their answering machine."

"I'll make sure she doesn't get charged for the extra day."

This was the kind of helping out she liked. Just like what her father had said this morning. *We can help her by just being here.*

"Anything else?"

"I don't know if she's in any condition to drive, but if she's going to return that stuff tomorrow—"

"I'll offer to drive it for her, if she'll let me."

Dozens of other things were running through Heather's mind. Léa needed to see a doctor about the stitches pretty soon. And there was still the...

"She needs a friend more than a protector."

Her father's comment drew her attention. "I want to help her."

"I know you do. You are helping her. But I don't think she'll let you take over her life, any more than she'll let me."

"Jeez. For a second, shades of Natalie came alive in me." She shuddered and actually found herself able to smile.

"Well, they say we become our parents."

"What are you trying to do, scare me?"

"I'm not saying I'm any better, but you do have two parents, you know."

"I'm glad I have you."

Heather felt herself getting flustered at the choked-up look on his face.

"I...I think I'll go to bed, too. I did more work today than I've done in ages." She started for the door, but then turned to him. "Do you think she'll get too stiff sleeping in the chair all night?"

He nodded. "I'll bring her upstairs."

Heather didn't offer to hang around and help. She and Léa had already established a pretty cool friendship. Maybe her father would work on taking *his* relationship with her to the next level.

Yeah. She could definitely live with that.

Mick didn't know what was it exactly that Léa had said to Heather, but it was like magic. Sure, Heather still had her new look, but beyond that he felt as if he had his old daughter back again.

He owed Léa more than she knew.

It was only nine-thirty, but he was dead tired, too. He took Max out to do his business for the night. Standing in the dark backyard, Mick glanced at the house next door. Despite all the repairs that still had to be done, the house was starting to look alive.

Mick wondered if Léa even knew that she had the touch.

This acknowledgment, albeit to himself, certainly added a new twist to his life. He was attracted to her. Heck, in spite of everywhere he'd gone and everyone he'd talked to today, Léa had always been on his mind.

She wasn't like any other woman that he'd dated over the last few years. Maybe ever. Her focus was outward. She was accustomed to giving and not asking—never mind taking. She was independent and relied on no one for help. She didn't allow people inside her life. No friends. No close acquaintances. He'd read that much in the newspaper article this morning.

He looked up at Heather's darkened window. Hearing his daughter's enthusiasm, he could tell that Léa had obviously let *her* inside those walls.

Maybe Mick had a chance.

The dog responded to his whistle and ran up the back steps ahead of him.

Mick turned off the lights as he went through the house. In the living room, the sight of Léa curled up in his favorite chair tugged hard at his heart.

For a long moment, gazing at her now, he didn't see the desirable woman he was getting to know but rather the brave young girl he could never stop worrying about when he was younger. He remembered how, when he was about fourteen, he'd found her sitting beside her overturned bike in the park. The gash on her ankle had been deep, but she hadn't complained at all as he'd walked her all the way up the hill to her house. His father had told him later that night that he'd ended up giving Léa six stitches. Mick's gaze was drawn to her slim ankle. He could see the faint half-moon scar still there.

Max put a quick end to his master's thoughts when he decided it was time to get close enough to lick her face. Mick grabbed the dog by the tail and dragged him back before the beast could lay a tongue on her.

Mick crouched before her. The dressing on her head was dirty and needed to be changed. Her hands were tucked under her chin. Her breathing was deep. Her lips were slightly parted, and Mick's mind filled with other ideas that had nothing to do with the child he'd known and everything to do with the woman before him now.

When he reached under her knees and back and lifted her against his chest, Léa's eyes fluttered open.

"Mick. You're back."

"Shush, go back to sleep." He stood up, carrying her easily.

"What are you doing?" Léa's arms flew around his neck, and she held on tightly.

"Taking you to bed." Seeing her hazel eyes grow round, he smiled mischievously. "Not my bed. Your bed."

The relief in her expression told him that she had a few doubts about where their relationship was going, and his ego, he realized, was a little bruised.

"I really can walk."

"Heather told me you worked too hard today. Hit that switch for me, will you?"

She reached with one hand and flipped the wall switch, immersing them in darkness.

"Where's Heather?"

"Already sleep."

"This is totally unnecessary," she said much more quietly. "I am perfectly…"

Her arms tightened around his neck, and she hid her face in his neck as Mick started up the stairs.

"You're not afraid of heights, are you?"

"No. I'm afraid of you dropping me."

"You think I'd do something like that?" Mick shifted her weight in his arms, and her arms tightened even more.

"You are the devil, Mick Conklin," she whispered in his ear.

"And you are strangling me."

"Good! That's not *all* I'm going to do to you."

"Promises, promises."

No light showed under Heather's bedroom door. "Do you want to use the bathroom first?"

"I can manage that by myself, thank you. Put me down."

"Not yet." He walked into the dark of the guest bedroom. "Wanna turn that light on?"

"I won't. Put me down first."

"Okay." He took her to one of the beds. "At least, reach over and pull those covers back."

"I will not, Mick. Put me down."

"You sound like a broken record." He lowered her on the quilt. "Now, that wasn't so bad, was it?"

Léa's arms were still wrapped tightly around his neck.

The moonlight from the window cast a soft glow. Mick saw her eyes study his face and then focus on his lips. And then she was kissing him. Deeply. Her mouth was soft and willing and gave as sweetly and passionately as it took. Mick's control was about to snap when she pulled back.

"Not too bad at all," she said, releasing him and sinking back on the pillow. "Good night, Mick."

"And you say I'm the devil?" His eyes lingered on her smiling face and then trailed over the gentle rise and fall of her breasts beneath the coveralls, and even lower to her bare legs and feet. He looked back into her eyes. "You're playing with fire."

"Am I?"

He nodded once. "A very hot fire, in fact."

"How hot?"

"Do you know what I want to do to you right now?"

She shook her head.

"I want to unsnap your coveralls and peel them off your body. I want to push your T-shirt over your head and slide your underwear down your legs. I want to taste every inch of your skin from your lips all the way down to your toes." Mick watched her lips part slightly, heard the breath catch in her throat. "I want to unzip my pants and have you sit on my lap and take me deep inside your body. I want to feel your heat close around me as you ride me to…"

He paused for an endless moment. Their breathing was the only sound.

Then, suddenly, with a half smile, he pushed himself to his feet. "I'm going to take a cold shower now. Good night, Léa."

Seventeen

They were all here.

Jason Shanahan stared at the pictures. Marilyn on all fours with her ass in the air. Marilyn leaning against the wall with him behind her. Marilyn bent over a chair and Jason holding her hips, ready to drive into her again.

He remembered that like it was yesterday and began to grow hard. The look on her face in every picture was priceless.

"You missed your calling," he said aloud. "You should have been a porn star."

A screechy voice erupted from the police scanner before subsiding into static. Jason had been a little surprised to see it when he came in, and he had turned it on. He reached over now and switched it off.

He gathered up the photos from the table and stuffed them in an envelope. Focusing his attention back on the steel box that contained several dozen similar envelopes, he held up the second of the two that had his name on it. He dumped it on the table and spread the photos out.

"You slut. You did take more," he muttered. He didn't realize she'd even taken these. She must have used a remote, maybe. Or a timer. Yes, they were definitely taken on a different day than the pictures she'd sent Brian.

He liked these, actually. His muscle definition looked better in these photographs than in the other set. He paused, looking at a particularly good shot of Marilyn going down on him against the sliding door.

They'd screwed a few times, and it had been nothing special. She'd come after him at the health club, and he'd thought she was discreet. What a laugh! After she'd taken the pictures and joked about having posters made from them, it was only natural that he'd get a little pissed off. That had been the second, or maybe third, time they'd met at her cottage. But Marilyn had given him the roll of film like it was no problem, laughing and teasing him. Even when he'd exposed the film, she'd laughed.

But she wasn't quite done with the shit.

A week later, Marilyn had mailed some pictures to Brian.

There had been hell to pay. Jason scowled at the memory of how pissed Brian had been. He'd been mad enough to kill the bitch...and him. That night, Brian had kicked him out onto the street.

Marilyn was the first woman Jason had screwed around with since hitching up with Brian Hughes. She wasn't the first *time* though. There was that muscular college kid over in New Hope and that biker he'd met in the club in Philadelphia. That guy had been fun for six months. But none of it meant shit, and he figured Brian never had to know about any of it. They had a good thing going between them. Jason was younger than Brian, but the old queen was still good in bed, money was never a problem and he really cared for Jason. Brian was definitely a good thing.

Until Marilyn almost succeeded in ruining everything.

It was the answer to Jason's prayers when the slut was murdered.

And there she was, smiling like a prom queen as she bent over the kitchen table with his prick up her ass.

Knowing his lover's forgiving nature, Jason had crawled back to him on his hands and knees once the bitch was gone, and Brian had taken him back.

After that, life had gradually gotten back to normal...until this week, when this shithead decided to open up that can of worms again.

Jason picked up a crumpled brown paper bag off the floor and stuffed the two envelopes of pictures and negatives into it.

It had started just like the last time. A couple of pictures in the mail, addressed to Brian. No letters. No request for some outrageous amount of money. Nothing to hint at who was behind it. Jason cringed even now, thinking about how Brian had almost gone through the ceiling again. But the pictures were some of the same ones that had been sent last time. Marilyn and him and yadda yadda yadda. But she was already dead.

Jason couldn't understand it at first. It was bad enough that somebody was messing with their minds, but he realized quickly something new was firing up the pot. Brian was afraid this time. Afraid that the police would find the pictures. Afraid that someone might think the two men had motive enough to knock off the bitch.

His argument that Ted was going to fry for the murder wasn't good enough. Jason had to get to the bottom of it. He had to find out who had the freaking pictures.

A little digging and it had been as easy as putting two and two together. Or maybe Jason Shanahan just had that good old Irish luck working OT for him. Whatever it was, once he knew who it was, it was easy to see that Marilyn would trust the loser to keep this stuff hidden for her.

He closed the paper bag. He had what he came for. It was getting late. He looked at the other packages of photos in the steel box. It was just too much of a temptation. He thumbed through the envelopes, reading the names.

He pulled one out and quickly leafed through the set of pictures. Then another. It was like a Who's Who of Stonybrook. And then it dawned on him.

There was some *serious* blackmail stuff here. The third envelope was even better than the first two.

"You cradle robber!" he muttered.

Going through the next two sets of pictures, Jason realized his jeans were feeling pretty tight in the crotch. The next set left him whistling sharply.

"Damn, there's a fortune to be made here." He let out a coarse laugh. "Done right, that is."

Jason put all of the photos back into the steel box and closed it. He never heard the footsteps behind him as he straightened with the box in his hands. He only heard the rush of air just before his head crumpled like a plastic ball from the impact.

Léa used a hand towel to wipe the steam off the mirror in the bathroom and stared at the blood oozing from the ugly stitches on her forehead.

The thought that maybe she shouldn't have taken a shower was quickly dismissed. She hadn't been able to stand the grime caked in her hair anymore. She carefully combed the wet hair away from the cut and wrapped a towel tightly above her breasts.

A glance at the round clock on the wall told her that it was only a quarter to six. Léa sneaked out of the bathroom and tiptoed quietly along the hall and down the stairs. There wasn't a stitch of clothing in her duffel bag that wasn't stained with blood or covered with filth from working on the house, so she'd started her load of laundry before jumping in the shower.

Max was lying by the back door when she walked into the kitchen. He raised his head sleepily and gave her a couple of wags of his tail as she moved to the closed door of the laundry room. Reaching for the knob, Léa heard the quiet rumble of the dryer and stopped.

"I hope everything in there could go in the dryer."

Every inch of Léa's body tingled with excitement at the

low growl of Mick's voice behind her. She half turned and saw him leaning against the kitchen doorway. He looked as if he'd just climbed out of bed and pulled on the khaki shorts he was wearing. He was wearing no shirt, and she noticed with a definite jump in her pulse that he hadn't quite gotten around to buttoning the top of the shorts.

"I hope you don't mind that I used your washer. I had nothing left that was clean and…" Her hand clutched the doorknob tightly as the words that he'd whispered to her last night came back to her. Unconsciously, her hand went to the edge of the towel, just above her breast. Last night he'd said something about "peeling," she recalled.

"Your clothes won't be dry yet. I just put them in."

"I didn't mean to wake you up." His arms and chest had the powerful look of an athlete who'd grown into a working man. His stomach wasn't flat like a teenager's, though. It, too, was muscled, but with the solid, rippled thickening that comes with manhood.

"This is the time I normally get up. I thought I'd get a caffeine jump start this morning before getting in the shower." He crossed the kitchen and started to make coffee. The broad span of his tanned back, tapering trimly to his shorts, kept her gaze riveted to the floor.

She shook off the thoughts running through her head. "Caffeine? You didn't sleep well?"

"Not really. I was…a bit distracted. How about you?"

"I passed out," she lied.

The look he gave her over his shoulder made Léa blush to the roots of her hair. She also became acutely aware of how little the towel she was wearing covered.

She turned the knob and pushed open the door to the laundry room. "Some of these things *must* be dry already."

"They won't be." He put the coffeepot on the stove and turned to her. "While you're waiting, though, let me see those stitches."

Léa was torn between locking herself in the laundry room or physically attacking Mick right here in the middle of the kitchen. She'd often felt the first impulse with men in the past, but never the second. She took a couple of deep breaths.

He pulled a chair away from the table and gestured toward it. "Come and sit. That cut doesn't look too good from here."

As he went into the pantry, she pushed herself to take the couple of steps and sit on the chair. The smooth wood of the chair's seat was quite cool on her legs, and she double-checked the tuck of the towel above her breasts. Mick reappeared with his first aid kit, putting it on the table beside her. He stood in front of her, and she flinched slightly when he pressed a gauze against the stitches.

"Don't be such a baby. I'm only cleaning it up."

"I've heard *that* before. By the way, the stitches don't come out yet."

"Oops," he deadpanned. "You should have told me before."

Léa gave him a swat on the side of his leg, but immediately she knew that she shouldn't have. His skin was too warm to the touch, and her gaze was drawn uncontrollably to the unbuttoned waistband and the curls of hair that disappeared there.

She closed her eyes and willed the stirring between her legs to go away.

His hands were sure as he worked around her wound. "So what do you have on the agenda today?"

This was what she needed. Safe ground. "First thing this morning, I have to return that load of equipment back to the rental place."

"Done with everything?"

"For now. I was a little too ambitious in my planning. Next time, I'll rent one thing at a time."

"Let me return them for you."

The tuck of the towel had gotten loose. She shifted on the seat and readjusted it. "I can really handle—"

"I have to go there this morning, anyway." He reached for a tube of ointment in the first aid kit. "Trust me, it won't be out of my way."

"What are you going to do with that?"

"I'm open to suggestions."

Léa bit her lip to hide a smile, then winced again at the cold sting of the ointment on the cut.

"I have to do more than just return the stuff. I'm sure I owe them money. The equipment was supposed to go back yesterday afternoon."

"All the more reason for me to go. You had an unexpected injury yesterday. Let me handle it. I send tons of business Doug's way every year, and he and I have learned to speak the same language."

When she started shaking her head, Mick took her chin and raised it until she was looking into his eyes.

"You have way too much on your plate this week. So, if you can't accept my help as a friend, then how about as the guy you're driving insane?"

"It's the towel, isn't it?"

"It's what's under the towel." He let go of her chin.

"You can return the equipment," she croaked, forcing herself to look anywhere but at that waist button…or any points south of it.

"What else do you have to do?"

"I have to call Sarah Rand." Léa tried to focus on his hands as they stripped the wrapping off a sterile gauze pad. "And I have to ride over to Doylestown to get some things out of the hotel room I rent there." She decided not to tell him about her ten o'clock rendezvous at the bench' on Main Street at the entrance to the park. She had a strong feeling he wouldn't approve of her going to meet some lunatic letter writer by herself.

His leg brushed against hers as he carefully applied the

nonstick pad to her stitches. Léa couldn't stop her gaze from fixing on the front of his shorts...the heavy ridge extending down one leg was too prominent against the khaki. She swallowed hard.

"A...a lot of...what..."

"Is something distracting you?" There was mischief in his voice, flustering her even more.

"No! Nothing!" She stared at his hands and the roll of gauze he was now holding. "Everything else depends on the outcome of my conversation with Sarah Rand."

"I think it'd be safest if I wrap this the same way they did it in the hospital. You shouldn't leave that exposed until you see a doctor."

"Right. Exposed is not good."

"Well, that depends." Mick moved behind her and started wrapping the gauze around her head. "Lean back."

Her head rested against his warm, firm stomach. She could feel a matching warmth spreading fluidly through her.

"Is it okay if I make an appointment for you with Heather's doctor for sometime tomorrow? And don't worry, he's not a pediatrician."

Léa had to move her head slightly forward and then back again to help him.

"Yeah...sure. Getting too low on my forehead." She touched her brow. "I want to be able to see."

"But I thought the mummy look was in this year." Mick unwrapped the gauze a little and rewrapped it. Léa touched her head as he did it, checking the tightness.

"Hold this end right here, so I can get a piece of tape."

Léa did as she was told and watched him cut off a piece. He taped the end and she let go.

"Would you let me drive you to your hotel in Doylestown?"

"I can drive okay. Mick, your work—"

"We can go during my lunchtime."

"Kind of a long lunch." The towel started to loosen again. Léa reached up to fix it, but Mick's hands took hold of hers, stopping her.

"Leave it."

Léa shivered as she felt his warm breath on her bare shoulder. His mouth kissed and tasted the skin on her neck.

"I'm going crazy like this. I want you." His whisper sounded hoarse in her ear. He raised her hands slowly, looping them behind his neck. She closed her eyes and felt herself lulled by the seductive pulse of his voice.

"Open your eyes. Léa. Look at how beautiful you are."

She opened her eyes and saw the loosening tuck of the towel. The white curves of her breasts were rising and falling as if trying to escape the confines of the cloth. He bit on her earlobe, and she dug her fingers into his short hair. The tuck gave way, and she saw the towel slip down and pool around her waist.

His large hands slid under her breasts, lifting them a little as his thumbs caressed the tingling nipples. Léa turned her head and found his hungry mouth. They attacked each other in a frenzy of need—tasting, taking, giving. Her breath caught in her throat when his hand moved down over her belly and cupped her mound. She rose up from the chair and as their mouths kept up the relentless duel, his fingers teased her wet folds. Turning slightly, Léa slipped her hand inside Mick's shorts and wrapped her fingers around his pulsating shaft.

That was all it took. Léa was barely able to snatch the towel off the chair before he whisked her into the laundry room and shut the door behind them.

He tried to suckle her breasts. She fought to unzip his shorts. The dryer rumbled on in the small room, masking the noises caused by their impatience.

"I know I promised you slow." He lifted her onto the dryer.

"Slow is overrated." She locked her legs around his waist.

He drove into her. Léa's hands and legs and mouth drew him close. Never in her entire life had she felt more alive than she did now.

Mick took hold of her buttocks and thrust himself deep into her at a quickening pace. Léa met his every stroke, rocking on the warm machine to receive him…to pull him deeper into the very core of her. He was so large, so potent. The fit was perfect. The rising thrill almost unbearable. The sounds he was making in her ear so primeval.

As she cried out from the power of her release, she felt his entire body go rigid as he, too, exploded in ecstasy. They clung to each other for several moments, a breathless tangle of limbs and bodies.

As if on cue, the dryer buzzer sounded.

Eighteen

"I just have to meet a couple of people downtown. But are you sure you can't call someone to come and stay with you?"

"Stop worrying!" Heather grabbed Léa by the shoulders and started pushing her toward the front door. "Just go and come back. Dad said he's picking you up here at noon. Just do it."

Léa planted her feet. "Then you're coming with us to Doylestown. You and Mick could get some lunch while I go to the hotel for my things."

"Wrong again, contestant, but thank you for playing." Heather opened the door. "I want to make a couple of calls to my friends. You two will just have to last a couple of hours without me."

"Heather! I…" Léa turned in the open doorway. "I'm worried about you being alone here. Some creep did really knock me in the head in the backyard."

She gave the anxious woman an incredulous look. "Daytime. Every busybody in the neighborhood is awake now and on guard at their windows. Léa, I'm fifteen. I have a killer dog. And I'm half a foot taller than you."

"In your dreams! Okay, maybe with your clogs on."

Heather stood up straight, looking down on Léa. "Besides, my looks are intimidating enough to scare the shit out of anyone."

Léa flung her arms around the teenager. "Well, that's definitely not true."

The unexpectedness of the hug threw Heather for a loop. Then she shocked herself further by returning the embrace.

She pulled back abruptly. "Get going."

"Here's my cell phone." Léa stuffed the thing in Heather's hand. "Turn it on. Leave it on. And take it with you if you leave the house. And everything next door can wait until we get to it together later."

"Get going!" She pushed her new friend out the door.

Heather held on to Max's collar and leaned in the doorway as she watched Léa walk down the street.

"Time to go to work," she announced excitedly to the dog the minute Léa disappeared from sight. She charged upstairs and into her room.

The thought of doing something nice for Léa had been tugging at Heather's mind since yesterday morning when she'd read that article. She had been thinking about how much Léa must have been doing without over the past few years. As the solitary caregiver for someone with late-stage Alzheimer's, as the problem solver for a brother who was in a jam he would probably never get out of, as the provider of everything, Léa was a person who needed to have something given back to her. But presents weren't what Heather was thinking about.

An old pair of blue jeans were ready on Heather's bed. After changing into them and pulling a white T-shirt over her head, she took a second look in the mirror at the new stranger staring back.

How weird to see that stranger smiling at her in the mirror.

Max stayed right on her heels when she went down into the basement for some work gloves and a painter's cap. A couple of minutes later, she clipped the phone onto her belt, and the two of them darted out the back door.

She was going to do one little thing for Léa, anyway. The idea had come to her this morning after Léa had mentioned at the breakfast table that she had some errands to run downtown. And then her father had said he was going to pick Léa up at noon.

No sweat, Heather had thought. She would have the front room painted by the time they got back. It was perfect.

The full garbage bags and the old, rolled carpets and the other junk they'd dragged out yesterday were all still piled at the end of the driveway by the carriage house. Heather had hinted about them to her dad again this morning before he left for work. He'd promised to have someone come and pick the stuff up today.

She and Max walked in through the back door. The place already looked so much more livable without all the junk cluttering up the place. Heather found the gallons of paint and the rollers and brushes in the dining room. Luckily, Léa had picked the same boring color of eggshell for every room.

Max followed Heather down to the basement. There was a pile of old sheets and blankets she'd spotted the day before. They stank, but they'd make perfect drop cloths.

When she came back upstairs, the dog stayed behind. To him, the cellar must have had more interesting smells than a cat convention in July. She dropped the bundle of cloths in the back parlor, shook a large sheet loose and turned to walk inside the living room.

A face was pressed to the glass panel of the front door, and Heather screamed once and jumped backward.

Max was up those basement stairs in a shot. Heather covered her mouth in embarrassment and leaned against the wall to catch her breath. She recognized Chris, waving at her through the glass, but Max didn't. The dog jumped up against the door, barking furiously.

"Sorry. I didn't mean to scare you." Chris's muffled

voice came through the door. Heather could barely make out what he was saying over the growling and barking of the dog. She shook her head and crossed the room to open the door.

"You scared the shit out of me, Chris Webster."

Max was still going bonkers, so Heather held on tight to his collar.

"I didn't know if anyone was in or not," Chris said guiltily, keeping a safe distance from the dog and standing near the broken front steps.

"I think Miss Manners generally includes 'knocking' in her answers on this topic. I don't recall 'look in' being on her list of appropriate ways to approach a home you don't live in."

"I had to deliver some flowers for my boss, and—"

"You work for the flower shop?"

"No, the drugstore," Chris replied over Max's continued fierceness. Chris threw him an uncomfortable glance. "Mr. Rice, the pharmacist, picked out this thing for Ms. Hardy. He told me to drop it off while I was doing my prescription deliveries this morning."

Two days ago, Heather had hated Andrew Rice for not filling her prescription. By this morning, however, the man had been reestablished as "pretty okay" in her mind. Right now, though, she wasn't sure how she should feel about him, considering he was sending Léa flowers. Well, staying neutral was probably the best course of action, she decided. After all, she couldn't definitely be sure what the pharmacist's intentions were toward Léa.

"So where are they?"

Chris looked confused.

"The flowers. Where are they?"

"Oh! Hang on. I'll get them." The lanky teenager hopped easily over the broken steps and went to his old station wagon parked out front. In spite of her misgivings, Heather had to approve of the pharmacist's taste when

Chris took the big basket of wildflowers out of the back of the car.

"Where should I leave them?"

"Why don't you bring them in?"

He looked warily at the growling dog.

"Come on! Max won't bite." She stepped inside, pulling the dog with her and giving the teenager plenty of room to come in. "Right there, in the parlor. Yeah, right there by the window looks good."

As soon as he put the flowers down, she let go of Max. The dog rushed over and started sniffing at Chris's sneakers and cuffs.

"He likes to smell everything. You can pet him if you want. He really won't hurt you."

He tucked his hands inside his front jeans pockets instead. Heather studied him quietly for a couple of seconds. Now that she wasn't mad at the world, she admitted more readily that he had turned out pretty cute. He was tall, maybe even as tall as his dad, Reverend Webster, the Presbyterian minister in town. And he was getting broad and muscular across the chest. It wasn't just his buff looks, though. There was also a sense of confidence about him that Heather liked. He was obviously not happy with the dog's attentions, but he was definitely not afraid.

"Sorry I don't have any money with me, so I can't tip you or anything," she said, just to start up the conversation.

He shook his head and actually smiled. "By the way, what are you doing here?"

"Working." She picked up one of the sheets and shook it out again. "Scraping, painting, doing repairs. Whatever needs to be done."

"Is your dad renovating this dump?"

"No, I'm working with Léa. The two of us are working on it. And it's not a dump."

He rolled his eyes at her.

"Well, it won't be when we're done."

Chris started walking around and peeking into the rooms. Heather motioned to Max to sit and stop sniffing.

"So the rumors are true. She *is* sticking around."

Heather somewhat selfishly wanted it to be true, and she found herself nodding at him in answer when he glanced at her over his shoulder. "Looks like it."

"And the famous kitchen." He stood in the doorway, staring in. "I'm surprised she doesn't freak out every time she walks in here."

"I don't know why she should." The comment irritated Heather. "That happened twenty years ago. Plus, she has her head screwed on tighter than most of us."

He turned to her. "That's not what they say."

"Who? The people in this pathetic little nothing town. What would *they* know? Léa hasn't been around since she was eleven years old. And since then, she's done a lot with her life. Didn't you read that article in the paper yesterday?"

He shook his head. "I was just telling you what people say."

"Well, don't! People don't have any license to gossip about her just because she's a Hardy." Heather took the sheets and blankets to the front room and started spreading them on the hardwood floor. Chris followed her and stood in the doorway.

"No reason for you to get so p.o.'d, Heather. People always gossip."

"No, they don't." She pushed the edges of a blanket against the walls with her shoe. "I wasn't deaf or blind the last time I was around. I saw the shit that was going on with Marilyn."

"What do you mean?"

"You know what I mean. Everybody in town saw it, too. But God forbid that anyone should whisper a word about the daughter of one of our oldest families. The woman was a whore, but would anyone even…''

The words caught in Heather's throat as she looked into Chris's face. She hadn't seen him walk across the room. His blue eyes looked almost fierce as he stared at her.

''You're looking even hotter now than when you left.''

''I—''

''And I thought you were a babe, then.'' His hand reached out and he gently fingered the earrings that lined her ear. ''Did you really mean it on Saturday when you said you were permanently unavailable?''

A shiver ran through Heather's body when his finger skimmed over her neck, just below the ear. When she said nothing, he smiled and let his hand trail down her back, finally hooking a finger into the low waistline of her jeans.

''I…I wasn't in too good a mood that day.''

She slipped away from him and moved a couple of steps toward the door. She felt hot. Excited. But also out of her league. All of a sudden, he seemed so much older, more experienced than she was. He'd changed a lot.

''I have tons to do here, Chris.'' She gave him a quick glance over her shoulder. ''I think you should go.''

His hands were once again tucked into his pockets.

''Can you get out tonight?''

She hesitated.

''We'll take it really slow, Heather.'' His eyes were soft, gentle. He looked again like the teenager that she used to know. ''We'll go to a movie, and I'll bring you back.''

''Okay,'' Heather said on impulse. ''I have a doctor's appointment at five. Pick me up at six-thirty, next door.''

He beamed her a smile as he walked out the front door, and she stood staring out the window at his back.

Who'd have thought that Chris Webster would turn out so hot, after all?

* * *

"This is not the same person that I married. It's impossible to believe she is the mother of my children."

"I know this is difficult for you to swallow." The lawyer gathered up the investigator's report Ted was scanning. *"But going up against someone with her kind of money and her connections, it never hurts to be prepared."*

Prepared? They were more than prepared! There was enough dirt here to bury that woman for eternity. And right now, after everything she'd put him through, that was exactly what he wanted to do. Bury her.

Nineteen

Léa took her time walking downtown. She had so many things racing through her mind…so many feelings whirling within her. Everything was becoming so complicated. She needed to simplify.

She stopped to pick up a newspaper. The woman at the register remembered her from before and was actually very friendly. Léa bought stamps at the post office. Still, she arrived at her destination fifteen minutes early.

She slowly passed the empty park bench on Main Street. The words Gift of the Torchbearers of Freedom were emblazoned on it. It felt far too awkward and obvious just to sit down and stare at everyone passing by. She walked to the next intersection and glanced at the line of storefronts on both sides of the street. Reaching the last building on the park side of Main Street, she noticed a preppy, slightly overweight man hurrying across the street. The balding, middle-aged man had a newspaper tucked under his arm, and he looked right past her. There was something vaguely familiar about him, though, that made Léa pause and look again.

She remembered seeing him in the courthouse, during the trial.

The man seemed oblivious to everything and everyone on the street, as if the weight of the world were on his stooped shoulders. It wasn't until she saw him take a key out of his pocket and open the front door to Hughes Grille that she realized the connection.

He was a Hughes. Certainly too young to be the Mr. Hughes who had run the Grille in her own father's time, but perhaps a son, she thought.

Léa glanced back at the bench near the entrance to the park and wondered if she should consider this man among the people mentioned in the letter. Marilyn's Hate Club.

She turned around and headed back along the street to the bench. A moderate amount of traffic rolled past. Léa recognized Stephanie's gray Cadillac, parked across the way in front of the Franklin Trust Bank.

Bob Slater, the founder of the bank, had run it for at least thirty years. He was also Stephanie's second husband. Charlie Foley, Stephanie's first husband and Marilyn's father, had been the owner of the mill and at one time had owned practically everything worth having in Stonybrook. He'd passed away some ten years ago, leaving everything to his wife and daughter. Bob Slater, at that time a healthy middle-aged widower, had married Stephanie a year later.

During the few short years that Ted and Marilyn had lived together as a couple outside of Stonybrook, Léa had seen Bob and Stephanie maybe a half-dozen times—all on the occasion of one of the girl's christenings or birthdays. At the beginning, Léa had chalked up the couple's coldness to the normal divisiveness of social and class difference. She'd thought that because of those barriers, perhaps the Slaters would never accept the Hardys, regardless of the marriage. But as the years had passed, Léa had seen a steady warming of Stephanie toward Ted. In fact, after his separation from Marilyn, Léa had heard her brother say that his mother-in-law was in favor of him getting custody of the girls. None of that mattered, though, after Ted was arrested for his family's murder. Stephanie—understandably—had lashed out at him harder than anyone else.

Léa took a deep breath, forcing herself to focus on why

she was here. She sat down at one end of the bench and opened the newspaper on her lap. She lowered her sunglasses and glanced over the top of the paper at the people coming and going on the street. She looked at the cars pulling into parking spaces and the strangers getting out of them. The buildings were all familiar, but the faces meant nothing. Twenty years was a long time to be away, and Léa questioned how she would make any sense out of the cryptic letter when she couldn't even identify the people.

Reaching inside her purse, she took out the envelope and read the words again.

Ten o'clock Monday morning sit on the bench by the Main Street entrance to the park. You'll meet Marilyn's Hate Club. They will all...

"Léa!"

She folded the letter and stuffed it and the envelope inside her purse. A buxom redhead, a little older than herself, was careering across the street toward her. She was squeezed into a black top with matching tights, and her outfit accentuated every curve. Her makeup had been applied with tremendous care and her hair was fashionably cut. Léa watched her approach with growing curiosity.

"You *are* Léa Hardy, aren't you?"

Léa dropped the newspaper onto the bench beside her as she nodded hesitantly. The woman had the friendliest green eyes, and she was stretching out her hand before she even reached the bench.

"Sheila. Sheila Desjardins. I went to high school with your brother. You remember me, don't you?"

Léa smiled and stood up, accepting the handshake. "I think I do. You used to live a couple of streets up from us, didn't you? Your parents had an old St. Bernard that slept in the shade in front of the garage door."

"That was us!" The woman beamed. "My parents sold that house back in '93 and moved to Florida. I really wanted to buy the place myself, but it was just too big a mortgage for one person to handle. But I'm renting an apartment just up the street from the house now. Are you waiting for someone? Can I sit with you?''

"Sure." Léa gathered up the papers, making room for her to sit.

"It's so nice out here. A perfect spot." Sheila did a quick survey of the people walking past and sat down next to Léa on the bench, crossing her legs. "You're probably wondering what the heck I'm doing wandering the streets with no purse or anything."

"No, actually, I wasn't, but—"

"My cut-color-foil appointment called and canceled five minutes ago. Can you imagine the woman's nerve?''

"I can't.''

"You know, first I was really teed off. Then I was looking out the window and saw you go by across the street. So I just thought I'd pop out and say hi. That's my shop across the way.''

Léa looked in the direction Sheila was pointing.

"Right there. Desjardins Hair Impressions. Rich says it's a mouthful, but I don't care. For the last three years I've been the only show in town, and I don't hear any of my customers complaining.''

"How about the canceled appointment? You don't think she was trying to make a statement about the name?'' Léa was very proud that she was able to get more than two words in.

Sheila looked startled for a second, then her eyes rounded in mock horror. "Do you really think so?''

"Hey, this is Stonybrook. Who knows?''

The skin around the green eyes crinkled when Sheila smiled. "You know, you look darn cute this close, and one heck of a lot better than you do in those pictures in the paper. But that thing on your head, when are they taking it off?''

"The stitches come out in ten days. The bandages should get smaller long before that, though." Léa paused, surprised that Sheila had not asked about how she'd gotten the injury to begin with. "How did you know about it?"

"Honey, nothing gets by me." She lowered her voice and slid closer to Léa. "As the long-suffering girlfriend of the chief of police, there isn't much that goes on in this burg that I don't hear about. But—" Sheila put a hand on Léa's knee "—you shouldn't blame Rich. You see, he has this control problem. You know, when we have sex. Especially when I wear this one-piece, see-through leopard thing I bought through this great catalog I get. So, anyway, I saw this sex therapist or something on one of the afternoon shows, and she said to help him—never mind him, to save *your* sex life—you need to take the pressure off him by talking to him and getting him to talk while we're—"

"Really, Sheila, I don't think I—"

"And it worked! I just have to get him talking. It gets his mind off his Little Chief and we've been known to go at it for—"

"Sheila, please, I—"

"That's okay, honey. But you know, there's nothing improper about Rich telling me stuff. I mean, half the people in Stonybrook have one of those police scanners sitting next to their sugar bowl, and the other half have them sitting on top of their TVs. You'd think with cable adding the Playboy Channel on to the pay-per-view a couple of years ago, things would get better. But no way! Stonybrook is full of Peeping Tom busybodies who like to know just what everyone is getting into. I have no time for them, myself."

Léa couldn't sort out in her own mind how she was feeling about chatting away with the girlfriend of one of her enemies. But it didn't matter; Sheila started right in again.

"You know, two weeks ago—after the Spring Fling Art Festival we have downtown here—I got him to tell me about each and every one of the fifty-four parking violations, the six drunken driving cases, the case of theft from an open car, and about the pair of teenagers they caught going at it in the back seat of a police car that was parked in that building's parking lot—the gate was left open. It was like a miracle."

Léa glanced at the police station down the street and across the way, and wondered how Rich Weir would feel about a Hardy getting the scoop on Little Chief and his sexual "shortcomings." Her lips twitched as it occurred to her that this might just be the origin of the word.

"But that wasn't even the good part." A mischievous smile broke out on the perfectly painted lips. "After we were done at my place, I made him bring me downtown and show me exactly what it was that those kids were doing in the back seat of that car. That was the *best* sex I've had in a long time."

She fanned herself with her hands and took another quick look around at the passersby.

"So, how's *your* sex life, honey?"

Léa found herself gaping.

"Well, I heard you're staying at Mick's." Sheila's thinly plucked eyebrows went up and down meaningfully.

"He and Heather gave me a ride back from the hospital yesterday. That was it." Léa tried not to think of the incredible sex they'd had in the laundry room this morning. She forced herself not to think of the promise he'd whispered in her ear before leaving for work earlier. Something about lunchtime and a hotel room in Doylestown and what he was planning to do to her. And this time, *very* slowly.

"Oh, I thought you were staying at his place."

"Well, I did...but in the guest room, and only for last night." She didn't know what was making her answer. It was nobody's business. But then again, she thought, it was probably good to set the record straight with Sheila. It was obvious that this woman's ability to trumpet information was better than publishing it in the paper.

"He is one hot number." Sheila picked up one of the folded newspapers off Léa's lap and fanned herself. "There is not a woman in this town who hasn't dreamed of being where you are right now, honey."

"We were under the same roof, not in the same room."

"Okay, if you say so. God knows, as Mick gets older—and better, I might add—he's been getting pretty darn picky."

"I'm sure that with a teenager in the house, discretion and…and appropriateness are an issue with him."

Sheila raised one eyebrow for a moment and then shrugged. "That might be it, honey, or it might not. I think this change in him started even before Heather came back. I really believe it has to do with getting sick and tired of the same selfish babes who've been hanging on him all of his life. The man is thirty-eight years old and every relationship he's had went like this… Mick gives. Mick buys. Mick takes care of her. Mick plays the nice guy and lets her put her life and needs ahead of his. In short, Mick spoils the heck out of her. I mean, if your love life was like that, wouldn't you get a little sick of it?"

Léa found herself hanging on every word that was being said. Sheila waved at a police cruiser that was driving slowly past.

"I mean, look at his ex-wife. Smart, pretty and spoiled. She hooked him in college, had a baby and used him until she was out of that West Coast med school and didn't need him anymore. Then…what, nine years ago…he comes back home, fresh from his divorce, and who does he start going out with? The reigning queen of selfishness, Marilyn Foley."

Sheila nodded seriously at Léa, for she must have read the disbelief in her face.

"Don't worry, that was during the year before Ted and Marilyn got married. Luckily, Mick must have seen right through her. He dumped her before she could dig her claws too deep into him. Now, after that, the women were less screwed up than Marilyn—and maybe his ex—but there was still not much improvement that I could see."

"There have been a lot of women?" Léa asked, feeling an empty ache that she knew she had no right to feel.

Sheila gave a meaningful nod. "Maybe not as many as he could have. But there was the weather girl on the Jersey cable station. A lawyer who moved to D.C. An engineer at one of those pharmaceutical companies down the road. There were others, too. I've lost track over the years. But you've got to give him credit. He doesn't like them dumb."

Sheila smiled at the couple crossing the street toward them. "Hi, Reverend Webster. Don't forget you're coming in for a cut this afternoon, Pat."

The clergyman was a very distinguished-looking man with graying reddish hair. The small-built woman looked hard at Léa and then steered her husband past them.

"Now, what was I saying?" Sheila said, turning back to Léa. "Oh, yeah. Mick. I think he's been getting sick and tired of this whole thing for a while now. Trust me, I notice these things. He's been dating less and less lately. But who could blame him with all the sharks in the water."

Léa felt slightly ill, thinking of herself as the next one in a line of sharks.

She'd never been a taker and yet here she was, dragging Mick and even Heather into her dismal situation. She pushed her sunglasses higher on the bridge of her nose and wished she could forget how wonderful every minute she'd spent with him had been.

"Joanna! Joanna!"

Sheila's voice pulled Léa's attention back to the present.

A gray van with wildflowers stenciled on the side of it had just pulled into a parking spot two cars down from them.

"*Jo!* Over here!"

A tall and very striking-looking young woman with long curly brown hair, wearing a flowered sundress, paused after closing the driver's door. She glanced in their direction.

"Come over here, Jo. There's someone I want you to meet."

Léa saw the woman push a large woven handbag up onto her shoulder and start slowly toward them with obvious reluctance.

"Joanna Miller and her sister Gwen own and run Miller Flower Shop," Sheila whispered quietly to Léa. "Gwen is a bitch, but Jo has always been an outsider with the old townies…kind of like you, I guess."

A warm spot immediately formed inside Léa at the comment. She got to her feet and shook Joanna's hand as Sheila made the introductions.

"You two weren't classmates or anything. I think Jo was a couple of years younger. But there's no way you would have recognized her, anyway. Back then, she wasn't wearing any size double-D bra like she does now!"

"Look who's talking? Miss Jellyfish Implants herself!" Jo's brown eyes glared at Sheila over the top of her shades before turning to Léa. "Watch out for her. She charges an arm and a leg."

"Speaking of which, you do need a trim, you wild woman." Sheila took a few strands of Joanna's hair and shook her head disapprovingly after a close look at the ends. She turned to Léa next. "And you need a *total* makeover. Look at her, Jo, with those eyes and her high cheekbones. I could cut her some bangs…maybe layer the sides and back. A little makeup here and there. I say she'll look just like that movie actress. What's her name? David Duchovny's wife…"

"Téa Leoni."

"That's it," Sheila said excitedly. "I can fit you in this afternoon if you want to come over."

"Thanks. I think I'll have to take a rain check for now," Léa answered.

"Suit yourself. But don't put it off too long. You want to impress that number you're living with."

"I am *not* living with anyone."

"Say what you want, honey." Sheila gave a knowing wink to Joanna. "She's staying with Mick Conklin and not playing doctor with the boy."

"You're staying with Mick?" Joanna asked, her surprise showing in her face.

"Just temporarily."

"Same as you and Andrew Rice have been *temporarily* screwing each other's brains out for I don't know how long!"

"Sheila!" Jo complained.

"At least one of us is not in denial." The hairdresser waved off their glares and glanced across the street. Rich Weir was heading in the direction of her store. "Sorry, girls, but I have to go. I believe I'm in for a backroom tabletop treat. I just hope that there are lots and lots of crimes on the Big Chief's mind. Well, enough to give Little Chief time to do it right. I'll tell you all about it later."

Totally amazed, Léa watched Sheila hurry across the street after her beau. "Will she really try to tell us about it later?"

"You can count on it."

Léa couldn't hold back her bubble of laughter. When she turned to Joanna, she found her smiling, too.

"So is it true? About you and Mick?"

This time Léa blushed. "We're friends. Old neighbors."

Jo gave her an I-don't-believe-you look over the top of her sunglasses.

"Do I have something tattooed on my forehead?"

"With Sheila doing the interrogating, you don't need a tattoo." Jo's expression was softer, friendlier when she took off the shades. "How did you like the flowers?"

"What flowers?"

"The ones Andrew Rice had delivered to your house this morning."

"I didn't see them. I must have left before they came." Sheila's comment about Jo and Andrew flickered in Léa's mind. "Andrew and I were friends when we were kids. I know he bought the pharmacy that my great-grandfather owned eons ago, but I haven't seen or talked to him for a long, long time. Why is he sending me flowers?"

"I think to make me jealous," Joanna said wistfully. "I've been the one, well, in favor of keeping our affair hush-hush, and he's not too happy about it."

Léa didn't know how it was that they'd become so comfortable with each other so fast, but she decided this probably wasn't the right time to analyze it.

"Are you in a situation that you want to get out of?" she asked.

"Hardly!" Jo shook her head adamantly. "God, being with Andrew is the only thing that makes me want to stay around in this stinking town. He's everything to me, but—"

The sound of a woman's scream echoed off the storefronts. The driver's door to the gray Cadillac was open wide. Stumbling out from behind the wheel, Stephanie Slater was nearly hysterical, crying and calling out incoherently. She was clutching a small object in one hand.

A number of pedestrians stopped and were staring at her from a safe distance, but none approached the distressed woman.

"*Hanna!*"

This time Léa had no difficulty understanding the older woman's wrenching cry.

"Maybe we can talk later," she said, touching Joanna's arm absently and taking a couple of steps into the street.

She stopped. Of anyone in this town, Léa knew she would be the last one Stephanie would want to see right now. The distraught woman was leaning against the car, wiping at her eyes with one hand.

Léa looked around again for any sign of someone else going to her. At the entrance to the park, not far from the bench where she had been sitting, a ragged-looking homeless man stood watching the spectacle across the street. Longer hair, a bit dirtier than she remembered from her childhood, his back slightly more rounded. But she remembered Dusty. If ever a smile could be described as nasty, his was it.

"Hanna! Please...*Hanna!*"

Stephanie's choked cries brought tears to Léa's eyes. When she looked back again at Dusty, he was disappearing into the park.

"Hanna, where is your sister? Get your sister."

A couple of cars had slowed down, but no one was stopping. Faces were staring out of windows of stores, but no one was coming out. Léa pushed her doubt aside and crossed the street.

"Hanna!"

Léa reached out and touched Stephanie's arm. The older woman whirled and looked at her.

"Have you seen my granddaughter? Oh! It's you." She started crying even harder now. "You! What have you done with my children? Bring them back...monster!"

Léa didn't back up. "It's me, Stephanie. It's Léa."

"You killed them. You took them away from me."

"I loved them, just like you. Stephanie, listen to me." She caught the hysterical woman by the arm. She was clutching a small stuffed animal tightly to her chest. She was shaking violently. Ignoring her weak attempt to struggle, Léa wrapped her arms around her and just held on.

"Give them back to me," Stephanie sobbed. "I want my girls back."

"I want them back, too." Léa opened the back door of the car and gently got her to sit. She crouched down on the street before her. Stephanie's eyes were riveted on the stuffed tiger.

"Hanna is here. She's downtown somewhere. Find her for me." She was not lashing out at Léa anymore, but pleading. The tears and the mascara were streaking her face. She grabbed Léa's hand. "Please, get her!"

"I would if I could." Léa cried with her. "But she's gone, Stephanie. Hanna's in heaven now."

"No. She's here." The older woman shook her head. "She left me this...in the car...when I was inside." She pushed the small toy tiger into Léa's hands. "She is here. She must be."

The stuffed animal was identical to one that had belonged to Hanna. The little girl and the tiger had been inseparable. But it was also identical to thousands of others that were sold in toy stores all over America. Léa pushed herself to her feet and looked around at the bystanders who were watching the old woman's misery as if it were a leisure activity. She wondered which one of them could be cruel enough to drop something like that into the car.

"Do you see her?" Stephanie persisted, her hand tugging on Léa's arm.

"No, I don't." She looked down at the broken woman and dashed away her tears. "I don't think she's going to come back."

A painful sob escaped the grandmother, but there was no denial left in her. The shivering hand moved down Léa's arm. Then, for the briefest of seconds, she squeezed Léa's hand before collapsing back against the seat.

"I want to go home."

Léa felt a soft touch on her shoulder. She turned and saw Joanna standing behind her.

"I'll drive her home."

Twenty

Traffic was moving at a crawl. On the chance that Léa might still be downtown, Mick tried to keep an eye open for her on both sides of Main Street as he followed the slow-moving line of cars. There was a small crowd of people standing together near Hughes Grille, staring across the street. The traffic came to a stop again, and Mick saw a throng on the sidewalk and in the street in front of the Franklin Trust building, as well.

Just as he was ready to step out and check out the reason for the jam, the crowd in the street parted and a gray Cadillac started to nose out into traffic. He recognized Stephanie Slater's car, but the driver was Joanna Miller.

The line of traffic in front of him started again, and he saw Léa back away from the Cadillac. She was still talking to someone in the back seat, and she looked upset. Mick pushed open the truck door, ignoring the honk of horns from the cars behind him, and went to her.

"Léa!"

She turned in surprise. There were traces of tears glistening in her hazel eyes. Without any regard to the dozens of onlookers, he put his arm around her.

"What happened here?"

"Somebody played an ugly joke on Stephanie." She held on to him, and her voice wavered. "They left a toy... like one of Hanna's...on her front seat. She thought...she thought Hanna was still alive. She was confused and upset.''

She was shivering and Mick held her tightly against him.

''She wasn't blaming you, was she?''

Léa shook her head. ''She was just confused for a moment or two. That's all. But I think it's so cruel for someone to do that.''

The crowd was drifting off, but he knew the tongues would already be wagging. He didn't really give a damn. ''Did you see who did it? Did anyone see who put it there?''

Léa shook her head again and let go of him, looking suddenly shy.

''I'm sorry. I'm a mess.'' She wiped at the tears on her face and pulled on her sunglasses. ''What are you doing here?''

The traffic in the street was honking and trying to pull around his truck.

''I've come to pick up my date, remember?'' He took Léa's hand and started for the idling vehicle. ''Come on.''

She glanced down at her watch as he held the door open for her to climb in. A slight smile had turned up the corners of her beautiful mouth. ''It's early. It's only eleven-thirty. How did you know I was down here?''

He went around and got behind the wheel first, dropping the shift lever into gear. ''Heather called and told me.''

''Is she okay?''

''She's fine. You left your phone with her this morning.''

''I know. I was worried about her going out alone.''

''After you left the house, Sarah Rand called and tried to get hold of you on your cell phone.''

Léa took off her glasses. ''She did?''

''She asked Heather to have you call her here.'' He took out a piece of paper with a number scribbled on it from his pocket and handed it to her. "Heather got hold of me and passed on the message."

"She must not want the case."

Mick heard the note of nervousness in her tone. He reached over and squeezed her hand. "It could *only* be good news. Hadn't you left it with her that you would call *her* this afternoon?"

"Yeah. But I gave her my number, too."

"Why would she call if she didn't want to handle the case?" He could see that she didn't look convinced. He took his cell phone off his belt and put it on her lap. "Why don't you call her right now and find out."

"I can call her from the house."

"We're not stopping there. We're going straight to the hotel."

She shot him an anxious look. "Well, maybe I'll call from there."

"I'm afraid you won't have any time for phone calls. I am planning on taking up every minute we have alone together."

He glanced over at Léa and saw the blush that had crept into her beautiful cheeks. The recollection of her, naked and wrapped around him, rushed back into his mind's eye. This morning, more than anything else, he'd wanted to take her back up to his bedroom and take his time making love to her again. He had to put those plans on hold, though, when they heard the shower running in Heather's bathroom.

"Look, Mick. I'm serious now—"

"So am I! I've had a hell of a time focusing on any work this morning. This keeps up, I'll have to go into some other line of business." Mick saw the trace of a smile, but he could tell she was still very tense. "Maybe marketing. Yeah, we could start a whole new ad campaign for clothes dryers. We could even sell accessories to go along with them. Cushions for the top. First aid kits with lots of gauze for wrapping and unwrapping your partner. And towels. Very skimpy towels.''

''I'd buy anything with *you* in them.''

Her quiet remark made Mick's loins tighten. The light at the intersection leading out of town turned yellow. Though he usually would have run the thing, he now stopped the truck and reached for her.

A small sigh of surprise escaped Léa's lips when he crushed his mouth on hers. In the next instant, though, she was kissing him back with enough hunger and passion to drive him right over the edge. When the light turned green, an impatient driver behind them tapped on his horn.

Mick reluctantly ended the kiss and drove on through the intersection. ''I'm going to break all kinds of land-speed records getting us to that hotel room.''

''Then I guess I'd better call that lawyer now.''

Mick saw her hand tremble a little as she punched in the number. He tried to keep his attention on the road. She said few words, but her voice was strong.

As she spoke to the attorney, he found himself once again admiring her courage and her ability to face challenges despite the distractions. And Mick knew he was the distraction now. Not that he would change a thing, even if he could. She was inching her way under his skin, and he loved the feel of it. The feel of her.

Sarah seemed to be doing most of the talking. When Léa finally ended the call and turned to him, the look on her face made him pull off onto the shoulder and stop the truck.

She undid her seat belt and slid across the seat and into his arms. ''She thinks there is hope. More than just hope. She thinks there are real grounds for getting a retrial.''

Mick held her tight for a minute before she pulled back, misty-eyed.

''What else did she say?''

Léa clutched his hand. ''Before she even read the trial

transcripts, she said that Ted's lack of cooperation and his attempt to kill himself in prison might give us grounds for appealing the death penalty. She said state-assisted suicide doesn't go over big these days. But now, having read through the material, she thinks Browning's arguably ineffectual defense work provides even more possibilities for appeal. Beyond that, Sarah suspects there might be evidence regarding Marilyn's murder that was not handed over to the defense by the prosecutor's office. There is nothing in there about her lifestyle or others who might have had a motive to kill her. Very little evidence of the crime scene, other than what pointed at Ted, was presented in court. She believes that means Browning was asleep or that he just didn't receive information that he should have. She didn't want to go into detail about police procedures over the phone, but she thinks there is a lot to work with there. Bottom line, she's very optimistic about getting a new trial.''

"Sounds like she's going to take the case?"

Léa pulled back and wiped her face. "Not yet. At least, not until after we meet with Ted tomorrow. She said she wants the two of us to talk to him before she'll give me her final answer.''

"You're on your way." He stroked her cheek with the back of his hand.

"I don't know. What happens if Ted decides to give Sarah the silent treatment, too? What if she decides that if he's not interested in his own defense, then she's not going to fight for him?''

"I think she wants to meet him so she can get a gut reaction of whether she thinks he is guilty or innocent. If I were a lawyer, I'd want to meet my client before taking a case.''

"I hope you're right." Léa unfolded and refolded the piece of paper with the attorney's phone number. "It's going to take forever for tomorrow to come.''

Mick's hand slid onto her bare knee. He gently caressed the silky skin. "It doesn't have to. I can think of a few distractions to fill the time."

She gave him a shy smile. "I thought you promised to break the land-speed record to the hotel?"

"Buckle your seat belt, love. You're in for a ride."

Brian Hughes left the bustling kitchen and passed through the lunchtime crowd in the dining room to take the phone call on his private line in the small office behind the bar.

"Please have some good news for me, Jane," he pleaded into the phone.

"Sorry, Brian, but there's been no sign of him around the health club at all this morning. I had to get another trainer to take his 9:30 and 10:45 appointments."

Using the letter opener, he started ripping open the day's mail sitting on his desk.

"How about the other stuff, Jane? The weight room? His tanning session? I don't know, the other places he hangs out there?"

"He was a no-show for his regular time in the spa, and nobody has seen him anywhere else on the facility, either. I'm sorry, Brian. I wish I could help you, but…you know…" The woman paused, obviously trying to choose her words carefully. "This is not the first time that Jason has been a no-show. Maybe he got hung up someplace. Maybe he's with family. Or friends…and he forgot to call you and…"

Jane's words trailed off, but Brian knew exactly what she was trying to tell him. She was saying that maybe Jason was cheating on him.

Christ! The bastard was screwing around again and everybody else knew it! Brian felt a lump swell in his chest until he thought he would die. Right there. The pain was tearing at him and he squeezed his eyes shut.

Everyone knew it, but he had been too blind to see it himself until a couple of years ago, when that bitch Marilyn had made sure he knew.

The photographs were bad enough, but the words in the letter she'd sent him separately had burned themselves into his brain. She'd said, in the most graphic terms, how she'd hired Jason as a weight trainer, and what a time they'd had after hours. On the weight machines. On the tanning beds. And in the men's sauna and shower. And how he used to come up to the cottage she rented on the lake, where they could really have a great time. She'd repeated over and over how obsessed Jason seemed to be with her tight ass. She wondered whether Brian really wanted everyone in Stonybrook to see these pictures.

The crazy bitch didn't care that she was in them, too. Everything to her was a pissing contest. And if Brian decided to go through with helping Ted, then she wanted him to know he'd pay the price. Period.

"Are you still there, Brian?"

The letter opener slid out of his fingers, and he stared at the deep gashes he'd carved in the surface of the antique wooden desk.

"Yeah. I'm here. Thanks for checking, Jane." He ran his fingers over the grooves and slid the desk calendar over it. "Will you please call me if he shows up?"

"Sure thing. And Brian...I'm sorry."

He hung up the phone and for a long time stared at the collection of framed pictures he had around his office. Most of them were of Jason, or they had the handsome son of a bitch in them. His fingers traced the smile of the younger man on a larger frame on the desk. Then, abruptly, he turned the picture facedown.

"You won't do this to me again. Do you hear me? You gave me your word, you bastard. That's the last time I trust you."

His throat was knotted, and he wanted to die. But the

feeling of doom hanging over him—that something was terribly wrong—was almost a source of hope. He knew it was twisted, but he found himself hoping that something had happened to Jason. That he was out there somewhere. Maybe his car had broken down or he'd gone off in a ditch. Maybe he couldn't get to a phone to call. Maybe he was in a coma.

In a few minutes, Brian let the noise of the crowd in the restaurant draw him out of the office. He went around the end of the bar and tried to make small talk with some of the regulars. Then he spotted Chief Weir and Sheila having lunch at a quiet table away from the window.

On impulse, he found himself walking to the table.

"I *love* this stuffed flounder, Brian. What did you—?"

"Excuse me, Sheila." Brian laid a hand on the woman's shoulder and turned his attention to Rich. "Chief, how long do you have to wait before you can report a missing person?"

His abrupt question obviously took the police chief by surprise, and it also caught him with a mouthful of food.

"Who's missing?" Sheila immediately piped in.

"Jason," he answered flatly, turning his attention back to the policeman.

"I saw him working behind the bar here last night," Sheila offered.

"I know. He disappeared after that."

She glanced at her watch. "But that's less than twelve hours!"

"Are you on the chief's payroll now?" Brian snapped. "I only asked a simple question. How long do I have to wait before I officially report him missing?" He drawled each word for emphasis.

Rich Weir leaned back in his chair and looked up at him. "It depends, Brian. Do you have any suspicion that there might be foul play involved?"

"How would I know that?"

"You tell me. You're the one who's worried."

"Do you mean did I see someone put a gun to his head and stuff him in his own trunk before driving away? No, I didn't see that."

Brian's attempt at sarcasm only drew a sharp look from the chief. Between the feeling of betrayal preying on him and the scenario he'd just described, he felt sick to his stomach.

"I'm sorry. I'm just so worried," he continued. "It's not like Jason not to tell me where he's going and when he's coming back. He wouldn't just drive off like this."

"Have you called everyone you know?"

Brian knew he couldn't explain the fear in his gut that something terrible had happened to Jason. He definitely didn't want to say anything about the lunatic who was out there getting his jollies off by sending pictures of Marilyn and Jason to them.

"I called the health club. He didn't show up for work today." He glared in the direction of the kitchen door as two waitresses almost collided going in and coming out. "I have to get back to work."

"Look, Brian. Without some evidence of foul play or violence, I can't put his name in the nationwide missing persons computer. Not yet. But there are a few things that both of us can do at this point. First, why don't you make a list of people to call? Everybody you know or Jason knows. It's hard to call people and say your friend is missing, but you need to pursue every possibility. While you're doing that, I'll put out an 'overdue motorist' for him with the area departments. That way, our guys will be on the lookout for his car, too."

"Thanks, Chief. I'll do what you suggested right now."

As Brian walked away, he wished he could be satisfied with that. But he wasn't. That gnawing feeling in his gut was still eating him alive.

* * *

"*Things have certainly shifted your way this past week,*" *Marilyn's lawyer commented brightly.* "*Twice already, Ted's lost his temper in public, and we have statements from witnesses about his 'unstable and erratic behavior.' And all but one of the people who were prepared to speak against you have withdrawn the statements they made.*"

"*Let me guess. My mother is still holding out.*"

"*Ah...yes. And frankly, she could be the most damaging character witness of all.*"

Marilyn sat back in the chair and crossed her legs. "*Don't worry, counselor. I'm working on her.*"

Twenty-One

The keys, the mail, the phone, the purse, the glasses—all had been dumped on the small table near the door. Stretching from there to the single twin bed, a trail of hastily discarded clothing lay scattered on the floor. In the bed itself, the two of them clung to each other, wrapped in the blissful aftermath of their frenzied lovemaking...and each with a vague fear that if they let go, one of them would end up on the floor.

"So much for going slow." Mick nibbled on her ear before propping himself up on his elbows to support some of his weight.

Léa wrapped her arms around him, cherishing the feel of him inside of her, loving the sensations that continued to ripple through her body. The sanctuary of this moment—thrilled and desired and protected by him as she felt—was already etched firmly in her mind.

"At least we made it to the bed," she purred.

"And, amazingly enough, this time I managed to put a condom on."

As he withdrew from her and shifted his weight to the side, Léa felt the warmth leave and the anxiety return. All morning she'd successfully avoided thinking about that—the consequences of what they'd done earlier.

As one who had always preached to her students the importance of safe sex—and preferably *no* sex at all until they were older and more secure in their relationships—

she'd broken her own rules today. But there was no ignoring it anymore. Despite her uneasiness, there was a
very important question that hung unanswered between
them.

"I haven't been physically involved with anyone for a
very long time," she started. "And I'm a firm believer in
regular physical checkups."

Mick lifted her chin until she was forced to look into
his blue eyes. "Since my divorce from Natalie, this morning was the first time that I haven't used a condom."

"Well, that settles that," Léa responded as brightly as
she could, but he didn't let go of her.

"No, it doesn't. What about birth control?"

She was uncomfortable about discussing any of this
with him now. Not while she was feeling so naked, inside
and out. "I'm okay. You don't have to worry about that."

Léa tried to roll off the bed, but his arm across her
stomach trapped her. "I'm *not* worried. I want to know."

"Look, I'm thirty-one years old. I've been around the
block a few times. We don't need to have this discussion."

"I say we do." His voice was low and serious.

Léa found it unsettling to have his attention so purely
focused on her, as if he could see through her and read
her mind. She wished she could lie, but she couldn't.

"Okay, I'm not using any birth control. But it doesn't
matter. It's the wrong time of the month."

"That doesn't wash with me. I'm a doctor's son. My
father used to claim that half of his patients were con-
ceived at the wrong time of the month."

Léa couldn't understand the contradiction of his serious
tone and the smile tugging at his lips. "I've answered your
question."

"But I have more."

"Well, I'd say you've reached your quota." She managed to sit up and swing her legs over the side of the bed.

"I didn't know you'd set any, so I'm grandfathered in."

Léa reached for her shirt on the floor. Sheila's words about Mick taking care of the grasping type of women he normally dated flooded her consciousness. He was doing it right now—moving into his "generous" mode while she was expected to slide into the "self-centered" one. He was already worrying about what he would do if she got pregnant.

"You're upset."

"I am not." She pulled the shirt over her head. "But I hope you know that I was and still am a consenting adult in this relationship."

"I certainly do."

She felt his hand caressing her back, but Léa wouldn't allow herself to turn around and fall once again under his charm. "And I also want you to know that I am perfectly capable of taking care of myself."

"I know that too."

"Good." Léa grabbed her underwear and shorts off the floor and darted toward the bathroom.

In the protection of the tiny bathroom, Léa turned on the cold water in the sink and splashed her face with it. She was feverish and trembling. Angry for no reason.

Léa could hear him moving around in the other room. She was an adult. They'd made love twice. They were having an affair. This was what adults did. At least, adults who did not ignore their personal lives for more than a decade at a time.

Then why the hell was she letting Sheila's account of Mick's past girlfriends bother her? She was *not* one of them. She was *not* like them. She was *not* going to use him. So why couldn't she let it go and just enjoy the few days they might have together?

"Was your aunt a weak woman?"

"What?" Léa was surprised to see him push his way inside the small bathroom. He was still stark naked. "No! Why do you say that?"

"Then Ted must be the weak one."

She tried to keep her eyes on his face in the mirror. "If this is some game you're playing, then you should know I don't play unless I know the rules."

"Why? Are you afraid of losing?"

Léa shook her head and watched him move behind her.

"Then are you afraid that others might not think too highly of you?" His hands slipped around her waist. Watching her in the mirror, he lifted the hem of her T-shirt up enough to expose one of her breasts, then lowered it again. "Are you concerned that you might not measure up?"

"I don't know what you're talking about."

"Then just answer my question. Was Ted weak?"

"No." Léa was fighting a losing battle with the tingling sensations running through her body.

"But you took care of him, didn't you?"

"We took care of each other."

"How about your aunt? You did all the work and—"

"No! Janice took care of us for years before she got sick. She was strong. Vibrant. Capable. She was a very independent woman."

"Then I'm betting she had the strength and intelligence to manage everything in her life. It takes that balance to keep life from throwing you. God knows, raising teenage kids isn't easy."

"I'm sure it wasn't."

"She must have allowed friends and neighbors and teachers to help her. And letting them be part of the action didn't make her less strong or less independent, did it? It certainly didn't make her needy. Her ego was not bruised because other people cared."

"I know what this is all about. You're bringing all these things up because I'm not behaving like the other women you go out with." She turned around and faced him. "I'm not asking you to run my life, so I don't fit the expected mold.''

''Wrong on all counts. I don't compare people, and I'm finding it challenging enough running my own life.'' He drew her tightly to him. She could feel his fully aroused manhood pressed intimately against her. ''And the only thing I know about molds is that we make an *incredible* fit together.''

It would have been so much easier to let go of everything but this minute. Léa knew she had the power to distract him. She could let him make love to her right now. They would both stop thinking and questioning why she was scared, why she felt the need to run, even why he couldn't let her draw away from him.

But that, too, would be using him. She couldn't do that.

''What do you want from me, Mick?''

His blue eyes darkened. His hand came up and cradled her cheek. ''That's easy. Friendship. Passion.''

''I want that, too.''

''And trust,'' he added. ''But I know that is something earned and not given.''

Léa felt herself wavering again. He had given her his trust, through Heather. But what had she given?

''I do trust you, Mick.'' Her voice trembled as the words came out.

''Do you?'' He forced her to look up at him again. ''Do you trust me enough to confide in me, to ask for help, to let me be there for you when you are alone? Do you trust me enough to let go of this belief that your independence is bruised by me wanting to share in the hard things and the joys?''

This was the core of it all. Not the independence, but the sharing. Being alone for so long, she had learned to survive on her own as a matter of necessity. Léa didn't know how to put any of this into words, how to communicate the fears that regardless of what was going on between them now, one day soon she was going to be there again. Alone.

He was waiting for an answer.

"I…I can try," she finally got out. "But no promises. The problem is not with you, it's with me. I know it takes great patience dealing with me. But I need to learn how to do these things. How to function with someone. Be nice to them, I guess."

"You don't have to be nice to anybody but me." He wrapped his arms around her. "Maybe Heather, too. You could be nice to her, I suppose."

Léa was relieved to hear his tone lighten. "No hard feelings? No 'do it my way or else'?"

He shook his head and kissed the tip of her nose. "No running away?"

She looped her arms around his neck and let out an unsteady breath. "No running away."

"Good." He swept her off her feet and stood her in the tub, climbing in after her.

"What are you doing?"

"Commemorating our agreement with a wet-T-shirt contest."

"I cannot believe what a kid you can be."

She laughed as he turned on the spray and stretched the fabric over her breasts.

"Well, maybe I should just soap you up while we're in here."

"If you insist," he replied, taking her mouth in a kiss.

He was back from physical therapy.

The buzz of the van's lift lowering the wheelchair to the gravel drive drifted in through the open windows. A minute later, Bob's wheelchair rolled up the ramp, and Stephanie saw the driver open the front door of the house ahead of her husband.

"Afternoon, Mrs. Slater."

"Hello, Sandy." Stephanie dropped the pictures and the envelope from her lap onto the coffee table. She crushed out one cigarette and reached for another.

"You would have been very proud of this guy today. The therapists said he worked really hard." She held the door back until Bob came through in his chair. "Come and see him sometime. When I went to get him, he was finishing up his balance exercises. You wouldn't believe how much better he's getting."

Stephanie left the comment unanswered, lit the cigarette and leaned back in the chair. She watched her husband maneuver his wheelchair around the furniture until he was in front of the pile of mail she'd left on an end table. This was the one thing that he looked forward to since his stroke.

Sandy looked down at her clipboard. "I have you down for Wednesday at ten and Friday at one o'clock for this week."

"R-right," Bob answered absently, thumbing through the envelopes.

"Have a good one, Mrs. Slater. See you later, Bob." The woman gave a half wave before closing the door behind her.

Stephanie took a deep drag from the cigarette and stared at her husband's profile. His gray hair was thinning. His face had grown pudgy and pale. Since his stroke, he'd put on a lot of weight, and there were at least two distinct rolls added to his gut. She leaned forward and picked up the pictures again.

The one she'd left on top was the most flattering of the bunch. Bob was wearing his bathing suit and a short-sleeved shirt with the buttons left open. Marilyn, of course, had to be topless in the picture. The slut was sitting on his lap on her backyard patio. He definitely had no gut, but his erection was clearly visible in his bathing suit.

Bob must have sensed her staring at him, for he turned his chair around to face her.

"G-good day?"

"No. It was horrible."

His legs were much skinnier now than before, too. Stephanie leafed through the pictures until she found the one of him lying on the bed with Marilyn preparing to suck his cock. He definitely used to have nice muscles.

"W-what happ-pened?"

"Somebody is trying to put me in an institution, and they've almost succeeded."

She took another deep drag and looked to see if there were any shots of him standing up.

"T-tell me. W-what happ-pened?" He moved his chair forward until his leg bumped against the coffee table.

"When I was at the bank, someone put a stuffed animal on the front seat of my car. One like the tiger Hanna used to carry around. I lost it for a couple of minutes. I got confused...again." Her hands were trembling again, so Stephanie leaned over and crushed the cigarette out in the ashtray.

"M-maybe acc-cident. S-some kid l-left it there."

"It was no frigging accident." Out of reflex she reached for the cigarette pack, but then leaned back and clutched the pictures instead. "This wasn't the first time something like this has happened. Last week, some creep jammed a tricycle under my car when I was at the cemetery. It looked just like the one I bought Emily on her fifth birthday."

"Y-you d-didn't tell me."

Stephanie shrugged and tried to keep her voice steady. Her body calm. "I told Rich Weir."

"Y-you should...have t-told me."

"Why? You don't tell *me* everything." She looked down at the pictures again. "There's not a single one of

you standing. I don't think I have a picture of you standing.''

"What's th-that?"

"Oh, didn't I tell you? These came in today's mail from
some unknown admirer of yours…or maybe an admirer of
mine, since the envelope was addressed to me.''

She tossed the pictures lightly onto the coffee table, and
they spread like a fan in front of him. Bob with his hand
on his stepdaughter's crotch. Bob squeezing Marilyn's tit
as he humped her from behind. And all the others.

"There are twelve of them in there and not one of you
standing.''

She lifted her gaze from the disgusting pictures to her
husband's face. He was pale, and she could hear him
wheezing. His eyes were closed, and she could see every
one of his eyelashes. She could have counted them. It
struck her as almost funny how clear and distinct things
became sometimes, particularly after those confused moments. Colors. Lines. The line between light and shadow.

"I assume," she said coolly, "this is not the first time
you're seeing these.''

"I…m-made mis…mistake. She p-promised y-you
wouldn't know. She s-said she'll des…stroy these. She
l-lied…l-lied.''

"That she did," Stephanie commented tersely. "But I
had the good fortune of not having to wait for these pictures. She called me. Yes, she did. She told me in graphic
detail how she was screwing my husband. *Graphic* detail.
My own daughter! She warned me that I'd better shut up
and mind my own business about the custody of those two
girls, or there was no saying what she might do to em-
barrass you and the bank and all of us.''

Every nerve in her body was jumping. The focus was
shifting, distorting. Her anger at the betrayal was stabbing
at her mind, puncturing her brain, cutting out chunks of
her reason. She could feel the confusion coming on again,

and she fought against it. She grabbed for a cigarette and somehow lit it.

"I should have told her to go and fuck herself. I should have taken the girls away. Pushed Ted to speed up the divorce."

The tears began to roll down her face. He'd loved them. Ted had loved them. But then he'd killed them. He'd betrayed those children, too. He'd betrayed their trust. Her trust. Hers. She'd been burned, too. Twice burned. Damn the fathers. Damn all men.

"I tried to protect you. To save your reputation. Your name. I tried to give you the benefit of the doubt. She was a viper. A slut. An unnatural monster. I didn't want to believe her." The tight control she'd been fighting for snapped and fell away. "But you weren't worth it."

"I h-hated her. *Hated her.*" Bob's hand shook violently. "Sh-she sent you these bef-fore she died. Sh-she said sh-she wouldn't, but did. I saw th-them first. I des-stroyed them... because I loved you. I was t-tricked. Tricked. I was...am... s-sorry."

"*Sorry?* Sorry for what? Sorry that after she died, you couldn't find another whore like her? Sorry that you had a stroke and turned into the half man you are now?"

"S-sorry I d-didn't s-stop her soo-ner. She was evil. She...she d-deserved to die. She *had* to die!"

She had to die! Stephanie had given birth to the devil's own spawn. Dusty and Marilyn. They were cut from the same vile cloth. Father and daughter, living only to taint anything within their reach. The only good that had come from her—ever—was Emily and Hanna. But...but it was because they had Ted's heart. She closed her eyes and saw the convicted and broken man in her mind. Grieving. In pain.

Sorry I didn't stop her sooner. Bob's words echoed in her mind again. Stephanie's hand, the cigarette dangling and forgotten, dropped onto the arm of the chair.

"Stop her sooner?" She peered at him through the tears clouding her vision.

"I did. I f-fell for her…and saw her sh-shed her s-skin. S-snake. Evil. Sh-she planned to de-destroy you…me…us. Sh-she had to die."

Bright shafts of light were blinding her. Stephanie didn't think she could stand the glare.

"That night—the night she and the girls were murdered—I was down in Delaware. You were here alone."

"Y-yes."

"I called you. Several times. But you never answered the phone."

He looked away. "L-long t-time ago."

Stephanie felt her claws come out. She'd been blaming Ted. She'd been crushed by the pressure of his betrayal. But she was wrong. "*You* killed her!"

"N-no. N-no. No!" he shouted.

"My precious girls were in that house. Those innocent babies were upstairs." She rose to her feet.

"No…*No!*" Tears were coursing down his face. "I… d-didn't."

Stephanie couldn't control the violent quaking of her body. The cigarette dropped from her fingers, but she didn't notice. She stared at the ruined man who had been her husband for nearly a decade. She glanced at the array of photographs that depicted his betrayal.

"Just once. Now. Tell me the truth. I need to know. *You killed Marilyn.*"

"No!" He moved his head slightly. "N-not me."

Her vision was clearing. The beams of light were softening. Bending over the table, she hurriedly scooped up the pictures and stuffed them into the envelope.

"W-what you do…with th-them?"

"I'm taking them to the police. I'm not holding back. I'm not protecting you or anyone else anymore." She headed for the door. "I want Rich to figure who is trying to punish me now. So late in the game."

Twenty-Two

"Léa was really touched by what you did today."

"I just painted a room." Heather turned to her father. She still couldn't shake off the warm fuzzy feeling that had surrounded her when she'd seen Léa's reaction. She'd laughed. She'd cried. And then she'd taken Heather in her arms and hugged her so hard and so long that she could hardly breathe. Heather had been embarrassed...but she'd also loved every minute of it. "It was no big deal."

"It *was* a big deal." Mick reached over and squeezed her hand, keeping half an eye on the road ahead. "I'm very proud of you. And, of course, I am a little ticked off."

"Why?"

"Because it doesn't matter what I do for her now. It could never top your surprise."

"Well, don't get her a flower basket. She won't even notice it."

When he threw a questioning look her way, she continued. "That big, expensive basket of wildflowers in the living room? That was sent by Andrew Rice this morning. She didn't even give it a second glance."

"Now, could that be because you had a drop cloth half covering it?"

"No! I told her about it before we even walked into her house. Before she saw the room. No. I just don't think of Léa as a flowers-and-chocolate kind of woman. She's more the touchy-feely type. You know…holding hands, hugging, good conversation…lots of sex.''

''Heather!''

She rolled her eyes at his shocked protest. ''I'm just trying to help!''

''I think I should be able to manage in that department by myself, thank you.''

She hid a smile and turned her eyes on the houses and neighborhoods they were passing. ''You did make an appointment for her to have those stitches checked out, didn't you?''

''For tomorrow afternoon.''

''And you *are* going to drive her.''

''Yes, I am. Anything else?''

''Take her someplace nice for dinner.''

''She doesn't want to go out. You saw her before we left. She was already in her work clothes and determined to burn the midnight oil in that house.''

''Yeah, but still…bring something nice home for dinner.'' She looked at him sternly. ''And no pizza. We had that last night.''

''Yes, ma'am.''

She glanced down at her watch. Seven-thirty already.

The doctor's office had been jammed. They'd been told all the appointments were running forty-five minutes to an hour late. By the time Heather had been in and out, it'd been more like an hour and a half. But she didn't care too much. She'd called Chris once she realized how late they'd be. He'd suggested a quick bite to eat before going to a second show.

Heather fidgeted as she thought about how this was like a real date. Things were going to be just fine, she told herself.

''Why didn't you mention your sleeping problems to the doctor?''

''Because I don't have them anymore.'' She glanced

over at her father's serious profile. "I think I was just too wound up or something. But I don't need the pills anymore."

He didn't say anything, but she could tell he was relieved.

"Are you going to be okay for dinner?"

"Sure! Chris thought we could stop at Hughes Grille or swing by a fast-food place, depending on what time I get to his house."

"What movie are you two going to see tonight?"

"Something triple-X." She laughed at his fierce glare. "Relax, Dad. I'm just kidding."

"Just remember that sixteen-year-old boys, with their hormones running wild, shouldn't be kidded in that department."

"Yes, sir." Heather gave him a mock solute. "And to answer your question, sir, we are probably going to see whatever is playing downtown."

"I want you home right after it."

"*Dad!*" she drawled loudly and exaggeratedly. "I'm not a kid."

"No, you're not. You are mature far beyond your years." He pulled the car to the curb in front of the Websters' house and turned to her. "But *he* is a kid, and I want you home right after the movie."

A week ago, she would have argued the heck out of this. But right now, Heather liked this new rapport between them.

"Fine!" she grumbled, opening the door.

"Take my cell phone." He handed it to her. "Léa has already been chewing my ear off on the safety of having it when you're out alone."

Heather tucked it into her shoulder bag. "Does this mean I'll be getting one of my own soon?"

"Yes, brat. Probably tomorrow."

"Cool! I should get her talking to you about the safety

of having a sports car.'' She hopped out. ''Red, convertible, preferably late model. Nothing like *this* tank, got it?''

''Keep dreaming, babe!''

Heather was smiling as she walked up the driveway to the Websters' house. Despite being waved to go, Mick sat in the Volvo waiting until she'd rung the bell. Even then, it wasn't until Chris opened the door that she heard the sound of the car moving off.

''Hi! Sorry I'm late.''

''Hey, no problem. In fact, your timing is perfect.'' He stepped back, motioning for her to come in. ''My parents just sat down to eat.'' He lowered his voice. ''They were wondering if we wanted to hang around and have dinner with them before the movie, but I didn't commit us to anything. So, whatever you say.''

''Whatever!'' Heather replied, breathing in his spicy cologne as she stepped through the door. He looked gorgeous, showered and shaved and wearing a tan polo shirt and a pair of khakis. ''I think I'm underdressed.''

As he closed the door, she looked down at the old jeans and T-shirt she was wearing. A couple of inches of midriff showed.

''You look great!''

She was surprised when he placed a kiss on her neck.

''It's nice to see you again, Heather.''

At the sound of the woman's voice, Heather practically leaped out of her skin. In the dim light of the long hallway, she hadn't seen Chris's mother standing at the other end.

''Uhh, hi. Nice to see you, too, Mrs. Webster.''

''I thought you were eating, Mom.'' Chris wrapped a hand around Heather's bare waist and started urging her along the hall.

''It's been a long time.''

The son's comment went unanswered. The woman's attention was focused totally on Heather…and on Chris's hand on her skin.

"Yes, it has. About two years."

"You've changed quite a bit."

Heather didn't miss the critical inflection in the woman's tone. She also didn't miss the disapproving scrutiny of her looks.

"That's what everybody has been telling me."

"And I am sure you understand why."

"Well, you know what they say. Kids grow and change and grow some more."

"Yes. Like weeds, some of them."

Though she would normally have lashed out at anyone with such a condescending attitude, Heather found herself biting her tongue. Mrs. Webster's insulting manner was making her feel extremely uncomfortable right now. Even vulnerable. All she wanted to do was get out.

"Come on, Mom. I've heard Dad say that roses are weeds, too. And they're the best-smelling flowers in the garden."

Chris's mother was a thin little thing, maybe five feet at the most, but right now the woman looked more like seven feet tall. She was like a mother bear ready to tear an intruder apart. Heather tried to casually brush off Chris's hand, but he hung on, slipping a couple of fingers into the waistband of her pants and pulling her closer.

"And you definitely smell good," he whispered against her ear, his fingers inching a little along the waistline. Heather caught his wrist.

Patricia Webster didn't miss a thing.

"So what'll it be?" Chris said brightly. "Her cooking or should we fly the coop?"

"Whatever," Heather whispered, finding herself tongue-tied.

"How come you're all standing in the dark?" The overhead light in the hallway came on at that moment as Chris's father appeared in the doorway to the kitchen.

"Hello, Heather. Great to see you back here. How is your mother?"

"Just great." She managed to unhook Chris's fingers and went on to answer Reverend Webster's rapid-fire questions about California and the family. The whole time, though, she could feel Patricia Webster's eyes burning a hole through her skin.

"So, are you kids staying for dinner?" the minister finally asked.

Chris looked at Heather for an answer.

She was having a hard time not making a dash for the door. "If you don't mind, I think I'll take a rain check. Perhaps some other time."

"No problem," Allan Webster replied cheerfully.

"I'll be waiting up, Chris," his mother said sternly. "Don't forget you have to be at work early tomorrow morning." With a last frowning glance at Heather, the woman turned around and disappeared into the kitchen.

"Say hello to your dad for me, will you?" Reverend Webster said, following his wife.

Heather let out a breath that she didn't know she was holding.

"Sure thing," she replied.

As Chris led her out the front door, it was all she could do to keep from running for the car.

"Never mind my mother. I don't know what's wrong with her these days," he commented, holding the door of his station wagon open for her to get in.

Heather climbed in and glanced back uneasily toward the house. "I know what's wrong with her. She doesn't like me."

The only noise in the house was the echo of Max's paws on the plastic drop cloths as he made his rounds, sniffing every corner. The sun had disappeared in the west, and the darkness was gradually crowding the fringe of yellows and reds and deepening purples toward the horizon. The overhead fluorescent light of the kitchen shining through open, curtainless windows threw quadrangular shapes of white on the backyard lawn and the driveway.

Léa looked at the stripes of paint she'd just applied around the edges of the ceiling. She flexed her arms and tried to shake out the burn she was already feeling in her muscles from the overhead work. Taking a deep breath, she picked up the heavy can and poured paint in the roller tray. After setting the tray on the stepladder, she carefully climbed up, ready to roll a coat of paint on the kitchen ceiling.

Max wandered in and looked at her for a second before stretching out in the kitchen doorway.

"Good boy," she said. "I wouldn't get too close, either, if I were y—"

Without any warning, Max leaped up, growling and barking furiously as he charged past her to the door leading to the mudroom. Her heart in her throat, Léa nearly fell off the stepladder. She climbed down in an instant, staring uncertainly at the dog scratching and barking at the door.

"What is it, Max? You scared the dickens out of me." She put the paint roller in the tray and crossed the room to the scratching and growling dog. The animal obviously had only one thing on his mind, and that was getting out.

The mudroom that separated the kitchen door from a second outside door was small and the overhead light was on. A row of coat hooks lined one wall, and a small broom closet was on the opposite wall. Both doors had glass panels in the upper half, but neither had a lock that worked...so far as Léa knew.

She peered through the mudroom door. The little room was empty, and she tried to see through the glass of the outside door. She couldn't see anything of the concrete porch and steps down to the backyard.

"What is it, good boy?" She crouched beside the agitated dog, holding his collar, petting him, trying to get his attention away from whatever it was beyond the doors. But he continued to bark and listen and growl. "What is it, a skunk out there?"

Léa froze at the sound of the outside doorknob turning. Despite her hold on him, Max leaped up at the glass again, standing now on his hind legs and barking ferociously.

She slowly pushed herself to her feet.

Dusty was inside the mudroom, facing her.

Twenty-Three

Every light in Léa's house appeared to be on, and every window open. Mick drove past the house and pulled into his driveway, parking next to his truck. Popping the trunk for the groceries, he grabbed a single long-stem rose off the passenger seat.

The smell of summer permeated the night air. A good night for cooking on the grill and eating dinner by candlelight on the back porch, he thought, taking the bag of groceries out of the trunk.

Mick was just coming around the truck when he heard the sharp scream. It took only an instant for him to realize it was coming from the Hardys' house. *Léa.* The bag of groceries hit the driveway and the flower fell onto the grass somewhere near it. He covered the ground around the back of his house at a dead run.

Max was barking furiously. Out of the corner of his eye, Mick spotted a two-legged shadow disappear through the thick brush behind the carriage house. He instinctively veered toward the carriage house and then hesitated, undecided for a split second whether to run down the intruder or go to Léa. Turning to the house, Mick went up the back steps three at a time. Cold panic washed through him when he saw the outside door to the mudroom was wide open. Max's paws were pressed against the glass on the kitchen door and his fangs were bared.

"Léa!" He banged on the door when he didn't see her.

The dog recognized him, and the tone of his bark changed. Mick tried to push open the door, but a weight at the bottom was holding it shut. He peered downward through the glass. Léa was on the floor, her back braced against the door.

"Léa! It's me, Mick." He turned the knob on the door and gently tried to push it as he knocked. Max's barks were now playful. The dog's tail was wagging when he jumped on the door in greeting. "Let me in, Léa."

She shifted her weight to the wall beside the door, and Mick went in. The sight of her curled up and shaking ripped at his heart.

"Are you okay? Please tell me you're okay...." He knelt beside her, touching her face, checking for bruises, cuts. "What happened?"

"Dusty." She raised her head off her knees. She was pale, trembling badly. "He was here...in the mudroom. He had a knife. He...he gestured that he was going to cut my throat." Her hands were shaking as she imitated the motion. "He...he's going to kill me."

Max had moved off to the cement landing on the back steps, barking into the night. Mick drew Léa into his arms and she came willingly, clutching on to him as if he were her lifeline. "Did he come in? Did he touch you?"

"No." She shook her head. "When I screamed, he...he walked away. He didn't run. He grinned at me...like he was telling me that he was going to get me, anyway. And then he just walked away."

"Do you have your phone?"

Léa motioned toward the counter.

"Neither one of us is too confident about the Stony-brook police right now, but I still think this is a good time to call them."

She nodded and pushed away from him. It was obvious she was trying hard to compose herself. "This was *not* my imagination. He was really here."

''I believe you. And when I'm done with them, they'll believe you, too.'' Mick dialed the number for the police department and reported to a dispatcher what had happened. He also left a message to have Rich Weir call or stop by at the house.

When he ended the call, Léa was standing at the kitchen sink, attacking the paintbrushes and rollers, trying to wash the paint out of them. He was relieved to see her shaking off the fear, fighting back.

''Why?'' she asked angrily.

''Everybody in town says Dusty's deck got shuffled when he was in the service. But he's been around a long time, and as far as I know, this is the first time he's been a threat to anyone.'' Mick folded the stepladder and put it against a wall. As much as he just wanted to hold Léa and take her out of here, he understood her need for answers.

''What have *I* ever done to him? Why is he doing this to me?''

''I've heard talk that Marilyn was always good to him. Maybe out of some twisted sense of loyalty, he hates you because of Ted.''

She glanced over her shoulder at him. ''But he hates Stephanie, too. I saw him today. Downtown by the entrance to the park. He thoroughly enjoyed it when she fell apart on the street.''

''Well, they have a past.'' Mick put the lid back on the can of paint and stood up. ''It goes back to before he got drafted.''

Léa shut off the water and turned to him. She had gained some of the color back in her face. The fear was gone, too.

''What kind of past?''

''I am not the best source of gossip in this town.'' Mick tore off some paper towels from a roll on the counter and started drying Léa's hands. The need to touch her, to make sure she was really okay, was overwhelming. ''But from what I remember hearing years ago, before he went in, Dusty was the town bad boy, always running wild. And Stephanie—despite her family and money—was practically his shadow. They were definitely an item. But then he went off to Vietnam, and Stephanie immediately ran off with Charlie Foley—''

''Whose family owned the mill and half of Stonybrook with it.''

He nodded and stuffed the paper towels into a trash bag. ''And Marilyn was born the same year.''

''Did Stephanie's husband put him up in that trailer on the mill property?'' she asked.

''I think he did. He's been there for as long as I can remember. It could be that Stephanie asked him to because Dusty was in pretty bad shape when he came back. He'd always worked there. He was one of the gatekeepers when the mill was operating. Later, he just lived there as a kind of watchman. It was perfect for him.''

''Mick, could Dusty be Marilyn's father?''

''I really don't think anybody can answer that but Stephanie,'' Mick answered honestly. ''But I can tell you this, as much as they tried to hush it up, there have always been rumors to that effect floating around Stonybrook.''

Mick wrapped his arms around her. Without a murmur, she settled against his chest.

''The Hardys have never been the only ones with problems in this town,'' he said gravely. ''The sad thing is, when Ted married Marilyn, I don't think he had a clue how truly messed up that family was.''

''You're right. He didn't.''

Max ran back into the house. The flashing lights of a police car pulling up to the curb drew their attention to the front of the house.

''What happens if they don't believe me again?''

''I'll unleash the dogs,'' Mick assured her. ''My lawyers, the politicians I know, the reporter that did that article on you. Rich won't brush this off.''

Léa didn't object. She didn't insist that she didn't need his help or that she was going to take care of this all by herself. She simply entwined her fingers with his and walked with him toward the front door.

''I don't think this is such a good idea.'' Heather glanced uncomfortably at the dark countryside whizzing by her window. ''I told my father we were going to a movie, and I promised I'd come home right after that.''

''I'll get you home at exactly when the movie gets out.'' Chris put a reassuring hand on her knee. ''Come on, Heather, for old times' sake. It'll be fun. Remember how we used to go to the lake all the time when you lived here before?''

''That last summer we were thirteen and fourteen, and we used to drive our bikes out here in the *daylight*. There's a big difference betw—''

''We used to go swimming,'' he said, cutting her short and putting his hand back on the wheel. ''That was fun. Remember the time we drove our bikes off the dock in front of my folks' cottage? It was like flying into the lake.''

Heather couldn't stop herself from smiling back at him. ''I didn't drive my bike off. You *pushed* me off. And it was freezing.'' She punched him on the arm. ''That was like the week after Easter. There were still ice chunks in that water.''

''But I jumped in after you, didn't I?''

Heather felt the jagged edges of anxiety sawing away at her brain as Chris turned down the winding gravel driveway. She remembered the route.

''Listen, Chris, I told you I don't want to go to the lake.''

"Come on. Don't be such a spoilsport. We'll only stay a couple of minutes."

He steered the station wagon into the short driveway beside his parents' cabin. The beams from the headlights skimmed out over the lake's surface as he stopped. With a smile at her, he undid his seat belt.

Dark thickets of oak and pine cut them off, providing a privacy Heather did not feel comfortable with at the moment. She looked at him, though, and tried not to show her nervousness. "Looks the same as it used to. Not much building going on around here, I guess."

"Actually, there is some." He turned off the headlights, and they were immediately immersed in darkness. "There are about six more cabins being built down at the far end of the lake." He leaned over to point them out to her. "And just over there, around the curve of the lakeshore, your father's company is renovating the Lion Inn and all its cottages."

Heather already knew about that, but she wanted to keep him talking so that things wouldn't get too serious. "Your parents have had this cabin for a while, haven't they?"

"Yeah." He undid her seat belt. "How about a twenty-five-cent tour of the inside?"

So much for keeping him talking. She took a peek past him at the dark windows of the cabin. The closest lights that she could see were across the lake.

"No way, Chris. It's too creepy out here alone." She felt much better once she'd said it. "I'll come back in the daylight if you want to invite me back again. But I'd just as soon stay in the car right now."

Heather stared straight ahead but felt the weight of his gaze studying her. She knew what he was thinking. This was the same thing she'd run into with the boys in L.A. They all looked at her "mod-Goth" look, listened to her sassy tongue and automatically assumed she'd be an easy hookup. What none of them guessed was that she was still intact.

"I understand."

His quiet acceptance was a surprise. She gave him a quick glance. He was looking at the lake, seemingly content. Heather felt the knot of worry in her stomach loosen a bit.

"Thank you," she whispered.

"You're welcome."

She smiled and looked at his handsome profile again. "But if you think you're going to lay a guilt trip on me by being so nice, it won't work. I'm not going in."

"I don't want to go in anymore, either."

"Then what are you doing, sulking?"

"I'm not sulking." He turned to her and smiled. In that moment, she thought he was more than hot. Chris Webster was solar. "I'm remembering."

"Remembering what?"

"Our first kiss. Right there, by those rocks. On that small ledge by the water."

"That wasn't our *first* kiss," Heather protested. "That was the first time you tried French-kissing me."

"I don't remember you complaining too much."

She hadn't complained at all. She'd been thirteen, but even back then he was hot, and he knew exactly what to do with his mouth. It had been two years now, and Heather thought none of the boys on the West Coast even came close to him in the kissing department. She took a quick look at his mouth and wondered if he was going to kiss her tonight before they went home.

Somewhere along the shore near the Lion Inn, Heather saw a vehicle pull in, facing the lake. A minute later the headlights went out.

"So, is this place still a big hangout for high school kids to come out at night and fog up their car windows?"

"It sure is." He smiled. "Do you want to do some window-fogging with me?"

"No!" She shot him a scornful look.

"How about some innocent kissing?"

She shifted in the seat, until her back was against the door. "There is *nothing* innocent about your kissing."

"I think you're making more of me than I am." He slid a few inches toward her. Heather felt her entire body heat up at the way his gaze focused on her lips. "How about if you try me out a little...just for old times' sake."

She pressed back against the door. She wanted him to kiss her. At the same time, things were different now. They were both older, and she was pretty sure she could keep everything under control. The fact that Chris was a full-grown man, though, made her want to be cautious. She drew one of her knees up against her chest.

"I don't know. This is only the first time we've been out toge—"

"Since you've been back." Chris slid toward her. "Just once. You don't have to do a thing."

Before she could protest, his lips were gently pressing against hers. His mouth was warm, gentle, and Heather silently talked herself into just enjoying the moment.

"This is not so bad, is it?" he murmured against her lips.

"No, it's not."

He shifted his weight to the edge of the seat and she drew her other leg up, too. "Just relax."

His tongue flicked at the seam of her lips, and Heather felt her entire body tingle with excitement. She opened her mouth and his tongue swept in, tasting, exploring, teasing. When he gently straightened her legs out along the seat, she gladly let him. She wrapped her arms around his neck, but he pulled back from the kiss.

"There's plenty of room in the cottage."

She shook her head. "This is just fine."

"How about the back of the station wagon?"

"Too dangerous," she whispered. "This is working for me."

He smiled. "Okay. But let me do it right."

Heather's body was beginning to hum with a soft buzz. She watched him push open the driver's door. He wrapped an arm around her back and slid her across the seat and then laid her down on it. Her feet were dangling out of the car.

"What are you doing?"

"I just had a thought." He smiled and then took both of her hands and tucked them behind her head.

"Chris, I'm not having sex with you," she said seriously.

"No sex," he agreed, sounding genuine. "Come on, Heather. I won't do anything you don't want me to do."

His mouth came down, and she was lost in the kiss that followed. She tried to move her hands once, but he stopped her and only deepened the kiss. She tried to raise her knees, but he gently pressed them down. The next time that he lifted his mouth off of hers, Heather's entire body was on fire.

"I have something to confess." Chris's lips hovered over hers.

"What?" she cooed, arching her back, wanting him to kiss her again.

"I've been obsessed with seeing your breasts since the first time we went swimming together down here."

A giggle rose up in her. She tried to move her hands again, but he tucked them back behind her head.

"Laugh if you want. But you had—you still have—these perfect round breasts with nipples that stick out on your shirt or bathing suit whenever you're cold…or wet…or when we kiss."

He looked down at her shirt, and Heather felt her nipples tingling.

"Can I look at them?"

Normally, Heather would have been out of here if one of her other dates had asked that. But with Chris, they'd been kissing for minutes, and he'd not once groped at her. And he was being so darn polite.

"Can I, Heather? Just look?"

She felt excited and embarrassed at the same time. "I don't generally go around showing my boobs to boys, you know."

"I know."

He kissed her deeply again. When he pulled back, her insides were quivering like Jell-O.

"You're not saying no." His finger started playing with the ring in her belly. "I told you I won't do anything you don't want me to do."

Heather watched him sit up straight and slowly push the tight shirt up to her neck. When he started to undo the clasp of the bra, she closed her eyes.

"Why close your eyes? You're beautiful."

The clasp opened and her white flesh poured out, her nipples hard and extended.

"This is the way I always imagined you would look. Like a goddess." His warm hand slid caressingly over her stomach. Round and round. Again and again. The circles growing ever wider.

Heather couldn't understand her body's shivering. She *wanted* him to touch her breasts now, and his touch was light. When his hand moved to the metal button of her jeans, no objections came out of her mouth. He slowly undid the button and lowered the zipper. He carefully pushed down the waistband of her underwear until just the top of her dark pubic hair was showing. He withdrew his hand.

"This is not so bad, is it?" he asked, coming and kissing her again deeply. She closed her eyes.

A need that she couldn't understand was rising in her.

She wanted to move her hips against him. She wanted him to touch her. She heard a sound of the glove compartment opening and looked at him in surprise.

"What are you doing?"

"Never mind." His hand caressed her stomach, again inching lower. He stopped and took his hand off her. "Can I kiss your breasts?"

She almost groaned out loud when he wrapped his hot mouth around her nipple without waiting for an answer.

There was a click and a blinding flash in the car.

"What was that?" Heather leaped off the seat, but Chris held her down.

"It's okay. It's okay. It was me." He smiled, showing her the camera. "I took a picture of us."

"What for?" She struggled to free her hands, but he was trapping them above her head with one hand.

"For fun. Don't you think it'll be cool to look at a picture of me sucking your breasts…or licking you?"

"No!" she spat out. "That's sick."

"Come on, Heather. It's all very cool. Wait till you see."

"You're sick, Chris."

He shook his head, his smile slipping a little. He was holding her hands tighter now, and she bucked when he slipped his hand inside her open pants, cupping her hard.

"Who are you kidding? You're all wet."

She twisted on the seat. "Let me go! *Stop* touching me!"

"Come on, Heather. You're getting upset over nothing. I didn't try to fuck you." She kicked futilely as he forced down the pants and underwear over her hips. He held down her legs with one of his own and took another picture. "Now, *that* would be a picture…the two of us making it."

She raised her head and bit down hard on the inside of his arm.

"Jeez," he cried out in pain, yanking his arm away and dropping the camera on her.

The moment he let her go, she frantically kicked herself free and shot out the open driver's door. As she went, the camera came with her and she grabbed it.

With her pants pushed down, Heather fell like a sack on the grass.

"Wait! Heather! Please wait."

She scrambled to her feet, pulling her pants up and lowering her shirt as she took off at a run toward the woods along the lake.

"I'm sorry!" he shouted at her back as she passed through the line of trees. "Heather!"

She was scared and angry. Angry for being such an idiot. Angry for falling for his stupid act. Angry for thinking the asshole was any different from the other walking hard-ons she seemed to attract.

She was also scared. Scared about how close she'd come to having this creep…jerk…asshole take porno shots of her. She felt suddenly queasy, thinking of them plastered all over the Web.

But they weren't going to show up on the Web or anywhere else, she thought as she came out onto a path that ran along the lake. She held up the camera in the dim light and smashed it against a tree. Opening it up, she ripped out the film and exposed the whole roll. Satisfied, she moved to the edge of the lake and threw the film and the camera as far as she could out into the dark water.

Heather turned and looked around her. There was no sign of Chris. There were lights on in a couple of the cottages she could see along the water. She redid the clasp of her bra, zipped and buttoned her pants.

A week ago, she realized as she started along the path toward the cottages, something like this would have torn her apart. But now she was stronger. Léa had told her she had to deal with her emotions, to express them. Well, she wanted to kick the shit out of Chris. Forget about being scared. She wanted to cut his balls off.

She remembered her bag was in his car. The cell phone was in it. What she really wanted was to call home and have her dad come and get her.

"You're pretty far from home, little girl."

Heather's heart almost stopped beating in her chest. The voice was deep. The words slightly slurred. Mocking. She stood still as pure fear caught at her throat.

Dusty was leaning against a tree beside the path not fifteen feet ahead of her, and she could smell the liquor from where she stood.

He'd always scared her. Disgusted her. Even when she was younger, his lecherous, hawklike look when he stared at her had always been filled with malice. She remembered how he used to hang out in the woods behind Marilyn's house whenever she baby-sat for the girls. That used to scare the heck out of her.

"So where's your new boyfriend?"

Heather's gaze was drawn to the blade of the knife in his hand. He was carving the bark off a stick of wood.

"You outta-town bitches sure got friendly with each other in a hurry. Just the same, you and that Hardy bitch."

She took a step backward and glanced nervously around her. She could jump in the lake and try to swim away. She could run toward the road. Or she could just hide her fear and walk casually away. For years Heather had heard everybody say that Dusty was harmless.

He pushed away from the tree. Even in the darkness, she could see his eyes narrow. He looked like an animal ready to pounce. Everybody was wrong.

"Don't even think about going anywhere, little girl. We have an account to settle, and you owe me big."

Heather took another step back.

"I should've gone upside your head when you opened your fat mouth that night. It was 'cuz of your screaming that I didn't finish the Hardy bitch. You pissed me off big time.'' He took a step toward her. She took two back. ''Of course, if you get on your knees right now, I might just take it easy on you…this time.''

Heather gasped out loud as she backed into something behind her. Or rather, someone.

''Stop right there, shithead.'' Chris wrapped an arm protectively around her waist and drew her to his side. Relief and gratitude instantly replaced her anger at Chris.

''Well, if it ain't Christopher Robin, Boy Wonder.'' The ragged man laughed and started toward them again. ''We'll have a fucking orgy. Okay, Boy Wonder, you hold her and let me go first and—''

''I said stop!''

Dusty glared at Chris. ''Fine, big boy. You do her first, and then I go.''

''Are you fucking deaf?'' Chris shouted. ''I said *stop* right there.''

For the first time, Heather saw the pocketknife Chris was holding. Dusty seemed to notice it, too.

''Oh, no!'' he said, sarcasm in his voice. ''I'm just *so* scared.''

In spite of his tone, Dusty did stop, though. He lowered his own knife, grinning like a lunatic.

''You just stay right where you are, pal.'' Heather felt Chris pulling her backward, and she willingly followed his lead.

''What the fuck, kid?'' Dusty put his hand on his crotch. ''No need to run off. Shit…if you want, you do it and I'll watch. It'll be just like the old days.''

''I'm going to take Heather home now, Dusty. Don't follow us.'' Chris drawled each word, as if he were talking to a child.

''What's wrong?'' the older man shouted after them. ''I'm not good enough to watch you anymore? The Boy Wonder's too fucking good for me?''

"Let's go." Chris took Heather's wrist, and they started walking away.

Dusty didn't follow but continued shouting at their backs. "I am *watching*, Christopher Robin. I'm *watching*. I know you marked your territory down here. I know, Boy Wonder. Chri-is!" The shouts became singsong in quality. "Boy Won-der! I know what you are up to!"

Heather continued to hear the taunts until they were almost back to the Websters' cabin.

"I'm really sorry, Heather," Chris started as soon as they could see his car. "I behaved horrible tonight. I put your life in danger by acting like some hard-up jerk."

She yanked her hand free and lengthened her steps. He kept up with her, talking nonstop.

"It's just that I've been wanting you so long. And I was trying to impress you because I thought I could never match up to those West Coast guys. I could only imagine the moves you're used to. I acted like a total—"

"Asshole! I know." Her heart was still racing. The fear of every shadow being Dusty made her almost frantic to get out of this place as soon as she could. "Give me your car keys."

"I'll drive you home."

"Give me your car keys!" She repeated sharply as they stepped into the clearing. The cabin and his car lay straight ahead.

"You don't have your license yet." He was starting to whine. "Look, I promise not to touch you. I won't come near you. I'll take you straight home."

Heather rounded on him when they reached the car. "You give me your fucking car keys right now, or I'm going to go straight to the chief of police when we get back to town."

"What for?"

"Does the term *date rape* mean anything to you?" She held out her hand.

He reached into his pocket and took out the keys. "We didn't do it."

"But you had every intention of it, and you know it. I am only fifteen, and your father is a goddamn minister in this town." Heather snatched the keys out of his hand and got behind the wheel. When he tried to get in on the passenger side, she locked the door.

"At least give me a ride back to town."

"No chance. You can walk," she snapped at him. "And as far as coming around to get your car, don't bother. I'll have a couple of my father's bruisers deliver it to your house when they're done trashing it."

She turned on the engine, slammed the station wagon in reverse and gunned it up the gravel driveway.

And as Heather ran over a small shrub marking the end of the drive, she swore that she was never going on a date again until she was at least thirty.

Twenty-Four

Bright spotlights from the cruisers flooded the gate and the yard immediately beyond the perimeter fence around the mill property. The padlock was open. The gate had been left ajar.

"Dusty?" the police officer called out. The small construction trailer that sat near the gate was dark. She peered into the partially open door. The silence, as heavy as midnight, stretched on for a minute.

A second officer came around the trailer.

"His truck is gone," he said in a low voice.

He motioned to Robin that they should take a look. She nodded and drew her baton. The other officer kept his hand on his gun as they advanced.

The stench of the place hit the two police officers as soon as they stepped into the trailer. It smelled more like a kennel than a living space for humans.

The switch beside the door did nothing when Robin tried it. Turning on her flashlight, she spotted a string dangling from the bank of fluorescent ceiling lights, and she gave it a tug. After a second, the lights blinked and came on.

The furniture was mostly old and broken, no doubt taken from the mill offices and from the town dump. A swivel chair with a cracked green seat sat by a card table against one long wall. An army cot with a bare mattress was visible by the end wall beneath a tiny window. Standing where she was, Robin could see the counters on either side of the little sink were covered with garbage, fast-food containers, empty bottles of liquor and more filth that was unidentifiable. The doorless cabinets beneath were loaded with more of the same. Jeff, at the far end of the trailer, was shining his light into a small room that appeared to be in a similar condition. Or worse.

In her six years as a police officer, Robin had never seen squalor like this. She hadn't thought it even existed in Stonybrook. She looked at her partner, who was now peering at the wall above the card table.

Photographs and clippings covered a large section of the paneling. Glancing around, she saw that a large corkboard on the other wall contained many more. Beneath the clippings and pictures, small carvings of animals and large-breasted women were visible. She noticed Jeff reaching up to flatten out a clipping.

"Don't touch anything," she barked.

"He's even got a picture of you."

Robin frowned and looked at the clipping Jeff was pointing to. It was the time Marilyn Hardy had given her a medal that her family sponsored. She looked at the photographs around it. They were all of Marilyn. Every one. Going back to high school. And grade school, even.

In a partially open drawer beneath, she saw a stack of photographs. Jeff tried to reach for them.

"Only stuff in plain view," she reminded him, and he withdrew his hand.

They both noticed the police scanner at the same time.

Exchanging a look with her partner, Robin turned and crossed the trailer to look at the other wall. It was covered with material about the murder trial, and one very mangled clipping with Léa Hardy's face missing. "I'd say she has every right to be nervous."

Jeff walked to the end of the trailer where the cot sat against the wall. Newspapers and magazines were stuffed underneath. "I can't tell what's junk and what's not. Do you think he's flown the coop?"

"Where is he gonna go?"

She cast a final look around the kitchenette area. More junk. A couple of grinding stones. Several carving knives. A good-sized block of wood. More piles of newspapers stacked next to a plug-in single-burner stove.

It smelled worse here than in the rest of the trailer, if that were possible. She glanced into the sink. One look at the two decomposing rats, and she almost lost her dinner.

"There's a box by the bed with more pictures," Jeff said, coming toward her.

"We need a search warrant," Robin said, moving quickly for the door.

"Yeah." Jeff followed his partner out. "Just be glad we're not the poor bastards who'll have to do it!"

Mick was surprised to see Heather driving Chris Webster's station wagon. He was even more surprised when she parked the car in front and got out alone. There was no sign of the other teenager.

He sat in his leather chair and pulled the newspaper back on his lap, trying to hide the fact that he'd been pacing the length of the living room nonstop for the past half hour. Max was less subtle. The animal was ready to jump through the screen door in his excitement at seeing her coming up the steps. A sharp "No!" from Mick kept the dog from doing any damage.

One look at her pale face and puffy eyes, though, and Mick shot to his feet.

"I'm fine," Heather said in response to his immediate question. She lifted both hands in his direction. "Nothing happened, Dad."

Totally ignoring the excited dog, she dropped her bag and the keys by the foot of the stairs, kicked out of her shoes and started up. She hadn't climbed three steps when she hesitated, then came back down and into his arms.

Mick hugged her fiercely to him. "Are you okay?"

"I'm okay now." She was shivering. "It's so good to be home."

It felt like a lifetime since she'd come to him like this. But as much as he treasured the moment, he was already primed to kill the little bastard who'd scared her so badly.

"What happened, baby?" he asked, trying to keep his voice calm.

She pulled back, and he was afraid that she wouldn't trust him enough to tell.

"I want something to eat." She started toward the kitchen, but then stopped in the doorway. "Do you want to sit with me?"

Mick bit back his raw emotions. He simply nodded and followed her through the house.

At that moment, she looked frail and young. Very young. What was most obviously missing was the attitude and the confidence that had always—and even more so lately—been part of her. When she reached for the bottle of milk in the fridge instead of a can of soda, he knew how bad things were.

"I'm going out there to wring that scrawny little bastard's neck right now."

She whirled on him. "Dad, sit!"

"Heather," he exploded. "You're not at fault. I am *not* mad at you. But I need you to tell me if Chris did anything…well, if he hurt you in any way. If he—"

"Dad, *sit* and I'll explain."

Mick forced back his temper and sat down in the chair she was pointing to. He watched her bring the jar of cookies and put it in the middle of the table. He thought he'd go crazy when she meticulously folded a couple of napkins and set them out for the two of them.

"Do you want a glass of milk, too?"

"No. I don't. Thanks."

Heather sat down across the table from him. "Where's Léa?"

"Sleeping."

"Is she feeling okay?"

"I'm not answering any more questions until you tell me what happened tonight."

Heather dipped a cookie in the milk and popped it into her mouth. "We didn't go to the movies tonight."

It took great effort, but Mick managed not to comment on that.

"It wasn't my idea. Chris had…this stupid notion that I might want to see his parents' cabin by the lake. So he took me there."

"Against your will?"

"I didn't kick or scream or put up a fuss, if that's what you mean. And once we got there, when I told him I'd prefer not to go inside the cabin, that was fine with him." Heather must have seen a murderous look in Mick's eyes, for she reached over and put a hand over one of his white-knuckled fists. "Really, Dad. He didn't force me to go in there. He didn't force me to do anything."

He felt sick. "What *exactly* are we talking about?"

She took another cookie out of the jar and kept dipping it in the milk. She was avoiding looking up at him. Half of the cookie broke off and sank to the bottom of the glass.

"Heck, you're my father. I guess you might as well know, too." Her voice had turned shy. "Despite all my big talk the other day, I'm…well, I'm still a virgin."

"There's no crime in that, Heather."

"Yeah, well, boys don't always believe that, for some reason. So anyway, I told Chris that we were not going all the way."

"And he didn't believe you, either."

"He did, after a while. I'm cool with him now."

Mick was relieved beyond words, and yet he sensed there was something else she was holding back.

"How come you drove his car home?"

She leaned against the back of the chair and let out a long, shaky breath. Her fear showed in her face. "When we were at the lake, I got out of Chris's car. I was definitely mad enough to walk back home. But then, as I was walking along the lake, I ran into Dusty…Dusty Norris. No kidding, Dad, that guy scared the shit out of me."

"Dusty was at the lake? Did he hurt you?"

"No. Chris was right behind me. He stood up to Dusty, and we ran away." She shivered and rubbed her arms. "That guy is too creepy."

Heather stood up and took the glass of milk to the sink, dumping it out. She reached inside the fridge for a can of soda.

"I was so ripped at Chris for taking me out there that I took his keys and told him he could walk home." She turned to him. "So here I am. And he's probably still walking."

"Did Dusty threaten you?"

"He didn't touch me or anything, if that's what you mean. But that guy is *always* scary. He had a knife on him, too. And he said some stuff that made me pretty sure he was the one who clocked Léa the other night." She shivered again and looked at the open windows. "I think he's been watching Léa's house and hanging around here."

"I think you're right." Mick pushed himself to his feet. "They've issued a warrant for his arrest. We're going to take care of that problem."

Heather became immediately alert. "Did something happen to Léa?"

Mick nodded. "She's okay, though. Dusty came into her house, as far as the mudroom, earlier tonight. Trying to scare her.'' He started closing the windows. "She's tired and scared, but she'll be okay.''

Heather put the can of soda in the sink and headed for the door. "I won't wake her up, but I think I'll check on her.''

Mick felt the emotions well up in him when he watched his daughter go. She was back, but even better, it seemed. Somewhere along the line, she'd become a young woman. Strong, independent, smart, beautiful...and now affectionate, even.

And he couldn't wait to wring Chris Webster's neck for messing around with her.

Mick picked up the phone in the kitchen and dialed the number Rich had left him.

Stonybrook's chief of police had sounded serious about wanting to take care of this problem. Of course he'd be serious, Mick thought. Over the years, Dusty Norris had become an eyesore in Rich Weir's perfect landscape. Now the man was becoming more than a nuisance...he was becoming a menace.

"Monday. The court date is for this Monday!" Ted repeated, satisfaction evident in his voice. "And I'm picking Emily and Hanna up tomorrow night for Aunt Janice's birthday. I was thinking of keeping them until the hearing."

"How is Marilyn dealing with the whole thing finally coming to an end?" Léa asked.

"She's pissed. For a while her lawyer had her believing that she was sitting pretty, but now she knows better."

"Why is she putting you both through this? I always thought the girls were cramping her style, anyway. Why doesn't she just make some kind of time and schedule arrangement and be done with it?"

"Because she's determined to punish me. Her one goal right now is to make me suffer, just because I love my daughters. She knows that they mean more than life to me."

Twenty-Five

After introducing Sarah Rand to Ted, Léa sat back and let the attorney do all the talking. For almost forty-five minutes, the woman explained to Ted the problems she'd discovered in reading the transcripts of the first trial. Sarah talked about the possibility of key evidence that might never have been passed from the prosecutor to the defense team. She emphasized the importance of time in the appeal process, and how he should not let any more of it expire.

With the exception of a brief glance at the bandages on Léa's head when he'd first been brought into the visiting room, Ted maintained his silence, though Léa had a sense that he was, at least, listening.

As the hands of the clock clicked forward on the wall of the visiting room, Léa began to feel the edges of fear seeping in. Ted was still not responding in any way. As she looked at him sitting on the other side of the glass, she began to think that all her hopes would be trampled in this meeting. Based on her brother's response, how could Sarah ever consider taking the case?

But Léa would not give up on Ted. She had never considered conceding to be an option. Never, during these past two years, had she considered simply accepting Ted's fate. She knew he was not the murderer of his own family. She would *not* let him rot in jail or die of a lethal injection for a crime he did not commit.

Sarah was giving her a look that said "take heart." Then the lawyer nodded slightly and turned back to Ted.

"I've been doing a lot of talking, Ted. Is there anything *you* want to tell me?"

Stony silence was again the convicted man's answer, and Léa's chin sank onto her chest as she closed her eyes. But then again, what power did she have? How could she make a difference when he refused to help her?

"The death of children, under any circumstances, is a horrible thing. It is so sad, so tragic, because it completely defies the natural order of life. Children do not die before their parents." Sarah's softly spoken words brought Léa's head up. "It is well documented that when children are murdered, the parents who are left behind are often completely devastated. It is so horrible, so illogical, so unnatural that the parent sometimes can't even begin to understand *what* has happened, never mind *why*."

Sarah pressed the palm of her hand against the wire-reinforced glass that separated them from Ted.

"I believe them when they say that the grief of a parent for a child is far more intense than any other kind of grief. Sorrow, depression, anger…these are feelings that are difficult to resolve."

"Save your pretty textbook words, counselor." Ted looked directly at Sarah. "You haven't got any idea what I'm going through."

"You're wrong about that, Ted," Sarah answered quietly. "I don't suffer as you do, but after talking to Léa and meeting you, I'd have to be blind not to see what you are going through. It's not only sorrow and anger and depression. There is also the question of blame."

Ted rested his forehead on his fists. Léa could see his eyes were squeezed shut.

"You *do* blame yourself, don't you, Ted?" the attorney persisted. "You have convinced yourself that you should have—that you *could* have—prevented the murder. That it was your fault that your girls were not protected.''

Ted pounded his two fists on the ledge in front of him. "Damn it, it *was* my fault."

Léa felt the tears well up in her eyes. This was the first outburst of anger he'd expressed since this all started the night of the murders.

"How, Ted? How did you have the power to stop the killer?''

"I had the power to stop Marilyn from taking my girls back to the house. I hugged them. I held them in my arms in that restaurant. But then I let her manipulate me. I let her make a scene and grab my children and go. I should have stopped her right then and there, no matter how ugly a public scene that was.''

"But you tried to stop her. You went after her.''

"Emily wanted me. She cried when Marilyn yanked her away from me in the restaurant.''

"You arrived at the house after them. Why didn't you get them then? Why didn't you get the girls out of the house?''

"I couldn't." Ted started crying. "It was on fire. They were in there, and the doors were locked…the place was burning…I couldn't get to them. God, they were right there…and I couldn't reach them.''

Léa could not swallow the sob rising in her throat. After calling on his cell phone for help, he'd repeatedly tried to charge back into the house. But he'd been too late. Ted's clothes had been singed. He'd had burns and cuts on both his hands. He was in shock by the time the police had taken him into custody.

Sarah's blue eyes were misty when they connected with Léa's. It was a silent message, but in that moment Léa knew that the attorney had decided to take the case.

"Someone *did* stab your estranged wife, Ted. Someone *did* set that house on fire. And in the process, that person

killed your children.'' Sarah paused. ''While you refuse
to fight for your innocence, while you insist on doing nothing, while you fail to exercise your right to appeal, the
killer of your children is hiding in the shadows.''

When he closed his eyes again and tried to shut them
out, Sarah pressed her palm against the glass again. ''Ted,
this monster is free, striking again at those you love. Léa,
your sister—the only person you have left in this world—
is the next target.''

Ted's gaze shifted to Léa's head.

''Eighteen stitches in one attack. A concussion. Threatened last night with a knife.'' The lawyer's tone was full
of challenge. ''Survivor guilt is a horrible thing to deal
with, never mind overcome. You have every right to stew
in it forever. But wouldn't you turn back the clock if you
could do it to save your children? Don't you know you
can do it now for Léa, before it's too late?''

It took him a long time to move his gaze from Léa to
Sarah and then back to his sister. ''Is that true, what she's
saying? Something happened to you because of me?''

''Not *because* of you, Ted,'' Léa answered him.
''Someone is trying to hurt me because of the murder. To
Stonybrook, you've already given up, but I haven't. Now
someone wants *me* to shut up and go away, too. But I
won't.''

''You owe it to your kids, Ted. You owe them justice.''

The answer was some time in coming. Léa found herself
holding her breath when he raised his head again to speak.

''What do you want me to do?''

''I said I don't want to talk about it right now.'' Chris
tried to close the bathroom door on his mother's face, but
Patricia Webster caught it and shoved it open.

''You are *not* putting me off any longer, young man.''
She folded her arms across her chest and stood stubbornly
in the doorway. ''You don't get home until one-thirty in

the morning. You're walking. Your car is…somewhere. You've slept most of the morning, missing work. You won't answer any of my questions.''

''I answered your questions last night.'' He glowered at her in the mirror while trying to shave. He'd showered and pulled on a pair of pants, but as soon as he'd opened the door to let the steam out, his mother was there, ready to attack. ''You just didn't like the answers.''

''Who would?'' she snapped. ''What mother would be happy hearing that her own son has been tricked by some scheming bimbo into lending her his car—''

''Don't say that about Heather.'' He pointed the razor at her momentarily before wiping his hand on the towel he had slung over his shoulder. He went back to shaving. ''I told you she'll return it this morning. It was an emergency.''

''What emergency?'' she sneered. ''Emergency to go out with her gangster friends and smoke dope and get drunk? Emergency to spend the night out with her devil cult doing Lord knows what?''

Chris turned on his mother. ''I am sick and tired of you freaking every time I like a girl. It's jealousy, Mom, pure and simple. And it's disgusting. Heather hasn't done a single thing to you. So stop talking about her like she is some monster.''

''But she *is* a monster! She's the devil.'' Mrs. Webster's voice rose. ''I saw her in the hallway last night. I saw the way she was eyeing you. Touching you. She couldn't keep her wicked little hands off you long enough to get out of here first—''

''I was touching *her,* Mom.'' He dropped the razor in the sink. ''Do you really want to know why she took off with my car last night? I tried to fuck her. Against her will, I tried to *fuck* her.''

Patricia's face became ashen, and she took a step back.

"Are you happy now, Mom? Do you have all the answers you were looking for?"

"She lured you out. She enticed you to—"

"Wake up, will you?"

"That's enough!" Chris was shocked to hear his father's stern command.

A moment later, as his wife disappeared down the hall, Allan Webster came to the bathroom door.

"Your car was just returned."

Chris didn't dare speak a word. The anger he saw in his father's face was unlike any he'd ever seen there before.

"Mick Conklin returned it. I just finished speaking to him in my office." The minister spoke slowly, methodically.

Chris noted with shock that his father's hands were doubled into fists.

"Make yourself decent…on the outside, at least…and come down to my office. You and I have a great many things to discuss."

"On top of all that, no independent psychiatric examinations were ever done. Ted has so much working for him in the appeal process. And this time, before he goes to court again, we'll make sure that he receives the treatment he needs." Sarah patted Léa's hand reassuringly. "We want him strong and competent and completely prepared to aid in his own defense."

"I am still a little dumbfounded at how you were able to break through that shell he'd built around himself."

"Not me, Léa. He came out of it because of you."

She knew better than to believe that. Sarah Rand had done her homework. The lawyer had known she needed to focus totally on Ted's grief for his daughters. By pulling that block from the wall supporting his depression, the whole structure had come down.

Curiously, Mick had known it would be this way. He'd suggested that she fire the other lawyer. Whether Sarah Rand worked out or not, he'd felt that she needed new representation. He was right.

Sarah pulled her car into the first available parking spot across the street from the building where her office was located. Léa had met her here this morning, and they'd ridden over to see Ted together.

"Are you sure I can't drop you at your doctor's office?"

Léa shook her head and smiled. "You've done so much already. When Mick and Heather dropped me off this morning, he was planning on coming back and picking me up. He is insistent about playing the part of my bodyguard until Dusty Norris is arrested. Not that I'm complaining!"

"I know exactly what you mean." Sarah laughed as the two of them got out of the car. "Sometime, when we can get together just to socialize, I'll tell you about the week in my life when I was supposedly dead and trying to hide with Owen."

"Mick mentioned it to me. Sounds like a horrendous experience."

"It was pretty bad, but I can see now that it turned out to be the start of something incredible." They left the parking lot and started crossing the street. "Talk about incredible—this guy was not supposed to come for me until one o'clock. A whole hour early."

Léa had no difficulty recognizing Owen Dean, waiting by the crosswalk. No one else passing on the street had any difficulty recognizing him, either.

Sarah had barely stepped onto the sidewalk before her husband drew her into his arms and kissed her.

"Sorry, we haven't seen each other since this morning," he said to Léa, as Sarah tried to regain her professional composure. The movie star-turned-producer smiled broadly and extended a hand in Léa's direction. "You must be Ms. Hardy."

"Léa." She shook his hand. It was fascinating to see the transformation in Sarah now that she was with her husband. The tough attorney had been replaced by a blushing woman who was obviously very much in love.

Despite the polite introductions, Owen's eyes never strayed too far from his wife, either. They made a stunning couple.

"I was talking to Mick on the phone this morning," he said as soon as Sarah had pulled herself from his arms. Léa noted that she managed to keep him happy by holding hands. "We thought maybe the four of us could get together for a drink or something over the weekend. Of course, my wife can only drink milk."

Sarah jabbed him in the arm.

"Okay, a milk shake."

She shook her head and smiled. "We only found out yesterday that we're expecting. For the most private guy in the world, he's become the biggest blabbermouth."

"You know there are no secrets. The tabloids probably knew before we did." He stole another kiss. "Besides, I had to tell Mick this morning when I talked to him about another addition."

"You are incorrigible, Owen Dean." Sarah turned to Léa. "The most important thing is that this will not affect what I'll be doing for Ted."

"I know that." She brushed the attorney's arm gently. "And that's great news. I'm so happy for you both."

They all turned as Mick's Volvo stopped in the street near the sidewalk. His door opened and his smiling face appeared above the roof of the car.

Léa quickly made some arrangements with Sarah about when they'd be talking again and rushed to the waiting car. Mick was waving and exchanging pleasantries with the complaining drivers as they tried to maneuver around his double-parked vehicle.

"I'm getting pretty good at blocking traffic these days."

He kissed her long and hard before moving the car, to the obvious amusement of Sarah and Owen.

For an insane moment, as Léa watched him concentrating on the traffic, an image of being pregnant with Mick's child rushed through her mind. She quickly tried to erase the unlikely vision.

"So tell me," he said impatiently, giving her a quick glance, "how did it go with Ted?"

"First, please tell me that Heather is not home alone."

"She's not home alone. After we dropped you off, we stopped and bought her a cell phone. After that, I dropped her off at my office. She's charging me an arm and a leg to do some filing for my office manager."

Léa had heard a brief version of what had happened to Heather last night from Mick before the teenager came down for breakfast. It was horrible to think that Dusty had threatened Heather, too. Even with Max around, she didn't want her alone for a second on that street.

"But what about the meeting with Ted?"

Léa filled him in about what had transpired at the prison. As she finished, though, she recalled the telephone discussion that she'd had with Sarah's office manager earlier this morning, before she even met with the attorney.

"Have you made some financial arrangement for Ted's legal fees without telling me?"

"What do you mean?"

Léa stared at Mick's profile. "I was told not to worry about the fees. That they were all taken care of. Sarah is quickly becoming one of the top attorneys in the region, and I would never have approached her if I thought she would consider it a charity case."

"She can afford to work on this case without emptying your pockets. Think of the publicity when she gets your brother off."

"Mick." She leaned toward him. "Remember our conversation about trust? I need to know what you have done.''

Frowning, he pulled the car into the nearest parking lot and turned off the engine. Léa tried to restrain her own jumble of emotions and waited until he swung around to face her.

''I called Sarah after seeing what I thought was a very suspicious case of vandalism at my job site on Sunday. The place that was wrecked used to be rented by Marilyn. I felt our police chief was brushing it off, but I had no doubt that it was somehow connected to the murder trial.''

''What did you ask Sarah to do?''

''Nothing. I simply called and offered the information I had…including things I knew about Marilyn's life that had not surfaced during the trial.''

''Is this why she called me on Monday? Because of your relationship with Owen and her?''

''No. I believe she called you because she thinks your brother has a valid case.''

Léa tried to keep in mind the effect of all of this on Ted's welfare. She was having a hard time, though, getting around her own feelings about just being another one of those women who took Mick for his money.

''But what about her fees?''

He turned and looked straight ahead.

''Mick, I'm not angry with you. In fact, I'm very grateful.'' She placed her hand on his arm. ''But I need to know what I owe you. I intend to pay it all back.''

''That's something I'll settle with Ted—but not before he gets out, that is.''

His answer threw her for a loop.

''That might take some time.''

''I can afford to wait.''

''Mick, be reasonable.''

''I am.'' He took her hand tightly in his own. ''You know, there is a reason why I didn't form an opinion about the trial or get involved sooner. After my divorce, I went out with Marilyn a few times. That was enough for me. To this day, I remember very clearly what a piece of work she was. Marilyn was capable of making a perfectly normal person crazy enough to want to punch her lights out. And I'll tell you something else. I don't believe she was capable of a monogamous relationship. In fact, I think she met Ted on one of our last dates. She was something else.''

Léa had always kept a safe distance from Ted and Marilyn's marriage, fearful of the very things Mick was saying.

"She used people, openly, and it seemed to me that any number of men in town might have wanted to kill her. But they arrested Ted, and I thought maybe he'd really done it. What I couldn't understand, though, was leaving his children in the house.''

"What changed your mind?'' she asked softly.

His intense blue eyes met hers. "You. Your belief in him was the start. Then, when I really looked around me and saw the attitudes of some of the people involved, I thought this could have been another case of rushing to justice.''

Léa's fingers remained entwined with his. "I can only say that I'm blown away by all you have done. By all your generosity. The house I'm trying to sell belongs to both of us. It's Ted's only asset right now, too. Once I sell it, I want you to accept—''

"No,'' he said stubbornly. "I don't want to talk money with you. I don't want to think how much we owe each other. What we have between us has nothing to do with sympathy or generosity.''

This close, Léa not only drowned in the deep sea blue of his eyes, but she found herself looking into his soul, reaching for his heart.

"I don't know what to say. What to do. I'm sinking.''

"So, go with it.'' He kissed her lips tenderly. "We're sinking together.''

Twenty-Six

Joanna nearly danced as she hung up the phone. Calming herself down, she did a ten-second cleanup of the workbench, put her tools in the correct drawer and whipped off the apron she was wearing. She ran a hand down the front of her new green flowered sundress to smooth out the wrinkles.

Gwen was behind the cash register in the front of the shop, tallying an order, when she came out. The older sister looked up in surprise as Joanna burst into the room.

"I'm going out for lunch. Do you need anything while I'm gone?"

"Where are you going?"

"I don't know. Maybe to the Grille. Maybe to that new Mexican restaurant near the highway." Joanna slipped behind her sister to get her purse and her keys.

"Who are you going with?"

"Andrew." She hadn't paused. She hadn't stopped and looked at Gwen to gauge her sister's reaction. She'd just said it, and she felt great about it. "I called and asked him if I could take him out for lunch, and he said yes."

"Joanna, I've had four calls in the past half hour for new orders. I have a delivery coming at twelve-thirty. I need you to stay here and take care of them."

The subtle change in Gwen's tone was repulsively clear. Joanna felt as if she'd been kicked in the stomach, but she was not stopping now. Her hands closed around the keys in the drawer, and she picked up her purse off the shelf under the counter. She turned to her sister.

"Sorry, my date can't wait."

"Joanna, I am running a business here. There are expectations—"

"I quit," she said simply, starting around Gwen.

The older woman backed up, blocking her. "You can't quit. This is as much your business as mine. You can't just walk out and quit."

"Yes, I can. Just watch me." She wasn't going to get angry. She wasn't going to lose her temper.

"But this is our livelihood. You can't—"

"*Your* livelihood," she corrected. "Your life might be tied to this business, but let's not forget that this is *all* yours. God knows, you've reminded me of that many times in the past."

When Gwen started to speak, Joanna raised a hand. "I'm not being critical of you over that. I think it's great that you have something that you feel so passionately about. But your lifestyle is not for me. I'm turning thirty next year, and there are a heck of a lot more things I want to do with my life than just cutting and arranging flowers."

When she attempted to pass again, Gwen blocked her exit. "You'll throw everything away just to go and have sex with...with some guy?"

"That guy has a name, Gwen. His name is Andrew. Andrew Rice. And it's not sex. We're not a couple of teenagers who have to run off to the barn." She shook her head. "We're both way past that stage."

"So what are you trying to tell me?" she snapped. "You're just going to go and flaunt your affair in front of everyone in Stonybrook?"

"What we do is nobody's business, Gwen."

"You've got to be kidding me!" she responded with a mirthless laugh. "You should know very well how they'll behave. They'll ruin you and Andrew both. They'll ruin me. We've been here before, Joanna. Or have you forgotten so quickly?''

"So quickly?'' she challenged. "God, Gwen! Listen to yourself. Cate is gone. Our sister is dead. But you can't stop blaming everyone else for what happened to her. You've never forgotten.''

"How can I forget when I still have you to worry about?'' She threw the order pad she still clutched in her hand onto the floor. "Cate tried to be different. Look what they did to her. You're trying to do the same thing and I'm going to lose you, too.''

Joanna shook her head disbelievingly. "Nobody did anything to Cate. She was a lesbian. That was who she was. And the choices she made were her own. For all her life, she wanted to escape this town. Like a lot of people, she also fought with bouts of depression from the time she was a teenager. Why don't you remember any of that?''

"Because it's not the truth. Marilyn started everything with her lies. And then the rest of them jumped on the wagon, and…''

Joanna looked down at the keys in her hand and listened to her sister's all-too-familiar rant about how everyone else was responsible for the fate of their sister. Jo had listened to this same broken record too long, though.

"But I'm *not* going to let the same thing happen to you. Do you hear me? They are *not* going to run you down because of a fling with some black man.''

Joanna pushed her way angrily past her sister and stalked toward the door.

"I'm leaving, Gwen.''

"You can't go.''

"You just don't get it.'' Jo paused briefly by the shop door. "It wasn't Marilyn or the rest of this town that pushed Cate out. It was you, Gwen. You and your ugly, narrow, prejudiced thinking. It was you and your denial of who she really was. Well, guess what? I'm not going to let you do the same thing to me."

"Would you please let Stephanie know that I called?" There was a pause. "Yes, Léa Hardy…"

Heather stood outside the doorway of her father's office, waiting for Léa to finish her call. There was something very right about seeing her here in their house, sitting in her father's chair. It just seemed so completely natural, coming downstairs in the morning and seeing her puttering around the house. Last night, before going to bed, Heather had gone to the guest room and stared for a few minutes at Léa while she slept. The whole time, she was thinking how wonderful it'd be if she stuck around.

They had taken the bandages off Léa's head, but a long nonstick pad, held on with tape, still protected the stitches. Heather couldn't wait until they arrested Dusty. It was time the creep paid up. When Léa put down the phone, the teenager burst in.

"You called the Slaters? You actually talked to them?"

"I talked to Bob."

"Wow!" Heather sat on her father's desk. "How come you called them? I thought all they did was go around badmouthing you and Ted."

"I don't know anything about that." Léa stood up. "But Stephanie didn't look too good yesterday when I saw her downtown, and I haven't been able to stop thinking about it. Anyway, this is my new motto. Don't waste energy worrying when there is something you can do about it."

"I like that!" Heather said enthusiastically. "And on the same note, I want you to know I've made an appointment for us."

"Appointment for what?"

"For haircuts," Heather said, hopping off the desk. "Actually, I'm hoping that Sheila will do a little more

than just give me a haircut. I'm getting a little sick of this
purple hair.''

"What's the next color?'' Léa asked.

"I was thinking about something of a checkered design,
with red and green on top.'' She struck a pose. "And
maybe some neon striping down the back.''

"You are a fashion statement, babe.''

"Not just a statement. I am a goddess!''

"Okay, goddess.'' Léa pushed Heather out of Mick's
office and into the kitchen. "So, do I have time to get
some work done next door before the appointment?''

"Sorry, but I'm afraid you don't. Dad said he'll be back
about five, so I had to make the appointment early enough
for us to have time to get really adventurous.''

"This is sort of like a 'girls' afternoon out.' You know,
I don't think I've ever had one of those.''

It was impulsive and mushy, but Heather didn't care.
She gave Léa a quick hug.

"Me, neither.'' She quickly pulled back and reached for
the fridge door, taking a can of soda out.

There was a long silence behind her. She didn't want
to turn around, thinking that maybe she'd choked Léa up
again. She somehow managed to do that to her a lot.

"I think I'll get my hair done however you have yours
done,'' Léa said finally. "And maybe if we have time after
Sheila's, we can go to one of those places in the mall
where I can get a couple more holes in my ear, too. I don't
know about this navel ring…but heck, I'll try it. Eyebrow
rings. A stud for the nose. The whole nine yards.''

"Now, why would you want to do all that?''

"To look like you, of course.''

"But *why?*''

"Because you are my idol.''

Heather couldn't hold back her smile. "Yeah, right.''

"I *am* proud of you,'' Léa said softly. "And I'm so
impressed. I have to tell you that you got it together much

faster and a lot better than I ever did. I could do a lot worse than imitating you.''

Heather leaned against the sink and felt herself filling up with emotion.

''You're strong and brave and good…aside from being a goddess.''

Léa walked over to the kitchen table and fished around in her pocketbook for a couple of seconds before taking a bottle of pills out. Heather knew what it was before she handed it to her.

''I found this in the carriage house yesterday afternoon. I think they're yours.''

Heather stared down at the full bottle of sleeping pills. Neither of them spoke for a long moment.

''You know, when I was a teenager—a little younger than you—I tried to commit suicide, too.''

Léa stretched out her arms and turned her palms face up. Faint white slash marks were still visible on her wrists.

''I was lonely and very depressed. Ted had just gone to college. I loved my aunt, but I decided she would be better off without me.'' She dropped her hands. ''I was very lucky that she found me. But it took a long time—and therapy, when we could afford it—for me to recover. Even so, *you* were the one who was able to help me face that kitchen, and the memory of my parents' deaths.'' Tears were glistening in her hazel eyes. ''I admire you, Heather. Now, is it asking too much if I want to be just like you?''

Heather hugged her fiercely, dashing away her own tears.

''I don't need these anymore,'' she finally managed to say. ''I was so sure I wanted to die. I…I gave away all these favorite things I had. I even wrote everyone a letter. I walked into your carriage house ready to end it all. But now, I…I don't know what I could have been thinking. The problems I thought I had…well, they just seem to be nothing now.''

"No. The problems I think you've been dealing with are real, but you've somehow gotten yourself to a place where you are working your way through them. This is what life is all about. Challenges and changes. We have to face them. We have to make ourselves survive the tough times so that we can enjoy the good moments around the corner."

Heather wiped the tears off her face and uncapped the bottle of pills. She dumped them all into the sink and ran the water. Watching them disappear down the drain, she decided to tell Léa about last night.

"You say I'm a good person, but that's not the feeling I got when I met Chris's mom."

"What happened?"

Heather told Léa about Patricia Webster's treatment of her. She even went on and described Chris's attitude and how he'd been ready to take advantage of her in more ways than one. She didn't hold anything back, either, as she had when she'd talked to her father, and she told Léa so.

"You didn't tell your father about Chris trying to take a picture of you?"

Heather shook her head. "Dad would have really hurt him. As calm and as collected as he is, I have no doubt that he would have lost his head and maybe done some damage."

"But that's maybe what Chris needs to learn a lesson."

Heather looked up in surprise. Léa looked upset. "What happened to your compassionate understanding of teenagers?"

"Hey, this is different. Chris is messing around with my idol." She took Heather's hands in hers. "But seriously, I have very little compassion when it comes to anyone who tries to abuse and manipulate others."

Heather pretended that she was considering that information, instead of showing how happy she was that Léa would say that she was her idol, even jokingly.

"I think I took care of it, though," she said finally.

"Listen, if he comes near you again—"

"I'll tell Dad everything. I promise." She didn't want to see Léa this upset. She glanced down at her watch. "Hey, we're going to be late for our appointment."

It took Léa a minute to compose herself. Then she grabbed her purse.

"So, what color did we finally decide on?" she asked Heather.

"I've changed my mind again. I want to have the same color hair as you have. Being an idol has its responsibilities."

"How are you boys doing this afternoon?"

Sheila didn't wait for the answers from the half-dozen police officers and office staff, but marched right past the Official Business Only sign and down the hallway to the office of the chief of police.

Tom Whiting was inside talking to his superior. Both men's heads snapped up in surprise at seeing her.

"Sheila, what are you doing here?"

"Tom, will you excuse us for a minute?"

At Sheila's request, the young officer looked at the chief, who nodded. As he left the office, she shut the door behind him and then proceeded to close the blinds on the large office window that looked out over the desks of nearly everyone in the department.

"What's going on, honey?" Rich asked, concerned, half rising from his chair.

Sheila went around to him and shoved him right back down in his seat. "Spill it."

"Spill what?"

She planted her hands on her hips. "I just spent the past two hours cutting and coloring the hair of two of the nicest women that have ever stepped foot in this sorry little burg.''

''They must have been *really* nice.''

''No cracks out of you, or I'm giving away my new bunny costume to the Salvation Army.''

He opened his mouth to say something but wisely closed it.

''I want to know what the heck you're doing to help Léa Hardy.''

''Honey, that's still—''

''Don't give me that honey stuff! The woman was knocked in the head and threatened with a knife in *your* town. And then Heather, that poor child, was scared out of her wits by the same brute.'' She glowered at him. ''Now, I want to know right this minute if you are doing one damn thing about it.''

''Honey, I—''

''Are you going to pick up Dusty or not?''

''I am.''

''Is that a *When I get to it, I am?* or a *Right now, I am?*''

''Right now, I am. Starting last night, when Mick called me. There is some serious shit going on around here, Sheila. We already have a warrant out for Dusty's arrest.''

He wrapped his hand around her wrist and tugged once. Sheila let herself land on his lap. ''Now, was that the only reason why you came to see me?''

She stopped his hand from roaming. ''Does this mean that you believe what she says?''

''I believe now that somebody is trying to hurt her.''

''What else?'' She let him slip his hand under her shirt.

''I believe she didn't come back to Stonybrook to cause trouble.''

''You're getting there.'' She guided his hand to the clasp of her bra, and he undid it. Her breast came to life in his hand. ''Keep going.''

"I believe there is some nutcase out there trying to cause trouble by sending old pictures of Marilyn and her...playmates around."

"You mean somebody other than Dusty?"

"Tom and I were working on that when you came in."

Sheila shot to her feet. Pulling her shirt up to her chin, she very slowly redid the clasp of her bra. Rich's eyes watched the slow movements of her hands.

"Well, you get *lots* of work done, and I'll have a real treat for Little Chief when you get home tonight." She gave him a deep, mouthwatering kiss before sauntering out of his office.

"Sorry, gang, but no slacking off this afternoon," she announced to the room. "You kids have lots of work to do."

Twenty-Seven

As usual, there was a line of people outside Hughes Grille. While Léa and Mick waited on one of the park benches, Heather went in to check where their name was on the list.

"I don't think it was such a good idea to come here for dinner," Léa said softly. "Everybody is staring at me."

"They're staring because you look absolutely gorgeous." Mick pulled Léa closer to him on the bench. The knee-length linen dress she was wearing climbed up a couple of inches, and he admired the stretch of smooth leg. He left his arm wrapped around her shoulder. "And you look sexy as hell, too."

She smiled and looked up and their gazes locked. "Why didn't you tell me sooner that you like short hair?"

"It's not just the hair. It's the rest of you. Do you realize it's been twenty-seven hours since the last time we had sex?"

"That long?"

"Yes, indeed. And you're not helping matters at all, I want you to know. I almost lost it when you were emptying the dryer before we left the house."

"I was looking for my bra and underwear. They somehow managed to get tangled up with your boxers in the laundry." She put her hand innocently on his knee. "I could have used your help."

His arm tightened around her, drawing Léa even closer.

His mouth hovered just above her smiling lips. "What do you say we take a quick walk to my office? It's only on the next block."

Her hand moved an inch up the inside of his leg. "I don't think, in your condition, you're decent enough for us to walk in public."

"And getting less decent by the moment. We could sneak through the park."

"Heather's coming."

She tried to pull back, but Mick kissed her lips hard before releasing her. Léa was blushing when he finally let her go. "Just a down payment for later."

"Can't you two keep your mouths and hands off each other?" Heather grumbled, shaking her head. "I mean, jeez, people, we're in public here."

"Just because you got your hair color back to normal and got rid of a couple dozen rings and studs, that doesn't make you the boss."

Heather beamed down at her father. "Of course it does. With my hair short like this, Sheila says I'm the 'very head off of Mick.' Don't you just love it?" She touched her short locks of sandy-blond hair.

"I do." He took her hand and pulled her down next to them. "Of course, I can see I have years of worrying ahead of me about all the boys who'll be chasing after you."

"Don't worry, I won't be dating again until I'm thirty."

"Yeah, I'll be sure to remind you of that next week." He ruffled her hair. "So what's the wait?"

"Forty-five minutes. I think it's only because my last name is Conklin, though." Heather glanced around at the groups of people waiting before them. "You know, I've been out of Stonybrook for only two years, but I don't remember any of these people. Do you recognize any, Léa?"

"Not a soul. People's looks change a lot over the years."

"Actually, there are very few people still around who were here twenty years ago." Mick had been waiting for the right opportunity for making Léa understand this. "With the exception of a handful of diehards, Stonybrook is filling up with young professional families who don't know and don't care what the cheap gossip was around here five, ten or twenty years ago. These days, everybody here starts fresh and with a clean slate."

He held Léa's gaze.

"Are you hoarding the whole bench or can we sit down with you?"

Mick smiled up at Andrew Rice, who was looking particularly content in the company of Joanna Miller. They were waiting for a table, too, and after a few minutes of catching up on old times, they changed their reservation to have dinner all together.

Walking inside the restaurant a half hour later, Mick couldn't have been happier about this little change in their plans. This was part of everything he wanted Léa to see about Stonybrook.

She wasn't an outsider. She had old friends, like Andrew, and she would make new friends, too, like Joanna, if she gave Stonybrook a chance.

As he watched her walk across the restaurant ahead of him, Mick realized that he very much wanted her to stay. He wanted Léa to give the town—and the two of them—a chance.

Chris stood behind the ornate Oriental screen that shielded the kitchen door from the dining room, and stared through a small opening between the panels.

Heather looked very different with the new hairdo, but not the way she used to a couple of years ago. She looked older now—and very hot—in the short, button-front dress.

She'd dumped the purple hair and the black outfit. He wondered if she was wearing her belly ring under that light blue dress.

The five of them were sitting at a table near the window. Heather was sitting next to her father and Léa Hardy. He had come out the minute he heard the waitress tell the chef who the order was for. He watched them carefully for a few minutes. Their meal hadn't been delivered. Then, just as he'd hoped, Heather got up and started for the ladies' room.

The hallway that led to the rest rooms was off the bar. Beyond the two doors and the pay phone, another door led to the kitchen, and Chris went back through the kitchen and came out that door. By the time he'd gotten there, though, Heather had disappeared into the rest room.

He waited, every nerve in his body jumping. Some guy came out of the men's room and squeezed by Chris. He could hear laughter coming from the tables in the bar, and heard Brian talking to the bartender.

As soon as she stepped out, he started in immediately.

"Heather, I've been trying to call you all day, but you weren't home and I didn't want to leave a message."

Her look was stone cold.

"I am so sorry about last night."

"I don't want to talk about it." She tried to get by, but he blocked her.

"But we have to. I just feel terrible for acting like that. I was such a jerk."

"Forget it." She tried to pass him, but he grabbed her arm.

"It was just everything. From the way my mother acted to what I thought would happen...to...jeez, it was just everything. And I want to make it up to you."

"No, Chris. You can't make it up to me. We're done. Finished. Kaput."

She tried to pull her arm free, but he grabbed the other

arm, too. "Come on, Heather. I said I made a mistake. I'm sorry."

"I forgive you." She tried to twist herself free. "Let me go."

"Not until you tell me when we can go out again."

He brought her closer to his body. Her arms became trapped against his chest. As she struggled, he felt himself getting hard.

"Come on. Last night wasn't all bad," he whispered against her ear. He ground his hips against her. "You liked *some* of the stuff we did."

She stepped hard on his foot and managed to pull away. "You are sick, Chris. You need some serious help."

He contemplated reaching for her again, but a woman was coming toward the rest rooms.

"Don't *ever* come near me again, Chris," Heather hissed, passing him.

As she disappeared back into the dining room, he hammered his hand against the wall.

"Shit. Shit. Shit."

Rubbing his hand over his face, Chris shoved open the door into the men's room. Crossing to the sinks, he turned on the water and splashed handfuls of it on his face and neck.

His head felt like it was about to explode, and he turned and kicked at one of the stall doors. The thing buckled as it slammed back against the wall of the next stall. He stood stock-still for a long moment, watching it swing crookedly on its hinges. Forcing himself to calm down, he gradually regained control over himself.

He had to take a leak and went to the urinal.

She'll come around, he thought. She liked him. She was hot for him.

He washed his hands, dried them and started for the door. As he reached for it, though, the door flew open in his face. Before he could react, Mick Conklin had him by the throat and was jacking him up against the wall.

"You listen to me, you little scumbag." Conklin's face was about an inch from his own. "I am about a hairbreadth away from breaking you in two. Do you understand that?"

"Yes, sir. I understand, sir. I've told Heather I'm sorry. Honest."

"You're not half as sorry as you'd be if I hadn't given her my word I wouldn't turn you into a goddamn grease spot."

"I...I'm sorry. Really. I don't know what came over me. I...I'm sorry for everyth—"

"Clearly, talking to your father wasn't enough. So let me tell you right now."

Heather's father slammed him hard against the wall to make his point, and Chris felt the air knocked from his body.

"If you ever come near Heather again, I will break you into sixteen little pieces and put your head on my flagpole. Am I making myself perfectly clear?"

"Yes, sir...flagpole."

Mick Conklin shoved him toward the urinals, and Chris staggered before regaining his balance and backing away. "Never! You don't come within a mile of her."

"Yes, sir. I'm sorry. I won't."

Chris cringed as Conklin kicked a trash can across the bathroom before turning and going out the door.

Léa found Mick in his study, poring over some papers on his desk. Judging from the tension in his jaw and the stiffness in his shoulders, though, she doubted he was getting anything done.

He looked up at her when she walked into the room. "How is she?"

"Still angry at Chris. And worried about you. And the dating timeline has been pushed back till she turns forty.

But I think she feels very good about herself and the way she handled it.'' She moved behind his chair and started kneading his shoulders. ''How are you?''

''Still pissed as hell at that son of a bitch.''

Léa kissed the top of his head and continued to work on his shoulders. ''Heather is also proud of the way *you* handled everything. She was especially proud when, after talking to Chris, you came out and we all stayed for dinner, with no ugly public scene.''

''*Did* we stay for dinner?''

''Yes, we did.''

''Did I eat?''

''Heather and I fought off Andrew and split your dinner between us.''

''That's good. I do remember talking to Brian Hughes before we left. I believe he said he'll send me a bill for any damages to the bathroom.''

''I'm glad to hear that.'' She massaged the back of his neck. ''We don't want to have to bail you out of jail.''

He leaned his head back against her stomach and closed his eyes when Léa started gently massaging his temples and his scalp. ''So you weren't upset that I lost it?''

''When I saw Heather come back to the table as upset as she was, I was amazed you let him walk away in one piece.'' She rubbed her chin against his short hair. ''But there will be consequences that Chris will have to live with, at least for this summer. Andrew was angry enough that I think he'll fire him. More than likely, Brian Hughes got the gist of what happened tonight, so I'll be surprised if he doesn't let him go, too. Through your direct intervention and everyone else's secondary reinforcement, Chris *will* learn a lesson.''

''Do you deal with many like him in your job?''

''Sometimes, but they're few and far between.''

''What happens to kids like him?''

"For the most part, they reform, with enough education, pressure and guidance."

"And those that don't?"

"You're going to drive yourself crazy thinking about that." Léa leaned around so she could look into his face. "Chris was an exception. Heather will meet and go out with lots of boys her age, and they'll be model citizens."

"After I'm done with them."

She smiled and brushed a kiss against his forehead. "You're a great father, Mick."

"I used to be better. I do really well with babies." He trapped her hand on his shoulder. Léa inwardly shivered at the way his eyes studied her face. "I was envious today."

"You were? Envious of what?"

"Sarah and Owen are expecting a baby."

"I heard about that."

"Maybe we could have one."

Léa was speechless. She felt suspended in air. Frozen in time and space. Mick drew her around the chair. She found her knees wobbling, though the butterflies in her stomach were in a full waltz. He pulled her onto his lap.

"Your new hairdo hides the stitches." He played with the bangs on her forehead before stroking her face. "I shocked you."

"You…I…"

He kissed her lips so tenderly that Léa thought she would melt. When he drew back, she was leaning into him.

"I love you, Léa."

She closed her eyes to hold back the sudden surge of emotion. His words made her heart dance. But it was to a song she hardly knew. As she felt the music in her soul swell to a crescendo, she realized that she'd been waiting a lifetime to hear those words. Her parents, Ted, Aunt Janice…none of them had ever said those words. Their affection was understood, but the words were never spoken. Not once.

"My life and Heather's changed the moment you walked in here." As he spoke, she looked into his misty deep blue eyes. "Because of you, we're beginning to find the family closeness that we'd lost. You've helped us to discover what it is like to love again—as a family. We were just going through the motions before—and failing—and we didn't even know it."

His arms wrapped around her, and he pulled her tighter against him.

"In my entire life, I've never wanted anyone to be part of my life more than you. Even with Heather's mother, it was nothing like this."

He kissed the tears from her cheeks.

"With you, I'm finding myself dreaming again. Thinking of kids that we could have or adopt. Thinking of what it will be like watching Heather bloom into womanhood. Thinking of you and me making love on the dryer…and on the stove…and the kitchen table. I even think of us growing old together and me still chasing you around the house."

She laughed through the tears. He kissed her again.

"I don't want you to give me an answer now." He smiled guiltily. "I don't want to risk getting rejected, because you have too many other things on your plate right now. But I want you to think about it. About us. Will you do that?"

Léa nodded and then kissed him with all the passion in her heart. With all the love she had for him but was afraid to put into words.

The heat of their kiss spread through her and she knew he was feeling it, too.

"Would you like to come to my bed tonight? It doesn't have a buzzer like the dryer, but it's wide enough to maneuver around in comfortably."

"Actually, I like the idea of the stove the best. There's something very adventurous-sounding about it." She brushed kisses on his cheek, along the taut muscles of his neck. "But the kitchen table is definitely a close second."

"Is that right?"

She stifled a laugh as Mick scooped her up and carried her out of the office and into the kitchen. He kicked the door shut and grinned at her mischievously.

"What'll it be, ma'am? The burners or the table?"

Léa reached over and turned off the light switch. The light from the moon and the neighboring houses blanketed them in a soft glow. He stood her on her feet, and her hand caressed the muscles of his chest and stomach and finally the hard shape pressing against the front of his pants.

"I'm betting you can manage both...*and* the bed."

"Then how can we lose," he said, scooping her up in his arms again and laying her on the table.

Twenty-Eight

Before the chief of police could say a word, Brian felt that cold, sick feeling settle into the pit of his stomach. It was early Wednesday morning, and for two days he had failed to find even a single bit of news of Jason. As far as anyone knew, the younger man had never left Stonybrook. And yet, he seemed to have vanished off the face of the planet.

The last place he'd been seen was here at the Grille.

The restaurant was not open yet. Only the kitchen staff were working, and Brian could hear them laughing and talking in the back as he took Chief Weir and the uniformed officer to his office behind the bar.

He was glad the police had come here. He couldn't deal with hearing news of Jason in their apartment. Brian needed to be surrounded by his work. This place had been his escape so often in the past. The Grille was the only thing that had kept him sane during these difficult days.

All the picture frames with Jason's photos sat in a pile against a wall. He hadn't been able to deal with his face looking at him.

Brian sat at his desk. The two officers sat in chairs between him and the door.

The chief started in immediately. "Late last night, Jason's car was found in the lake. He was inside."

Brian closed his eyes as the grief overtook him.

"After just the initial stages of the investigation, we

suspect that the car and the body have been submerged in the water for maybe two days or so. Of course, after the autopsy we'll have more definite answers.''

"What happened?'' Brian managed to get out. "Did he drive off the road?''

Rich's voice was gentle. "We suspect it's a homicide. The car was found in the water near the town boat launch. There are lacerations on the back of the head. Our initial guess is that some type of blunt-force injury might have been the cause of death.''

"And not from an accident in the car.''

"No.''

Brian's head sank in his hands. He continued to rub the aching pain in his forehead as Rich went on to explain what was in the works right now. They were expecting him to come to the hospital and make a positive identification before the autopsy.

"Do you have any idea what time he left here on Sunday night or where he was headed?''

All the strength was draining out of Brian, and he was feeling sick to his stomach. He tried to draw a deep breath, but he only did so with difficulty. He had no doubt that as Jason's lover he could be the prime suspect. He pushed himself to his feet and went to the small safe he kept on the floor behind the door. The uniformed officer's eyes watched his every movement.

He opened the safe and took out the envelope of pictures. He handed them to Rich and sank into his chair again.

"Jason was looking for whoever it is that's sending these…these pictures to me. I got them in the mail at the end of last week.''

The police chief took out the photos and leafed through them. His face creased into a frown.

"These pictures were sent to you? Not to Jason.''

"That's correct.''

"Was he being blackmailed, Brian?"

"No." He smiled bitterly. "They came the same way Marilyn sent them the first time. Just the pictures, with her best wishes. That bitch was sick. She was pissed off because I had sided with Ted before her divorce. Because of that, she just wanted to make me suffer. To see Jason and me break up."

"But you didn't break up."

"No. I took him back. I—" He shook his head and forced back his tears.

"Can I take these?"

Brian nodded. "Chief, I don't know who this asshole is or why he's sending them. But Jason was convinced that he'd figured it out."

"But you're sure Marilyn was the one who sent you these pictures before?"

"Yes."

"What was your reaction when you saw them?"

"I was ready to kill the bitch, and Jason along with her."

"Did you?"

Brian looked up at the police chief. "No. Somebody else took care of that before me."

Stephanie pushed the pack of cigarettes away on the table. "I was going to call you back, but I didn't have your number."

Bob motored his wheelchair in through the back door. He noticed immediately how relaxed his wife looked. She was sitting in her bathrobe at the kitchen table, a steaming cup of coffee in front of her.

"Yes. Much better. I'm…I'm grateful for…well, for the way you stepped in like that." Pause. "Nonetheless, I don't think I could have managed, myself." Longer pause. "I know. I think so, too."

Bob slid the back door shut as he realized Stephanie

had turned the air-conditioning on. He wheeled his chair around again and watched curiously as she talked. Whatever the person on the phone said, it actually brought a momentary glimmer of a smile to her lips.

"Thank you. Perhaps…perhaps we should." Pause. "All right. How long are you staying?"

He moved his chair to the table.

"That would be fine. I could do it next week." Pause. "No, these things are never easy, but you're right…and I'll try." Pause. "Yes. Next week. I'll talk to you then. Goodbye."

Bob watched Stephanie hang up the phone and sit thinking for a moment. When she turned to him, he could see she was feeling quite pleased as a result of the phone call.

"I hope you don't mind me putting the air on," she said to him. "It's supposed to be god-awful hot today."

Bob shrugged. "Wh-who was on the ph-phone?"

"Léa," the older woman replied easily. "She called again to make sure I was okay. We're going out for coffee some time next week."

Bob didn't know what to say. He'd been hesitant even to mention that the Hardy woman had called the day before. So much of Stephanie's anger had been directed toward Léa during the trial. The young woman had been the enemy for so long now. She had been the only constant supporter of Ted from the beginning.

He couldn't understand this, and it must have shown on his face.

"Léa Hardy was the only one in this town who had either the guts or the compassion to come and help me on Monday. Even that kid you've been paying to look after me—what's his name?"

Bob didn't know she had guessed. "T.J."

"Even he wouldn't help me." Stephanie turned away. "I…I have to learn to let go of some things. There is a great deal I need to rethink. Léa has suffered, too. In that alone, we have much in common.''

"Heather and I will be just fine by ourselves. We have Max here, too, to protect us. Mick, you can't take the day off.''

"As a matter of fact, I can. I made a couple of phone calls, and everything is all set.'' He tucked a pair of work gloves into the back pocket of his jeans. "I'm actually itching to get going on a little honest labor. I'm starting on those porch steps this morning.''

As he reached inside one of the kitchen drawers for the key to his toolshed, Léa moved behind him and wrapped her arms around his waist.

"And here I thought you'd be exhausted,'' she whispered. "I was sure I did a good job keeping you up last night.''

Mick caught Léa's arm and brought her around. He pushed her back against the counter, his body pressing intimately against hers.

"A good job keeping me up? Yes.'' He kissed her long and deep. His hands roamed caressingly over the curve of her firm bottom as he felt himself growing hard against her. "Exhausted? I don't think so. It just seems I can't get enough of you.''

She obviously felt it, too, and tore her mouth away. "Your daughter went up to change into a T-shirt and shorts. She'll be back down here any minute.''

"Then we need to negotiate right now about work breaks.'' He pressed his lips to the skin of her neck and inhaled deeply. He loved the fresh smell of her. "I demand a ten o'clock break with the boss.''

"Really. With the boss?''

"That's right. That's nonnegotiable.''

"Okay. And where will we be taking that break?''

"I don't care. We could start trying out the closets upstairs."

She slid out of his arms at the sound of Heather whistling as she came down the stairs. Mick noticed that his daughter had picked up a habit of singing or calling Max or drumming her hands on the walls before coming into a room where he and Léa were alone together. That girl was getting pretty clever about giving them time to pull themselves together.

"I'm ready," the teenager announced, strolling into the kitchen. "And what have you two been up to? Just standing around?"

Léa's blush was always a dead giveaway.

He grinned and ruffled Heather's hair. "Enough yakking. Time to get to work."

They all stopped briefly in the backyard while Mick got his tool belt from his truck. Max was running around, sniffing out the track of every squirrel that had stepped foot in the yard during the night.

"Oh, shoot. I forgot the key," Léa said, running back inside the house to get it. Because of the Dusty incident Monday night, he'd sent over one of his men yesterday to install new locks on Léa's front and back doors.

Slinging the tool belt around his hips, Mick unlocked the shed and took out a long level and a couple of saws.

"Good job sending her to bed early, Dad," Heather said slyly, as soon as Léa was inside. "She not only looks well rested, but about the happiest I've seen her."

Mick couldn't bring himself to look at her. He'd tried reasonably hard to be discreet last night. Léa had slipped out of his bed and into her room about five this morning. The only sleep either of them had last night was after that.

As Léa came out his back door and down the steps, the image of her sprawled naked in his bed flashed in Mick's mind. She had the most beautiful body and the most erotic mouth. And he loved that little sound she made in the back

of her throat when she was ready to climax and how her
hazel eyes got misty and turned a deeper shade. He didn't
even mind it when she looked at him as if he was some
kind of miracle.

Most of all, though, he loved staying inside of her afterward. Deep inside. Feeling as if their two bodies were
one.

"Uh, excuse me." Léa smiled and tugged on his hand,
leading him toward her back door. "It's not break time
yet. Let's go."

"That obvious, huh?"

"As someone said to me recently, it's tattooed on your
forehead."

"What's tattooed on his forehead?"

"His eagerness to fix my front steps," Léa said brightly,
going up to the back door of her house ahead of them.

She stopped abruptly at the door.

"Wait. Heather, stay back."

Mick heard the sharp change in Léa's tone and went
around his daughter and up the steps in two strides. She
hadn't put the key in the door yet, but it was already open.

He looked at the basement window on the left of the
landing and saw it was smashed.

"Heather, go and call the police."

"Dad, don't let Léa go in," the teenager warned before
running back toward their house.

The golden retriever took that moment to race up the
steps and through the door before Mick could grab his
collar. Taking his hammer out of his belt, Mick followed
the dog in. The second door, beyond the mudroom, was
open, too. Inside the kitchen, he stared in stunned disbelief
at the mess. Bright red paint was dripping down from the
ceiling and the walls. There were large dents in the plaster
walls. Deep gouges had been cut into the layers of old
paint on the cabinets.

Max was sniffing a yellow puddle on the floor, but without getting that close Mick could tell it was urine.

"But I...I haven't done anything to him. Why is he doing this?"

He turned around at the sound of Léa's wavering voice. She was frozen in the doorway. Shock was etched on her face, and he pulled her into his arms.

"This all has to do with Marilyn. They'll find him, my love. I promise you, they'll find him."

"We don't have the manpower, Reverend Webster," Tom Whiting explained. "We can't just sit at the mill, waiting for him to show up. Besides, there have been sightings of Dusty along that northwestern section of the lake. The chief is asking for the cooperation of everyone to let us take a look in the cabins at that end of the lake. We figure he may just be hiding in one of them."

"I'll be glad to help in any way I can, Tom. But—"

Chris stepped back from the open window of his bedroom. The Help Wanted section of the newspaper was spread next to his computer. He picked up the letter and the envelope from the printer tray. He meticulously folded the page and stuffed it in.

It was not too cool getting fired from two jobs in the same day. And cutting grass didn't pay shit. He tucked the newspaper and the envelope under his arm and headed out.

But at least he knew who was to blame.

Dusty reeled forward and kicked viciously at the green swivel chair. The thing tumbled the length of the trailer, coming to rest against the cot.

They'd been in here. Messing with his stuff. He stared at the printed note in his hand, but the words were running together. The sheet had been taped to his door.

Fucking cops.

He slammed the door before picking up the bottle of vodka from the floor. He looked around as he drank deeply. What were they doing coming in here? So what if he paid a visit to the Hardy bitch. What did they care?

Fuck 'em.

He'd seen the squad cars watching the mill property when he got back from the lake yesterday morning. No big deal. He'd gone back out to the lake and returned today. The fucking assholes were finally gone.

"Hot," he muttered, shedding his ragged jacket.

He took another drink, finishing the bottle. Turning, he flung the empty thing against the paneled wall. The bottle didn't break, but only bounced off and fell behind the piles of newspapers on his bed.

But they'd be back.

Dusty went into the room at the far end of the trailer and dumped empty bottles and rags out of a couple of plastic grocery bags. Coming back, he pulled open a cabinet door and drew out another bottle of vodka. Tipping the bottle up to his lips, he kept it there until a quarter of the bottle was gone. He lowered it, spun the cap back on and dropped it into one of the bags.

With jerky movements, he lurched around, piling things into the bags. Wooden carvings. A dirty rag. A frying pan. An empty vodka bottle. His jacket.

His knives were nowhere in sight. The cops must have taken them.

"Fucking assholes."

The room was spinning a little, and he leaned against the counter.

"Merl," he muttered, stumbling across the trailer.

He stopped dead, trying to focus. The plastic bags fell to the floor at his feet.

The pictures were gone. Every one of them. "Not Merl…no…"

Dusty yanked his knife from its sheath. With a roar, he

attacked the wall, stabbing at it and carving away chunks of paneling. He was tiring fast, and as he jabbed at the place where the pictures had been, the blade suddenly snapped off an inch from the hilt, cutting his cheek as it flew past his shoulder.

He stopped and leaned on his hands on the counter. He was so tired. Drops of blood were falling from his face onto his wrist and hand. He thought of Marilyn and closed his eyes.

She was dead. His Merl was dead, stabbed and burned in that stinking house by the river. Dead.

Dusty heard a metallic click from the trailer door and turned in time to see the flames racing toward him across the gasoline that covered the floor.

He charged the door, but the curtain of smoke and flame swallowed him up before he reached it.

Twenty-Nine

Other shoppers in the building supply store veered out of Léa's way as she raced down each aisle with Mick on her heels.

"I am *not* going to let him do this to me." She piled three gallons of white semigloss paint next to the five cans of flat paint into the cart. "He is *not* driving me out of this town."

"That's the spirit. I think I'll push this thing," he said, maneuvering the cart to catch the dozen brushes and rollers as she swept them off the shelf.

"Rich Weir said there are only so many places he can hide. Well, then, they should find him and drag him out. They should smoke his sorry, cowardly ass out of the hole he's hiding in and arrest him." She pulled a gallon of industrial-strength cleaning solution off the shelf.

"I agree. But I believe Rich is doing his best this time." He caught the huge bag of sponges and a pair of floor mops she flung back toward the cart. "With Jason Shanahan's body turning up today, and Dusty seen up by the lake recently, I'd say that the chief has got a lot more than just us nipping at his heels to produce him."

Léa stopped abruptly and turned to him.

"God, I am such a jerk." She looked angry and upset. She kicked the cart once and then walked into his embrace. "Here I am, upset about repainting a couple of walls, and poor Brian Hughes is trying to deal with losing someone he loved.''

Mick held her tightly in his arms. "I'd say you have every right to be as upset as you are. You've put up with more than your share of harassment in this town.'' He kissed her temple, then Léa pushed out of his arms as a couple of men coming down the aisle said hello to Mick.

"Sorry,'' she whispered, falling in beside him as he pushed the cart along. "Guys and hardware stores. I hope I didn't ruin your reputation draping myself all over you.''

"You can drape yourself all over me, anytime and anywhere.'' He kissed her mouth. "And incidentally, my stock will only go up being seen with a knockout like you.''

Léa blushed and took a couple of bottles of disinfecting spray off the shelf. She tossed them into the cart.

"You know exactly how to make me forget my troubles.'' She gave him an affectionate smile. "You are the most sensitive person in this world, Mick.''

"Uh, well…that's the first time I've ever heard that,'' he said with a laugh. "But I'm going to quote you when I'm pressuring you for an answer.''

Getting in line to check out, as she started helping Mick unload everything at the register, she couldn't brush off the moment of hope that swept through her. Spending her life with Mick was a happily-ever-after ending that she wouldn't have imagined possible for herself in a million years. He offered the balancing weight of passion, happiness and love that she'd always lacked on fortune's scale. He offered her a future.

Mick also had the ability to wipe away her worries, to make life livable. This morning, after talking to the chief and the officers who had come to see Dusty's latest handiwork in her house, Mick had announced she needed to go shopping with him at some "serious" hardware stores. Léa understood that he wanted to take her away from the house so she could get her mind back in order. Heather had been less than thrilled about spending the day in places where "Nine Inch Nails" referred to something you hammered into wood, and had asked to be dropped off at Mick's office.

Left to themselves, Mick had taken Léa for a late breakfast before checking out kitchen cabinets. Though he'd insisted on looking at every possibility, Léa hadn't been ready to make that kind of investment in a house she needed to sell. After browsing through two more places that specialized in doors and then bathroom fixtures, Léa hadn't bought anything, but she'd felt much better.

With the day almost over, though, her thoughts of having wasted a day began to prey on her and she felt herself growing tense. Mick had happily taken her to the building supply store when she'd insisted that they needed to buy paint and cleaning stuff for the mess they were going back to. Just the thought of how much extra work and money Dusty had caused her, though, was enough to wind her up again.

As Léa signed the credit card slip, she wondered if maybe she hadn't gotten carried away a little with her purchases.

"Don't forget your receipt," Mick said, reminding Léa when she almost walked away without it. She tucked the paper into her pocket.

"This should be enough stuff to clean and paint every house in the neighborhood," he commented as they loaded the supplies into his truck.

"Well, if I do this long enough—or often enough— maybe I'll pick up scraping and painting as a profession."

"Cool! I'm always looking to hire painters, especially sexy ones who have hazel eyes and tons of stitches on their forehead and who like to check out appliances around the house."

In a minute they were in the truck and on the road.

"With that kind of job description coming from *you*, Stone Builders might find every woman in three counties getting hazel-colored contact lenses and banging their heads with two-by-fours."

"Well, they'll be out of luck. That position has already been filled by the sexiest woman alive, and I have my eyes on her right now."

His smile hit her somewhere deep in her chest. She undid her seat belt and slid across the seat.

"You always say the nicest things." Laying her head against his shoulder, Léa slipped her fingers under his shirt and caressed the warm skin of his chest.

"Excuse me, ma'am. Should I pull off to the side of the road?" he asked huskily.

"No. It's still daylight." She kissed his neck. "We might get arrested for what I want to do to you."

"Then you'd better put your seat belt on. I'm having a little difficulty focusing on the road."

Léa buckled on the middle seat belt, but her hand immediately returned to where it had left off. "So where were we?"

"You were working on getting us arrested."

"Oh, yes. You know, now that you have both of your hands on the wheel—" She slid her hand down his stomach and felt every muscle contract. "You do have your hands tight on the wheel, don't you?"

"Uh, yes, I do." His knuckles were white.

"Good, because there are a few things I've been dying to tell you, too." She stretched up and kissed his jaw before nibbling on his ear. "*You* are the sexiest man alive."

He opened his mouth to say something, but Léa ran her fingers down over the front of his jeans. A growl was the only thing that left his throat.

"And the most giving."

She undid his belt.

"And the most considerate."

She lowered the zipper.

"And the most loving."

She slipped her hand into the pant leg of his jeans and took hold of the stiffening shaft.

"And I love you."

The car bounced, and Léa turned to see that Mick had steered the car off the main highway and down a dirt road into the woods.

"Where are you going?"

"Somewhere that we won't get arrested—at least not right away." He pulled the car sharply into the woods and came to a stop by a barbed-wire pasture fence.

The black-and-white cows in the field were moderately interested, but Léa didn't care. As she was undoing her seat belt, Mick was tugging down her shorts. She only had time to kick off one sneaker and get one leg out her shorts before he slid across to her. In an instant, she was straddling him on the seat.

Léa lowered herself onto him, taking him in deeply. They writhed together like starved lovers. Neither had patience to go slow, and Léa rode him hard as he lifted her T-shirt and bra out of the way of his mouth.

Their bodies rocked together in a wild and rhythmic dance of love. A fever took hold of her, filling her with pleasure that pulsed within her. Then, when Léa thought she could take no more, the truck and the pasture and the golden summer afternoon all disappeared as they exploded together in a tumult of passion.

They clung together, breathless in the aftermath.

"We didn't use a condom again," he whispered in her ear.

Léa felt a giggle rise up in her chest. "Well, if I ever do get pregnant, we have a wide range of names we can call her or him."

"That right?"

"Westinghouse...or GE...or Jenn-Air...or Amana...or Ford..."

"I went to college with a guy whose first name was Ford. We called him Fordie."

"Well, now you know where he got the name."

"Never mind about him. Just think, we can go to the World Appliance Home Show for our honeymoon."

Léa kissed him deeply. "You are the most romantic man in the world."

He hugged her tightly. "I'm very glad you appreciate me."

Mick's cell phone began to ring. He grumbled and looked at the number of the incoming call. "It's Heather."

Léa worked her way off his lap as he answered the phone. He nodded to her calmly after a minute of talking. She sighed with relief.

"We're on our way home." He handed Léa her sneaker as he talked to Heather. "Where are we? I don't know. All I see are fields."

She searched under the car seat and in the glove compartment for something they could use to clean up. She found a package of tissues.

"Yup. We'll be home in about ten or fifteen minutes. Bye."

"Is she okay?" Léa asked as soon as he hung up.

"Yes. She's fine. She's back at the house."

"We should hurry," Léa said urgently. "She shouldn't be alone there, and..."

Mick took her face in his hands and kissed her hard. There was a smile tugging at his lips when he pulled back.

"She'll be okay," he said, reassuring her.

Léa found herself drifting in a haze of blissful pleasure for the rest of the ride home. When Mick pulled onto Poplar Street, she was surprised to see all the lights in her house on.

"I hope Heather didn't come here to work alone again."

She got out of the car and climbed up the broken steps. Through the open windows on the porch, she heard voices coming from inside. She glanced over her shoulder and found Mick standing behind her.

"Go in." He shrugged. "I think she left it unlocked."

Léa's hand was shaking when she pushed the door open.

She stood gaping at the number of people inside. Some wore tool belts, others just wore old work clothes spattered with paint. A man and a woman were coming down the stairs, paint brushes and rollers in hand. Some of the smiling faces were familiar, others were just friendly strangers. She was dumbfounded.

Heather came out from the back of the house. Joanna was right behind her.

Léa heard Andrew Rice's voice from the sidewalk. "Am I too late for the work party?"

"For the work part, yes," Joanna called to him. "For the party part, you're just in time."

Heather gave Léa a big hug. "Come on, we have so much to show you."

As the teenager started pulling her into the house, Léa turned and reached for Mick. He took her hand.

"Did you plan all of this?"

"Everyone did. We want you to stay, Léa." He smiled at her. "We *all* do."

Stephanie stood by the counter and put the phone down.

With a trembling hand, she picked up her glass of iced tea and attempted to bring it up to her lips. The ice cubes rattled. The liquid sloshed over the rim onto the front of her dress. There was moisture on the outside of the glass, and before she could get a good grip, it slipped through her fingers and crashed on the tile floor. Splinters of glass flew in every direction.

"Wh-what Rich w-wanted?"

She stared down at the jagged pieces scattered across

the kitchen floor. Bob had been watching her when she was on the phone. He was always watching her. She raised her eyes and looked at the wheelchair. At his partially paralyzed body. At the face that had once been handsome. And caring.

He was still caring. He always looked after her.

"There's been a fire on the mill property. Rich called to let me know." Stephanie tore a few sheets of paper towel off the roll and knelt down on the floor, soaking up the liquid.

"N-no one h-hurt?"

Her hand passed over a jagged piece of glass. Blood streamed out of a cut onto the paper towel. With no regard for it, she continued to wipe the floor.

"Yes. It seems the fire started in Dusty's trailer. There's a burned body. They suspect it might be him."

"Y-you're b-bleed-ing."

"I am not."

"S-Steph…"

"I wanted him to die. I never wanted him to come back from the army. We were finished." The wet towel was red with blood. "Finished. But he came back, anyway. Of course, everyone felt sorry for him. He was broken. Lost. No mind left. It was the war. He was harmless. Even I was fooled. I was…fooled."

Tears fell on her bleeding hand. She stared at them for a moment and then wiped her cheek with the towel, leaving a scratch and a smudge of blood there just below her eye. She dropped the towel on the floor.

"I didn't realize…he was full of hate. He was evil. Crazy evil. Just loved to punish me. He…he did it…through Marilyn."

The shards of glass were sharp, piercing the skin of her fingers and the palms of her bare hands as Stephanie swept the glass into a pile.

"He told her. Dusty told her when he was ready. She

was not even a teenager. He waited and then told her, when he was ready, that he was her father. That I had betrayed him. Him and his love for me. That I married for money. That *I* betrayed *him*. Can you imagine?''

Another needle of glass stabbed her. She didn't even wince from the pain. She looked curiously at the long sliver protruding from her skin before picking up the paper towel again.

"His methods worked. And she was just like him. In every way she was like him. Punishing me. But then that wasn't enough. She was never happy. Everyone had to suffer.''

Stephanie sat back on her heels and looked out into space.

"She went after Charlie when she was still in school. As far as everyone knew, he was her father. But that didn't stop her. I think…no, I *know* she made sure that I saw them. Walked in on them. The two of them. She made sure I saw.'' She looked at Bob. "And she did the same thing to you. And to me…again.''

More tears rolled down her face. Her hands squeezed the paper towel. The blood and spilled drink dripped out of it onto her dress.

"I learned to hate her as much as I hated Dusty. I wanted to see her dead. My own daughter. She was part of me, and yet I wanted to wrap my hands around her throat and watch her gasping for breath.''

Stephanie tore the paper towel in two and carefully laid the pieces down, side by side like two paper dolls. But these were red with blood and glistening with the shards of splintered glass. She touched each one tenderly.

"But Ted shouldn't have done it. He was good. The girls had a chance for a life with him. They were a family. My family. My babies. He should not have taken them away from me.''

She rocked a little on her heels. The pain lay all around

her like a bloody mist. The grief was taking her under again. She closed her eyes and a sob racked her body.

"I didn't see the evil in him. He betrayed me, too. He lied. Like Dusty. Like Marilyn. He waited like some monster and then killed them. He stole the only two good things in my life."

"He d-didn't."

Stephanie continued to rock. The tears wouldn't stop, squeezing through her closed eyelids.

"Ted d-didn't kill."

She opened her eyes and saw Bob through a haze of tears.

"I got th-there f-first. House was on f-fire. I d-didn't go in. Ted c-came af-after. He pulled in af-after. I saw him go c-crazy…t-trying to g-get in."

Stephanie's body was shaking violently when she tried to push herself to her feet. She held on to the counter to steady herself. Bob's face was wet with tears. He looked a hundred years old.

"I went th-there, because she'd sent th-the pictures in the m-mail…th-that day. But I didn't k-kill her. I got th-there after…and Ted…t-too…got th-there after."

"Why?" she breathed in disbelief. "Why didn't you say any of this sooner? Why not two years ago?"

"I was af-fraid th-they'd arrest me. I th-thought you d-didn't know about Maril-lyn and m-me. I was mad… c-crazy m-mad. Enough to k-kill her. I c-could have…"

As she stood up, broken glass stabbed her feet.

"S-so…s-sorry. For-give me. I love you, S-Steph."

She reached for the phone on the counter and handed it to him.

"Show me."

Thirty

"**I** don't have any way of getting up to the cabin. My car's at the garage, and they're closed today," Chris complained into the phone. "And besides, you've taken my keys away, remember?"

"Where's your mother?" Reverend Webster asked shortly at the other end.

"Out at some charity breakfast. And I don't know when she's coming back." The teenager paced back and forth in the kitchen.

"Well, I still want you to get up there. You're the only one who's been using the cabin this spring, and I want you there to let them in."

Chris took the lid off Patricia's cash cookie jar and took out three twenty dollar bills, stuffing them deep in his pocket.

"You be ready," his father continued. "I'll call Chief Weir and ask him to send one of his patrol cars to pick you up on their way to the lake. If he wants to go through my cabin so badly he's not waiting for a warrant, I don't think he'll be balking at giving you a ride out there."

"I'll be waiting by the phone. Thank you, Sarah, for everything."

Léa didn't know how to contain her emotions as she hung up the phone. She turned to Mick and hugged him hard in the middle of the kitchen. "I can't believe it. God, I can't believe this is happening."

"I tried to get bits and pieces out of your side of the phone call. Good news?"

"There is a new development in the case. A witness has voluntarily stepped forward to testify on Ted's behalf. It's too early to tell if there is a need for a retrial, but she is pushing to get a hearing right away. Everything is shut down today, but she thinks maybe tomorrow." Reining in her feeling of exultation, she kissed him tenderly. "Did you have something to do with this, too?"

"You give me way too much credit." He laughed, kissing her back. "Who's the witness?"

"She didn't know yet, but she said she'll call as soon as she hears something more."

Heather appeared in the kitchen door. "Aren't you two tired of all this hugging and kissing, yet? Christmas, I can't turn my back on you for a minute. I hope I missed breakfast."

Before the teenager could reach for her morning can of soda, Léa gave her a bear hug, too.

"Okay. What's wrong with her?" she asked her father with a smile.

When Mick told Heather the news, she hooted loudly and hugged Léa back. Releasing her, the teenager paused and smacked her own forehead with her palm.

"I can't believe I forgot to give you something last night." Heather searched on the countertop where Mick piled his mail. She picked up an envelope. "Before we started working on the house yesterday, I found this inside the front door. It kind of looks like that other one you got."

A brief moment of anxiety took hold of Léa as she handled the familiar white envelope. Like the last, it was addressed but not stamped. She didn't even pause and tore it open.

I'm taking care of everything. Now you can go.

She stared at it in confusion.

"What is it?" Mick asked. "Who is it from?"

Before she could answer, Max charged at the front door, barking as he raced through the house. Mick went to see who it was, and a minute later Léa heard Rich Weir's voice as the two men walked back toward the kitchen. The police chief had been surprisingly civil to her lately, and Léa wondered if it had something to do with Sheila's influence.

"Sorry I didn't get over to the house last night. I got tied up with a few things. Sheila said you had lots of help, though."

Léa was stunned that he'd even considered it. "Yes. Thank you."

"Cup of coffee?" Mick offered.

"No, thanks," he answered. "I'm on my way up to the lake. We're going through some of the cottages."

"No sign of Dusty yet?"

Rich looked at her and frowned. "I guess you haven't heard. There was a fire at the mill yesterday afternoon."

"I heard. One of my guys called me last night to tell me." Mick filled his own cup. "We lease one of the buildings in the back for storage. All he said was that the fire didn't come anywhere near the storage area."

"No. The whole thing was pretty much contained to Dusty's trailer. He was in it."

"Dusty is dead?" Léa asked in shock.

"We didn't get the final ID on the body until this morning. But it was him."

Léa sat down on a chair. This whole thing was like some self-solving puzzle. She had a hard time believing it.

"We're still investigating the fire scene. But there was another reason why I stopped by." He turned to Heather. "I know today is a holiday and all that, but I was wondering if you wouldn't mind coming up to the lake and showing us where exactly you saw Dusty. We're trying to hammer out his movements in the investigation of Jason Shanahan's death, and it would help us a lot to know where you saw him.''

Heather looked at the chief. ''Can my dad or Léa drive me out there?''

''Absolutely.''

''When do you want her?'' Mick asked.

''The sooner the better. If you can do it this morning, I'd appreciate it.''

''Why don't you take her out there now?'' Léa offered. ''I'll hang by the phone.''

Mick didn't seem too comfortable with the idea.

''I'll stay right here by the phone. I promise, Mick.''

''I'll go get my shoes.'' Heather ran to the front of the house, the dog on her heels.

''Ms. Hardy,'' Rich started as soon as Heather left the kitchen. ''You should know that we've had some new information with regard to your brother's case. We're doing everything possible to pursue the matter, and the Stonybrook Police Department is a hundred percent behind you.''

For the second time in minutes, Rich Weir left her speechless.

''I don't know where the kid went, but there was nobody answering the doorbell at the rectory,'' Jeff said through the open window of his patrol car.

Robin frowned at the other officer. ''Tom said he'd talked to Reverend Webster and arranged it.''

''He wasn't there. I'm telling you.''

''Well,'' she said thoughtfully, looking at the Websters' cabin. ''I say we go in. We've got the owner's permission and a dozen more cabins to check. What are the chances of the place having a lock on the door?''

Her partner nodded and called it in on his radio handset. In a minute they were crossing the leaf-strewn gravel to the cabin. A steady rain had started to fall.

The front door turned out to be locked, after all, but they circled the building, peering in and trying the windows as they went along. When they reached the back porch, Robin went up and pulled on the sliding glass door. It opened easily.

"What did I tell you?"

They called into the cabin, identifying themselves. Getting no answer, they entered. A quick look around told them that the place was empty.

The cottage was neat and tidy. Everything in its place. The furniture had that comfortable worn look that showed care, in spite of its age. The books on the shelves, a mix of mysteries and biographies, were recently dusted. The beds were covered with spreads but unmade. The refrigerator was on and the shelves were spotless. A police scanner sat unplugged on a clean counter, but there wasn't a TV in sight. In the sitting room, cushions for the porch furniture were stacked neatly against a wall and covered with a beach towel.

Robin had worked her way to the back door when she saw Jeff on one knee by the kitchen counter.

"What is it?" she asked, crossing the cabin and crouching beside him.

"You tell me."

She looked hard at the white wood showing from the deep chip in the pine floorboard. It looked like the corner of something had struck the floor, denting it and chipping the wood. She shone her flashlight on it and a moment later pointed to a spot about three feet from the mark. Two thin dark lines ran along the grooves between the floorboards for almost a foot and then stopped.

"Look at that," she said softly. "I'll bet you a paycheck that's blood."

* * *

The summer rain continued steadily, falling in huge droplets from the leaves of the trees overhead.

Chris hated being wet, but he waited until the police car, followed by Heather and her old man in the Volvo, left the street. Climbing over the stone wall, he saw the old Honda was still parked in the Hardys' driveway.

He needed a car. He had to get away from Stonybrook. He had to run, even though he still didn't know where.

The Hardy house looked all shut up. The windows were closed and the lights turned off. He peered around the decrepit carriage house and noticed the basement window he'd used to get in Monday night had a piece of plywood hammered over it. She wouldn't keep her keys inside there, anyway, he thought, running up the driveway toward the car.

He tried the doors. Locked.

Heather's dog was barking somewhere inside their house next door. He heard the Hardy woman call something to the animal. A minute later, he watched through the railings of her porch as she came out the Conklins' front door.

Her voice carried across the lawn. She was talking to the dog. "Not much of a storm to watch."

Chris saw her sit down on one of the wicker chairs with the dog at her side. He took off around the back of the houses.

Everybody kept their keys in their kitchen. Everybody.

His shoes barely made any noise at all as he climbed the back steps. The Conklins' back door was open. Chris quietly opened the door and went in.

He knew the layout of the house. The last time Heather was staying with her father, he'd been in and out of this house a few times. He glanced toward the front door. Through the length of the house, he saw the closed screen door to the front porch. He shot a quick glance at the walls for a key rack. There was none.

He looked on the counters for Léa's pocketbook, for anywhere she might drop the keys. Nothing.

"It's raining, Max. Your father's right, you are an idiot." She was joking with the stupid dog. He froze as he saw her shadow pass in front of the screen door.

"Okay, just a quick walk around the block."

The front door opened, and he drew back behind the door into the kitchen. He breathed again when she didn't come into the house, at all. He heard the door again, and realized she was reaching for the dog's leash in the basket by the door.

As soon as her voice drifted off the porch, he moved out of the kitchen. Conklin's truck keys would do, too, even though the business lettering on the side would make it easier to spot on the road. He quickly looked inside the study. There was nothing on the desk. He hurried through the house and up the stairs. He went past Heather's door to the guest room where he assumed Léa was staying.

He spotted her purse on a bureau. Rushing now, he dumped the contents of the purse onto one of the beds. The keys dropped out with the rest, and he pocketed them. He quickly went through her wallet and took all the cash and a credit card.

He strode back out of the room but couldn't help but stop at Heather's doorway. The furniture was the same as he remembered from before, but the room was messier now. He saw a pair of her underwear near the door and picked it up. He felt the silky texture, rubbed it against his cheek. It was as soft as Marilyn's.

He remembered the feel of Heather's wet warmth when he touched her Monday night. He should have fucked her. She wouldn't have complained much if he'd gone all the way. Marilyn always said she liked it rough. The rougher the better.

Chris thought he heard a noise outside. Quickly, he stuffed the underwear in his back pocket and hurried downstairs.

"Chris, what are you doing here?" Léa was standing with a leash in her hand inside the front door.

"I...I was looking for Heather."

Léa hoped her surprise at finding him here hid her fear. At the sound of Chris's voice, Max started barking furiously from outside the screen door. She reached back to open the door and let the dog in.

"Don't!" the teen said sharply. "Leave him out there."

"Sure. Whatever." She forced herself to stay calm. The dog jumped up on the screen, scratching to get in.

"Close the door."

Léa turned and closed the front door.

"Drop the leash."

She dropped it in the basket. "Heather's not home right now, but I'll be glad to tell her when she gets in that you stopped by."

"Yeah, right, so she can tell me to get lost again."

His face was flushed and his breathing obviously uneven. When she'd first spotted him, his hand had gone into his jeans pocket. It came out now holding a closed pocketknife. She had faced a number of angry and aggressive students who were ready to explode in her career, but none of them had ever pulled a knife on her.

"She confuses the hell out of me." He took a step down. "One minute she's hot for me, and the next she's stomping on my foot and shoving me away."

Léa maintained an open stance and kept her voice calm. "I know what you mean."

"I don't like girls my age. I never have. But Heather was always different. She doesn't think like the rest of them. She doesn't go around trying to get a new boyfriend every other day. I don't know how many guys she had when she was in California, but since she's been back, I'm the only one that she's gone out with."

"That's true." Léa realized that he was in no rush to get out. "Is there anything I can do for you, Chris?"

The phone started ringing. She looked at the portable one on the coffee table a few steps away. "I'm expecting a call from my lawyer. She knows I'm here."

She didn't ask him if it was okay to pick it up. She calmly walked over and answered it.

"Léa." Mick's voice was a welcome sound. "I've got more news."

"Hi." She casually turned to face Chris. He was standing at the bottom of the stairs, facing her. The knife was now open, the blade pressed against his leg.

"We're up at the lake. The police have found blood in the Websters' cabin. Rich also just got a report from the fire investigators that it looks like someone may have used a crowbar or something to jam the door to Dusty's trailer shut from the outside. Somebody set the thing on fire with him inside. I want you to be careful. I don't know what the heck is going on, but I'm worried about you."

"Thanks, Sarah!" she said brightly. "Call me again if you find something else."

Léa turned off the phone and laid it back down on the coffee table.

Thirty-One

"We've searched the kid's car at the garage," one of the officers was saying to the chief. "They found a steel box containing photographs of Marilyn Hardy, and others, in the trunk."

Mick leaned for a moment more against the cabin's back railing, staring at his phone. Then her words clicked.

"Somebody is at the house," he said, starting for his car with Rich and Heather following. "Léa's in trouble."

"It could be the kid." The police chief whipped out his cell phone. "The closest cruiser we have is at the mill."

Heather barely had her seat belt on when Mick threw the car in reverse and sped back up the drive. She looked pale, and he could see she was shaking.

"Please, God, let her be okay. Please, God," she whispered. She turned to Mick. "He tried to take a picture of me, Dad. He's sick, like Marilyn was. She always had cameras in the house. I should have stopped him. I—"

"This is *not* your fault," Mick said grimly. "And Léa will be okay. We'll be there in a few minutes. But she'll know how to deal with him. I just know it. She can handle him."

Léa could see the muscles tensing in the teenager's arm. The blade of the knife still pointed to the floor.

"That was Sarah Rand," she offered, as if there were nothing wrong. "She's Ted's new lawyer, and she's darn good. Hey, I could go for a glass of iced tea. Would you like some?"

As casually as she could muster, she started toward the kitchen. The back door was unlocked. Léa considered if she had a chance running out of it.

"I like iced tea." He was right at her shoulder.

No chance of running. When she reached inside a cabinet for a couple of glasses, Chris moved to the back door and closed it. Léa noticed the teenager's gaze fall on the white envelope she'd left on the counter.

"You should have listened to him. You should have gone."

"I couldn't go before thanking him...before thanking you."

His eyes were cold when they fixed on her face. "You knew it was me?"

She managed to laugh as naturally as possible.

"It doesn't matter, but you just told me. You knew what was in the letter without looking at it." She handed him one of the glasses of iced tea. "So...thanks, Chris."

He didn't say anything, and Léa sat back against the kitchen table. The kid looked lost. His eyes swept the floor. Clearly, he didn't know what he wanted to do next.

Bits of information started fitting together in her mind. Chris had all the markings of a class-A sexual predator. So did Marilyn when she was alive. He wanted to manipulate and control Léa with those letters. Marilyn had the same behavioral characteristics.

"So you believe Ted's innocent," she said, keeping her tone conversational.

"I didn't say that."

"That's what your letters said."

"I was only saying what you wanted to hear, jerking you around. I wanted you to come back to Stonybrook." He smiled. "And you bought it."

"Why did you want me back here?" Léa asked, knowing full well that with each question she might be pushing him in the wrong direction. The dog was still barking furiously at the front door.

"Like I said, to jerk you around. And to pit the wolves against one another. To stir things up. Everyone who Marilyn hated. You. Mr. Slater. Stephanie. Brian. Jason. There were others, too. It was just like the good old days, with Marilyn."

"I had nothing to do with her."

"She hated you when she was still married to him." He shrugged. "Anyway, you had to be a stand-in for your brother. How was I going to have fun watching the shit hit the fan when there's no one standing in for Ted?"

"Clever." Léa took a sip of her iced tea. "The stuffed toy in Stephanie's car was also very clever."

"That was okay. I liked sending pictures better."

"I never saw them."

"That's because she didn't have any of herself with her husband."

"Where did you get them, Chris? She's dead."

"She gave me some of the negatives to get copies." He shrugged. "I got the rest from her cottage before the police got to it."

Léa put her glass down. Sitting in the middle of the kitchen table was a disposable camera Heather had used to take some pictures of the work party the night before.

"So that was it? You just wanted a little group activity where you could tease everybody for a couple of days?"

"Not tease. Make them suffer," he corrected her. "I had to finish what Marilyn started. She hated those people."

She took another sip of iced tea and put it back down on the table, closer to the camera this time.

"I have to hand it to you, Chris, you are good. So, did you kill Dusty? And Jason? Did you kill everybody?"

"I didn't want to kill those two creeps. But shit happens." He leaned against the counter. With the blade of his knife, he started carving something into the countertop.

"Brian will suffer because Jason is gone."

"I always liked Brian. He didn't need that asshole."

"What about Bob Slater and Stephanie?" she asked. "You just wanted to drive her over the edge? That's it?"

"That's enough. He's a useless cripple, anyway."

"And what about me?"

"If you'd left town when I told you, then you would only have had to watch your brother fry. But now—" He straightened up from the counter. "I don't like loose ends. Everything in its place."

Léa didn't get up. She didn't cringe when she saw the light change in Chris's face. She had no doubt that this was the face of a killer, but Mick was coming, she told herself. He'd be here any minute now.

"Was Marilyn good to you?"

"Yeah, she was unbelievable."

The fact that she wasn't standing up and backing away or putting up a fight, or even behaving fearfully, was obviously throwing him for a loop. He halted a couple of steps from her.

"You loved her, didn't you, Chris?"

"Of course I did. And she loved me, too."

"Then why did she screw around with all those other guys when she had you?" She casually reached for the camera and held it up. "Why the big deal about the pictures?"

"She only did that to get even. She really only loved me."

"You're too smart a kid to believe that baloney. But I can tell you I treat my boys a lot better than that. And I don't lie to them."

"Your boys?"

"Of course. You think Marilyn is the only woman in the world who likes younger men? We know a stud when we see one. That's what she used you for, Chris. Nice, strong young body. Quick learner. Somebody she could use to follow her around like a puppy and do her bidding. I'll bet she even had you take some of those pictures for her.''

''So what?''

She noticed the goose bumps rising on his bare arms. She held the camera against her cheek. ''Didn't you hate her for it, Chris? Weren't you jealous at all?''

''Sometimes.'' He took a step closer. ''I couldn't help it. But she loved me.''

He was in striking range. ''Didn't you want to kill her for using you?''

''No! I loved her.''

''Didn't you want to be in those pictures yourself?''

A victorious look showed on his face. ''I *was* in some of them. A *lot* of them. She took her time when she was with me. Let me do whatever I wanted to her. Anything at all.''

''And who did she send those pictures of you to?'' Léa asked, casually bringing the camera to her eye and looking through the viewfinder at him. ''Was she using you to hurt someone else? Your parents? Or was she really trying to hurt you?''

He was trembling all over. Through the viewfinder, she saw him raise the knife.

Léa lowered the camera a little and looked straight into his eyes. ''You can admit it. You're among friends. You see, I'm just like Marilyn. I'd have used you, Chris, the same way she did. You're a toy. Nothing else. Just the means of hurting more people. But you're a smart boy, Chris. You should have figured that out by yourself.''

''I did.''

''I thought so. And you hated her.''

''Yes.''

''Enough to want to kill her?''

"Yes!"

The camera flash exploded in his eyes just as he drew back the knife. Léa threw herself back across the table and went tumbling to the floor, just as Mick hurtled across the kitchen and slammed Chris's body against the wall.

In an instant, the kitchen was filled with police.

Léa just lay there on the kitchen floor in shock. All her gung-ho courage of a moment ago was gone. She realized she was shaking like a leaf.

Chris wasn't putting up any fight. She watched with a strange sense of disconnectedness as someone read him his rights while another officer put handcuffs on him.

Léa found Mick's arms around her. "Are you okay? Tell me you're okay."

"I'm okay."

She clung tightly to him. She'd seen Mick at the kitchen door just as she lowered the camera. That had given her the courage to ask the last question.

"How did you get in?"

He was touching her arms, her face, as if he had to check for himself to make sure she was okay.

"The front door. With all Max's barking, I was hoping I could sneak up on him. I can't believe how close he came to really hurting you."

"Where is Heather?"

"She's in the car. She almost went crazy, worrying about you."

Léa sat up, still holding on to Mick. She tried to get her bearings.

"I don't know what you said to him before," Rich Weir said, crouching in front of her as a couple of the officers took Chris out. "But I loved hearing that last answer. Anytime you're looking for a job as an interrogator—"

"Get in line, pal." Mick helped her to her feet and wrapped an arm around her. "She owes *me* a couple of answers before we discuss any jobs with *you*."

She turned to Mick and nestled against his chest. She could feel his strength flowing into her.

"Léa!" Heather ran into the room. "Is it really over?"

"Yes." She brought the teenager into their embrace. "This nightmare is really over."

Thirty-Two

"Just give me fifteen minutes."

"Are you sure you don't want me to come in with you?"

Joanna shook her head and kissed Andrew on the lips. "I have to do this alone."

She turned the collar of her coat up against the rain. She hurried up the pathway and passed beneath the trellis blooming with fragrant climbing roses.

A glance over her shoulder told her that the flower shop was already closed.

She rang the front doorbell once and waited for Gwen to answer. This had been as much her house as her sister's. Both of them—no, the three of them, she corrected—had been raised under this roof. But she had no ties to it. She made no claim on it.

The door opened wide, and Gwen stepped aside. "You're back?"

"No," Joanna said shortly. "I'm here to get my clothes. One suitcase should handle everything I care to take."

She didn't wait for a response, but strode quickly past her sister and up the stairs.

From her closet she took out the only large suitcase she had, and laid it open on the bed. Without any concern for tidiness, she removed her clothes from the drawers and placed them in the suitcase. She took a half-dozen dresses that she liked from their hangers and laid them in the case, as well.

It was amazing how little she owned, Joanna thought. But really, it made perfect sense, considering she'd never gone too far, either. She stacked three pairs of shoes and a pair of sneakers on top of everything.

At some point during the hasty packing job, Gwen had come upstairs. Joanna didn't slow down, though, totally ignoring her older sister as she looked on from the doorway.

"How long are you planning to be gone?"

"Forever," Joanna replied calmly, keeping all hostility out of her voice.

"What about the flower shop? I can't run that alone."

"I told you before. It's yours. Do what you want with it." Joanna picked up her delicate perfume bottles off the bureau and wrapped them gently in her socks.

"What are you planning to do with your life?"

"That's my business, isn't it?"

"You can't just stay at home and let him take care of you."

"*Him* has a name. His name is Andrew." Joanna's eyes were blazing when she looked up. "You know, it would have been a lot easier for me to come and take my things sometime when you weren't home."

Now that the floodgate was open, she couldn't hush the arguments inside her head.

"It actually would have been a lot less stressful not to have to see you *ever* again. I could have pulled a Cate and just walked away without ever saying goodbye. But I thought, what the heck, out of respect for you, we could both have a little closure. I'd even hoped we could walk away without hating each other. Without carrying grudges that would last a decade. But, once again, Gwen, you've managed to prove me wrong."

Joanna tucked the rest of the perfume bottles on top of

the clothes and zipped the case closed. She dragged the suitcase off the bed and went out through the door, giving her sister no more attention than the molding on the wall.

"What about me?"

Joanna found herself frozen at the top of the stairs, looking down. It was not the question but the sadness in the voice that stopped her there.

"I've focused my whole life on Cate…and you…and the business. I don't know what it's like to be alone. I don't know what to do with *me*."

She turned and looked into her sister's tearstained face. "You *will* survive, Gwen. In fact, I believe you will thrive."

The older woman shook her head and sank down on the floor, her back to the wall.

"I'm scared, Jo," she whispered. "I don't even know who I am…or what I want to do. And I am too old to make mistakes."

Joanna left her suitcase at the top of the stairs and walked back to her sister. She crouched down beside the weeping woman.

"Even though you act like some Victorian prude, you are *not* old, Gwen. You are only forty-one. God, that can be the beginning of a life! And who says there's anything wrong with making mistakes? For crying out loud, *make* some! Experience things. Take a trip. Sell the house and the business and go out and travel around the world. Find who you are. Find a cause to fight for. Have sex, for chrissake! None of that has to be a mistake…and who will care if it is?"

Joanna wiped the tears off her sister's face.

"I can't give you answers. But I can tell you that you can't hide behind me and Cate forever."

She stood up and walked back to her suitcase.

"Does this have to be it?" Gwen asked. "Can't you and I still be sisters?"

Joanna looked back at her. "I honestly don't know."

"Do you think...do you think Andrew would mind if I stopped by and visited with you two some time?"

Joanna stared at Gwen for a long time, feeling the years of anger and frustration draining away.

"No, Gwen, I don't think he'll mind. And I won't mind, either."

Picking up her case, she went down the stairs, out the door and along the walk to the waiting car.

"I love the smell of those roses," Joanna said as she handed Andrew the suitcase.

Thirty-Three

"Don't you think we might be setting a bad precedent, doing all this cooking and baking and spoiling him like this?"

"No, I don't think so. Check the cookies." Léa handed a pot holder to Heather. "After running in a dozen different directions for me in the past week, your father could use a little spoiling."

"Okay, but remember, you could be burning your own bridges here. I just don't want to hear any complaints from you three years from now when I'm in college, about kids and housework and Dad not doing his share."

Léa smiled and turned the burner down under the pot of boiling water she had ready for lobsters. "You're kind of assuming a lot, aren't you?"

"Another minute or so on these cookies." Heather slid the tray of cookies back in the oven and gave Léa a bear hug. "So when's the wedding? When? When?"

Léa returned the embrace. "We haven't even talked about it."

And they might not for a while yet, she thought wistfully. Not while Ted's case was still unresolved.

Things were moving well, though. In the past week, Sarah had been able to get a petition for a new trial approved. And while they were waiting, they'd been able to get Ted transferred to a hospital to get him ready. It had given Léa great joy to visit him there every day this week and see the progress he was making.

Chris Webster's lawyers, however, had pretty much shut down any further information from him. Though the prosecutor was still working on connecting him to the deaths of Marilyn and her children, the murders of Jason Shanahan and Dusty were clearly tied to him. Of course, there were the lesser charges of destruction of property with regard to the cottage at the Lion Inn, as well as the vandalism of Léa's house, but those were the least of his worries.

Ted's murder conviction, though, was still the main thing on Léa's mind. Sarah had assured her that the fact that Bob Slater's decision to take the stand voluntarily as a witness for Ted, along with Chris's apparent guilt, would pretty much mean that Ted would go free. But Léa was still not ready to relax until she saw that really happen.

"You two are not going to elope or anything, are you?" Heather asked, taking another peek in the oven at the cookies.

"If we do, we'll make sure we take you along."

"And my grandparents. Dad is the only kid, you know. They'd be so excited to come to the wedding!"

"I can't wait to see them again."

"And how about Ted? Wouldn't you want him to be at your wedding?"

At the very thought of it, Léa felt her throat close up with emotion. She nodded.

"Yes. I'd love to have him there."

"Dad said the doctors are really hopeful."

"Ted will probably always carry mental scars from his loss. But they think he'll soon be able to function in society, at least. After that, it's up to him…and up to us to help him, as well."

Heather smiled and reached into the oven for the cookies. Léa went back to setting the table. Tonight was for

Mick, she reminded herself. He'd been everything to her during this ordeal. Her support. Her strength. He had put his own life and job and everything else on hold to help her. To be there for her.

God, she loved him! If she had the power to spoil him for life, she would.

The cookie jar crashed to the floor.

"Jeez! Dad loves that thing. I can't believe I dropped it."

"No big deal." Léa pushed the excited dog aside, crouched down and started picking up the larger pieces of the ceramic jar. "This gives us an excuse for you and me to go shopping tomorrow. We can buy him a new one as a present."

Since getting their hair done together, shopping with Léa had become one of Heather's passions. Léa knew it wasn't what they bought that drew the teenager, but the personal connection they were making.

"Don't cut your hand. I'll get the dust pan and the broom."

Heather ran toward the small pantry but reappeared immediately.

"I left them in the kitchen at your house," she said, grabbing Léa's keys off the counter and running out the back door. "I'll be right back."

With the sun falling in the west, the shadows lay long and heavy across the yard. The sounds of the day were giving way to the silence of evening, and the coolness of the earth was beginning to rise. In the deep shadow of the carriage house, imposing in its decay, the trespasser stood and watched the two houses and waited.

It wasn't long before the unholy demon came out of one house and ran blithely across the lawn. The keys in her hand jangled as she mounted the steps, unlocked the door and went in.

Moving noiselessly, the shadow stepped out of the darkness and crossed the lawn to the house.

Léa dropped a few of the larger pieces of the broken jar in the trash can. As she reached for a couple of paper towels, her gaze was drawn to the window over the sink. She saw Heather on the back porch of the house next door. The teenager unlocked the back door and went in. A second later the overhead light in the kitchen went on.

"I see you eyeing those crumbs," she warned Max over her shoulder. The dog was lurking a couple of steps away. She pushed the tray of cookies back from the edge of the counter and suddenly a movement from the other house caught her eye. She stared into the kitchen window across the way in horror.

The blade of the knife flashed as it arced through the air before sinking into Heather's back.

"*No!*" she screamed.

As she raced out the back door and across the lawn, her feet hardly touched the ground. She leaped up the back steps and tore open the door.

"Please," she sobbed. "No."

She burst into the house and saw Heather lying facedown in her own blood on the kitchen floor. She wasn't moving.

Another memory blinded her momentarily. The image of her mother, lying dead in her own blood, in this same kitchen.

She'd been too late that day, as well.

Léa saw the descending blade and turned, just as Patricia Webster brought the knife down. Her arms shot up in defense, and sharp pain cut through her as the woman struck again and again. Léa's arms spewed blood from deep slashes on her forearms.

"No!"

* * *

"Oh, it's you." Marilyn turned on the kitchen light. *"I told your husband on the phone this morning. There was no need for you to come here."*

She went to the stove and turned on the light above it, as well.

"That is, so long as the two of you shut your mouths during my divorce hearing on Monday, you won't get any more surprise packages of pictures. And neither will…"

"You told me you'd stop touching Chris. You had him here last night."

"He's the one doing all the touching these days. Chris has a wonderful talent." Marilyn laughed. *"One of these days, I should extend an invitation to your husband, too. It'll be something to get the two of them going at me at the same time. Maybe I'll send you some pictures."*

She turned to gauge the woman's reaction. Instead, she only saw the blade of the knife flashing down at her.

Chris's mother raised the knife to strike again, but Léa kicked her hard and stumbled backward herself.

"Why?" she gasped, facing the woman.

Despite her small size, Patricia Webster was strong and quick. She raised the kitchen knife again. "I killed her once, but she came back again to abuse my boy. I'll kill her again."

The knife sliced toward her and Léa jumped to the side, but the blade still managed to pierce the flesh of her biceps.

Heather made a small noise on the floor and Patricia turned.

"You will *not* take my Christopher away again. I'll kill you first."

Léa threw herself against the woman, grabbing hold of her wrist. The two of them landed hard on the kitchen floor, but Patricia's grip on the knife never loosened.

"I won't let you," Léa panted, pummeling the woman's face with a bloody fist. "I won't let you."

The knife cut her somewhere high on her shoulder, but Léa was beyond feeling pain. Her body was covered with blood—her vision blurred with tears—but she could not give up the fight. Like a wild creature, she used her fists and her legs, anything to stop the she-devil from taking Heather's life. Grabbing hold of the woman's hair, she pounded Patricia's head on the floor.

At some point, the knife dropped from the woman's hand, but Léa didn't stop. She continued to bang the head on the floor until she realized, some time later, that her enemy was no longer moving.

"Léa—" Heather whispered weakly from the other side of the kitchen.

It was only then—after hearing that voice—that Léa allowed herself to fall forward and give in to the pain.

Thirty-Four

"Neither of us is going to look too good in a bathing suit this summer."

Mick saw Léa laugh at Heather's quip, and his heart soared with joy. He'd come so close to losing both of them yesterday. Fear had chilled him when he'd walked into his empty house, then turned to horror when he'd gone to Léa's back door and seen all the blood. The police, the ambulances, the emergency room doctors—none of them could have moved fast enough for him.

Heather's injuries had consisted of a stab wound along the shoulder blade and a bruise on the head from the fall that had more than likely saved her life. Léa, on the other hand, had more than twenty cuts up and down her arms and shoulders. She'd lost a lot of blood.

Patricia Webster had suffered a concussion, but Mick was having a little difficulty mustering any sympathy. She was already out of the hospital and in the custody of the police.

Two years of lies had come undone in one night.

Chris had confessed, over his lawyers' efforts to stop him. His mother was too insane to care about consequences, and her version of the night of Marilyn's murder had spilled out in her hospital bed as her husband sat by, holding her hand.

The pieces all fell together in Mick's head.

Patricia Webster had stabbed Marilyn to death. Chris

had arrived in time to see his mother leave. Entering the house and witnessing what his mother had done, he had set the place on fire to cover his mother's crime. Killing the two little girls had been unintentional, but their murders were being added to the charges against him. According to Rich Weir, the prosecutor was considering trying him as an adult.

Bob Slater and Ted had both arrived after the fact.

For two years, Reverend Webster had known that his family's troubles ran deep, but he had chosen silence and prayer as his only course of action.

Mick closed his eyes momentarily and sent his own silent prayer of thanks heavenward for his family having been spared.

Family. His gaze locked with Léa's. Her hands were bandaged, but she reached for him, anyway, from the hospital bed.

"You can just let those lines in your forehead relax, my love," she whispered. "We're okay."

"I know." He brushed a kiss across her lips. "I love you. And you still owe me some answers."

"Well, I'm selling the house. Betty Walters called while you were at the police station. Some crazy writer wants to buy it."

"I'm looking for other answers," he persisted, kissing her again.

"Well? We're waiting," Heather said. The teenager's arm was in a sling, and she sat down carefully on the other side of the bed.

Léa smiled and looked from Mick to Heather and back to him. "Yes."

Sling or no sling, Heather's shouts woke up every hospital patient in Stonybrook.

AUTHORS' NOTE

We hope you enjoyed *Twice Burned* and are now ready to spend some quality time in beautiful Bucks County on your next vacation in Pennsylvania. It's perfectly safe. The murders have been solved, and the fictional town of Stonybrook has been neatly folded and put away in our imaginations. So enjoy your trip.

As most of our May McGoldrick readers already know, we delight in occasionally bringing you glimpses of characters from our past novels, and we loved doing it here. In *Trust Me Once*, we had the pleasure of introducing Owen Dean and Sarah Rand.

We'd like to thank our readers for their continuous support of our Jan Coffey and May McGoldrick books, and for their delightful question, "When is the next book coming out?" We love you.

In addition to our readers, we'd also like to thank Chief Paul T. Dickinson of the Perkasie (Pennsylvania) Police Department for all his enthusiastic help with our thousand or so questions. We salute, as well, the Perkasie Police Department, who we are happy to say were *not* the model for Stonybrook's finest. We also want to thank Kate Williams for writing the book *A Parent's Guide for Suicidal and Depressed Teens*. This book is an excellent resource for any parent or anyone dealing with teenagers…troubled or otherwise.

Lastly and as always, we'd like to thank our sons for

their love and patience and for accepting our promise to play more golf *next* summer!

As always, we love to hear from our readers. Write to us at:

Jan Coffey
c/o Nikoo & Jim McGoldrick
mcgoldmay@aol.com
www.JanCoffey.com

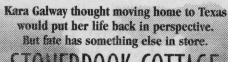

USA TODAY Bestselling Author

ANNE STUART

For Sophie Davis, turning Stonegate Farm into a quaint country inn is the fulfillment of a lifelong dream. She doesn't even mind that the farm was the scene of a grisly murder twenty years earlier….

When a stranger moves in next to the farm, Sophie believes the sense of peace she has created is threatened. Because there's something different about John Smith. It's clear he's come to Colby, Vermont, for a reason…and that reason has something to do with Sophie and Stonegate Farm.

Now her dream is becoming a nightmare. Who is John Smith? Why does his very presence make Sophie feel so completely out of control? And why is she beginning to suspect that this mysterious stranger will put in jeopardy everything she's dreamed of—maybe even her life?

STILL LAKE

"A master at creating chilling atmosphere."
—*Library Journal*

Available the first week of August 2002 wherever paperbacks are sold!

Just livin' *la vida loca*

Suzann Ledbetter

**On sale
July 2002
wherever
paperbacks
are sold!**

West of Bliss

As resident manager for the exclusive retirement community of
Valhalla Springs, Hannah Garvey is up to any challenge life throws
her way. But nothing can prepare her for what is about to happen.
At the going-away party of Eulilly and Chet Thomlinson, the restaurant
dishwasher suddenly opens fire. Chet, an ex-Secret Service agent,
manages to shoot the gunman, and is hailed a hero. The tragedy
is chalked up to a case of a disgruntled employee—with poor
Eulilly caught in the cross fire. But Sheriff David Hendrickson,
Hannah and the erstwhile senior sleuths of Kinderhook County
think the whole incident is just a little *too* cut-and-dried.

**"This novel [is] a winner that will send readers seeking
Suzann Ledbetter's first tale in this series and
demanding the next novel."**
—*Midwest Book Review* on *South of Sanity*

Jan Coffey

66859 TRUST ME ONCE   ___ $5.99 U.S. ___ $6.99 CAN.
(limited quantities available)

TOTAL AMOUNT $_____
POSTAGE & HANDLING $_____
($1.00 for one book; 50¢ for each additional)
APPLICABLE TAXES* $_____
<u>TOTAL PAYABLE</u> $_____
(check or money order—please do not send cash)

To order, complete this form and send it, along with a check
or money order for the total above, payable to MIRA Books®,
to: **In the U.S.:** 3010 Walden Avenue, P.O. Box 9077, Buffalo,
NY 14269-9077; **In Canada:** P.O. Box 636, Fort Erie, Ontario
L2A 5X3.

Name:_____
Address:_____ City:_____
State/Prov.:_____ Zip/Postal Code:_____
Account Number (if applicable):_____
075 CSAS

*New York residents remit applicable sales taxes.
  Canadian residents remit applicable GST and provincial taxes.

MIRA®